Margaret Sidney

MARGARET SIDNEY was born Harriet Mulford Stone in 1844 in New Haven, Connecticut. She wrote many books during her lifetime, but the favorite for generations of young readers remains her first novel, *Five Little Peppers and How They Grew*. The tales of the Pepper family were first published in *Wide Awake* magazine in 1880 as stories, under the name of Margaret Sidney, and were among the first children's stories about people in real-life situations. The Peppers' adventures were so popular that Daniel Lothrop, the publisher of *Wide Awake*, issued them the next year as a book, and devoted admirers followed the Peppers through eleven more books.

Harriet Stone married Daniel Lothrop in 1882, and for the next ten years they lived in The Wayside, Nathaniel Hawthorne's old home in Concord, Massachusetts. Harriet Lothrop continued writing novels for children, as well as stories and poems for *Wide Awake*, until her death in 1924.

YEARLING CLASSICS

Works of lasting literary merit by English
and American classic and contemporary writers

YEARLING BOOKS/YOUNG YEARLINGS/YEARLING CLASSICS are
designed especially to entertain and enlighten young people.
Charles F. Reasoner, Professor Emeritus of Children's Literature
and Reading, New York University, is consultant to this series.

For a complete listing of all Yearling titles, write to
Dell Readers Service, P.O. Box 1045,
South Holland, IL 60473.

Five Little Peppers at School

Margaret Sidney

With an Afterword by Barbara Cooney

Published by
Dell Publishing
a division of
The Bantam Doubleday Dell Publishing Group, Inc.
1 Dag Hammarskjold Plaza
New York, New York 10017

Yearling ® TM 913705, Dell Publishing Co., Inc.

ISBN: 0-440-40035-X

RL: 6.5

Printed in the United States of America

February 1988

10 9 8 7 6 5 4 3 2 1

W

Preface

*T*he story of young people's lives is not complete without many and broad glimpses of their schooldays. It was impossible to devote the space to this recital of the Five Little Peppers' school life in the books that showed their growing up. The author, therefore, was obliged unwillingly to omit all the daily fun and study and growth that she, loving them as if they were real children before her eyes, saw in progress.

So she packed it all away in her mind, ready to tell to all those young people who also loved the Peppers, when they clamored for more stories about them—just what Polly and Joel and David did in their merry schooldays. Ben never got as much schooling as the others, for he insisted on getting into business life as early as possible, in order the sooner to begin to pay Grandpapa King back for all his kindness. But Jasper and Percy and Van joined the Peppers at school, and a right merry time they had of it!

And now the time seems ripe to accede to all the insistent demands from those who love the Five Little Peppers, that this record of their schooldays should be given. So here it is, just as they all gave it to

MARGARET SIDNEY.

Contents

Five Little
Peppers
at School

Chapter 1

Hard Times for Joel

"**C**OME on, Pepper." One of the boys rushed down the dormitory hall, giving a bang on Joel's door as he passed.

"All right," said Joel a bit crossly. "I'm coming."

"Last bell," came back on the wind.

Joel threw his tennis racket on the bed and scowled. Just then a flaxen head peeped in, and two big eyes stared at him.

"Ugh!" Joel took one look. "Off with you, Jenkins." Jenkins withdrew at once.

Joel jumped up and slammed the door hard, whirled around in vexation, sprang over and thrust the tennis racket under the bed, seized a dog-eared book, and plunged off, taking the precaution, despite his hurry, to shut the door fast behind him.

Jenkins stole out of his room three doors beyond, and as the hall was almost deserted about this hour, so many boys being in recitation, he had nothing to do but tiptoe down to Joel's room and go softly in.

"Hullo!" A voice behind made him skip.

"Oh, Berry." It was a tone of relief. "It's you."

"Um," said Berry. "What's up now, Jenk?" He tossed back his head, while a smile of delight ran all over his face.

"Hush—come here." Jenk had him now within Joel's room and the door shut. "We'll have fun with the beggar now."

"Who—Dave?"

"Dave? No. Who wants to haul him over?" cried Jenk in scorn. "You are a flat, Berry, if you think that."

"Well, you are a flat, if you think to tackle Joe," declared Berry with the air and tone of one who knows. "Better let him alone, after what you got last term."

"Well, I ain't going to let him alone," declared Jenk angrily, and flushing all up to his shock of light hair. "And I gave him quite as good as he gave me, I'd have you know, Tom Beresford."

"Oho!" Tom gave a howl of derision, and slapped his knee in pure delight. "Tell that to the marines, sonny," he said.

"Hush—old Fox will hear you. Be still, can't you"—twitching his jacket—"and stop your noise."

"I can't help it. You say such very funny things," said Beresford, wiping his eyes.

"Well, anyway, I'm going to pay him up this term," declared Jenkins decidedly. He was rushing around the small room, the corners devoted to David being neatness itself, which couldn't truthfully be said of Joel's quarters. "I'm after his new tennis racket. Where in thunder is it?" tossing up the motley array of balls, dumbbells, and such treasures, that showed on their surface they belonged to no one but Joel.

"Great Scott!" Tom cried with sudden interest, and coming out of his amusement. "You won't find it."

"Saw him looking at it just now, before he went to class," cried Jenkins, plunging around the room. "Where is the thing?" he fumed.

Berry gave a few swift, birdlike glances around the room, then darted over to the end of one of the small beds, leaned down, and picked out from underneath the article in question.

"Oh! Give it to me," cried Jenk, flying at him and possessing himself of the treasure. "It's mine. I told you of it."

"Isn't it a beauty!" declared Berry, his eyes very big and longing.

"Ha, ha—ain't it? Well, Joe won't see this in one spell."

Jenkins gave it a swing over his head, then batted his knee with it.

"What are you going to do, Jenk?" demanded Berry presently, when he could get his mind off from the racket itself.

"Do? Ha, ha! Who says I can't pay the beggar back?" grinned Jenk, hopping all over the room and knocking into things generally.

"Hush—hush," warned Berry, plunging after him. "Here's old Fox," which brought both boys up breathless in the middle of the floor.

"She's gone by"—a long breath of relief. "And there she goes down the stairs," finished Berry.

"Sure?" Not daring to breathe, but clutching the racket tightly, and with one eye on Berry, Jenk cried again in a loud whisper, "Sure, Berry?"

"As if anyone could mistake the flap of those slipper heels on the stairs!" said Berry scornfully.

"Well, look out of the window," suggested Jenk suddenly. "She'll go across the yard, maybe."

So Berry dashed to the window, and gave one look. "There she sails with a bottle in her hand, going over to South" (the other dormitory across the yard). "Most likely

Jones has the colic again. Good! Now that disposes finely of old Fox," which brought him back to the subject in hand, the disposal of Joel's racket.

"Give me that," he said, hurrying over to Jenkins.

"No, you don't," said that individual. "And I must be lively before old Fox gets back." With that, he rushed out of the room.

"If you don't give me that racket, I'll tell on you," cried Beresford in a passion, flying after him.

"Hush!" Jenk turned on him suddenly and gripped him fast. "See here," he cried in a suppressed tone, and curbing his anger as best he could, "you don't want Joe to go into that match, this afternoon, with this racket." He shook it with eager, angry fingers.

"No," said Berry without stopping to think, "I don't."

"Well, then, you better keep still, and hold your tongue," advised Jenk angrily.

"Well, what are you going to do with it?"

"None of your—" what, he didn't say, for just then a boy flew out of his room, to tear down the long hall. He had his back to them, and there was no time to skip back into Jenkins's own room, for the two had already passed it. One wild second, and Jenkins thrust the racket into the depths of the housemaid's closet close at hand, under some cleaning cloths on a shelf. Then he stuck his hands in his pockets.

"Hullo!" The boy who was rushing along suddenly turned, to see him whistling.

"Oh, Jenk, is that you? See here, where's your Caesar?"

"Don't know—gone up the spout," said Jenkins carelessly, and keeping well in front of Beresford.

"Well, who has one? You haven't, Berry?" He turned to Tom anxiously.

"Not on your life he hasn't," Jenk answered for him.

"Botheration!" ejaculated the boy. "I've fifty lines to do, else I'm shut in from the game. And Simmons has run off with my book."

"Try Joe Pepper's room. He's in math recitation," said Jenk suddenly. "He has one, Toppy."

"You're a brick." Toppy flew down the hall, and bolted into Joel's room.

"Holy Moses, what luck! He'll prowl for an hour over Joe's duds. Come on." Jenk had his head in the cupboard, and his fingers almost on the racket, when Toppy's voice rang dismally down the hall: "Joe must have taken it."

Jenk pulled his fingers out, and had the door fast, and was quite turned away from the dangerous locality. "Well, I don't know what you'll do, Toppy," he said, controlling his dismay enough to speak. "Run down and skin through the fellows' rooms on first floor. Oh, good gracious!" he groaned. "It's all up with getting it now," as a swarm of boys came tumbling over the stairs.

So he mixed with them, laughing and talking, and Berry melted off somewhere. And no one had time to think a syllable of anything but the great game of tennis to be called at two o'clock, between the two divisions of Dr. Marks's boys. Some of the team of the St. Andrew's School, a well-known set of fellows at this sport and terribly hard to beat, were going to be visitors. So there was unusual excitement.

"What's up, Pepper?" A howl that rose above every other sort of din that was then in progress came from Joel's room.

"He's been in here!" Joel plunged out of the doorway, tossing his black, curly locks, that were always his bane, his eyes flashing dangerously. "Say, where's Jenk? He's been in my room," he cried, doubling up his small fists.

"What is it?" cried Jenkins, making as if just coming up the stairs. "What's all the row about?"

"You've been in my room," shouted Joel in a loud, insistent voice, "and taken my—" The rest was lost in a babel of voices.

"What? What's gone, Joe?" They all crowded into the small space, and swarmed all over the room.

"My racket," yelled Joel wrathfully. "Jenk has got it. He better give it up. Quick now." He pushed up the sleeves of his tennis shirt and squared off, glaring at them all, but making the best of his way over toward Jenk.

That individual, when he saw him coming, thought it better to get behind some intervening boys. Everybody huddled against everybody else, and it was impossible to get at the truth.

"See here now, Mother Fox will be after us all if you don't hush up," called one boy. "I guess she's coming," which had the desired effect. All the voices died down except Joel's.

"I don't care," said Joel wrathfully. "I wish she would come. Jenk has got my racket. He saw me with it before I ran to math, and now it's gone." All eyes turned to Jenkins.

"Is that so?" A half-dozen hands pushed him into the center of the group. "Then you've got to give him fits, Pepper."

"I'm going to," announced Joel, pushing up his sleeves higher yet, "until he tells where it is. Come on, Jenk." He tossed his head like a young lion, and squared off.

"I haven't your old racket," declared Jenk, a white line beginning to come around his mouth. It wasn't pleasant to see his reckoning quite so near.

"Then you know where it is," declared Joel.

"And give it to the beggar," cried several of the boys, with whom Jenkins was by no means a favorite.

"Give it to him worse than you did last term, Joe," called someone on the edge of the circle closing around the two.

"I'm going to," nodded Joel, every nerve tingling to begin. "Come on, Jenk, if you won't tell where you've put my racket."

"He's afraid," said the boy who had advised the more severe pummeling. "Old fraid cat!"

Jenkins, his knees knocking together miserably, but with a wild rage in his heart at these words, struck out blindly to meet Joel's sturdy little fists, and to find his Waterloo.

In the midst of the din and confusion that this encounter produced, steps that could never by any possibility be mistaken for those of a schoolboy struck upon their ears.

The circle of spectators flew wide, and before Joel and Jenkins realized what was coming, a good two dozen hands were laid on their collars, and they were dragged apart, and hauled into separate rooms, the rest of the boys scattering successfully. Tom Beresford fled with the rest, and the long hall was cleared.

"Boys!" The voice of the matron, Mrs. Fox, rang down the deserted, long hall, as she looked up from the stairway. "Humph! They are quiet enough now." She gave a restful sigh, and went down again. Jones and his colic were just so much extra on a terribly busy day.

"What did you fellows touch me for?" roared Joel, lifting a bloody nose. In his own room, Jenkins was in that state that recognizes any interruption as a blessing.

"Old Fox would have caught you if we hadn't rushed you both," cried the boys.

Tom Beresford worked his way up to say close to Joel's ear, "Don't speak, get into your room. I'll tell you where it is," then melted off to the outer circle of boys.

Joel looked up, gave a little nod, then broke away from the boys and dashed to Jenkins's door.

"See here"—he flung the words out—"you've got to finish sometime when Mrs. Fox isn't around."

Jenkins, who was under the impression that he had had quite enough, was made to say "All right," something in the boys' faces making it seem imperative that he should do so.

Quite pleased, Joel withdrew as suddenly as he had come.

Meanwhile, up the stairs, two at a time, came Davie, singing at the memory of the special commendation given by his instructor in the recitation just over, and secretly David's heart bounded with a wild hope of taking home a prize in classics for Mamsie!

"Everything's just beautiful this term!" he hummed to himself. And then, in a breathing space, he was in his room. And there, well drawn behind the door, was a boy with big eyes. "*Hush*," he warned.

"What's the matter?" asked David in astonishment. "And where's Joel?"

"Oh, don't speak his name. He's in disgrace. Oh, it's perfectly awful!" The boy huddled up in a heap, and tried to shut the door.

"Who?" cried David, not believing his ears.

"Joel—oh dear! It's perfectly awful!"

"Stop saying it's perfectly awful, Bates, and tell me what's the matter." Davie felt faintish, and sat down on the shoe box.

Bates shut the door with a clap, and then came to stand over him, letting the whole information out with a rush.

"He's pitched into Jenk—and they've had a fight—and they're all blood—and the old Fox almost got 'em both." Then he shut his mouth suddenly, the whole being told.

Davie put both hands to his head. For a minute everything turned dark around him. Then he thought of Mamsie. "Oh dear me!" he said, coming to.

"How I wish he'd had it all out with that beggar!" exploded Bates longingly.

David didn't say anything, being just then without words. At this instant Joel rushed in with his bloody nose, and a torn sleeve where Jenk in his desperation had gripped it fast.

"Oh, Joel!" screamed Davie at sight of him, and springing from his shoe box. "Are you hurt? Oh, Joey!"

"Phoo! That's nothing," said Joel, running over to the wash basin and plunging his head in, to come up bright and smiling. "See, Dave, I'm all right," he announced, his black eyes shining. "But he's a mean beggar to steal my new racket," he concluded angrily.

"To steal your new racket that Grandpapa sent you!" echoed David. "Oh, dear me! Who has taken it? Oh, Joel!"

"That beggar Jenkins," exploded Joel. "But I'm to know where it is." Just then the door opened cautiously, enough to admit a head. "Don't speak, Pepper, but come."

Joel flung down the towel and pranced to the door.

"No one else," said the boy to whom the head belonged.

"Not me?" asked David longingly. "Can't I come?"

"No—no one but Joe." Joel rushed over the sill tumultuously, deserting David and the Bates boy.

"Don't speak a single word," said the boy out in the hall, putting his mouth close to Joel's ear, "but move lively."

No need to tell him so. In a minute they were both before the housemaid's closet.

"Feel under," whispered the boy, with a sharp eye down the length of the hall.

Joel's brown hands pawed among the cleaning cloths and brushes, bringing up in a trice the racket, Grandpapa's gift, to flourish it high.

"Take care. Keep it down," said the boy in a hurried whisper.

"Oh, oh!" cried Joel, hanging to it in a transport.

"Um," the boy nodded. "Hush, be still. Now skip for your room."

"Beresford," said Joel, his black eyes shining as he paused a breathing space before rushing back to Davie, the new racket gripped fast, "if I don't pay Jenk for this!"

"Do." Tom grinned all over his face in great delight. "You'll be a public benefactor." And he softly beat his hands together.

Chapter 2

The Tennis Match

JOEL, hugging his recovered tennis racket, rushed off to the court. Tom Beresford, staring out of his window, paused while pulling on his sweater to see him go, a sorry little feeling at his heart, after all, at Joe's good spirits.

"He'll play like the mischief, and a great deal better for the row and the fright over that old racket. Well, I had to tell. 'Twould have been too mean for anything to have kept still."

So he smothered a sigh, and got into his togs, seized his implements of battle, and dashed off too. Streams of boys were rushing down to the court, and the yard was black with them. In the best places were the visitors. Royalty couldn't have held stronger claims to distinction in the eyes of Dr. Marks's boys, and many were the anxious glances sent over at the four St. Andrew's boys. If the playing shouldn't come up to the usual high mark!

"Pepper will score high," one after another said as he

dropped to the ground next to his chums, in the circle around the court.

"Of course." Nobody seemed to doubt Joel's powers along that line. "He always does." And cries of "Pepper—Pepper" were taken up, and resounded over the yard.

Joel heard it as he dashed along, and he held his head high, well pleased. But David followed his every movement with anxiety. "I'm afraid he was hurt," he said to himself. "And if he should lose the game, he'd never get over it. Oh dear me! If Mamsie could only be here!"

But Mamsie was far away from her boys, whom she had put at Dr. Marks's school for the very purpose of achieving self-reliance and obedience to the training of the little brown house. So Davie, smothering his longing, got into a front row with several boys of his set, and bent all his attention to the game just beginning.

Sharp at two o'clock the four went onto the court—Joel and Fred Ricketson against Tom Beresford and Lawrence Green, otherwise "Larry." And amid howls of support from the "rooters," the game began.

At first Joel's luck seemed to desert him, and he played wild, causing much consternation in the ranks violently rooting for him. David's head sank, and he leaned his elbows on his knees, to bury his hot cheeks in his hands.

"Wake up," cried Paul Sykes, his very particular friend, hoarsely, giving him a dig in the ribs. "Don't collapse, Dave."

"Oh!" groaned David, his head sinking lower yet, "I can't look. I simply can't. It will kill Joel."

"Stiffen up!" cried Paul. "Joe's all right. He'll come to. *Ha!*"

A shout, stunning at first, that finally bore down all before it in the shape of opposing enthusiasm, swept over the whole yard. Screams of applause, perfectly deafening, rent the air.

And look! Even the visitors from St. Andrew's are leaping to their feet, and yelling "Good—good." Something quite out of the common, even in a close tennis match, was taking place. David shuddered, and crouched down on the ground as far as he could. Paul gave him an awful whack on the back.

"You're losing it all," he cried as he stood on his tiptoes. "Hi! Hi! Tippety Rippety! Hi! Hi!"

It was Joel's especial yell. And there he was, as David scrambled up to see him, head thrown back, and black eyes shining in the way they always did when he worked for Mamsie and Polly, and that dealt despair to all opponents. He had just made a brilliant stroke, returning one of Larry's swiftest balls in such a manner that it just skimmed over the net and passed the boys before they could recover themselves, and fairly taking off from their feet the St. Andrew's men, who had been misled by Joel's previous slow playing in the first set, which Tom and Larry had won.

"Who is he? Gee whiz! But that's good form!" declared Vincent Parry, the St. Andrew's champion, excitedly.

"Pepper—don't you know Pepper?" cried a dozen throats, trying to seem unconscious that it was Parry, the champion, who was asking the question.

"Oh, is that Pepper?" said the St. Andrew's boy. While "Pepper—Pepper. Hi! Hi! Tippety Rippety! Hi! Hi!" rolled out, till there wasn't any other sound to be heard. And a regular tussle of boys were getting in the wildest excitement when it was announced that Pepper and Ricketson had won the second set, the referees trying to quiet them so that the game could proceed.

In the third set, Joel seemed to have it all his own way, and fairly swept Ricketson along with him. The excitement

was now so intense that the boys forgot to yell, afraid they
would miss some strokes.

David clenched his hands tightly. The net and flying balls
spun all together inextricably before his eyes as he strained
them to see Joe's brilliant returns. This was the deciding set,
as the cup was to go to the winners of two sets out of three.

Joel's last serve was what finished it, the ball flashing by
Tom with such impetus that even the St. Andrew's champion said he couldn't ever have returned it.

Everybody drew a long breath, and then the crowd rushed
and converged to Joel, surrounded him, fighting for first
place, the fortunate ones tossing him up to their shoulders to
race him in triumph around the yard.

"Take Ricket!" screamed Joel, red in the face. "Take him!"
he roared. "He beat too, as much as I." So a second group
seized Fred, and up he went to be trotted after, the crowd
swarming alongside, yelling, tumbling over each other, gone
perfectly wild—Joe waving the cup, thrust into his hand,
which would be kept by the winners for a year.

It was the middle of the night. Davie, flushed with the
happiest thoughts, had peacefully settled to dreams in which
Mamsie and Grandpapa, and Polly and Jasper, and all the
dear home people, were tangled up. And Phronsie seemed to
be waving a big silver cup, and piping out with a glad little
laugh, "Oh, I am so glad!" And now and then the scene of
operations flew off to the little brown house, that it appeared
impossible to keep quite out of dreamland. Someone gripped
him by the arm.

"Oh, what is it, Joe?" David flew up to a sitting posture in
the middle of his bed.

"It isn't Joe. Get up as quick as you can."

David, with a dreadful feeling at his heart, tumbled out of

bed. "*Isn't Joe!*" he found time to say, with a glance in the darkness over toward Joel's bed.

"Hurry up. Don't stop to talk." The voice was Tom Beresford's. "Get on your clothes."

Meantime he was scuffing around. "Where in time are your shoes?" But David already had those articles, and was pulling them on with hasty fingers. "Oh, tell me," he couldn't help crying, but "Hurry up!" was all he got for his pains. And at last, after what seemed an age to Tom, David was piloted out into the hall, with many adjurations to "go softly," down the long flight of stairs. Here he came to a dead stop. "I can't go another single step, Tom," he said firmly, "unless you tell me what you want me for. And where is Joel?" he gasped.

"Oh, bother! In another minute you'd have been outside, and then it would be safe to tell you," said Tom. "Well, if you will have it, Dave, Joe's finishing up that business with Jenk, and you're the only one that can stop it. Now don't keel over."

David clung to the door, which Tom had managed to open softly, and for a minute it looked as if Beresford would have his hands full without in the least benefiting Joel. But suddenly he straightened up. "Oh, tell me where he is," he cried, in a manner and voice exactly like Polly when she had anything that must be done set before her. And clear ahead of his guide when Tom whispered, "Down in the pine grove," sped Davie on the very wings of the wind.

"Gracious! Joel is nothing to Dave as a sprinter," said Tom to himself, as his long legs got him over the ground in the rear.

The two boys hugged the shadow of the tall trees and dashed across the lawn to the shrubbery beyond. Then it was but a breathing space, and a few good leaps to the depths of the pine grove. In the midst of this were two figures, busily engaged in the cheerful occupation of fisticuffing each other till the stronger might win.

"*Joel!*" called David hoarsely, his breath nearly spent as he dashed up.

Joel, at this, wavered, and turned. Seeing which, his antagonist dealt him a thwack that made his head spin, and nearly lost him his footing.

"That was mean, Jenk!" exclaimed Beresford, dashing up in time to see it. "You took advantage when Joe was off guard," he cried hotly.

"No such thing," roared Jenk, losing his head at what now seemed an easy victory, "and I'll settle with you when I get through with Joe, for being such a mean sneak as to turn telltale, Tom."

"All right," said Tom coolly. "Go it, Joe, and pay him up. You've several scores to settle now."

"Joel," gasped Davie. "Oh Mamsie!" He could get no further.

Joel's hands, out once more in good fighting trim, wavered again, and sank helplessly down to his side.

"Oh dear!" Tom groaned in amazement.

"Oho! You see how easy I could whip him," laughed Jenkins, raining down blows all over Joel's figure, who didn't offer to stir.

"See here, you!" Tom fairly roared it out, perfectly regardless of possible detection. "You beastly coward!" And he jumped in between Joel and his antagonist. "You may settle with me now if you like."

"Stop, Tom." Joel seized him from behind. Tom, in a fury, turned to see his face working dreadfully, while the brown hands gripped him tightly. "I forgot—Mamsie wouldn't—like—you mustn't, Tom. If you do, I'll scream for John," he declared suddenly.

John, the watchman, being the last person whom any of Dr. Marks's boys desired to see when engaged in a midnight prank, Beresford backed away slowly from Jenkins, who was delighted once more at the interruption, and fastened his gaze on Joel. "Well, I never did, Pepper!" he brought himself to say.

"Tom," said David brokenly, and getting over to him to seize his hand, "don't you know our Mamsie would feel dreadfully to see Joel doing any such thing? Oh, she would, Tom," as Beresford continued to stare without a word.

"Not to such a miserable beggar." Tom at last found his tongue, and pointed to Jenk.

"Oh, yes, she would. It's just as bad in Joel," said Davie, shaking his head. Joel turned suddenly, took two or three steps, then flung himself down flat on his face on the pine needles.

"Well, get up," said Tom crossly, running over to him. "John will maybe get over here, we've made so much noise. Hurry up, Joe, we must all get back."

Joel, thus adjured, especially as David got down on the ground to put his arms around the shaking shoulders, got up slowly. Then they turned around to look for Jenkins. He was nowhere to be seen.

"Little coward!" exclaimed Tom between his teeth. "Well, we'll have to skin it as best we may back. *Here comes John!*"

They could see his lantern moving around among the trees, and dashing off, taking the precaution to hug the shadow of the trees again, they soon made the big door to the dormitory. Tom reached it first and turned the knob. "It's locked," he said. "The mean, beastly coward has locked us out."

Chapter 3

A Narrow Escape

*J*OEL, in such an emergency, wiped his black eyes and looked up sharply. David sank on the upper step.

"Oh, no, Tom," cried Joel, crowding in between Beresford and the door, "it can't be. Get out of the way. Let me try."

"It is—it is, I tell you," howled Tom in what was more of a whine, as he kept one eye out for John and his lantern. "The mean sneak has got the best of us, Joe." He set his teeth hard together, and his face turned white.

Joe dropped the doorknob and whirled off the steps.

"Julius Caesar! Where are you going?" began Tom, as Joel disappeared around the corner of the dormitory.

"He's gone to see if John is coming, I suppose," said Davie weakly.

Tom, preferring to see for himself, skipped off, and disappeared around the angle. "Oh—oh!" was what David heard next, making him fly from his step to follow in haste.

What he saw was so much worse than all his fears as Tom gripped his arm pointing up over his head, that he screamed right out, "Oh, Joe, come back! You'll be killed!"

"He can't come back," said Tom hoarsely. "He'd much better go on." Joel, more than halfway up the lightning conductor, was making good time shinning along. He turned to say, "I'm all right, Dave," as a window above them was thrown up, and a head in a white nightcap was thrust out.

"It's all up with him now. There's old Fox," groaned Tom, ducking softly back over the grass. "Come on, Dave."

But David, with clasped hands and white face, had no thought of deserting Joel.

The person in the window, having the good sense to utter no exclamation, waited till Joel was up far enough for her to grasp his arm. Then she couldn't help it as she saw his face.

"*Joel Pepper!*"

"Yes'm," said Joel, turning his chubby face toward her. "I knew I could get up here. It's just as easy as anything."

Mrs. Fox set her other hand to the task of helping him into the dimly lighted hall, much to Joel's disgust, as he would much have preferred to enter unassisted. Then she turned her capfrills full on him, and said in a tone of great displeasure, "What *is* the meaning of all this?"

"Why, I had to go out, Mrs. Fox."

"Why?"

"Oh—I—I—had to."

She didn't ask him again, for the matron was a woman of action, and in all her dealings with boys had certain methods by which she brought them to time. So she only set her sharp eyes, that Dr. Marks's pupils always called "gimlets," full upon him. "Go to your room," was all she said.

"Oh, Mrs. Fox," cried Joel, trying dreadfully to control

himself, and twisting his brown hands in the effort, "I—I—had to go. Really I did."

"So you said before. *Go to your room.*" Then a second thought struck her. "Was any other boy with you?" she demanded suddenly.

Joel gave a sharp cry of distress as he started down the hall, revolving in his mind how he would steal down and unlock the door as soon as the matron had taken herself off.

"Here, stop—come back here! Now answer me—yes or no—was any other boy with you?" as Joel stood before her again.

Joel's stubby black curls dropped so that she couldn't see his face. As there was no reply forthcoming, Mrs. Fox took him by the arm. "You needn't go to your room, Joel," she said sharply. "You may go to Coventry."

"Oh, Mrs. Fox," Joel burst out, "don't—don't send me there."

"A boy who cannot answer me is fit only for Coventry," said Mrs. Fox with great dignity, despite the nightcap. "Wait here, Joel. I will get my candle and light you down." She stepped off to a corner of the hall, where she had set the candlestick on a table when startled by the noise outside. "Now we will go."

It was impossible that all this confusion should not awake some of the boys in the hall, and by this time there was much turning on pillows, and leaning on elbows, and many scuttlings out of bed to listen at doors opened a crack, so that nearly every one of the occupants on that particular hall soon knew that "old Fox" had Joel Pepper in her clutches, and that he was being led off somewhere.

And at last Joel let it out himself. "Oh, Mrs. Fox—dear Mrs. Fox, *don't* make me go to Coventry," he roared. He clutched her wrapper, a big, flowered affair that she wore on such nocturnal rambles, and held it fast. "I'll be just as good," he implored.

"Coventry is the place for you, Joel Pepper," said Mrs. Fox grimly. "So we will start."

Meanwhile David, holding his breath till he saw, in the dim light that always streamed out from the dormitory hall where the gas was left turned down at night, that Joel was safely drawn into shelter, frantically rushed around to the big door, in the wild hope that somehow admittance would be gained. "Joe will come by and by," he said to himself, sinking down on the steps.

"We're done for," said Tom's voice off in the distance.

"Oh, Tom, are you there?" cried Davie, straining his eyes to catch a glimpse.

"Hush!" Tom poked his head out from a clump of shrubbery. "Don't you dare to breathe. I tell you, Dave, our only hope is in staying here till morning."

"Oh, dear me!" exclaimed David in dismay.

"Oh, dear me!" echoed Tom in derision. It was impossible for him to stop talking, he was so keyed up. "It's paradise, I'm sure, compared to being in old Fox's grip."

This brought David back to Joel's plight, and he sighed dismally and leaned his head on his hands. How long he sat there he couldn't have told. The first thing he did know, a big hand was laid on his shoulder, and a bright glare of light fell full on his face.

"Oh, my soul and body!" cried John, the watchman, bending over him, "if here ain't one of th' boys dead asleep on the doorsteps!"

"Little goose, to sit there!" groaned Tom, huddling back into his bushes. "Now it's all up with him. Well, I'll save my skin, for I don't believe those boys will tell on me."

•   •   •

"Coventry" was a small square room in the extension, containing a bed, a table, and a chair, where the boys who were refractory were sent. It was considered a great disgrace to be its inmate. They were not locked in, but no boy once put there was ever known to come out unless bidden by the authorities. And no one, of course, could speak to them when they emerged from it to go to recitations, for their lessons must be learned in the silence of this room. Then back from the classroom the culprit must go to this hated place, to stay as long as his misdemeanor might seem to deserve.

It was so much worse punishment than a flogging could possibly be that all Dr. Marks's boys heard "Coventry" with a chill that stopped many a prank in midair.

But Joel didn't get into "Coventry" after all, for at the foot of the stairs another candlebeam was advancing, and back of it was the thin, sharp face of Mr. Harrow, one of the underteachers.

"Oh, Mr. Harrow," screamed Joel, breaking away from the matron to plunge up to him, "she's going to put me into Coventry. Oh, don't make me go there. It will kill my Mamsie, and Polly."

"Hey?" Mr. Harrow came to a sudden stop, and whirled the candlestick around to get a better view of things. "What's this, Mrs. Fox? And *Joel Pepper,* of all boys!"

"I know it," said Mrs. Fox, her candlestick shaking in an unsteady hand. "Well, you see, sir, I was going upstairs to see if little Fosdick had blankets enough. It's turned cold, and you know he's had a sore throat, and—"

"Well, come to the point, Mrs. Fox," said the teacher, bringing her up quickly. Joel clung desperately to his hand, shaking violently in every limb.

"Oh, yes, sir—well, and I heard a noise outside, so I

bethought me to look, and there was this boy climbing up the lightning conductor."

"Up the lightning conductor?" echoed Mr. Harrow.

"Yes, sir"—Mrs. Fox's capfrills trembled violently as she nodded—"Joel Pepper was climbing up the lightning conductor, sir. And I thought I should have dropped to see him, sir."

The underteacher turned and surveyed Joel. "Well, I think, Mrs. Fox," he said slowly, "if he's been over that lightning conductor tonight, we won't put him in Coventry."

"He wouldn't answer when I asked him if any other boys were there," said the matron, a dull red spot coming on either cheek.

"That's bad—very bad," said Mr. Harrow. "Well, I'll take Joel under my care. Do you go to bed, Mrs. Fox."

It was all done in a minute. Somehow Mrs. Fox never quite realized how she was left standing alone. And as there really wasn't anything else for her to do, she concluded to take the underteacher's advice.

"Now, Joel"—Mr. Harrow looked down at his charge—"you seem to be left for me to take care of. Well, suppose you come into my room and tell me something about this affair."

Joel, with his heart full of distress about David and Tom, now that the immediate cause of alarm over his being put into "Coventry" was gone, could scarcely conceal his dismay, as he followed Mr. Harrow to his room. He soon found himself on a chair, and the underteacher, setting his candlestick down, took an opposite one.

"Do you mind telling me all about this little affair of yours, Joe?" said Mr. Harrow, leading off easily. His manner, once away from the presence of the matron, was as different as possible, and Joel who had never met him in just this way, stared in amazement.

"You see, Joe," the underteacher went on, and he began to play with some pencils on the table, "it isn't so very long ago, it seems to me, since I was a boy. And I climbed lightning conductors too. I really did, Joel."

Joel's black eyes gathered a bright gleam in their midst.

"Yes, and at night, too," said the underteacher softly, "though I shouldn't want you to mention it to the boys. So now, if you wouldn't mind, Joel, I should really like to hear all about this business of yours."

But Joel twisted his hands, only able to say, "Oh, dear! I can't tell, Mr. Harrow." His distress was dreadful to see.

"Well," said the underteacher slowly, "perhaps in the morning you'll feel better able to tell. I won't press it now. You must get to bed, Joe," with a keen look at his face.

"Oh, Mr. Harrow—would you—would you—" Joel jumped out of his seat and over to the underteacher's chair.

"Would I what?" asked Mr. Harrow in perplexity, wishing very much that "Mamsie," whom he had seen on her visits to the school, were there at that identical moment.

"Would you—oh, might I unlock the—the back door?" gasped Joel, his black eyes very big with distress.

"Unlock the back door?" repeated Mr. Harrow. Then he paused a moment. "Certainly. I'll go with you." He got out of his chair.

"Oh, no, sir," cried Joel tumbling back. "I'll—I'll do it alone if I may. Please, sir."

"Oh, no, Joel, that can't ever be allowed," Mr. Harrow was saying decidedly, when steps were heard coming down the hall, and there was John, the watchman, hauling David Pepper along the dimly lighted hall to the extra gleam of the underteacher's room.

"I found this boy asleep on the steps," announced John, coming in with his charge.

"Why, David Pepper!" exclaimed Mr. Harrow in astonishment. Then he turned a cold glance on Joel, who flew over to Davie's side.

"Joel!" cried David convulsively, and blinking dreadfully as he came into the light. "Oh, I'm so glad you're safe—oh, so glad, Joey!" He hid his face on Joel's arm, and sobbed.

"You may go, John," said the underteacher to that individual, who kept saying "I found that boy asleep on the steps" over and over, unable to stop himself. "And don't say anything about this to anyone. I will take care of the matter."

"All right, sir," said John, glad to be relieved of all responsibility, and touching his cap. "I found that boy asleep on the steps," he added as he took himself off.

"Now, see here." Mr. Harrow laid his hand on David's shoulder, ignoring Joel for the time, and drew him aside. "The whole of this business must be laid before me, David. So begin."

"Oh, Dave!" cried Joel, springing up to him. "Oh, sir—oh, Mr. Harrow, it was all my fault, truly it was. David only came after me. Oh, Mr. Harrow, don't make him tell."

"You go and sit down in that chair, Joel," said Mr. Harrow, pointing to it. So Joel went, and got on it, twisting miserably.

"Now, then, David."

"You see," said David, the tears still rolling down his cheeks, "that—oh dear!—Joel was gone, and—"

"How did you know Joel was gone?" interrupted the underteacher.

"Oh dear!" David caught his breath. "Another boy told me, sir."

"Who?"

David hesitated. "Must I tell, sir?" not trusting himself to look at Joel.

"Certainly."

"Tom Beresford."

"Ugh!" Joel sprang from his chair. "He hadn't anything to do with it, sir. Tom has been awfully good. He only told Dave."

"Go back to your chair, Joel," said Mr. Harrow. "Now, then, David, go on. So you went out with Beresford to find Joel, eh?"

"Yes, sir," said David faintly.

"Any other boy?" asked the underteacher quickly.

"No, sir."

"Well, then, Tom is waiting out there, I suppose, now." Mr. Harrow got out of his chair.

"He didn't have anything to do with it, sir," cried Joel wildly, and flying out of his chair again, "truly he didn't."

"I understand." Mr. Harrow nodded. "I'm going to bring him in. Now it isn't necessary to tell you two boys not to do any talking while I'm gone." With that he went over to a corner, took down a lantern, lighted it, and passed out.

When he came back, both Joel and David knew quite well by Tom's face that the whole story was out; and Joel, who understood as well as anyone that Floyd Jenkins never by any possibility could be a favorite with instructors, any more than with the boys, unless he changed his whole tactics, groaned again at thought that he had made matters worse for him.

"Now all three of you scatter to bed," was all the underteacher said as he came in with Tom. "No talking now. Get up as softly as you can. Good night."

Chapter 4

Of Various Things

*A*ND the next day, the story which flew all over the yard, how that Joel Pepper was "put into Coventry" last night, was overtaken and set right.

"Huh! There, now you see," cried Van Whitney, coming out of his rage. He had cried so that his eyes were all swollen up, and he was a sight to behold. Percy, too miserable to say anything, and wishing he could ever cry when he felt badly, had slunk out of sight, to bear the trouble as well as he might. Now he came up bright and smiling. "Yes, now you see," he cried triumphantly.

"Oh, I hope that mean beggar Jenk will be expelled." There appeared to be but one voice about it.

"Well, he won't," said Van.

"Won't? Why not?" The boys crowded around him on the playground, all games being deserted for this new excitement. "Why not, pray tell?"

"Of course he will," said one boy decidedly. "Dr. Marks never'll keep him after this."

"Yes he will too," roared Van, glad he could tell the news first, but awfully disappointed that it must be that Jenkins was to stay, "for Joel got Dr. Marks to promise there shouldn't anything be done to Jenk. So there now!"

"What, not after locking that door! That was the worst." The boys, two or three of them, took up the cry. " 'Twas beastly mean."

"Contemptible! Just like Jenk!" went all over the playground.

"Well, he isn't to go," repeated Van with a sigh, "and Joel says he was as bad, because he went out at night to fight."

"Why, he had to—Jenk dared him. And he couldn't have it out in the dormitory. You know he couldn't, Whitney," said one of the boys in surprise.

"Oh, dear! I know," said Van helplessly. "Well, Joel says it's no matter that the racket was stolen out of his room, and—"

"No matter!" ejaculated the boys, a whole crowd of them swarming around him. "Well, if that isn't *monstrous!*"

"Oh, Joel's afraid that Dr. Marks will expel Jenk," Percy, very uncomfortable to have Joel blamed, made haste to say. "Don't you see?"

"Well, he ought to be turned out," declared one boy decidedly. "Never mind, we'll make it so hot for that Jenk, he'll want to go."

"No, you mustn't," declared Percy, now very much alarmed. "Oh, no, you mustn't, Hobbs, because, if you do, Joel won't like it. Oh, he'll be so angry! He won't like it a bit, I tell you," he kept saying.

The idea of Joel's not liking it seemed to take all the fun out of the thing, so Hobbs found himself saying, "Well, all right, I suppose we've got to put up with the fellow then. But you know yourself, Whitney, he's a mean cad."

There seemed to be but one opinion about that. But the fact remained that Jenkins was still to be one of them, to be treated as well as they could manage. And for the next few days Joel had awfully hard work to be go-between for all the crowd, and the boy who had made it hard for him.

"You'll have to help me out, Tom," he said more than once in despair.

"Pretty hard lines," said Tom. Then the color flew all over his face. "I suppose I really ought, for you know, Pepper, I told you I wanted at first that you should lose your racket."

"Never mind that now, Tom," said Joel brightly, and sticking out his brown hand. "You've been awfully good ever since."

"Had to," grunted Tom, hanging to the hand, "when I saw how mean the beggar was."

"And but for you I should never have found the racket, at least not in time." Joel shivered, remembering the close call he had had from losing the game.

Tom shivered too, but for a different cause. "If I hadn't told him, I'd always have hated myself," he thought.

"Well, Joe, I wouldn't after this give away a racket. Now you see if you hadn't bestowed your old one on that ragamuffin in town, you wouldn't have been in such a scrape." Tom tried to turn it off lightly.

"Oh, that made no difference," Joel made haste to say, " 'cause I could have borrowed another. But I'd got used to my new one. Besides, Grandpapa sent it to me to practice with for this game, and I really couldn't have done so well without it."

"Yes, I know—I know," said Tom remorsefully, "and that's what Jenk knew, too, the beggar!"

"Well, it's all over now," said Joel merrily, "so say no more about it."

But it wasn't all over with Jenkins, and he resolved within himself to pay Joel Pepper up sometime, after the boys had forgotten a little about this last exploit, if they ever did.

And that afternoon Joel stayed in, foregoing all the charms of a ballgame, to write Mamsie a complete account of the affair, making light of the other boys' part in it, and praising up Tom Beresford to the skies. "And oh, Mamsie," Joel wrote over and over, "Dave didn't have anything to do with it—truly he didn't. And Mr. Harrow is just bully," he wrote—then scratched it out although it mussed the letter up dreadfully. "He's fine, he is! And oh, I like Dr. Marks, ever so much, I do"—till Mrs. Fisher had a tolerably good idea of the whole thing.

"I'm not sorry, Adoniram," she said, after Dr. Fisher had read the letter at least twice, and then looked over his spectacles at her keenly, "that I agreed with Mr. King that it was best that the boys should go away to school."

"Now, any other woman," exclaimed the little doctor admiringly, "would have whimpered right out, and carried on dreadfully at the least sign of trouble coming to her boy."

"No, I'm not a bit sorry," repeated Mrs. Fisher firmly, "for it's going to be the making of Joel, to teach him to take care of himself. And I'd trust him anywhere," she added proudly.

"So you may. So you may, my dear," declared the little doctor gaily. "And I guess, if the truth were told, that Joel's part in this whole scrape hasn't been such a very bad one after all."

Which came to be the general view when Dr. Marks's letter arrived, and one from the underinstructor followed, setting things in the right light. And although old Mr. King was for going off directly to interview the master, with several separate and distinct complaints and criticisms, he was at last persuaded to give up the trip and let matters work their course under the proper guidance at the school.

"So, Polly, my child," he said on the following day, when the letters were all in, "I believe I'll trust Dr. Marks, after all, to settle the affair. He seems a very good sort of a man, on the whole, and I really suppose he knows what to do with a lot of boys, though—goodness me!—how he can, passes my comprehension. So I am not going."

"Oh, Grandpapa!" exclaimed Polly, the color flooding her cheek, and she seized his hand in a glad little way.

"Yes, I really see no necessity for going," went on the old gentleman, much as if he were being urged out of his way to set forth, "so I shall stay at home. Joel can take care of himself. I'd trust him anywhere," he brought up, using the same words that Mother Fisher had employed.

"Wouldn't you, Grandpapa!" cried Polly with sparkling eyes, and clinging to him.

"Yes, Polly, my chlld," said Grandpapa emphatically, "because, no matter into what mischief Joe may get, he always owns up. Goodness me, Polly, that boy can't go very far wrong, with such a mother as you've got."

Alexia Rhys, running through the wide hall, came upon the two. "Oh, beg pardon, and may we girls have Polly?" all in the same breath.

"Get away with you," laughed old Mr. King, who had his own reasons for liking Alexia. "That's the way you always do, trying to get Polly Pepper away when we are having a good talk."

"Oh dear!" exclaimed Alexia, doing her best to curb her impatience, and pinching her hands together, "we did so want—"

"I can't go now, Alexia," said Polly, still clinging to Mr. King's hand.

Grandpapa sent a keen glance over into Alexia's face. "I think you better go, Polly," he said. "You and I will have our talk later."

"Oh, goody!" cried Alexia, hopping up and down. And "Oh, Grandpapa!" reproachfully from Polly.

"Yes, Polly, it's best for you to go with the girls now," said old Mr. King, gently relinquishing her hands, "so run along with you, child." And he went into the library.

"Come right along," cried Alexia gustily, and, pulling Polly down the hall.

"There now, you see, you've dragged me away from Grandpapa," cried Polly in a vexed way.

"Well, he said you were to go," cried Alexia, perfectly delighted at the result. "Oh, we're to have such fun! You can't think, Polly Pepper."

"Of course he did, when you said the girls wanted me," said Polly, half determined, even then, to run back. "I'd much rather have stayed with him, Alexia."

"Well, you can't, because he said you were to come. And besides, here are the girls." And there they were on the back porch, six or eight in a group.

"Oh, Polly, Polly!" they cried. "Are you coming—can you really go?" swarming around her. "And do get your hat on," said Clem Forsythe, "and hurry up."

"Where are you going?" asked Polly.

"The idea! Alexia Rhys, you are a great one to send after her," cried Sally Moore. "Not even to tell her where we are going, or what we want her for!"

"Well, I got her here, and that is half of the battle," said Alexia, in an injured way. "And my goodness me! Polly won't hardly speak to me now, and you may go yourself after her next time, Sally Moore."

"There, girls, don't fight," said Clem sweetly. "Polly, we are going out to Silvia Horne's. Mrs. Horne has just telephoned to see if we'll come out to supper. Come, hurry up. We want to catch the next car. She says she'll send somebody home with us."

"Yes, yes, do hurry," begged the girls, hopping up and down on anxious feet.

"I must ask Mamsie," said Polly. "Oh, how perfectly splendid!" running off with a glad remembrance of lessons all ready for the next day. "Now, how nice it is that Mamsie always made me get them the first thing," she reflected as she sped along.

Mamsie said yes, for she well knew that Mrs. Horne was a careful person, and when she promised anything it was always well done. "But brush your hair, Polly," she said. "It looks very untidy flying all over your head."

So Polly rushed off to her own room, Alexia—who didn't dare to trust her out of her sight—at her heels, to get in the way, and hinder dreadfully by teasing Polly every minute to "hurry, we'll lose the train."

"Where are you going, Polly?" asked Phronsie, hearing Alexia's voice. And laying down her doll, she went into the blue and white room that was Polly's very own. "Oh, may I go too?" as Polly ran to the closet to get out her second-best hat.

"Oh dear me!" began Alexia.

"No, Pet," said Polly, her head in the closet. "Oh my goodness, where *is* that hat?"

"Oh dear!" exclaimed Alexia, wringing her hands, "we'll be late and miss the train. Do hurry, Polly Pepper."

"I'll find it, Polly," said Phronsie, going to the closet and getting down on her knees to peer around.

"Oh, it wouldn't be on the floor, Phronsie," began Polly. "Oh dear me! Where *can* it be?"

"Here it is," cried Alexia, "behind the bed." And running off, she picked it up and swung it over to Polly.

"Goodness me!" said Polly with a little laugh. "I remember now, I tossed it on the bed, I thought. Well, I'm ready now, thank fortune," pinning on her hat. "Good-bye, Pet."

"I am so very glad it is found, Polly," said Phronsie, getting up on tiptoe to pull Polly's hat straight and get another kiss.

"Come on, Polly," called Alexia, flying over the stairs. "Yes, yes, girls, she's coming! Oh dear me, Polly, we'll be late!"

Chapter 5

At Silvia Horne's

*B*UT they weren't—not a bit of it—and had ten minutes to spare as they came rushing up to the station platform.

"Oh, look—look, girls." Polly Pepper pointed up to the clock, pushing back the damp rings of hair from her forehead. "Oh dear me—I'm so hot!"

"And so am I," panted the other girls, dashing up. One of them sank down on the upper step and fanned herself in angry little puffs with her hat, which she twitched off for that purpose.

"Just like you, Alexia," cried one when she could get her breath. "You're always scaring us to death."

"Well, I'm sure I was scared myself, Clem," retorted Alexia, propping herself against the wall. "Oh dear! I can't breathe. I guess I'm going to die—whew, whew!"

As Alexia made this statement quite often on similar occasions, the girls heard it with the air of an old acquaintance, and straightened their coats and hats, and pulled themselves into shape generally.

"Oh my goodness, how you look, Sally! Your hat is all over your left eye." Alexia deserted her wall, and ran over to pull it straight.

"You let me be," cried Sally crossly, and twitching away. "If it hadn't been for you, my hat would have stayed where I put it. I'll fix it myself." She pulled out the long pin.

"Oh dear me! Now the head has come off," she mourned.

"Oh my goodness! Your face looks the worst—isn't it sweet!" cried Alexia coolly, who hadn't heard this last.

"Don't, Alexia," cried Polly. "She's lost her pin."

"Misery!" exclaimed Alexia, starting forward. "Oh, where, where—"

"It isn't the pin," said Sally, holding that out. "But the head has flown off." She jumped off from the step and began to peer anxiously around in the dirt, all the girls crowding around and getting dreadfully in the way.

"What pin was it, Sally?" asked Polly, poking into a tuft of grass beneath the steps. "Your blue one?"

"No, it was my best one—oh dear me!" Sally looked ready to cry and turned away so that the girls couldn't see her face.

"Not the one your aunt gave you, Sally!" exclaimed Clem.

"Yes—yes." Sally sniffed outright now. "Oh dear! I put it in because—because—we were going to Silvia's—oh dear me!"

She gave up now, and sobbed outright.

"Don't cry, Sally," begged Polly, deserting her grass tuft to run over to her. "We'll find it." Alexia was alternately picking frantically in all the dustheaps, and wringing her hands, one eye on the clock all the while.

"Oh, no, you won't," whimpered Sally. "It flew right out

of my hand, and it's gone way off—I know it has—oh dear!" and she sobbed worse than ever.

"Perhaps one of those old hens will pick it up," suggested Lucy Bennett, pointing across the way to the stationmaster's garden, where four or five fowl were busily scratching.

"Oh—oh!" Sally gave a little scream at that, and threw herself into Polly Pepper's arms. "My aunt's pin—and she told me—to be careful, and she won't—won't ever give me anything else, and now those old hens will eat it. Oh *dear* me! What shall I do?"

"How can you, Lucy, say such perfectly dreadful things?" cried Polly. "Don't cry, Sally. Girls, do keep on looking for it as hard as you can. Sally, do stop."

But Sally was beyond stopping. "She told—told me only to wear it Sundays, and with my best—best dress. Oh, do give me your handkerchief, Polly. I've left mine home."

So Polly pulled out her clean handkerchief from her coat pocket, and Sally wiped up her face, and cried all over it, till it was a damp little wad, and the girls poked around, and searched frantically, and Alexia, one eye on the clock, exclaimed, "Oh, girls, it's time for the train. Oh misery me! What *shall* we do?"

"And here it comes!" Lucy Bennett screamed.

"Stick on your hat, Sally—you've the pin part. Come, hurry up!" cried the others. And they all huddled around her.

"Oh, I can't go," began Sally.

"You must," said Clem. "We've telephoned back to Mrs. Horne we're coming. Do stick on your hat, Sally Moore."

Alexia was spinning around, saying over and over to herself, "I won't stay back—I won't." Then, as the train slowly rounded the long curve and the passengers emerged from the waiting room, she rushed up to the knot of girls.

"Go along, Sally Moore, and I'll stay and hunt for your old pin," just as someone twitched Sally's hat from her fingers and clapped it on her head.

"Oh my goodness me!" Alexia gave a little scream, and nearly fell backward. " Look—it's on your own head! Oh, girls, I shall die." She pointed tragically up to the hat, then gave a sudden nip with her long fingers, and brought out of a knot of ribbon, a gilt, twisted affair with pink stones. "You had it all the time, Sally Moore," and she went into peals of laughter.

"Well, do stop. Everybody's looking," cried the rest of the girls, as they raced off to the train, now at a dead stop. Sally, with her hat crammed on her head at a worse angle than ever, only realized that she had the ornament safely clutched in her hand.

"Oh, I can't help it," exclaimed Alexia gustily, and hurrying off to get next to Polly. "Oh dear me! Whee—*whee!*" as they all plunged into the train.

When they arrived at Edgewood, there was a carriage and a wagonette drawn up by the little station, and out of the first jumped Silvia, and following her, a tall, thin girl who seemed to have a good many bracelets and jingling things.

"My cousin, Kathleen Briggs. She just came today," said Silvia, "while I was at school, and so mother thought it would be nice to have you girls out to supper, 'cause they're only going to stay till tomorrow. Oh, it's so fine that you've come! Well, come and get in. Polly, you're going in the carriage with Kathleen and me. Come on."

Alexia crowded up close behind.

"I'm going with Polly Pepper, this time," announced Sally, pushing in between. "Alexia always gets her."

"Well, she's my very dearest friend," said Alexia coolly,

and working her long figure up close to Polly, as Silvia led her off, "so of course I always must go with her."

"Well, so she is our very dearest friend, too, Alexia Rhys," declared Clem, "and we're going to have her sometimes, ourselves." And there they were in a dreadful state, and Silvia's cousin, the new girl, to see it all!

She jingled her bracelets, and picked at the long chain dangling from her neck, and stared at them all.

"Oh my goodness!" exclaimed Polly Pepper with very red cheeks. "Alexia, don't—don't," she begged.

"Well, I don't care," said Alexia recklessly, "the girls are always picking at me because I will keep next to you, Polly, and you're my very dearest friend, and—"

"But Sally had such a fright about her pin," said Polly in a low tone. Alexia was crowded up close and hugging her arm, so no one else heard.

"Well, that old pin dropped in the ribbon. She had it herself all the time. Oh dear!" Alexia nearly went off again at the remembrance.

"She felt badly, all the same," said Polly slowly. She didn't even smile, and Alexia could feel that the arm was slipping away from her.

"Oh dear me!" she began, then she dropped Polly Pepper's arm. "Sally, you may go next," she cried suddenly, and she skipped back into the bunch of the other girls.

Polly sent her an approving little nod, and she didn't fail to smile now. Alexia ran over to the wagonette and hopped in, not daring to trust herself to see Sally Moore's satisfaction ahead in the coveted seat.

The other girls jumping in, the wagonette was soon filled, and away they spun for the two miles over to the Hornes' beautiful place. And before long, their respects having been paid to Mrs. Horne, the whole bevy was up in Silvia's pretty pink and white room overlooking the lake.

"I think it's just too lovely for anything here, Silvia Horne," exclaimed Sally, whose spirits were quite recovered now. She had her aunt's pin all safe, and she had ridden up next to Polly. "Oh, girls, she has a new pincushion and cover."

"Yes, a whole new set," said Silvia carelessly, as the girls rushed over from the bed where they were laying their things, to see this new acquisition to the beautiful room.

"Well, if I could have such perfectly exquisite things," breathed Alexia as they all ohed and ahed over the pink ribbons and dainty lace, "I'd be the very happiest girl."

Kathleen Briggs thrust her long figure in among the bevy. "That toilet set is very pretty," she said indifferently and with quite a young-lady air.

"Very pretty!" repeated Alexia, turning her pale eyes upon her in astonishment. "Well, I should think it was! It's too perfectly elegant for anything!"

"Oh dear me!" Kathleen gave a little laugh. "It's just nothing to the one I have on my toilet table at home. Besides, I shall bring home some Oriental lace, and have a new one: I'm going around the world tomorrow, you know."

"Oh my goodness!" exclaimed Alexia faintly. And the other girls fell back, and stared respectfully.

"Yes," said Kathleen, delighted at the effect she had produced. "We start tomorrow, and we don't know how long we shall be gone. Perhaps two years. Papa says he'll stay if we want to, but mamma and I may get tired and come home." She jingled her bracelets worse than ever.

"They've come to bid us good-bye, you see," said Silvia, to break the uncomfortable silence.

"Oh yes," said Polly Pepper.

"Well, if you've got your things off, let's go out of doors," proposed Silvia suddenly.

"Yes, do let's." The girls drew a long breath as they raced off.

"I think that Kathleen Briggs is too perfectly horrid for anything"—Alexia got up close to Polly as they flew down the stairs—"with her going round the world, and her sniffing at Silvia's toilet set."

"Hush—hush!" whispered Polly. "She'll hear you."

"Well, I don't care. And she's going round the world tomorrow, so what does it signify?" said Alexia. "Oh, don't go so fast, Polly. You most made me tumble on my nose."

"Well, you mustn't come with me, then, if you don't keep up," said Polly, with a merry little laugh, and hurrying on.

"I'm going to keep up," cried Alexia, dashing after, "but you go so fast," she grumbled.

"We're going to have tea out on the lawn," announced Silvia in satisfaction, as the bevy rushed out on the broad west piazza.

The maids were already busily setting three little tables, that were growing quite pretty under their hands.

"There will be four at each table," said Silvia. "Polly's going to sit with Kathleen and me, and one other girl—I don't know which one yet," she said slowly.

"Oh, choose me." Alexia worked her way along eagerly to the front. "I'm her dearest friend—Polly's, I mean. So you ought to choose me."

"Well, I shan't," declared Silvia. "You crowded me awfully at Lucy Bennett's party, and kept close to Polly Pepper all the time."

"Well, that's because you would keep Polly yourself. You crowded and pushed horribly yourself, you know you did." Her long face was quite red now.

"Well, I had to," declared Silvia coolly. "At any rate, you shan't have Polly today, for I've quite decided. Clem, you shall have the other seat at my table."

Clem hopped up and down and beat her hands together in glee. "There, Alexia Rhys!" she cried in triumph. "Who's got Polly Pepper now, I'd like to know!"

Alexia, much discomfited, fell back. "Well, I think that's a great way to give a party," she said, "to get up a fight the first thing."

But Silvia and Kathleen had got Polly Pepper one on each side, and were now racing down to the lake. "We're going to have a sail," called Silvia over her shoulder, so they all followed, Alexia among the rest, with no time for anything else. There was the steam launch waiting for them.

"Girls—girls!" Mrs. Horne called to them from the library. "Wait a moment. Mr. and Mrs. Briggs are going too."

"Oh bother!" began Silvia. Then the color flew into her face, for Kathleen heard.

"I shall tell my mother what you said," she declared.

"Dear me! No, you mustn't," begged Silvia in alarm.

"Yes, I shall too." Kathleen's bracelets jingled worse than ever as she shook them out.

"Well, I call that real hateful," broke out Silvia, a red spot on either cheek. "You know I didn't mean it."

"Well, you said it. And if you think it's a bother to take my mother and father out on your old launch, I shan't stop here and bring you anything when I come home from around the world."

Silvia trembled. She very much wanted something from around the world. So she put her arm about Kathleen. "Oh, make up now," she said. "They're coming," as Mr. and Mrs. Briggs advanced down the path. "Promise you won't tell," she begged.

"Yes, do," said Polly Pepper imploringly.

So Kathleen promised, and everything became quite serene, just in time for Mr. and Mrs. Briggs to have the girls presented to them. And then they all jumped into the steam launch, and the men sent her into the lake, and everything was as merry as could be under the circumstances.

"I haven't got to go to school tomorrow," announced Silvia when they were well off. "Isn't that too fine for anything, girls?"

"Dear me! I should say so," cried Alexia enviously. "How I wish I could ever stay home! But aunt is so very dreadful, she makes me go every single day."

"Well, I'm going to stay home to bid Kathleen good-bye, you know," said Silvia.

"You see we are going around the world," announced Mrs. Briggs. She was just like Kathleen as far as mother and daughter could be, and she had more jingling things on, besides a long lace scarf that was catching in everything, and she carried a white, fluffy parasol in her hand. "And we've come to bid good-bye to our relatives before we start. Kathleen, you shouldn't have come out on the water without your hat," for the first time noticing her daughter's bare head.

"None of the girls have hats on," said Kathleen, shaking her long light braids.

"Well, I don't see how their mothers can allow it," exclaimed Mrs. Briggs, glancing around on the group, "but I shan't let you, Kathleen. Dear me! You will ruin your skin. Now you must come under my parasol." She moved up on the seat. "Here, come over here."

"Oh, I'm not going to," cried Kathleen with a grimace. "I can't see anything under that old thing. Besides, I'm going to stay with the girls."

"Yes, you must come under my parasol." A frown of real

anxiety settled on her mother's face. "You'll thank me by and by for saving your complexion for you, Kathleen, so come over."

"No," said Kathleen, hanging back and holding to Silvia's arm.

"There's your veil, you know." Mr. Briggs hadn't spoken before, but now he edged up to his wife. "It's in my pocket."

"So it is," cried his wife joyfully, as Mr. Briggs pulled out a long green tissue veil. "I am so glad I had you bring it. Now, Kathleen, tie this all over your head. Your father will bring it over to you. And next time, do obey me, and wear your hat as I've always told you."

So Kathleen, not daring to hold back from this command, but grumbling at every bit of the process, tied on the veil, and then sat up very cross and stiff through the rest of the sail.

"I should rather never go around the world, if I'd got to be tied up like an old green mummy every step," Alexia managed to whisper in Polly's ear as they hopped out of the launch. And she was very sweet to Kathleen after that, pitying her dreadfully.

Chapter 6

The Accident

"*O*H dear me!" exclaimed Clem. They were all on the cars—the early train—going home; the governess, a middle-aged person who looked after the younger Horne children and who was going in to her sister's to pass the night, taking care of the party. "Now I've got to sit up till all hours when I get home, to get my lessons."

Polly Pepper gave a comfortable little wriggle under her coat. "Isn't it nice Mamsie makes me get my lessons the first thing, before I play!" she said to herself for about the fiftieth time.

"So have I," cried Lucy Bennett, echoing Clem's words.

"Well, I can't," cried Alexia with a flounce, "because my aunt won't let me sit up after nine o'clock—that is, to study. So I have to get up early in the morning. Oh dear!" with a grimace at the thought.

"So do I," said Amy Garrett. "Dear me! and I'm just as sleepy in the morning as I can be."

Alexia yawned at the very memory of it. "Well, don't let's talk of it," she begged. "Seems as if Miss Salisbury's eyes were all over me now."

"I have Miss Anstice tomorrow," said Amy, "and it's the day for her black silk gown."

"Horrors!" exclaimed Alexia, and "How do you know she'll wear the black silk gown tomorrow, Amy?" from the other girls.

"Because she said Professor Mills from the Institute is to be there tomorrow," said Amy. "He gives the art lecture to our class. And you know the black silk gown will surely go on."

"There's no help for you, you poor child," cried Alexia, exulting that she never would be gathered into Miss Anstice's class, and that she just hated art and all that sort of thing, despite the efforts of Miss Salisbury's younger sister to get her interested. "Yes, that black silk gown will surely be there. Look out now, Amy. All you girls will catch it."

"Oh, I know it," said Amy with a sigh. "How I do wish I never'd got into that class!"

"Well, you know I told you," said Alexia provokingly. "You'd much better have taken my advice and kept out of her clutches."

"I wish I had," mourned Amy again.

"How Miss Anstice can be so horrid—she isn't a bit like Miss Salisbury," said Alexia. "I don't see—"

"She isn't horrid," began Polly.

"Oh, Polly!"

"Well, not always," said Polly.

"Well, she is anyway when she has company, and gets on that black silk gown. Just as stiff and cross and perky and horrid as can be."

"She wants you all to show off good," said Alexia. "Well,

I'm glad enough I'm not in any of her old classes. I just dote on Miss Salisbury."

"Oh, Alexia, you worry the life out of her almost," said Sally.

"Can't help it if I do," said Alexia sweetly. "I'm very fond of her. And as for Mademoiselle, she's a dear. Oh, I love Mademoiselle, too."

"Well, she doesn't love you," cried Clem viciously. "Dear me! Fancy one of the teachers being fond of Alexia!"

"Oh, you needn't laugh," said Alexia composedly as the girls giggled. "Every single one of those teachers would feel dreadfully if I left that school. They would really, and cry their eyes out."

"And tear their hair, I suppose," said Clem scornfully.

"Yes, and tear their—why, what in this world are we stopping for?" cried Alexia in one breath.

So everybody else wondered, as the train gradually slackened speed and came to a standstill. Everybody who was going into town to the theater or opera began to look impatient at once.

"Oh dear!" cried the girls who were going to sit up to study. "Now isn't this just as hateful as it can be?"

"I don't care," said Alexia, settling comfortably back, "because I can't study much anyway, so I'd just as soon sit on this old train an hour."

"Oh, Alexia!" exclaimed Polly in dismay, with her heart full at the thought of Mamsie's distress, and that of dear Grandpapa and Jasper. Phronsie would be abed anyway by the time the early train was in, so she couldn't worry. But all the others—"Oh dear me!" she gasped.

"Don't look so, Polly," said Alexia. "We'll start pretty soon, I guess."

The governess, Miss Baker, came over from the opposite

seat to stand in the aisle. "I think we'll start soon," she said.
But her eyes looked worried.

"What is it—oh, Miss Baker, what is the reason we're
stopping?" cried two or three of the girls.

"I don't know," said the governess.

A man coming in from outside, where a lot of gentlemen
were pouring out of the cars to investigate, furnished the
information.

"Driving wheel broken," he said, being sparing of words.

"Oh, can't we go out to see?" cried Alexia, hopping out
of her seat. "Come on," and she was prancing down the
aisle.

"No, indeed," said Miss Baker in displeasure. "And do you
come directly back," she commanded.

"Oh dear me!" grumbled Alexia to Sally, who had tumbled out after her. "She's worse than Miss Anstice—stiff,
precise old thing!" She came slowly back.

"That a young lady under my care," said Miss Baker,
lifting her black gloves in amazement, "should so far forget
herself as to want to run out on that track with a lot of men! I
am astonished."

"There's a girl out there," said Alexia, sinking into her
seat crossly, and peering over Polly Pepper's head.

"And there's another," proclaimed Sally triumphantly.

"Well, if they've forgotten themselves so far as to go out
there under such circumstances, I shall not let any young
lady in my care do it," said Miss Baker emphatically.

So, swallowing their disappointment at not being allowed
to see all that presented itself, the girls settled back and
made themselves as comfortable as possible. Meantime almost everybody else poured out of their car. But it seemed
to Polly Pepper as if she never could keep still in all this

world. And she clasped her hands tightly together and hoped nobody would speak to her just yet.

"Polly"—Alexia gave a little push as she leaned over—"isn't it perfectly dreadful to be mewed up here in this way? Say, Polly, do talk."

"Go right away, Alexia." Polly gave a little flounce, and sat quite straight.

"Oh dear me!" exclaimed Alexia in astonishment, and falling back.

"And I wish you would let me alone," cried Polly, quite aghast at herself, but unable to stop.

"Oh dear me!" Alexia kept saying quite faintly, and rolling her eyes.

"Well, I'm glad Polly has made you behave for once," said Clem, who never could forgive Alexia for getting Polly so much to herself.

Alexia stopped saying "Oh dear me!" and sat quite still. Just then Polly turned and saw her face.

"Oh, Alexia!" she cried, flying at her, when an awful bump, and then another much worse, and then a grinding noise, perfectly terrible—and everybody who was left in the car went tumbling out of their seats.

"Oh, we're run into!" screamed half a dozen of the girls. Miss Baker, who had been standing in the aisle, was down in a heap on the floor.

"Oh, oh!" Polly had her arms around Alexia and was hugging her tightly. "Are you hurt?" as they wriggled out of the bunch of girls into which they had been precipitated, up to their feet.

"N-no," Alexia tried to say. Instead, she wobbled over, and laid her head on Polly's arm. "Girls—girls—Miss Baker!" called Polly, not seeing that lady, in the confusion of the other passengers, staggering along the aisle, her bonnet knocked over her eyes, and a girl on either hand to help her along. "Clem—oh, somebody help me! Alexia is hurt." But nobody heard in the general tumult.

"Oh dear! Alexia, do open your eyes," begged Polly, quite gone now with distress. "And to think I was so cross to her!" And she turned quite white.

"Dear, dear Alexia," she cried. And because there was nothing else to do, she leaned over and dropped a kiss on Alexia's long face, and two tears dropped down as well.

Alexia opened her eyes. "That's very nice, Polly," she said. "Do so some more."

"Aren't you ashamed!" cried Polly, the rosy color coming back to her cheek. And then, remembering, she hugged Alexia tightly. "Oh, I'm so glad you're not hurt, Alexia, so very glad!" she cried gratefully.

"Ow!" exclaimed Alexia, shrinking back.

"Oh, now you are hurt," cried Polly. "Oh, Alexia!" And she turned very white again. "Tell me where it is." And just then some of the girls rushed up with the news, corroborated by the other passengers, that the down express had run into them—been signaled, but couldn't stop in time, etc., etc. —till Polly thought she should go wild before the babel could be stopped. "Don't crowd around so," she cried hoarsely. "Alexia is hurt."

"Alexia?" The noise, as far as Miss Salisbury's girls were concerned, stopped at once, and at last the other passengers were made to understand how it was. And Alexia, quite faint now, but having sense enough to hang to Polly Pepper's hand, was laid across an improvised bed made of two seats, and a doctor who happened to be on the train, one of the party going in to the theater, came up, and looked her over professionally.

"It's my arm," said Alexia, opening her eyes again. "It was

doubled up someway under me. Oh dear me! I'm so silly to faint."

"You're not silly at all," cried Polly warmly, and holding her well hand, while her eyes searched the doctor's face anxiously. "Oh, is it broken?" they asked, as plainly as possible.

"Not a bit of it," said the doctor cheerfully, feeling it all over again to make quite sure, while Alexia set her teeth together, trying not to show how very much it hurt. "It's badly strained—the ligaments are—but fortunately no bones are broken."

"Oh dear!" groaned Alexia. "Now, why can't it be broken?"

"Oh, Alexia!" cried Polly. And now the tears that had been kept back were rolling down her cheeks. "I'm so happy, I can't help it," she said.

"And the very idea, Alexia Rhys," exclaimed Clem, "to wish your arm had been broken!" And she gave a little shiver.

"It hurts just as much," said Alexia, trying to sit up straight and making an awful face, "so it might as well be. And I've never been in a railroad accident. But a sprained arm isn't anything to show. Any baby can have that—oh dear me!"

"Well, you better lie still," counseled Miss Baker tartly. "Dear me! I little thought when I took charge of you young ladies that any such thing would occur."

"She acts as if she thought we did it on purpose," said Alexia, turning her face over to hide it on Polly's arm again, and wishing her own needn't ache so dreadfully. "Oh dear! Such a time as we've had, Polly Pepper, with those dreadful Briggses—I mean Mrs. Briggs—and now to be all banged up, and this cross old thing to see us home! And now I never'll be able to get through the term, 'cause I'll have to stay at home with this old arm, and aunt will scold." She was quite out of breath with all her woes.

"Oh, yes, you will," cried Polly reassuringly. "I'll run over every day and study with you, Alexia. And you'll soon be all well again. Don't try to talk now, dear." And she patted the poor cheeks, and smoothed her hair. All the while she was trying to keep down the worry over the home circle, who would be thrown into the greatest distress, she knew, if news of the accident should reach their ears.

"Can't somebody telephone them?" she cried. "Oh, Miss Baker"—the doctor had rushed off to other possible sufferers— "and tell them no one is hurt? I mean seriously?"

"There is," said the governess, quite calmly. "A man has been killed."

"Oh dear!"

"A brakeman," Miss Baker hastened to add. "Don't be frightened. None of the passengers."

"Now I know he was brave, and trying to do something to save us," cried Polly, with kindling eyes.

"Yes," said a passenger, coming up to their group. "He was running back with a lantern to signal the train, and he slipped and fell, and the express went over him. But it stopped just in time for us."

"Oh, the poor, poor man!" Polly was quite gone by this tine, and Alexia forgot her pain in trying to comfort her.

"But suppose he had children," cried Polly. "Just suppose it, Alexia."

"I don't want to suppose it," said Alexia, wriggling. "Ugh! You do say such uncomfortable things, Polly Pepper."

"I know it." Polly swallowed hard, and held Alexia's hand tighter than ever. "Well, I won't talk of it any more."

The governess, who had moved away a bit, now came back with vexation plainly written all over her face. "I must go and see if there isn't some way to get a message to Grandpapa King, Alexia," said Polly. "I'll be back as soon as I can." She dropped a kiss on the nearest cheek.

"Don't be gone long," begged Alexia.

"I will go with you," said the governess, stepping off after her.

"Very well," said Polly, going swiftly down the aisle, to see below the car steps a crowd of passengers all in a tumult, and vociferating angrily. In the midst of them, Polly saw the face of the doctor who had just fixed Alexia's arm.

"Oh, sir," she began.

He looked up, and caught sight of the brown eyes. "Is the little girl worse?" And he sprang over toward her.

Polly, not stopping to think how furious Alexia would be, who was quite the tallest of their set, to be designated as a little girl, made haste to say, "Oh no, sir. But oh, could you tell me how to let my grandpapa and my mother know we are safe? Could you, sir?" Poor Polly, who had held up so bravely, was clasping her hands tightly together, and the brown eyes were full of tears.

"Well, you see," began the doctor, hating to disappoint her, "it's a difficult matter to get in communication with them at once. We are only five miles out, but—"

"Five miles?" echoed Polly. "Oh then, someone can go to the nearest station, and telephone, can't they, sir?"

"To be sure, and that's been done. But your family, little girl—how can we reach them?"

"Oh, I can run," cried Polly happily, "to the station myself, sir." And she began to clamber down the car steps.

"Come back," commanded the governess, lifting her hands in horror. "I never heard of such a thing. The very idea! What would your grandfather, Mr. King, say to such a thing, Polly Pepper?"

"Mr. who?" cried the doctor. "Stay, little girl," seizing her arm. "Mr. who?" he demanded, looking up to the governess on the car steps.

"Mr. Horatio King," she replied with asperity, "and you'd better be occupied with something else, let me tell you, sir, instead of encouraging his granddaughter to run off on such a wild-goose errand as this."

"I certainly shall take pleasure in performing the wild-goose errand myself," he said. "Now, Polly, I'll send the message. Don't you worry." And he sped off down the track.

Chapter 7

The Salisbury Girls

AND then somebody rushed in, saying, "We've another locomotive. Now we're going!" And everybody else who was outside hurried into the cars. The new propelling power was attached to the other end of the train, and after a deal of switching, there they were at last—off on the way home!

Polly gave a long breath of relief and clasped Alexia's hand closely. "Oh, by this time they know at home it's all right," she cried.

The doctor came smilingly down the aisle. "Well"—he nodded to Polly—"yes, it's all right," he said. "I must really call you Polly Pepper now, for I know your grandfather, and Dr. Fisher—well there! Indeed I know him."

"Do you?' cried Polly with blooming cheeks, well pleased to find a friend at such a time.

"Yes, indeed. I'm fortunate enough to meet him in hospital work. Now then, how is our little friend here?" He leaned over and touched Alexia's arm lightly.

"Oh, I'm all right," she said.

"That's good," in a gratified tone. "Now keep plucky, and you'll get out of this finely." Then he sat down on the arm of the seat, and told such a funny story that no one supposed it could be the home station when the train came to a stand-still, and he was helping Alexia out.

"There now—drop Polly's hand, if you please," the doctor was saying. "I'll assist you."

"But I don't want to," said Alexia, hanging to it for dear life. "I want Polly."

"I presume so," laughed the doctor, "but I think it's best for me to help you." Miss Baker and all the girls crowded up in a bunch. "Easy there," he said. "Don't hurry so. There's plenty of time." And he got between them and Alexia's lame arm.

And there, down by the car steps—Polly could see him as he waited for the stream of passengers to get out—was Jasper, his eyes eagerly searching every face, with an impatience scarcely to be controlled. And back of him were Dr. Fisher's big glasses, shining as the little doctor pranced back and forth, unable to keep still.

"There they are—there they are!" Polly exclaimed. "Oh, if we could hurry and let them know we're all right!" But they were wedged in so, there was nothing to do but to take their turn and let the passengers in front descend.

"Jasper—oh, Papa Fisher!" At last Polly was out on the platform, where she stood on her tiptoes and waved her hand.

"Are you all right?" asked Jasper eagerly, craning his neck to see for himself.

"Yes—yes!" cried Polly. And then presently they had her on either hand! "Oh, help Alexia," she cried, turning back.

Dr. Fisher took one look through his big glasses. "Well, well, Pennell," he exclaimed, "you here?" and he skipped over to them.

"I really believe so," laughed Dr. Pennell.

"Dear me!" Little Dr. Fisher glanced at Alexia quickly.

"Nothing but sprained," the other doctor said quickly. "Still, it needs careful attention."

And then it came out that Alexia's aunt had heard a chance word dropped about the accident, and had run down to Mr. King's in her distress, so she was there awaiting them, and the fathers and brothers of the rest of the "Salisbury girls" took off their charges, much to the relief of the governess. So presently Jasper had his party all settled in the carriage, Dr. Pennell saying, "Well, I resign my responsibility about that arm to you, Dr. Fisher." He lifted his hat and was off.

"Oh, wait!" cried Polly in great distress as Thomas was just starting off with a dash. "I must speak to him."

"Polly—what is it?" cried Jasper. "Wait, Thomas!" So Thomas pulled up.

"I must—I must," declared Polly. Her foot was on the step, and she was soon out.

"I'll go with you," said Jasper, as she sped down through the streams of people pouring along the platform, to thread her way after the tall figure, Jasper by her side. "Dr. Pennell—oh, please stop."

"Hey?" The doctor pulled up in his brisk walk. "Oh dear me! What is it?"

"Will you please tell me—do you know who the poor man was who was killed?" she gasped.

"Oh, Polly," cried Jasper. "Was there someone killed?"

"Yes, he was a brakeman, Polly," said Dr. Pennell.

"Oh, I know—but where did he live?" cried Polly. "And had he any children?" all in one breath.

"A big family, I understand," said the doctor gravely.

"Oh dear me!" exclaimed Polly with a sorry droop to the bright head, and clasping her hands. "Could you, Dr. Pennell, tell me anything more?"

"That's all I know about the poor fellow," said the doctor. "The conductor told me that."

"I'll find out for you tomorrow, Polly," said Jasper quickly. "I'll run down to the railroad office and get all the news I can."

"And I'll go with you," said Polly, "for I most know Grandpapa will let me. He was so very good to us all—that poor man was," she mourned.

"Yes, Polly, there's no doubt of that," Dr. Pennell said abruptly. "You and I maybe wouldn't be standing here if it were not for him."

Jasper shivered and laid hold of Polly's arm. "Well now, run along and get home," finished the doctor cheerily, "and look out for that plucky little friend of yours, and I'll try and find out, too, about that brakeman, and we'll talk the thing over." So Polly and Jasper raced back again down over the platform, clambered into the carriage, and away they went home to Grandpapa and Mamsie!

And Alexia and her aunt stayed all night. And after the whole story had been gone over and over, and Grandpapa had held Polly on his knee, all the time she was not in Mamsie's lap, and Alexia had had her poor arm taken care of, and all bandaged up, Dr. Fisher praising her for being so cool and patient, why then it was nearly eleven o'clock.

"Dear me! Polly," cried Mother Fisher in dismay, looking over at the clock—they were all in the library, and all visitors had been denied—"the very idea! you children must get to bed."

"Yes—or you won't be cool and patient tomorrow," said Dr. Fisher decidedly, and patting Alexia's bandages. "Now run off, little girl, and we'll see you bright as a button in the morning."

"I'm not cool and patient," declared Alexia, abruptly pulling down, with her well hand, the little doctor till she could whisper in his ear. "Oh, aunt does fuss so—you can't think. I'm a raging wild animal."

"Well, you haven't been raging tonight, Alexia," said the little doctor, bursting out into a laugh.

"Oh, hush, do," implored Alexia, who wasn't in the slightest degree afraid to speak her mind, least of all to Dr. Fisher, whom she liked immensely. "They'll all hear us," she brought up in terror.

"What is it, Alexia?" cried her aunt from the sofa, where Dr. Fisher had asked her to be seated, as it was well across the room. "Oh, is she worse?" she exclaimed, hurrying over nervously.

"There, now, you see," cried Alexia tragically, and sinking back in her chair. "Everything's just as bad as can be now."

"Not in the least, Miss Rhys," the little doctor said in his cheeriest tones. "Only Alexia and I had a little joke all by ourselves." And as he waited coolly for the maiden lady to return to her seat, she soon found herself back there. Then he went over to Mamsie and said something in a low tone.

"Yes, Adoniram." Mother Fisher nodded over Polly's brown head. "She ought to have a good night's sleep."

"Polly," said Dr. Fisher, leaning over her, "it's just this: that aunt of Alexia's—she's a good enough sort of a woman, I suppose," wrinkling his brows in perplexity to find the right words, "but she certainly does possess the faculty to rile folks up remarkably well. She sets my teeth on edge; she does really, wife." He brought out this confession honestly, although he hated professionally to say it. "And Alexia—well, you know, Polly, she ought to be kept quiet tonight. So your mother and I—we do, don't we, dear?" taking Mamsie's hand.

"We certainly do," said Mrs. Fisher, not waiting for the whole story to be told, "think it's best for you to have Alexia with you tonight."

"Oh, goody!" exclaimed Polly, sitting quite straight in Mamsie's lap.

"You are not to talk, Polly, you know," said Dr. Fisher decidedly.

"Oh, we won't—we won't," promised Polly faithfully.

"You can have the red room, Polly," said Mamsie, "because of the two beds. And now, child, you must both hop off and get into them as soon as you can, or you'll be sick tomorrow."

So Polly ran off to bid Grandpapa good night. And then as he held her in his arms, he said, "Well, now, Polly, you and Jasper and I will take that trip down to the railroad station tomorrow."

"Oh, Grandpapa!" cried Polly, clasping her hands, while her cheeks turned rosy red, "I am so very glad. We can go right after school, can't we?"

"School? Oh, you won't go to school tomorrow," said old Mr. King decidedly. "Yes, yes, Mrs. Fisher, in just a minute— Polly shall go to bed in a minute. No, no, Polly, after such an excitement, school isn't to be thought of for a day or two."

"Perhaps she'll be all right in the morning, father," Jasper hurried to say, at sight of Polly's face.

"Oh, I shall—I shall." Polly flashed a bright glance at

him. "*Please*, Grandpapa, let me go. I haven't been absent this year."

"And it's so awfully hard to make up lessons," said Jasper.

"Make up lessons? Well, you needn't make them up. Bless me! Such a scholar as you are, Polly, I guess you'll stand well enough at the end of the year, without any such trouble. Quite well enough," he added with decision.

Polly's brown head drooped, despite her efforts to look bravely up into his face. "Good night, Grandpapa," she said sadly, and was turning away.

"Oh bless me!" exclaimed old Mr. King hastily. "Polly, see here, my child, well—well, in the morning perhaps—dear me!—we can tell then whether it's best for you to go to school or not. Come, kiss me good night again."

So Polly ran back and gave him two or three kisses, and then raced off, Jasper having time to whisper at the door, "I most know, Polly, father'll let you go. I really and truly believe he will."

"I believe so too," cried Polly happily.

And sure enough, he did. For the next morning Polly ran down to breakfast as merry as a bee, brown eyes dancing, as if accidents were never to be thought of, and Grandpapa pinched her rosy cheek and said, "Well, Polly, you've won! Off with you to school." And Polly tucked her books under her arm and raced off with Jasper, who always went to school with her as far as their paths went, turning off at the corner where she hurried off to Miss Salisbury's select school, to go to his own.

"Oh, here comes Polly Pepper!" The girls, some of them waiting for her at the big iron gate, raced down to meet her. "Oh, Polly—Polly." At that a group of girls on the steps turned and came flying up too. "Oh, tell us all about the awful accident," they screamed. "Tell, Polly, do." They swarmed all over her.

"Give me the books"—and one girl seized them. "I'll carry them for you, Polly."

"And, Polly, not one of the other girls that went out to Silvia Horne's is here this morning."

"They may come yet," said Polly. "It's not late."

"Oh, I know. We came early to meet you. Well, Silvia isn't here either."

"Oh, she can't come, because of her cousin," said Polly, "and—"

"Well, I don't care whether she ever comes," declared Leslie Fyle. "I can't abide that Silvia Horne."

"Nor I," said another girl. "She's so full of her airs and graces, and always talking about her fine place at Edgewood. Oh dear me! I'm sick of Edgewood!"

A little disagreeable laugh went around.

"Oh, I'll tell you of the accident," said Polly. "Come, let's sit down on the steps. We've ten minutes yet."

"Yes, do, do," cried the girls. So they huddled up together on the big stone steps, Polly in the middle, and she told them the whole story as fast as she could. Meantime other girls hurrying to school saw them from a distance, and broke into a run to get there in time.

And Polly gave Alexia's love all round, as she had been commissioned to do.

"We'll go up to your house to see her," cried Leslie. "Perhaps this afternoon."

"Oh, no, you mustn't," said Polly. "I'm dreadfully sorry, girls, but Papa Fisher says no one must come yet, till he sends word by me."

"I thought you said Alexia was all right."

"And if her arm isn't broken I should think we might see

her," said a big girl on the edge of the circle discontentedly. She had private reasons for wishing the interview as soon as possible, as she and Alexia had quarreled the day before, and now it was quite best to ignore all differences, and make it up.

"But she's had a great strain, and Papa-Doctor says it isn't best," repeated Polly very distinctly, "so we can't even think of it, Sarah."

"Polly? Is that Polly Pepper?" exclaimed a voice in the hall.

"Oh, yes, Miss Anstice," cried Polly, hopping up so quickly she nearly overthrew some of the bunch of girls.

Yes, she had on the black silk gown, and Polly fancied she could hear it crackle, it was so stiff, as Miss Anstice advanced primly.

"I hear that there was an accident, Polly Pepper, last night, which you and some of the other girls were in. Now, why did you not come and tell me or sister at once about it?"

"Oh dear me! Do forgive me," cried poor Polly, now seeing that she had done a very wrong thing not to have acquainted Miss Salisbury first with all the particulars. "I do hope you will forgive me, Miss Anstice," she begged over again.

"I find it very difficult to overlook it, Polly," said Miss Anstice, who was much disturbed by the note she held in her hand, just delivered, by which Professor Mills informed her he should be unable to deliver his address that morning before her art class. So she added with asperity, "It would have been quite the proper thing, and something that would naturally, I should suppose, suggest itself to a girl brought up as you have been, Polly, to come at once to the head of the school with the information."

Polly, feeling that all this reflected on Mamsie and her

home training, had yet nothing to do but to stand pale and quiet on the steps.

"She couldn't help it." The big girl pushed her way into the inner circle. "We girls all just made her stop. My! Miss Anstice, it was just a mob here when we saw Polly coming."

"Sarah Miller, you have nothing to say until I address you." A little red spot was coming on either cheek as Miss Anstice turned angrily to the big girl. "And I shall at once report you to sister, for improper behavior."

"Oh dear, dear! Well, I wish 'sister' would fire old black silk," exclaimed a girl on the edge of the circle under her breath. "Look at her now. Isn't she a terror!" And then the big bell rang, and they all filed in.

"Now she won't let us have our picnic. She'll go against it every way she can," cried a girl who was out of dangerous earshot. And the terror of this spread as they all scampered down the hall.

"Oh dear, dear! To think this should have happened on her black silk day!"

"No, we won't get it now, you may depend," cried ever so many. And poor Polly, with all this added woe to make her feel responsible for the horrible beginning of the day, sank into her seat and leaned her head on her desk.

The picnic, celebrated as an annual holiday, was given by Miss Salisbury to the girls, if all had gone well in the school, and no transgressions of rules, or any misdemeanor, marred the term. Miss Anstice never had looked with favor on the institution, and the girls always felt that she went out of her way to spy possible insubordination among the scholars. So they strove not to get out of her good graces, observing special care when the "black silk days" came around.

On this unlucky day, everything seemed against them, and as Miss Anstice stalked off to sit upon the platform by "sister" for the opening exercises, the girls felt it was all up with them, and a general gloom fell upon the long schoolroom.

Miss Salisbury's gentle face was turned in surprise upon them as she scanned the faces. And then, the general exercises being over, the classes were called, and she and "sister" were left on the platform alone.

"Oh, now she's getting the whole thing!" groaned Leslie, looking back from the hall, to peer in. "Old black silk is giving it to her. Oh, I just hate Miss Anstice!"

"Sarah, why couldn't you have kept still?" cried another girl. "If you hadn't spoken, Miss Anstice would have gotten over it."

"Well, I wasn't going to have Polly Pepper blamed," said Sarah sturdily. "If you were willing to, I wasn't going to stand still and hear it, when it was our fault she told us first."

"Oh, no, Sarah," said Polly, "it surely was my own self that was to blame. I ought to have run in and told Miss Salisbury first. Well, now, girls, what shall I do? I've lost that picnic for you all, for I don't believe she will let us have it now."

"No, she won't," cried Leslie tragically. "Of that you may be sure, Polly Pepper."

Chapter 8

"We're to Have Our Picnic!"

AND that afternoon Polly kept back bad recollections of the gloomy morning at school as well as she could. She didn't let Alexia get the least bit of a hint about it, although how she ever escaped letting her find it out, she never could quite tell, but rattled on, all the messages the girls had sent, and every bit of school news she could think of.

"Were the other girls who went to Silvia's at school?" asked Alexia suddenly, and twitching up her pillow to get higher in bed, for Dr. Fisher had said she mustn't get up this first day—and a hard piece of work Mother Fisher had had to keep the aunt out of the room.

"I wouldn't go in," Mamsie would say. "Dr. Fisher doesn't wish her to be disturbed. Tomorrow, Miss Rhys." And it was all done so quietly that Alexia's aunt would find herself off down in the library again and busy with a book, very much to her own surprise.

"I'll shake 'em up," Polly cried, and hopping off from the foot of the bed, she thumped the pillows, if not with a merry, at least with a vigorous hand. "There now," crowding them in back of Alexia's restless head, "isn't that fine?"

"I should think it was," exclaimed Alexia with a sigh of satisfaction, and giving her long figure a contented stretch. "You do know just the best things to do, Polly Pepper. Well, tell on. I suppose Amy Garrett is perfectly delighted to cut that old art lecture."

"Oh, Professor Mills didn't come at all," said Polly. That brought it all back about Miss Anstice, and her head drooped suddenly.

"Didn't come? Oh dear!" And Alexia fell to laughing so, that she didn't notice Polly's face at all. But her aunt popping in, she became sober at once, and ran her head under the bedclothes.

"Oh, are you worse? Is she, Polly?" cried Miss Rhys all in a flutter. "I heard her cry, I thought."

"No, I was laughing," said Alexia, pulling up her face red and shining. "Do go right away, aunt. Dr. Fisher said Polly was to tell me things."

"Well, if you are not worse," said her aunt, slowly turning away.

"No," said Alexia. "Polly Pepper, do get up and shut that door," she cried. "Slam it, and lock it."

"Oh, no," said Polly, in dismay at the very thought. "I couldn't ever do that, Alexia."

"Well, then, I will." Alexia threw back the bedclothes with a desperate hand, and thrust one foot out.

"If you do," said Polly, not moving from where she sat on the foot of the bed, "I shall go out of this room, and not come back today."

"Shall you really?" cried Alexia, fixing her pale eyes on her.

"Yes, indeed I shall," said Polly firmly.

"Oh, then, I'm not going." Alexia drew in her foot and huddled all the clothes up over her head. "Polly Pepper," she said in muffled tones, "you're a perfectly dreadful creature, and if you'd gone and sprained your arm in a horrible old railway accident and were tied in bed, I'd do just everything you said, I would."

"Oh, I hope you wouldn't," said Polly.

"Hope I wouldn't!" screamed Alexia, flinging all the clothes away again to stare at Polly out of very wide eyes. "Whatever do you mean, Polly Pepper?"

"I hope you wouldn't do as I wanted you to," said Polly distinctly, "if I wanted something that was bad."

"Well, that's a very different thing," mumbled Alexia. "Oh dear me!" She gave a grimace at a twinge of pain in her arm. "This isn't bad. I only wanted that door shut."

"Oh now, Alexia, you've hurt your arm!" cried Polly. "Do keep still, else Papa-Doctor won't let me stay in here."

"Oh dear, dear! I'll keep still," promised Alexia, making up her mind that horses shouldn't drag any expression of pain from her after that.

"I mean, do sit up straight against your pillows—you've got 'em all mussed up again," cried Polly. So she hopped off from the bed and thumped them into shape once more.

"I wish you'd turn 'em over," said Alexia. "They're so hot on that side." So Polly whisked over the pillows, and patted them straight, and Alexia sank back against them again.

"Wouldn't you like me to smooth your hair, Alexia?" asked Polly. "Mamsie does that to me when I don't feel good."

"Yes, I should," said Alexia, "like it very much indeed, Polly."

So Polly, feeling quite happy, albeit the remembrance of the morning still lay deep in her mind, ran off for the brush and comb. "And I'm going to braid it all over," she said with great satisfaction, "after I've rubbed your head."

"Well, now, tell on," said Alexia, as Polly climbed up back of the pillows and began to smooth the long light fluffs of hair, trying to do it just as Mamsie always did for her. "You say Professor Mills didn't come—oh dear! and think of that black silk gown wasted on the girls. Well, I suppose she was cross as two sticks because he didn't come, wasn't she, Polly? Oh dear me! Well, I'm glad I wasn't there." She hurried on, not waiting for a reply. "I'd rather be in with this old bundle"—she patted her bandages—"Oh Polly!" She started up so suddenly that the brush flew out of Polly's lap and spun away across the floor.

"Take care," said Polly. "Oh, there goes the comb now," and she skipped down, recovered the articles, and jumped up to her post again. "What is it, Alexia?"

"Why, I've just thought—you don't suppose Miss Salisbury will appoint the day for the picnic, do you, while my arm is lame?"

The color in Polly's cheeks went out, and she was glad that she could get well behind the pillows.

"Oh, no, Alexia," she made herself say. "We wouldn't ever in all this world have the picnic till you were well. How could you think it, Alexia?"

"I didn't believe you would," cried Alexia, much gratified, and huddling down again, without once seeing Polly's face. "But most of the girls don't care about me, Polly, and they wouldn't mind."

"Oh yes, they do," said Polly reassuringly. "They're very fond of you, most of them are."

"Well," said Alexia, "I'm not fond of them, so I don't really expect them to be, Polly. But I shouldn't like 'em to go off and have that picnic when I couldn't go. Was anything said about it, Polly?" she asked abruptly.

"Miss Salisbury or Miss Anstice didn't say a word," said Polly, trembling for the next question.

Just then Mother Fisher looked in with a smile. "Polly, you are wanted," she said. "Grandpapa and Jasper are ready to go to the railroad station. I'm going to stay with Alexia and finish her hair just as I do for Polly."

Alexia looked up and smiled. It was next best to having Polly, to have Mrs. Fisher. So Polly, happy to have a respite from Alexia's questions about the picnic, and happier still to be going to find out something about the poor brakeman's family, flew off from the bed, set a kiss on Alexia's hot cheek, and another on Mamsie's, and raced off.

"I'm coming, Jasper," she called. She could see him below in the wide hall.

"All right, don't hurry so, father isn't ready yet. Dear me! Polly, you can get ready so quickly for things!" he said admiringly. And in the glow of starting, he couldn't see that Polly's spirits seemed at a low ebb, and he drew a long breath as he tried to make himself believe that what he had noticed at luncheon wasn't really so at all.

And Polly, between Grandpapa and Jasper, tried to make them have such a good time that really it seemed no walk at all, and they were all quite surprised when they found themselves there.

"We must go up into the superintendent's room," said Mr. King. So up the long stairs they went, the old gentleman grumbling at every step because there was no elevator, and at all other matters and things that were, as he declared, "at loose ends in the whole system." At last they stood before the desk.

"Have the goodness," began old Mr. King to the official, a short, pompous person who came up in the absence of the superintendent and now turned a cold face up to them, "to give me some information regarding a brakeman who was killed last night in the accident to the train due here at 7:45."

"Don't know anything about him," said the official in the crispest accents. He looked as if he cared less, and was about to slam down the window, when Mr. King asked, "Does anybody in this office know?"

"Can't say." The official pulled out his watch, compared it with the big clock on the wall, then turned away.

"Do any of you know who the man was who was killed last night?" asked the old gentleman, putting his face quite close to the window, and speaking in such clear, distinct tones that every clerk looked up.

Each man searched all the other faces. No, they didn't know—except one, a little, thin, wizen-faced person over in the corner, at a high desk, copying. "I only know that his name was Jim," he said in a voice to match his figure.

"Have the goodness to step this way, sir, and tell me what you do know," said Mr. King in such a way that the little man, but with many glances for the pompous individual, slipped off from his high stool, to advance to the window rubbing his hands together deprecatingly. The other clerks all laid down their pens to see the interview.

"What was his name—this brakeman's?" demanded Mr. King.

"I don't know, sir," said the little, thin clerk. "Jim—that was all I knew him by. I used to see him of a morning when I was coming to the office, and he was waiting to take his train. He was a steady fellow, Jim was," he added, anxiously scanning the handsome face beneath the white hair.

"I don't doubt that," said old Mr. King hastily. "I don't in the least doubt it."

"And he wasn't given to drink, sir," the little, thin clerk cried abruptly, "although some did say it who shouldn't, for there were many after Jim's place. He had an easy run. And—"

"Yes, yes. Well, now what I want to know," said Mr. King interrupting the stream, Polly and Jasper on either side having a hard time to control their impatience, "is where this 'Jim,' as you call him, lived, and what was his last name."

"That I don't know, sir," said the little, thin clerk. "I only know he had a family, for once in a while when I had a minute to spare he'd get to talking about 'em, when we met. Jim was awful fond of 'em. That anyone could see."

"Yes. Well, now what would he say?" asked the old gentleman, trying to hurry matters along. The pompous official had his eye on the clock. It might go hard for the little, thin clerk in his seedy coat if he took too much time from office hours.

"Why, he had one girl who was crazy about music," said the little clerk, "and—"

"Oh dear me!" exclaimed Polly. Old Mr. King heard her sigh at his side, and he cried, "Well, what else?"

"Why, I've heard Jim say more'n once he'd live on bread and water if he could only give his daughter a chance. And there were his three boys."

"Three boys," echoed Mr. King sharply.

"Yes, sir. I saw 'em round the train once or twice. They were likely chaps, it seemed to me." The little, thin clerk, a bachelor with several unmarried sisters on his hands for support, sighed deeply.

"Well, now," cried Mr. King, thinking it quite time to bring the interview to a close, "I'd take it quite kindly if you'd find out for me all you can about this Jim. A member of my family was on the train last night, who but for this noble brakeman might—might—bless me! There is my card." The old gentleman pulled out one from his cardcase, then fell to wiping his face violently.

"What is your name?" asked Jasper, seeing that his father couldn't speak.

"Hiram Potter," said the little clerk. The pompous official drew near, and looked over his shoulder at the card. "Oh! Why—Mr. King!" he cried, all the pomposity suddenly gone. "I beg your pardon. What can I do for you, sir?"

"Nothing whatever, sir." Mr. King waved him away. "Well, now, Mr. Potter, if you'll be so very good as to get this information for me as soon as possible and bring it up to my house, I'll be very much indebted to you." With a bow to him, in which the official was nowise included, the old gentleman and Polly and Jasper went off down the stairs again.

"Finkle, you're caught this time. You're in a hole," the brother officials sang out when the card had been displayed around the office. "I wouldn't want to be in your shoes," said more than one.

Finkle tried to brave out the dismay he felt at having offended the powerful millionaire railroad director, but he made but a poor show of it. Meanwhile the little, thin clerk, slipping the precious card into his seedy coat pocket, clambered up to his high stool, his mind busy with plans to unearth all possible information concerning Jim, the brakeman, as soon as the big clock up on the wall should let them out of the office.

"Polly, my dear," old Mr. King kept saying, as they went down the stairs, and he held her hand very closely, "I think this Potter—a very good sort of a man he seems to be, too—will find out all we want to know about Jim. I really do, Polly, so we won't worry about it, child."

Nevertheless, on top of all the rest that was worrying her, Polly had a sorry enough time, to keep her troubles from showing on her face. And after dinner, when the bell pealed violently, she gave a great start and turned quite pale.

Jasper saw it. "I don't believe it's any bad news, Polly," he hastened to say reassuringly, and longing to comfort, though he couldn't imagine the reason.

"Oh, where's Polly?" She heard the girls' voices out in the hall and ran out to meet them. "Oh dear me!" she cried at sight of their faces that confirmed her worst fears.

"Yes, oh Polly, it's just as I said," cried Leslie Fyle, precipitating herself against Polly. "Now, girls, keep back. I'm going to tell her first."

"Well, we are all going to tell too, Les. That's what we've come for," cried the others, crowding up.

"Oh, what is it?" cried Polly, standing quite still, and feeling as if she never could hold up her head again now that the picnic was lost through her.

"I shall tell, myself," declared Sarah bluntly. "I'm the one, it seems, that made all the trouble, so it really belongs to me, I should think, to be the first speaker."

Polly folded her hands tightly together while the babel went on, feeling that if she didn't hear the dreaded news soon, she should fly off to Mamsie.

"Miss Salisbury said—" She could hear little scraps of chatter.

"I know—oh, do hurry and tell Polly."

"Oh, and just think, Miss Salisbury—"

"And Miss Anstice—" Then some of them looked around and into Polly's face. "Oh my goodness, girls, see Polly Pepper!"

With that they all rushed at her, and nobody told first, for they all shouted it out together: "Polly, Miss Salisbury has given us our picnic!" and "Polly, isn't it too splendid!" and "Polly Pepper, just think how perfectly elegant! Our picnic, Polly—only think!" till the circle in the library popped out their heads into the hall.

"Jasper," cried Polly, deserting the bunch of "Salisbury girls," to plunge up to him with shining eyes, "we're to have our picnic. We truly are, Jasper, and I thought I'd lost it to all the girls."

And just then Johnson advanced down the length of the hall. "It's a person to see you, sir," he said to old Mr. King. "Says it's quite important, sir, and that you told him to come. He's sitting by the door, sir."

"Oh, it's Mr. Potter, I think." said the old gentleman. "Show him into the library, Johnson. Polly, my child. Bless me! I don't see how you stand it with these girls chattering around you every minute. Now be off with you," he cried gaily to the group. He was much pleased at the success of his plan to find out about the brakeman, of which he felt quite sure from the appearance so promptly of the little clerk. "I have something quite important for Polly to attend to now, and I really want her to myself once in a while."

"Yes, I must go, girls," said Polly, turning a blooming countenance on them. "So good night. We won't have the picnic, you know, till Alexia is well," she added decidedly.

"Oh, that's what Miss Salisbury said," cried Leslie, turning back. "You see, I saw her after school—went back for my history—and I was to tell you that, Polly, only Sarah spoilt it all."

"Never mind," said Polly brightly. "It's all right now, since we are really to have our picnic." And then she put her hand in old Mr. King's, quite bubbling over with happiness—Jasper just as jubilant, since Polly was herself again, on the other side—to go in and meet the little, thin clerk, scared at his surroundings, and perched on the extreme edge of a library chair.

Chapter 9

All About
the Poor Brakeman

MR. POTTER was very miserable indeed on the edge of his chair, and twirling his hat dreadfully, and for the first moment after the handsome old gentleman spoke to him he had nothing to say.

Old Mr. King was asking him for the third time, "You found out all about poor Jim's family, eh?"

At last he emerged from his fit of embarrassment enough to reply, "Yes, sir."

"Now that is very good," the old gentleman cried approvingly, and wiped his face vigorously after his effort. "Very good indeed, Mr. Potter."

Hiram Potter now followed up his first attempt to find his voice, and trying to forget the handsome surroundings that had so abashed him, he went on now quite glibly.

"You see, sir, there's six of 'em—Jim's children."

"Dear me!" ejaculated old Mr. King.

"Yes, sir, there are." Mr. Potter's hat began to twirl uneasily again. "And the wife—she ain't strong, just got up from rheumatic fever."

"That's bad—very bad," said Mr. King.

"Those three boys of his are good," said Mr. Potter, brightening up a bit in the general gloom, "and the biggest one says he's going to be a brakeman just like his father. But the mother wants 'em all to go to school. You see, that's what Jim was working for."

"And the girl who wanted to play on the piano?" broke in Polly eagerly. Then she blushed rosy red. "Oh, forgive me, Grandpapa, for interrupting," and she hid her face on old Mr. King's arm.

"I was just going to ask about that girl myself," said Grandpapa promptly. "Tell us about her, Mr. Potter, if you please."

Hiram Potter set his hat carefully on the floor beside his chair. It was his Sunday hat, and evidently that, with his best clothes which he had donned in honor of the occasion, were objects of great care. He scratched his head and thought deeply. "Well, now, you see, sir," he said slowly, "that's almost a hopeless case, and I wish, as sure as I sit here, that girl hadn't never thought of piano music. But it's born in her, the mother said. The girl's grandfather was a musician in the old home in Germany, and so she can't help it. Why, she's just so crazy about it, she'll drum all up and down the kitchen table to make believe that—"

"Oh, Grandpapa!" cried Polly in the greatest excitement, and hopping up and down by his side, "that's just as I used to do in the little brown house—the very same way, Grandpapa, you know."

"Yes, she did, father," cried Jasper, bobbing his head scarcely less excited, just as if old Mr. King hadn't heard the story many times.

Mr. Potter, for want of something to do to express his amazement, picked up his hat, stroked it, and set it down again, staring with all his might.

"So you did, Polly. So you did, my child," cried Grandpapa, taking her hands in both of his and looking down into her shining eyes. "Well, well, to be sure. Now, Jasper, get the tablet, and write down the address of Jim's family as quickly as you can, my boy."

So Jasper ran over to the library table and brought back the tablet and pencil hanging to it, and pretty soon Jim's home was all described thus: "Mrs. James Corcoran, 5 Willow Court—third house from Haven Street."

"It's kinder hard to find," observed Mr. Potter slowly, "because Willow Court runs into Haven Street crisscross, and this number isn't on the house—it's got rubbed off. But if you follow up No. 3, and come up carefully, why, there you'll be where No. 5 was."

"Oh dear me!" said Mr. King. "Well, you may describe the house, for I am going down there tomorrow, and I certainly do not wish to waste my time walking about."

Polly and Jasper looked so very decidedly "Oh, may we go too?" that the old gentleman added quickly, "And my young people will accompany me," which really left nothing more to be desired at present.

"Well, it's a yellow house," said Mr. Potter, thinking very hard. "That is, it is in spots, where the paint is on, and it's low, and runs down to the back, and sets sideways. But I tell you how you'll know it. She's got—Mrs. Jim Corcoran has—the greatest lot of flowers in her window. They're chock full, sir."

"I shall know it, then," cried Polly in great satisfaction.

"I think there's no danger, sir, but what we will find the place all right." Old Mr. King was fumbling in his pocket in great perplexity. "It never would do," he decided, pulling his hand out. "No, I must contrive to send him something. Well, now—hem—Mr. Potter," he said aloud, "and where do you live? Quite near, I presume?"

"Oh, just the other end of the town, sir," said Mr. Potter. "I live on Acorn Street."

"Acorn Street?" repeated Mr. King, wrinkling his brows. "And where may that be, pray tell?"

"It's over at the South End, sir. It runs off from Baker Street and Highland Square."

"Oh yes, yes," said the old gentleman, without much more idea than before.

"I know where it is, father," and Jasper. "Dear me! You've had to take a good bit of time to get all this information, Mr. Potter."

Mr. Potter looked down busily on the carpet, trying not to think how tired his feet were, saving some carfare for their owner.

"Well, now, what number?" The old gentleman seeming to desire his whole address, that was soon given too: "23 Acorn Street, South End."

"And I suppose you have a family?" went on the old gentleman, determined to find out all there was to it, now he had commenced.

The little clerk began to hem and to haw, behind his hand. "No, sir, I haven't. That is, yes, I have considerable—I mean my four sisters, sir. We all live together."

"Oh—ah!" replied Mr. King. "Well, now, thank you very much, Mr. Potter. And as your time is valuable, and should be paid for—" He tucked a bill within the nervous hands.

"Oh, I couldn't take it, sir," cried Hiram Potter, greatly distressed.

"But it's your due. Why, man, I shouldn't have asked you

to take all this trouble, and spend so much time after I've found you had so far to go." Mr. King was really becoming irate now, so that the little clerk didn't dare to say more. "Bless me! Say no more—say no more!"

The little clerk was too much frightened to think of another word, and finding that the interview was considered closed, he picked up his hat and in some way, he could never remember how, he soon found himself out of the handsome house and skipping off nimbly in the fresh air, which quite revived him.

"I could offer him only a trifle," old Mr. King was saying. "Only what might repay him for his trouble and time tonight. But I shall speak to Fraser about him tomorrow, Jasper. That agent of mine is, curiously enough, in want of a clerk just at this time, and I know this little man can fit in very well, and it will get him away from that beastly office. Four sisters—oh my goodness! Well, Fraser must give him enough to take care of them."

"Oh, how fine, father!" exclaimed Jasper with kindling eyes. "And then the girl that wants to learn to play on the piano."

"Oh dear me, yes!" Old Mr. King burst into a merry laugh. "I must look after that little girl, or Polly won't speak to me, I am afraid. Will you, Polly, my child?" He drew her close to him, and kissed her blooming cheek.

"I am so very glad you are going to look out for her, Grandpapa," she cried, "because you know I did feel so dreadfully when I used to drum on the table in the little brown house," she confessed.

"I know—I know, child." Grandpapa's face fell badly, and he held her very close. It always broke him up to hear the Peppers tell of the hard times in the little brown house, and Polly hastened to add brightly, "And then you came, Grandpapa dear, and you made it all just beautiful—oh, Grand-papa!" and she clung to him, unable to say more.

"Yes, yes, so I did—so I did," cried the old gentleman delightedly, quite happy again, and stroking the brown hair. "Well, Polly, my girl, it isn't anything to the good times we are always going to have. And tomorrow, you and I must go down to see after poor Jim's family."

"And Jasper?" cried Polly, poking up her head from old Mr. King's protecting arm. "He must go too, Grandpapa."

"And Jasper? Why, we couldn't do anything without him, Polly," said the old gentleman in such a tone that Jasper threw back his head very proudly. "Of course my boy must go too."

And the next day, Pickering Dodge, who thought he had some sort of a claim on Jasper for the afternoon, came running up the steps, two at a time. And he looked so horribly disappointed, that old Mr. King said, "Why don't you take him, Jasper, along with us?"

Jasper, who would have much preferred to go alone with his father and Polly, swallowed his vexation, and said, "All right." And when he saw Pickering's delight, he brightened up, and was glad it all happened in just that way after all.

"Now, see here," said old Mr. King suddenly. They were turning out of Willow Court, after their visit, and Thomas had a sorry time of it, managing his horses successfully about the old tin cans and rubbish, to say nothing of the children who were congregated in the narrow, ill-smelling court. "Why don't you boys do something for those lads in there?" pointing backward to the little run-down-at-the-heel house they had just left.

"We boys?" cried Pickering faintly. "Oh dear me! Mr. King, we can't do anything."

" 'Can't' is a bad word to use," said the old gentleman

gravely, "and I didn't mean that you all alone should do the work. But get the other boys interested. I'm sure you can do that. Phew! Where are the health authorities, I should like to know, to let such abominations exist? Thomas, drive as fast as you can, and get us out of this hole." And he buried his aristocratic old face in his handkerchief.

Pickering looked over at Jasper in great dismay.

"We might have our club take it up," said Jasper slowly, with a glance at Polly for help.

"Yes, why don't you, Jasper?" she cried. "Now, that's what I'm going to propose that our club of Salisbury girls shall do. We're just finishing up the work for a poor southern family."

"You've had a bee, haven't you," asked Pickering, "or something of that sort? Although I don't really suppose you do much work," he said nonchalantly, "only laugh and play and giggle, generally."

"Indeed we don't, Pickering Dodge," cried Polly indignantly, "laugh and play and giggle. The very idea!"

"And if you say such dreadful things I'll pitch you out of the carriage," cried Jasper in pretended wrath.

"Ow! I'll be good. Take off your nippers," cried Pickering, cringing back down into his corner as far as he could. "Goodness me, Jasper! You're a perfect old tiger."

"Take care, and keep your tongue in its place then," said Jasper, bursting into a laugh.

"And we work—oh, just dreadfully," declared Polly with her most positive air. "We cut out all the clothes ourselves—we don't want our mothers to do it. And sew—oh dear me!"

"You ought to see our house on club day when Polly has the bee," said Jasper. "I rather think you'd say there was something going on for those poor little southern darkies."

"Well, I don't see how you can work so for a lot of disgusting pickaninnies," said Pickering, stretching his long figure lazily. "The whole bunch of them isn't worth one good solid afternoon of play."

Polly turned a cold shoulder to him and began to talk with Jasper most busily about the club of boys.

"Yes, and oh, Jasper, let's have one meeting of all you boys with us girls—the two clubs together," she cried at last, waxing quite enthusiastic.

"Yes, let us," cried Jasper, just as enthusiastic. "And oh, Polly, I've thought of something. Let's have a little play— you write it."

"Oh, Jasper, I can't," cried Polly, wrinkling her brows.

"Oh, yes, Polly, you can," cried Jasper. "If it's one half as good as 'The Three Dragons and the Princess Clotilde,' it will be just fine."

"Well," said Polly, "I'll try. And what then, Jasper?"

"Why, we'll give it for money—father, may we, in the drawing room? And perhaps we'll make quite a heap to help those boys with. Oh, Polly!" He seized both of her hands and wrung them tightly. "Oh, may we, father, may we?"

"Eh—what's that? Oh, yes." The old gentleman took down his handkerchief. "Dear me! What a mercy we are where we can breathe!" as Thomas whirled them dexterously past a small square. "What *are* the health authorities about, to allow such atrocious old holes? Oh, yes, my boy, I'm sure I'd be delighted to have you help along those three lads. And it's really work for boys. Polly's going to start up something for the girl."

"How perfectly fine!" exclaimed Jasper and Polly together, now that the consent was really gained. Then they fell into such a merry chatter that Pickering, left out in the cold, began to wriggle dreadfully. At last he broke out:

"Yes, I think it would be fine too," trying to work his head into the conference, where Polly and Jasper had theirs together buzzing over the plans.

But nobody paid him the slightest attention; so he repeated his remark, with no better success.

"I should think you might turn around," at last he said in a dudgeon, "and speak to a body once in a while."

"Why should we?" cried Jasper over his shoulder. "You don't think it's worth while to work for any of those people. No, Polly, we'll let him severely alone." Then he fell to talking again, busier than ever.

"Yes, I do," cried Pickering in a high, wrathful key, "think it's worth while too, so there, Jasper King!"

"Oh, he does, I do believe, Jasper," cried Polly, looking at Pickering's face.

"Why, of course I do," said Pickering.

"And so we must let him into the plans." So Polly turned around to draw Pickering in, and old Mr. King leaned forward in his seat, and the committee of ways and means got so very busy that they didn't even know when Thomas turned in at the big stone gateway, until Polly looked up and screamed out, "Why, we are home! Why, we *can't* be!"

"Well, we are, Polly, my child," said old Mr. King, getting out to help her with his courtliest air. "We've been gone just three hours and a half, and a very good afternoon's work it is too. For Jim's children will care twice as much for what you young folks are going to do for them as for anything I may do. Yes, Polly, they will," as he saw her face. "And I'm sure if I were in their places, I'd feel just the same way."

Chapter 10

Joel and His Dog

"**N**OW, children," hummed Phronsie, pausing in the midst of combing her doll's flaxen hair, "you must keep still, and be very good. Then I'll get through pretty soon." And she bowed to the several members of her numerous family set up in a row before her, who were awaiting their turn for the same attention. Then she took up the little comb which had dropped to her lap, and set herself busily to her task again.

Alexia looked in at the door of the "baby house," as Phronsie's little room devoted to her family of dolls was called. "Oh my goodness me!" she exclaimed, "don't you ever get tired of everlastingly dressing those dolls, Phronsie?"

Phronsie gave a sigh and went patiently on with her work. "Yes, Alexia, I'm tired sometimes. But I'm their mother, you see."

"And to comb their hair!" went on Alexia. "Oh dear me!

I never could do it in all this world, Phronsie. I should want
to run and throw them all out of the window."

"Oh, Alexia!" exclaimed Phronsie in horror. "Throw them
all out of the window! You couldn't do that, Alexia." She
tightened her grasp on the doll in her arms.

"Yes, I should want to throw every one of those dreadful
dolls out of the window, Phronsie Pepper!" declared Alexia
recklessly.

"But they are my children," said Phronsie very soberly,
trying to get all the others waiting for their hair to be fixed
into her arms too, "and dear Grandpapa gave them to me,
and I love them, every single one."

"Well, now, you see, Phronsie," said Alexia, getting down
on the floor in front of the doll's bureau, by Phronsie's side,
"you could come out with me on the piazza and walk around
a bit if it were not for these dreadfully tiresome dolls. And
Polly is at school, and you are through with your lessons in
Mr. King's room. Now how nice that would be, oh dear me!"
Alexia gave a restful stretch to her long figure. "My!" at a
twinge of pain.

"Does your arm hurt you, Alexia?" asked Phronsie, looking over her dolls up to Alexia's face.

"Um—maybe," said Alexia, nursing her arm hanging in
the sling. "It's a bad, horrid old thing, and I'd like to thump
it."

"Oh, don't, Alexia," begged Phronsie. "That will make it
worse. Please don't, Alexia, do anything to it." Then she got
up and went over with her armful of dolls to the sofa, and
laid them down carefully in a row. "I'll fix your hair tomorrow, children," she said. "Now I'm going away for a little bit
of a minute," and came back. "Let's go down to the piazza,"
she said, holding out her hand.

"You blessed child, you!" exclaimed Alexia, seizing her

with the well hand. "Did you suppose I'd be such a selfish old pig as to drag you off from those children of yours?"

"You are not a selfish old pig, Alexia, and I like you very much," said Phronsie gravely, trying not to hit the arm in the sling, while Alexia flew up to her feet and whirled around the room with her. "And, oh, I'm so afraid you'll make it sick," she panted. "Do stop."

"I just can't, Phronsie," said Alexia. "I shall die if I don't do something! Oh, the horrid old arm!" And she came to a sudden standstill, Phronsie struggling away to a safe distance.

"Papa Fisher would not like it, Alexia," she said in great disapproval, her hair blown about her face, and her cheeks quite pink.

"Oh dear me!" Alexia, resting the sling in the other palm, and trying not to scream with the pain, burst out. "It's so tiresome to be always thinking that someone won't like things one does. Phronsie, there's no use in my trying to be good, because, you see, I never could be. I just love to do bad things."

"Oh no, Alexia," said Phronsie, greatly shocked, "you don't love to do bad things. Please say you don't," and before Alexia could say another word, the tears poured down the round cheeks, wetting Phronsie's pinafore. And although she clasped her hands and tried to stop them, it was no use.

"There now, you see," cried Alexia, quite gone in remorse. "Oh, what shall I do? I must go and get Mrs. Fisher," and she rushed out of the room.

Phronsie ran unsteadily after her, to call, "Oh Alexia!" in such distress that the flying feet turned, and up she came again.

"What is it, Pet?" she cried. "Oh dear me! What shall I do? I must tell your mother."

"I will stop," said Phronsie, struggling hard with her tears, "if you only won't tell Mamsie," and she wiped her cheeks hard with her pinafore. "There, see, Alexia," and tried to smile.

"Well, now, come back." Alexia seized her hand, and dragged her up the stairs. "Now I'm just going to stay up here with you, if you'll let me, Phronsie, and try not to do bad things. I do so want to be good like Polly. You can't think how I want to," she cried in a gust, as she threw herself down on the floor again.

"Oh, Alexia, you never could be good like Polly," said Phronsie, standing quite still in astonishment.

"Of course not," said Alexia with a little laugh, "but I mean—oh, you know what I mean, Phronsie. I want to be good so that Polly will say she likes it. Well come on now, get your horrible old—I mean, your dolls, and—"

"I wish very much you wouldn't call them dolls, Alexia," said Phronsie, not offering to sit down. "They are my children, and I don't think they like to be called anything else."

"Well, they shan't hear it, then," declared Alexia decidedly. "So get some of them, and brush their hair, just as you were doing when I came in, and I'm going to read aloud to you out of one of your books, Phronsie."

"Oh—oh!" Phronsie clapped her hands in glee. Next to Polly's stories, which of course she couldn't have now as Polly was at school, Phronsie dearly loved to be read to. But she suddenly grew very sober again.

"Are you sure you will like it, Alexia?" she asked, coming up to peer into Alexia's face.

"Yes, yes, Pet, to be sure I will," cried Alexia, seizing her to half smother her with kisses. "Why, Phronsie, it will make me very happy indeed."

"Well, if it will really make you happy, Alexia," said Phronsie, smoothing down her pinafore in great satisfaction,

"I will get my children." And she ran over to the sofa and came back with an armful.

"Now, what book?" asked Alexia, forgetting whether her arm ached or not, and flying to her feet. "I'm going down to your bookshelf to get it."

"Oh, Alexia," cried Phronsie in great excitement, "will you—could you get 'The Little Yellow Duck'?"

As this was the book Phronsie invariably chose when asked what she wanted read, Alexia laughed and spun off, perfectly astonished to find that the world was not all as blue as an indigo bag. And when she came back two steps at a time up the stairs, Phronsie was smiling away, and humming softly to herself, while the hair-brushing was going on.

"She had a blue ribbon on yesterday—Almira did," said Phronsie, reflecting. "Now, wouldn't you put on a pink one today, Alexia?"

"I surely should," decided Alexia. "That pretty pale pink one that Polly gave you last, Phronsie."

"I am so very glad you said that one," said Phronsie, running over on happy feet for her ribbon basket, "because I do love that ribbon very much, Alexia."

"Well, now then," said Alexia, as Phronsie began to tie up the pink bow laboriously, "we must hurry and begin, or we never shall see what happened to this 'Little Yellow Duck.' "

"Oh, do hurry, Alexia," begged Phronsie, as if she hadn't heard the story on an average of half a dozen times a week. So Alexia propped herself up against the wall and began, and presently it was so still that all anyone could hear was the turning of the leaves and the ticking of the little French clock on the mantel.

"Well, dear me, how funny!" and Polly rushed in, then burst into a merry laugh.

"Polly Pepper—you home!" Alexia tossed "The Little

Yellow Duck" half across the room, flew to her feet again, and spun Polly round and round with her well hand.

"Yes," said Polly, "I am, and I've been searching for you two all over this house."

"Take me, Polly, do." Phronsie laid down Almira carefully on the carpet and hurried over to Polly.

"I guess I will. Now then, all together!" and the three spun off until out of breath.

"Oh dear me!" Polly stopped suddenly. "I never thought of your arm, Alexia. Oh, do you suppose we've hurt it?" It was so very dreadful to think of, that all the color deserted her cheek.

"Nonsense, no!" declared Alexia. "That spin put new life into me, Polly."

"Well, I don't know," said Polly critically. "At any rate, we mustn't do it any more. And we must tell Papa-Doctor about it as soon as he gets home."

"Oh, what good is it to worry him?" cried Alexia carelessly. "Well, Polly, tell all the news about school," as they hurried downstairs to get ready for luncheon.

"We must tell Papa-Doctor everything about it, Alexia," said Polly in her most decided fashion, putting her arm carefully around Alexia's waist, and with Phronsie hanging to the other hand, down they went, Polly retailing the last bit of school news fresh that day.

"And, oh, Alexia, Miss Salisbury said we are not to have the picnic until you get quite well. She said so in the big schoolroom, before us all."

"Did she, Polly?" cried Alexia, immensely gratified.

"Yes, she did." Polly stood on her tiptoes at the imminent danger of going on her nose, and pulling the other's down, to get a kiss on the long sallow cheek. "She said it very distinctly, Alexia, and all the girls talked about it afterward."

"Well, she's a dear old thing," exclaimed Alexia, with remorseful little pangs at the memory of certain episodes at the "Salisbury School," "and I shall try—oh, Polly, I'll try so hard to be nice and please her."

Polly gave her two or three little pats on her back.

"And don't you think," cried Polly, flying off to brush her hair, and calling back through the open door, "that the boys are going to have their club meet with ours. Just think of that!"

"Oh, Polly!" Alexia came flying in, brush in hand. "You *don't* really mean it!"

"I do. Jasper just told me so. Well, hurry, Alexia, else we'll be late," warned Polly, brushing away vigorously. "Yes, Phronsie"—for Phronsie had gone off for Jane to put on a clean apron—"we're ready now—that is, almost."

"When—when?" Polly could hear Alexia frantically asking, as she rushed back into her room, which was next to Polly's own.

"Oh, just as soon as you are able," called Polly. "Now, don't ask any more questions, Alexia," she begged merrily. "Yes, Mamsie, we're coming!"

That afternoon, Percy and Joel were rushing back to school from an errand down to the village, and hurrying along with an awful feeling that the half-past-five bell in the big tower on the playground would strike in a minute.

"Hold on," called Percy, considerably in the rear. "How you get over the ground, Joe!"

"And you're such a snail," observed Joel pleasantly. Nevertheless he paused.

"What's that?" pricking up his ears.

"I don't hear anything." Percy came up panting.

"Of course not, when you're puffing like a grampus."

"What's a grampus?" asked Percy irritably.

"I don't know," said Joel honestly.

"Well, I wouldn't say words I didn't know what they meant," said Percy in a patronizing tone, and trying not to realize that he was very hot.

"Well, do keep stlll, will you!" roared Joel. "There, there it is again." He stooped down, and peered within a hedge. "Something's crying in here."

"You'll get your eyes scratched out, most likely, by an old, cross cat," suggested Percy.

Joel, who cared very little for that or any warning, was now on his knees. "Oh, whickets!" he exclaimed, dragging out a small yellow dog, who, instead of struggling, wormed himself all up against his rescuer, whining pitifully.

"He's hurt," declared Joel, tossing back his stubby locks, and patting the dog, who stopped whining, and licked him all over, as much of his face and hands as he could reach.

"Oh, that dirty thing—faugh! How can you, Joel Pepper!" cried Percy in distress.

But Joel didn't even hear him, being occupied in setting the dog on the ground to try his paces.

"No, he's not hurt, after all, I guess," he decided, "but look at his ribs—he's half starved."

"I don't want to look at them," said Percy, turning his back, "and you ought to let him alone. That bell will ring in half a second, Joel Pepper!"

"True enough!" cried Joel. " Come on, Perky," this being the school name of the older Whitney, and he picked up the dog, and shot off.

"What are you going to do with that dog?" yelled Percy after him. But as well talk to the wind, as Joel arrived hot and breathless at the big door long before him.

Luckily for him, none of the boys were about, and Joel,

cramming the dog well under his jacket, plunged up the stairs and down the hall to his room.

"Joe!" roared two or three voices, but he turned a deaf ear and got in safely, slammed the door, and then drew a long breath.

"*Whew!* Almost caught that time," was all he had the wind to say. "Well, now, it's good Dave isn't in, 'cause I can tell him slowly, and get him used to it." All this time he was drawing out his dog from its place of refuge, and putting it first on the bed, then on the floor, to study it better.

It certainly was as far removed from being even a good-looking dog as possible. Having never in its life had the good fortune to hear its pedigree spoken of, it was simply an ill-favored cur that looked as if it had exchanged the back yard of a tenement house for the greater dangers of the open street. Its yellow neck was marked where a cruel cord had almost worn into the flesh, and every one of its ribs stuck out as Joel had said, till they insisted on being counted by a strict observer.

Joel threw his arms around the beast. "Oh dear!" he groaned, "you're starved to death. What have I got to give you?" He wrinkled his forehead in great distress. "Oh goody!" He snatched the dog up and bore him to the closet, then pulled down a box from the shelf above. "Mamsie's cake— how prime!" And not stopping to cut a piece, he broke off a goodly wedge. "Now then, get in with you," and he thrust him deep into one corner, cramming the cake up to his nose. "Stay there on my side, and don't get over on Dave's shoes. *Whee!*"

The dog, in seizing the cake, had taken Joel's thumb as well.

"Let go there," cried Joel. "Well, you can't swallow my thumb," as the cake disappeared in one lump. And he gave a sigh for the plums with which Mamsie always liberally supplied the school cakes, now disappearing so fast, as much as for the nip he had received.

The dog tured his black, beady eyes sharply for more cake. When he saw that it wasn't coming, he licked Joel's thumb, and in his cramped quarters on top of a heap of shoes and various other things not exactly classified, he tried hard to wag his stump of a tail.

"Whickets! There goes that bell! Now see here, don't you dare to stir for your life! You've got to stay in this closet till tomorrow—then I'll see what to do for you. Lie down, I tell you."

There was a small scuffle, and then the dog, realizing here was a master, curled himself on top of some tennis shoes and looked as if he held his breath.

"All right," said Joel with an approving pat. "Now don't you yip, even if Dave opens this door." Then he shut it carefully and rushed off down to the long dining room to the crowd of boys.

Joel ate his supper as rapidly as possible, lost to the chatter going on around him. He imagined, in his feverishness, that he heard faint "yaps" every now and then, and he almost expected to see everybody lay down knife and fork.

"What's the matter with you?" He was aroused by seeing the boy next to him lean forward to peer into his face. And in a minute he was conscious that on the other side he was just as much of an object of attention. He buried his face in his glass of milk, but when he took it out, they were staring still the same.

"Ugh ! Stop your looking at me," growled Joel.

"What's the matter with you, anyway?" asked the other boy.

"Get away—nothing," said Joel crossly, and bestowing as much of a kick as he dared on the other boy's shin.

"Ow! There is too."

"You're awfully funny," said the first boy. "You haven't spoken a word since you sat down."

"Well, I ain't going to talk, if I don't want to," declared Joel. "Do stop, Fletcher. Everybody's looking."

But Fletcher wouldn't stop, and Joel had the satisfaction of seeing the whole table, with the underteacher, Mr. Harrow, at the head, making him, between their mouthfuls, the center of observation. The only alleviation of this misery was that Percy was at another table, and with his back to him.

David looked across in a worried way. "Are you sick, Joe?" he asked.

"No." Joel laughed, and began to eat busily. When he saw that, David gave a sigh of relief.

Mr. Harrow was telling something just then that seemed of more than common interest, and the boys, hearing Joel laugh once more, turned off to listen. "Yes," said the underteacher, "it was a dog that was—"

"Ugh!" cried Joel. " Oh, beg pardon," and his face grew dreadfully red, as he tried to get as small as possible on his chair.

"It's a dog I used to own, Joel," said Mr. Harrow, smiling at him. "And I taught him tricks, several quite remarkable ones."

"Yes, sir," mumbled Joel, taking a big bite of his biscuit. And for the next quarter of an hour he was safe, as the funny stories lasted till back went the chairs, and the evening meal was over.

To say that Joel's life was an easy one till bedtime would be very far from the truth. Strange to say, David did not go to the closet once. To be sure, there was a narrow escape that made Joel's heart leap to his mouth.

"Let's have Mamsie's cake, Joe, tonight," said David in an aside to him. The room was full of boys. It was just before study hour, and how to tell David of the dog was racking Joe's powers of mind.

"Ugh! No, not tonight, Dave." He was so very decided that although David was puzzled at his manner, he gave it up without a question. And then came study hour, when all the boys must be down in "Long Hall," and Joel lingered behind the others. "I'll be down in a minute." He flew over to the closet, broke off another generous wedge of Mamsie's cake, stifling a second sigh as he thought of the plums. "You haven't eaten my half yet," he said as the dog swallowed it whole without winking. "Keep still now." He slammed to the door again and was off, his books under his arm.

And after the two boys went up to bed, David was too tired and sleepy to talk, and hopped into his bed so quickly that long before Joel was undressed he was off to dreamland.

"That's good—now I haven't got to tell him till morning." Joel went over to the other bed in the corner, and listened to the regular breathing, then tiptoed softly off to the closet, first putting out the light. "I know what I'm going to do." He got down on all fours and put his hand out softly over the pile of shoes, till he felt the dog's mangy back. "I'm going to take you in my bed. You'll smother in here. Now, sir!" The dog was ready enough to be quiet, only occupied in licking Joel's hands. So Joel jumped into his bed, carrying his charge, and huddled down under the clothes.

After being quite sure that he was really to remain in this paradise, the dog began to turn around and around to find exactly the best position in which to settle down for the night. This took him so long, interrupted as the process was with so many lickings of Joel's brown face, that it looked as if neither would get very much sleep that night; Joel, not averse to this lengthy operation, hugging his dog and patting him, to his complete demoralization just as he was about to quiet down.

At last even Joel was tired, and his eyes drooped. "Now go to sleep"—with a final pat—"I'm going to call you Sinbad." Joel, having always been mightily taken with Sinbad the Sailor, felt that no other name could be quite good enough for his new treasure. And Sinbad, realizing that a call to repose had actually been given, curled up, in as round a ball as he could, under Joel's chin, and both were soon sound asleep.

It was near the middle of the night. Joel had been dreaming of his old menagerie and circus he had once in the little brown house, in which there were not only trained dogs who could do the most wonderful things—strange to say, now they were all of them yellow, and had stumpy tails—but animals and reptiles of the most delightful variety, never seen in any other show on earth, when a noise, that at once suggested a boy screaming *"Ow!"* struck upon his ear, and brought him bolt upright in his bed. He pawed wildly around, but Sinbad was nowhere to a found.

Chapter 11

The United Clubs

*T*HE whole dormitory was in an uproar.

"*Ow!* help—help!" Mr. Harrow, having gone out after dinner, had retired late, and was now sound asleep, so another instructor scaled the stairs, getting there long before Mrs. Fox the matron, could put in an appearance.

In the babel it was somewhat difficult to locate the boy who had screamed out. At last, "In there, Farnham's room," cried several voices at once.

"Nightmare, I suppose," said the instructor to himself, dashing in.

But it was a real thing he soon saw, as a knot of boys huddled around the bed, where the terrified occupant still sat, drawing up his knees to his chin, and screaming all sorts of things, in which "wild beast" and "cold nose" was all that could be distinguished.

"Stop this noise!" commanded the instructor, who had none of Mr. Harrow's pleasant but decided ways for quelling an incipient riot. So they bawled on, the boy in bed yelling that he wouldn't be left alone.

Just then something skimmed out from the corner. The boys flew to one side, showing a tendency to find the door. Even the instructor jumped. Then he bethought himself to light the gas, which brought out the fact that there certainly was an animal in the room, as they could hear it now under the bed.

"Boys, be quiet. Mrs. Fox's cat has got up here, probably," said the instructor. But the boy in the bed protested that it wasn't a cat that had waked him up by thrusting a cold nose in his face and jumping on top of him. And he huddled worse than ever now that it was under him, yet afraid to step out on the floor.

Even the instructor did not offer to look under the bed, when Joel Pepper rushed in, his black eyes gleaming. "Oh, it's my dog!" he cried.

"It's Joe Pepper's dog!" cried the whole roomful, nearly tumbling over each other.

"And when did you begin to keep a dog, Joel Pepper?" hurled the instructor at him, too angry for anything, that he hadn't impressed the boys with his courage.

But Joel was occupied in ramming his body under the bed as far as possible. "Here, Sinbad," and he presently emerged with a very red face, and Sinbad safely in his arms, who seemed perfectly delighted to get into his old refuge again. David had now joined the group, as much aghast as every other spectator.

"Do you hear me, Joel Pepper?" thundered the instructor again. "When did you get that dog?" This brought Joel to.

"Oh, I haven't had him long, sir," he said, and trembling for Sinbad, as he felt in every fiber of his being that the beast's fate was sealed, unless he could win over the irritated teacher. "He's a poor dog I—I found, sir," wishing he could think of the right words, and knowing that every word he uttered only made matters worse.

"David," cried the instructor, catching Davie's eye, down by the door, "do you know anything about this dog?"

"No, sir," said David, all in a tremble, and wishing he could say something to help Joel out.

"Well, now, you wait a minute." The instructor, feeling that here was a chance to impress the boys with his executive ability, looked about over the table where Farnham's schoolbooks were thrown. "Got a bit of string? No—oh, yes." He pounced on a piece, and came over to Joel and the dog.

"What are you going to do, sir?" Joel hung to Sinbad with a tighter grip than ever.

"Never mind. It's not for you to question me," said the instructor, with great authority.

But Joel edged away. Visions of being expelled from Dr. Marks's school swam before his eyes, and he turned very white.

David plunged through the crowd of boys, absolutely still with the excitement. "Oh, Joel," he begged hoarsely, "let Mr. Parr do as he wants to. Mamsie would say so."

Joel turned at that. "Don't hurt him," he begged. "Don't, please, Mr. Parr."

"I shall not hurt him," said Mr. Parr, putting the cord about the dog's neck and holding the other end after it was knotted fast. "I am going to tie him in the area till morning. Here you, sir," as Sinbad showed lively intentions toward his captor's legs, with a backward glance at his late master.

"Oh, if you'll let me keep him in my room, Mr. Parr," cried Joel, tumbling over to the instructor, who was executing a series of remarkable steps as he dragged Sinbad off,

"I'll—I'll be just as good—just till the morning, sir. Oh, *please*, Mr. Parr—I'll study, and get my lessons better, I truly will," cried poor Joel, unable to promise anything more difficult of performance.

"You'll have to study better anyway, Joel Pepper," said Mr. Parr grimly, as he and Sinbad disappeared down the stairway. "Every boy get back to his room," was the parting command.

No need to tell Joel. He dashed through the ranks and flung himself into his bed, dragged up the clothes well over his stubby head, and cried as if his heart would break.

"Joel—Joel—oh, Joey!" begged David hoarsely, and running to precipitate himself by his side. But Joel only burrowed deeper and sobbed on.

And Davie, trying to keep awake, to give possible comfort, at last tumbled asleep, when Joel with a flood of fresh sorrow rolled over as near to the wall as he could get, and tried to hold in his sobs.

As soon as he dared the next morning, Joel hopped over David still asleep, and out of bed, jumped into his clothes, and ran softly downstairs. There in the area was Sinbad, who had evidently concluded to make the best of it, and accept the situation, for he was curled up in as small a compass as possible, and was even attempting a little sleep.

"I won't let him see me," said Joel to himself, "but as soon as Dr. Marks is up"—and he glanced over at the master's house for any sign of things beginning to move for the day—"and dressed, why, I'll go and ask him—" what, he didn't dare to say, for Joel hadn't been able, with all his thinking, to devise any plan whereby Sinbad could be saved.

"But perhaps Dr. Marks will know," he kept thinking. And after a while the shades were drawn up at the red brick house across the yard, the housemaid came out to brush off the steps, and various other indications showed that the master was beginning to think of the new day and its duties.

Joel plunged across the yard. It was awful, he knew, to intrude at the master's house before breakfast. But by that time—oh, dreadful!—Sinbad would probably be beyond the help of any rescuing hand, for Mr. Parr would, without a doubt, deliver him to the garbage man to be hauled off. And Joel, with no thought of consequences to himself, plunged recklessly on.

"Is Dr. Marks up?" he demanded of the housemaid, who only stared at him and went on with her work of sweeping off the steps. "Is Dr. Marks up?" cried Joel, his black eyes flashing, and going halfway up.

"Yes, but what of it?" cried the housemaid airily, leaning on her broom a minute.

"Oh, I must see him," cried Joel, bounding into the hall. It was such a cry of distress that it penetrated far within the house.

"Oh my! You outrageous boy!" exclaimed the housemaid, shaking her broom at him. "You come right out."

Meantime a voice said, "What is it?" And there was Dr. Marks in dressing gown and slippers looking over the railing at the head of the stairs.

"Oh, Dr. Marks, Dr. Marks!" Joel, not giving himself time to think, dashed over the stairs, to look up into the face under the iron-gray hair.

The master could scarcely conceal his amazement, but he made a brave effort at self-control.

"Why, Pepper!" he exclaimed, and there was a good deal of displeasure in face and manner, so much so that Joel's knees knocked smartly together and everything swam before his eyes.

"Well, what did you want to see me for, Pepper?" Dr. Marks was inquiring, so Joel blurted out, "A dog, sir."

"A *dog?*" repeated Dr. Marks, and now he showed his amazement and displeasure as well. "And is this what you have interrupted me to say, at this unseasonable hour, Joel Pepper?"

"Oh!" cried Joel, and then he broke right down, and went flat on the stairs, crying as if his heart would break. And Mrs. Marks threw on her pretty blue wrapper in a dreadful tremor, and rushed out with restoratives, and the housemaid who shook her broom at Joel ran on remorseful feet for a glass of water, and the master's whole house was in a ferment. But Dr. Marks waved them all aside. "The boy needs nothing," he said. "Come, Joel." He took his hand, all grimy and streaked, and looked at his poor, swollen eyelids and nose, over which the tears were still falling, and in a minute he had him in his own private study, with the door shut.

When he emerged a quarter hour after, Joel was actually smiling. He had hold of the master's hand, and clutched in his other fist was a note, somewhat changed in appearance from its immaculate condition when delivered by Dr. Marks to the bearer.

"Yes, sir," Joel was saying, "I'll do it all just as you say, sir." And he ran like lightning across the yard.

The note put into the instructor's hand, made him change countenance more than once in the course of its reading. It simply said, for it was very short, that the dog was to be delivered to Joel Pepper, who was to bring it to the master's house, and although there wasn't a line or even a word to show any disapproval of his course, Mr. Parr felt, as he set about obeying it, as if somehow he had made a little mistake somewhere.

All Joel thought of, however, was to get possession of

Sinbad. And when once he had the cord in his hand, he untied it with trembling fingers, Sinbad, in his transport, hampering the operation dreadfully by bobbing his head about in his violent efforts to lick Joel's face and hands, for he had about given up in despair the idea of ever seeing him again.

"He's glad to go, isn't he, Joel?" observed the instructor, to break the ice and make conversation.

But no such effort was necessary, for Joel looked up brightly. "Isn't he, sir? Now say good-bye." At last the string was loose, and dangling to the hook in the area wall, and Joel held the dog up, and stuck out his paw.

"Good-bye," said Mr. Parr, laughing as he took it, and quite relieved to find that relations were not strained after all, as Joel, hugging his dog, sped hastily across the yard again to the master's house.

Dr. Marks never told how very ugly he found the dog, but summoning the man who kept his garden and lawn in order, he consigned Sinbad to his care, with another note.

"Now, Joel," he said, "you know this payment comes every week out of your allowance for this dog's keeping, eh? It is clearly understood, Joel?"

"Oh, yes, sir—yes!" shouted Joel.

"Perhaps we'll be able to find a good home for him. Well, good-bye, Sinbad," said the master, as Sinbad, with the gardener's hand over his eyes, so that he could not see Joel, was marched off, Dr. Marks from the veranda charging that the note be delivered and read before leaving the dog.

"Oh, I'm going to take him home at vacation," announced Joel decidedly.

"Indeed! Well, now, perhaps your grandfather won't care for him. You must not count too much upon it, my boy." All the control in the world could not keep the master from smiling now.

"Oh, I guess he will." Joel was in no wise disturbed by the doubt.

"Well, run along to breakfast with you, Pepper," cried Dr. Marks good-humoredly, "and the next time you come over to see me, don't bring any more dogs."

So Joel, in high good spirits, and thinking how he would soon run down to the little old cobbler's where the master had sent the dog, chased off across the yard once more, and slipped in to breakfast with a terrible appetite, and a manner as if nothing especial had happened the preceding night.

And all the boys rubbed their eyes, particularly as Joel and Mr. Parr seemed to be on the best of terms. And once when something was said about a dog by Mr. Harrow, who hadn't heard anything of the midnight tumult in the dormitory, and was for continuing the account of his trained pet, the other underteacher and Joel Pepper indulged in smiles and nods perfectly mystifying to all the other people at the table, David included.

David, when he woke up, which was quite late, to find Joel gone, had been terribly frightened. But chancing to look out of the window, he saw him racing across the yard, and watching closely, he discovered that he had something in his arms, and that he turned in to the master's house.

"I can't do anything now," said Davie to himself in the greatest distress. Yet somehow when he came to think of it, it seemed to be with a great deal of hope, since Dr. Marks was to be appealed to. And when breakfast time came, and with it Joel so blithe and hungry, David fell to on his own breakfast with a fine appetite.

*   *   *

All the boys of the club, not one to be reported absent, presented themselves at Mr. Ring's on club night. And all the members of the "Salisbury School Club" came promptly together, with one new member, Cathie Harrison, who, at Polly's suggestion, had been voted in at the last meeting.

Alexia still had her arm in a sling; and indeed she was quite willing it should remain so, for she was in constant terror that her aunt, who had been persuaded to leave her, would insist on the return home. So Alexia begged off at every mention of the subject, as Grandpapa King and Mother Fisher were very glad to have the visit lengthened. She was as gay as ever, and tonight was quite in her element; it had been so long since she had had a good time.

"Oh, Jasper," she cried. "Can we all get into your den?"

"I think so," said Jasper, who had already settled all that with Polly, counting every member as coming, in order to make no mistake. "We're to have the business meeting in there, Alexia. And after that, father has invited us in to the drawing room."

"What richness!" exclaimed Alexia, sinking into one of the library chairs to pull out her skirts and play with her rings. "Oh, Jasper King, I shouldn't think you'd ever in all this world get used to living in this perfectly exquisite house."

"Well, I've always lived here, Alexia," said Jasper with a laugh, "so I suppose that is the reason I'm not overwhelmed now. Oh, here comes Clare. All right, old fellow, glad you've come. Now I'll call the meeting to order." For Clare was the secretary.

And the rest of the boys and girls assembling, the business meeting was soon begun in the "den," Jasper who was the president of the boys' club, flourishing his gavel in great style.

"Now we've come together," announced the president

after the regular business was disposed of, "to get up a plan by which we can accomplish something more than merely to have a good time."

"Nonsense!" interrupted Clare. "We want a good time."

"For shame!" Jasper pounded his gavel to restore order. "And to begin with, it is as well to announce at once that all unruly members will be put out," with a stern glance at the secretary.

"Oh, dear me!" exclaimed Clare, huddling down into his big chair.

"Go along, Prex," said Pickering, coming over from the other side of the room. "I'll sit on that old secretary if he makes any more trouble."

"Get away!" laughed Clare. "That's worse than being put out."

"Oh, I'll sit on you first, and then I'll carry out the pieces afterward. Sail on, Prexy, they all want the plan."

"Well"—the president cleared his throat—"hem! And in order to do good work, why we had to ask the girls' club to come to this meeting, and—"

"Not necessarily," put in Clare.

Pickering pounced for him, but instead of sitting on him, his long figure doubled up in the big chair, while the secretary slipped neatly out.

"Ha, ha! Did you ever get left?" giggled Clare, at a safe distance.

"Many a time, my dear child," said Pickering coolly, leaning back restfully, "but never in such a good seat. Thank you, Mr. Secretary. Proceed, Prexy."

"Good for you, Pickering," cried Alexia, while the laugh went around.

"Order!" cried Jasper, pounding away. "Now that our troublesome secretary is quieted, I will proceed to say that as

we want the plan to succeed, we invited the Salisbury Club
this evening."

"Thank you, Mr. President." The girls clapped vigorously.

"So now after I tell you of the object, I want you to
express your minds about the various plans that will be laid
before you." Then Jasper told the story of Jim, the brakeman; and how Grandpapa and Polly and he had gone to the
poor home, thanks to the little clerk; and how the three boys
who were waiting for education and the girl who was crazy to
take music lessons, to say nothing of the two mites of
children toddling around, made the poor widow almost frantic as she thought of their support; until some of the girls
were sniffling and hunting for their handkerchiefs, and the
boys considerately turned away and wouldn't look at them.

"Now, you tell the rest, Polly," cried Jasper, quite tired
out.

"Oh, no, you tell," said Polly, who dearly loved to hear
Jasper talk.

"Do, Polly," and he pushed the hair off from his forehead.
So, as she saw he really wanted her to, Polly began with
shining eyes, and glowing cheeks, to finish the story.

And she told how Grandpapa had ordered provisions and
coal for the poor widow, enough for many months to come,
and how—oh, wasn't that perfectly splendid in dear Grandpapa?—he had promised that the little girl (Arethusa was
her name) should take music lessons from one of the teachers
in the city. And Polly clasped her hands and sighed, quite
unable to do more.

"And what do you want us to do?" cried the secretary,
forgetting all about losing his seat, to crowd up to the table.
"Say, if that family has got all that richness, what do you
want the club to do?"

"Oh," said Polly turning her shining eyes on him, "there

are ever and ever so many things the boys and that girl will
need, and Grandpapa says that they'll think a great deal
more of help, if some young people take hold of it. And so
I'm sure I should," she added.

"It strikes me that I should, too," declared Pickering, all
his laziness gone. And getting his long figure out of the
chair, he cried, "I move, Mr. President, that we"—here he
waved his hands in a sweeping gesture—"the Salisbury Club
and our club, unite in a plan to do something for that
family."

"I second the motion," the secretary cried out, much to
everybody's surprise, for Polly was all ready to do it if no one
else offered to. So the vote was carried unanimously amid
the greatest enthusiasm.

"Now what shall we do?" cried the president, jumping to
his feet. "Let us strike while the iron is hot. What shall we
do to raise money?"

"You said you had plans," cried one of the girls.

"Yes—tell on," cried several boys.

"Well, one is, that we have a play," began Jasper.

"Oh—oh!"

Old Mr. King, over his evening paper off in the library,
laid it down and smiled at the merry din that reached him
even at such a distance.

"And another," cried the president, doing his best to
make himself heard.

"Oh, we don't want another," cried Clare, in which the
united clubs joined.

"Don't you want to hear any other plans?" shouted the
president.

"No, no—the play! Put it to vote, do, Jasper—I mean,
Mr. President," cried Alexia.

So the vote was taken and everybody said, "Aye," and as

there wasn't a single no, why the ayes had it of course. And after that they talked so long over the general plan, that old Mr. King at last had to send a very special invitation to come out to the dining room. And there was Mother Fisher and Mrs. Whitney and the little doctor and a most splendid collation! And then off to the big drawing room to top off with a dance, with one or two musicians tucked up by the grand piano, and Grandpapa smiling in great satisfaction upon them all.

Chapter 12

Some Everyday Fun

"**I**T can't rain," cried Polly Pepper, "and it isn't going to. Don't think it, girls."

"But it looks just like it," said Alexia obstinately, and wrinkling up her brows. "See those awful horrid clouds, girls." She pointed tragically up to the sky.

"Don't look at them," advised Polly. "Come on, girls. I challenge you to a race as far as the wicket gate."

Away she dashed, with a bevy at her heels. Alexia, not to be left behind staring at the sky, went racing after.

"Wait," she screamed. The racers, however, spent no time attending to laggards, but ran on.

Polly dashed ahead and touched the green wicket gate. "Oh, Polly got there first!" Almost immediately came another girl's fingers on it.

"No—I don't think so," panted Polly. "Philena got there just as soon."

"No, you were first," said the girl who plunged up next. "I saw it distinctly."

"Well, it was so near that we ought to have another race to decide it," declared Polly, with a little laugh, pushing back the damp rings of hair from her forehead. "Girls, isn't it lovely that we have this splendid place where we can run, and nobody see us?"

"Yes," said Alexia, throwing herself down on the grass, which example was immediately followed by all the other girls. "I just love this avenue down to the wicket gate, Polly Pepper."

"So do I," chimed in the others.

"Oh dear me! I'm just toasted and fried," declared Alexia. "I never *was* so hot in all my life."

"You shouldn't have run so, Alexia," said Polly reproachfully, patting the arm still in its sling. " Oh, how could you!"

"Well, did you suppose I was going to see you all sprinting off and having such fun, and not try it too? No, indeed. That's asking too much, Polly."

Then she threw herself at full length on the grass and gazed at her meditatively.

"Well, we mustn't have the second race, Philena," said Polly, "because if Alexia runs again it surely will hurt her."

"*Ow!*" exclaimed Alexia, flouncing up so suddenly that she nearly overthrew Amy Garrett, who was sitting next, and who violently protested against such treatment, "now I won't keep you back, Polly. Oh dear me! It can't hurt me a single bit. I'm all ready to take off this horrible old thing, you know I am, only Dr. Fisher thought—"

"He thought it would be safer to keep it on till after the picnic," Polly was guilty of interrupting. "You know he said so, Alexia. No, we won't run again, girls," Polly brought up quite decidedly.

"Polly, you shall. I won't run—I really won't. I'll shut my eyes." And Alexia squinted up her pale eyes till her face was drawn up in a knot. "I'll turn my back, I'll do anything if you'll only race. *Please* try it again, Polly."

So Polly, seeing that Alexia really wished it, dropped a kiss on each of the closed eyes. "Put your hand over them, and untwist your face from that funny knot," she laughed. "Come on, girls," and the race began.

Alexia twisted and wriggled, as the pattering feet and quick breath of the girls when they neared her resting place plunged her in dreadful distress not to look. "Oh dear—um! If I could just see once. Um—*um!* I know Polly will win. Oh, dear! She *must.*"

But she didn't. It was Cathie Harrison, the new girl—that is, new to them, as they hadn't drawn her into their set but a few weeks. She was a tall, thin girl, who got over the ground amazingly, to touch the green wicket gate certainly three seconds before Polly Pepper came flying up.

"You did that just splendidly, Cathie," cried Polly breathlessly. "Oh dear me, that *was* a race!"

"Goodness me!" cried Alexia, her eyes flying open, "my face never'll get out of that knot in all this world. My! I feel as if my jaws were all tied up. Well, Polly, this time you beat for sure," she added confidently, as the girls came running up to throw themselves on the grass again.

"But I didn't," said Polly merrily. "Oh dear! I *am* so hot."

"Yes, you did," declared Alexia stubbornly.

"Why, Alexia Rhys! I didn't beat, any such a thing," corrected Polly—"not a single bit of it."

"Well, who did, then?" demanded Alexia, quite angry to have Polly defeated.

"Why, Cathie did," said Polly, smiling over at her.

"What, that old—" Then Alexia pulled herself up, but it was too late.

A dull red mounted to Cathie's sallow cheek, that hadn't changed color during all the two races. She drew a long breath, then got up slowly to her feet.

"I'm going to play beanbags," announced Polly briskly. "Come on, girls. See who'll get to the house first."

"I'm going home," said Cathie, hurrying up to wedge herself into the group, and speaking to Polly. "Good-bye."

"No," said Polly, "we're going to play beanbags. Come on, Cathie." She tried to draw Cathie's hand within her arm, but the girl pulled herself away. "I must go home—" and she started off.

"Cathie—*Cathie*, wait," but again Cathie beat her on a swift run down the avenue.

Alexia stuffed her fingers, regardless of arm in the sling, or anything, into her mouth, and rolled over in dreadful distress, face downward on the grass. The other girls stood in a frightened little knot, just where they were, without moving, as Polly came slowly back down the avenue. She was quite white now. "Oh dear!" groaned Philena. "Look at Polly!"

Alexia heard it, and stuffed her fingers worse than ever into her mouth to keep herself from screaming outright, and wriggled dreadfully. But no one paid any attention to her. She knew that Polly had joined the girls now. She could hear them talking, and Polly was saying, in a sad little voice, "Yes, I'm afraid she won't ever come with us again."

"She must, she shall!" howled Alexia, rolling over and sitting up straight. "Oh, Polly, she shall!" And she wrung her long hands as well as she could for the arm in the sling.

"Oh, no, I am afraid not, Alexia," and her head drooped. No one would have thought for a moment that it was Polly Pepper speaking.

And then Amy Garrett said the very worst thing possible: "And just think of that picnic!" And after that remark, the whole knot of girls was plunged into the depths of gloom.

Jasper, running down the avenue with Pickering Dodge at his heels, found them so, and was transfixed with astonishment. "Well, I declare!" He burst into a merry laugh.

"You look like a lot of wax figures," said Pickering pleasantly. "Just about as interesting." Then they saw Polly Pepper's face.

"Oh, what is it?" cried Jasper, starting forward.

Polly tried to speak cheerfully, but the lump in her throat wouldn't let her say a word.

"If you boys must know," said Alexia, flouncing up to her feet, "I've been bad and perfectly horrid to that Harrison girl, and I've upset everything, and—and—do go right straight away, both of you, and not stand there staring. I don't think it's very polite."

"Oh, Polly," cried Jasper, gaining her side, "can't we help?" He was dreadfully distressed. "Do let us."

Polly shook her head. "No, Jasper, there isn't anything you can do," she said brokenly.

Pickering thrust his hands in his pockets and whistled softly. "Girls always get into such rows," he observed.

"Well, I guess we don't get into worse ones than you boys do, nor half as bad," cried Alexia crossly, perfectly wild to quarrel with somebody. "And besides, this isn't the other girls' fault. It's all my fight from beginning to end."

"Then you ought to be perfectly ashamed of yourself, Alexia," declared Pickering, not intending to mince matters in the slightest.

"Well, I am," said Alexia, "just as ashamed as I can be. Oh dear me! I wish I could cry. But I'm too bad to cry. Polly Pepper, I'm going to run after that horrible Harrison girl. Oh

misery! I wish she never had come to the Salisbury School."
Alexia made a mad rush down the avenue.

"Don't, Alexia, you'll hurt your arm," warned Polly.

"I don't care—I hope I shall," cried Alexia recklessly.

"It's no use to try to stop her," said Jasper, "so let us go up
to the house, Polly."

So they started dismally enough, the girls, all except
Polly, going over in sorry fashion how Cathie Harrison would
probably make a fuss about the little affair—she was doubt-
less on her way to Miss Salisbury's now—and then perhaps
there wouldn't be any picnic at all on the morrow. At this,
Philena stopped short. "Girls, that would be too dreadful,"
she gasped, "for anything!"

"Well, it would be just like her," said Silvia Horne, "and I
wish we never had taken her into our set. She's an old
moping thing, and can't bear a word."

"I wish so too," declared Amy Garrett positively. "She
doesn't belong with us, and she's always going to make
trouble. And I hope she won't go to the picnic anyway, if we
do have it, so there."

"I don't think that is the way to mend the matter, Amy,"
said Jasper gravely.

"Oho!" exclaimed Pickering. "How you girls can go on so,
I don't see, talking forever about one thing, instead of just
settling it with a few fisticuffs. That would be comfortable
now."

The girls, one and all, turned a cold shoulder to him after
this speech.

"Well, we shan't get the picnic now, I know," said Philena
tragically. "And think of all our nice things ready. Dear me!
Our cook made me the sweetest chocolate cakes, because we
were going to start so early in the morning. Now we'll have

them for dinner, and eat them up ourselves. We might as well."

"You better not," advised Pickering. "Take my advice. You'll get your picnic all right. Then where would you be with your cakes all eaten up?"

"You don't know Miss Salisbury," said Sally Moore gloomily. "Nothing would make her so mad as to have us get up a fuss with a new scholar. She was so pleased when Polly Pepper invited that Harrison girl to come to our bee for that poor family down south."

"And now, just think how we've initiated her into our club!" said Lucy Bennett, with a sigh. "Oh my goodness—look!"

She pointed off down the avenue. All the girls whirled around to stare. There were Alexia and Cathie, coming toward them arm in arm.

"Jasper"—Polly turned to him with shining eyes—"see!" Then she broke away from them all, and rushed to meet the two girls.

"There isn't anybody going to say a word," announced Alexia, as the three girls came up to the group, Polly Pepper in the middle, "because, as I told you, it was all my fight, anyway. So Pickering, you needn't get ready to be disagreeable," she flashed over at him saucily.

"I shall say just what I think," declared Pickering flatly.

"No doubt," said Alexia sweetly, "but it won't make a bit of difference. Well, now, Polly, what shall we do? Do start us on something."

"We came, Pick and I," announced Jasper, "to ask you girls to have a game of beanbags. There's just time before dinner—on the south lawn, Polly."

"Oh, good—good!" cried the girls, clapping their hands. "Come on, Cathie," said Philena awkwardly, determined to break the ice at once.

"Yes, Cathie, come on," said Amy and Silvia, trying to be very nice.

Cathie just got her mouth ready to say, "No, I thank you," primly, thought better of it, and before she quite realized it herself, there she was, hurrying by a shortcut across the grass to the south lawn.

"I'm going to stay with Alexia," said Polly, when they all reached there, and Jasper flew over to pull out the beanbags from their box under the piazza. "Come on, Alexia, let's you and I sit in the hammock and watch it."

"Oh, Polly, come and play," begged Jasper, pausing with his arms full. "Here, Pick, you lazy dog. Help with these bags."

"Can't," said Polly, shaking her head. So Alexia and she curled up in one of the hammocks.

"I'm just dying to tell you all about it, Polly Pepper," said Alexia, pulling Polly's cheek down to her own.

"Yes," said Polly happily, "and I can't wait to hear it. And besides, you can't play beanbags, Alexia, with that arm. Well, do go on," and Polly was in quite a twitter for the story to begin.

"You see," said Alexia, "I knew something desperate had got to be done, Polly, for she was crying all over her best silk waist."

"Oh dear me!" exclaimed Polly, aghast.

"Yes. She had sat down on the kitchen step."

"The kitchen step," repeated Polly faintly.

"Yes. I suppose she got beyond caring whether the cook saw or not, she was feeling so very badly. Well, there she was, and she didn't hear me, so I just rushed up, or rather down upon her, and then I screamed 'Ow!' And she jumped up, and said, 'Oh, have you hurt your arm?' And I held on to it hard, and made up an awful face, oh, as bad as I could, and doubled up; and the cook came to the door, and said could she get me anything, and she was going to call Mrs. Fisher. That would have been terrible." Alexia broke off short, and drew a long breath at her remembrance of the fright this suggestion had given her. "And Cathie fell right on my neck with, 'Oh, do forgive me,' and I said 'twas my fault, and she said, no, she oughtn't to have got mad, and I said she must hold her tongue."

"Oh, Alexia!" cried Polly reprovingly.

"I had to," said Alexia serenely, "or we should have gotten into another fight. And she said she would, and I just took hold of her arm, and dragged her down here. And I'm tired to death," finished Alexia plaintively.

"Alexia," exclaimed Polly, cuddling up the long figure in a way to give perfect satisfaction, "we must make Cathie Harrison have the best time that she ever had, at the picnic tomorrow."

"I suppose so," said Alexia resignedly. "Well, but don't let's think of it now, for I've got you, Polly, and I want to rest."

Chapter 13

The Picnic

*T*HE four barges were to leave the "Salisbury School" at precisely half-past eight o'clock the next morning. Miss Salisbury was always very particular about being prompt, so woe be to any girls who might be late! There was great scurrying, therefore, to and fro in the homes of the day scholars. And the girls hurried off with maids behind carrying their baskets; or, as the case might be, big family carriages filled with groups of girls collected among those of a set; or in little pony carriages. All this made the thoroughfares adjacent to the "Salisbury School" extremely busy places indeed.

Mother Fisher sent Polly's basket over to the school at an early hour, Polly preferring to walk, several of the girls having called for her. So they all, with Jasper, who was going as far as the corner with them, set out amidst a chatter of merry nonsense.

"Oh, girls, I *am* so glad we are going to the Glen!" exclaimed Polly, for about the fiftieth time.

"So am I," cried all the others in a chorus.

"Why, you haven't ever been to any other place for your picnic, have you, Polly?" cried Jasper, with a laugh.

"No," said Polly, "we never have. But suppose Miss Salisbury had decided to try some other spot this year. Oh, just suppose it, Jasper!" And her rosy color died down on her cheek. "It would have been just too dreadful for anything."

"We couldn't have had our picnic in any other place," declared Rose Harding. "It wouldn't be the same unless it was at the Glen."

"Dear old Glen!" cried Polly impulsively. "Jasper, it's too bad you boys can't all come to our picnics."

"I know it. It would be no end jolly if we only could," said Jasper regretfully, to whom it was a great grief that the picnic couldn't take in the two schools.

"Yes," said Polly, with a sigh, "it would, Jasper. But Miss Salisbury never will in all this world let the boys' school join."

"No, I suppose not," said Jasper, stifling his longing. "Well, you must tell me about it tonight, the same as always, Polly."

"Yes, I will, Jasper," promised Polly. So he turned the corner to go to his school. But presently he heard rapid footsteps back of him. "Oh, Jasper," cried Polly, flushed and panting, as he whirled about, "tell Phronsie I won't forget the little fern roots. Be sure, Jasper."

"All right, I will," said Jasper. "Dear me! do hurry back, Polly. You'll be late."

"Oh no, there are oceans of time," said Polly, with a little laugh. "I've the tin case in my picnic basket, Jasper, so they will keep all fresh and nice."

"Yes. Do hurry back," begged Jasper. So Polly, with a merry nod, raced off to the corner where the girls were drawn up in a knot, impatiently waiting for her.

Every bit of the fuss and parade in getting the big company started—for all the scholars went to the annual picnic—was a special delight to the girls. The only trouble was that the seats were not all end ones, while the favorite places up by the driver were necessarily few in each vehicle.

"Come on, Polly," screamed Alexia. Everybody had agreed that she should have one of these choice positions because of her lame arm, which Dr. Fisher had said must be carried in its sling this day. So there she was, calling lustily for Polly Pepper, and beating the cushion impatiently with her well hand. "Oh, *do* hurry up!"

Polly, down on the ground in a swarm of girls, shook her head. "No," her lips said softly, so that no one but Alexia who was leaning over for that purpose, could possibly hear. "Ask Cathie."

"Oh bother!" exclaimed Alexia with a frown. Then she smothered it up with a "Come, Polly," very persuasively.

"Can't," said Polly. "I'm going back here." And she moved down to the end of the barge.

"Then I'm going back too." Alexia gave a frantic dive to get down from the barge.

Miss Salisbury saw it. And as she had planned to give Alexia just that very pleasure of riding on the front seat, she was naturally somewhat disturbed. "No, no, my dear," seeing Alexia's efforts to get down, "stay where you are."

"Oh dear me!" Alexia craned her long neck around the side of the vehicle, to spy Polly's movements. "I don't want to be mewed up here," she cried discontentedly. But Miss Salisbury, feeling well satisfied with her plan for making Alexia happy, had moved off. And the babel and tumult

waged so high, over the placing of the big company, all the
girls chattering and laughing at once, that Alexia, call as she
might, began to despair of attracting Polly's attention, or
Cathie's either for that matter.

"You better set down," said the driver, an old man whom
Miss Salisbury employed every year to superintend the business, "and make yourself comfortable."

"But I'm not in the least comfortable," said Alexia passionately, "and I don't want to be up here. I want to get
down."

"But you can't"—the old man seemed to fairly enjoy her
dismay—" 'cause she, you know," pointing a short square
thumb over his shoulder in the direction of Miss Salisbury,
"told ye to set still. So ye better set."

But Alexia craned her neck yet more, and called insis-
tently, "Polly—oh, Polly!"

Miss Anstice looked up from the bevy of girls she was
settling in another barge. "Alexia Rhys," she said severely,
"you must be quiet. It is impossible to get started unless all
you girls are going to be tractable and obedient."

"Miss Anstice"—Alexia formed a sudden bold resolve—
"please come here. I want you very much," she said sweetly.

Miss Anstice, pleased to be wanted very much, or indeed at
all, left her work and went over to the front barge, where
Alexia was raging inwardly.

"Miss Anstice, I need Polly Pepper up next to me," said
Alexia, "oh, so much. She knows all about my arm, you
know. Her father fixed it for me. Will you please have her
come up here? Then if I should feel worse, she could help
me."

Miss Anstice peered here and there in her nearsighted
fashion. "I don't see Polly Pepper," she said.

"There she is! There she is!" cried Alexia, trembling in every limb, for her plan could not be said to be a complete success yet, and pointing eagerly to the end of her barge, "she's the fourth from the door, Miss Anstice. Oh, how lovely you are!"

Miss Anstice, quite overcome to be told she was lovely, and especially by Alexia, who had previously given her no reason to suppose that she entertained any such opinion, went with great satisfaction down the length of the barge, and standing on her tiptoes, said very importantly, "Polly Pepper, I want to place you differently."

So Polly, quite puzzled, but very obedient, crawled out from her seat, where she was wedged in between two girls not of her set, who had been perfectly radiant at their good fortune, and clambering down the steps, was, almost before she knew it, installed up on the front row, by Alexia's side.

"Oh, Polly, what richness!" exclaimed that individual in smothered accents, as Miss Anstice stepped off in much importance, and hugging Polly. "I'm so glad my sling is on, for I never'd gotten you up here without the old thing," and she giggled as she told the story.

"Oh, Alexia!" exclaimed Polly, quite shocked.

"Well, I may get a relapse in it, you don't know," said Alexia coolly, "so you really ought to be up here. Oh my goodness me! I forgot this man," she brought up suddenly. "Do you suppose he'll tell?" She peered around anxiously past Polly.

"Ef you'll set still, I won't tell that teacher," said the old man with a twinkle in his eye, "but ef you get to carryin' on, as I should think you could ef you set out to, I'll up an' give the whole thing to her."

"Oh, I'll sit as still as a mouse," promised Alexia. "Oh,

Polly, isn't he a horrible old thing!" in a stage whisper under cover of the noise going on around them.

"Hush," said Polly.

"Well, I'm not going to hush," cried Alexia recklessly. "I'm going to have a good time at the picnic today, and do just everything I want to, so there, Polly Pepper!"

"Very well," said Polly. "Then when we get to the Glen, I shall go off with the other girls, Alexia," which had the desired effect. Alexia curled up into her corner, and hanging to Polly Pepper's arm, was just like a mouse for quiet. And off they went, the old man's whip going crack—*snap!* as he led the way with a grand flourish, as much better than his efforts of former years as was possible!

The road led through winding, woodsy paths, redolent of sweet fern. The girls never tired of its delights, exclaiming at all the sights and sounds of country life at all such moments as were not filled to the brim with the songs that ran over from their happy hearts. So on and up they went to the Glen, a precipitous ravine some fifteen miles out from the city.

When the barges finally drew up with another grand flourish at the entrance, a smooth grassy plateau shaded by oaks and drooping elms, they simply poured out a stream of girls from each conveyance, the old man and his companion drivers laughing to see them tumble out. "Pretty quick work, eh, Bill?" said old man Kimball. "No screaming for first places now."

"It's the same beautiful, dear old Glen!" exclaimed Polly, with kindling eyes and dancing feet. "Oh, Alexia, come on!" and seizing the well hand, they spun round and round, unable to keep still, having plenty of company, all the other girls following suit.

Polly looked at her little watch. "In five minutes we must stop. It'll be time to get the flowers."

"Oh, can we?" cried Alexia. "Misery me! I'm so tired cooped up in that barge, I feel stiff as a jointed doll, Polly Pepper."

"Well, I don't," said Polly, dancing away for dear life. "Oh, Alexia, when Miss Salisbury gives the signal to explore, won't it be just fun!"

"I should say," cried Alexia, unable to find words that would just express the case.

There was always one routine to be observed in the annual picnic of the "Salisbury School," and no one thought for a moment of deviating from it. The maids collected the baskets taken from the wagons and set them in a cool, shady place among the rocks just within the Glen. The girls ran hither and thither to collect flowers and ferns to drape Miss Salisbury's seat of honor, and one as near like it as possible for Miss Anstice. These were big crevices in the rocks, that were as comfortable as chairs, and having backs to them in the shape of boulders, they were truly luxurious. Indeed, Miss Salisbury had declared, when the seats were discovered by Polly Pepper at the first picnic after she joined the "Salisbury School" that she never sat in one more comfortable, and she was so pleased when she was led to it and inducted therein, all flower-trimmed with little vines trailing off, and arching over her head.

"Why, my dears!" she exclaimed, quite overcome. "Oh, how pretty! And how did you think of it?"

"It was Polly Pepper who thought of it," said a parlor boarder. And Polly, blushing rosy red, a new girl as she was, was led up, and Miss Salisbury set a kiss on her round cheek. Polly never forgot how happy she was that day.

And afterward, when the girls were busy in various little

groups, Miss Salisbury had beckoned Polly to her side where she reposed on her throne, for it was beautiful and stately enough for two, and quite worthy of royalty itself.

"Polly," said Miss Salisbury, in quite a low tone only fitted for Polly's ear, "do you think you could find a seat, like this beautiful one of mine, for sister? I should really enjoy it so very much more if sister had one also, and she would prize the attention very much, Polly, from you girls."

So Polly, fired with the laudable desire to find one exactly like Miss Salisbury's very own, for "sister," at last was just so fortunate. So that was also flower-trimmed, with trailing vines to finish it off with. And every year, the first thing the girls did after dancing around a bit to rest their feet after the long drive, was to set to work to collect the vines and ferns, and decorate the two stone seats.

Then with quite a good deal of pomp and ceremony, the girls escorted the two teachers to their thrones, unpacked the little bag of books and magazines, and arranged some cushions and shawls about them. And then Miss Salisbury always said with a sweet smile, "Thank you, my dears." And Miss Anstice said the same, although, try as hard as she would, her smile never could be sweet like Miss Salisbury's. And then off the girls would go to "exploring," as they called rambling in the Glen, the underteachers taking them in charge.

And now Polly Pepper ran to her hamper, which she saw in a pile where the baskets had been heaped by the maids. "There it is," pointing to the tag sticking up. "Oh, help me—not you, Alexia," as Alexia ran up as usual, to help forward any undertaking Polly Pepper might have in mind. "Dear me! You might almost kill your arm."

"This old arm," cried Alexia. "I'm sick and tired of it."

"Well, you better take care of it," cried Polly gaily, "and

then it won't be an old arm, but it will be as good as brand new, Alexia. Oh, one of the other girls, do come and help me."

"What do you want, Polly?" cried some of the girls, racing up to her.

"I want to get out my hamper," said Polly, pointing to the tag sticking up "high and dry" amid a stack of baskets. "My tin botany case is in it. I must get the ferns I promised to bring home to Phronsie."

"You stand away, all of ye." The old man Kimball, his horses out of the shafts, and well taken care of, now drew near, and swept off with his ample hand the bunch of girls. "Which one is't? Oh, that ere one with the tag," answering his own question. "Well, now, I'll git that for you jest as easy as rolling off a log. One—two—three—there she comes!"

And, one, two, three, and here she did come! And in a trice Polly had the cover up, and out flew the little green tin botany case; and within it being an iron spoon and little trowel, off flew Polly on happy feet to unearth the treasures that were to beautify Phronsie's little garden, a bunch of girls following to see the operation.

The magazine fell idly to the lap of Miss Salisbury. She sat dreamily back, resting her head against the boulder. "Sister," she said softly, "this is a happy custom we have started. I trust nothing will ever prevent our holding our annual picnic."

"Yes," said Miss Anstice absently. She was very much interested in a story she had begun, and she hated to have Miss Salisbury say a word. Although she had on a stiff, immaculate white gown (for on such a festival as the annual picnic, she always dressed in white), still she was not in the same sweet temper that the principal was enjoying, and she held her thumb and finger in the place.

"Yes, the picnic is very good," she said, feeling that

something was expected of her, "if we didn't get worms and bugs crawling over the tablecloth."

"Oh, sister!" exclaimed Miss Salisbury, quite shocked. "It is no time to think of worms and bugs, I'm sure, on such a beautiful occasion as this."

"Still, they are here," said Miss Anstice. "There is one now," looking down at the hem of her gown. "*Ugh!* Go right away," slapping her book at it. Then her thumb and finger flew out, and she lost her place, and the bug ran away, and she added somewhat tartly, "For my own taste, I should really prefer a festival in the schoolroom."

When it came to spreading the feast, not one of the maids was allowed to serve. They could unpack the hampers, and hand the dishes and eatables to the girls, and run, and wait, and tend. But no one but the Salisbury girls must lay the snowy cloth, dress it up with flowers, with little knots at the corners, concealing the big stones that kept the tablecloth from flapping in any chance wind. And then they all took turns in setting the feast forth, and arranging all the goodies. And someone had to make the coffee, with a little coterie to help her. The crotched sticks were always there just as they had left them where they hung the kettle over the stone oven. And old man Kimball set one of the younger drivers to make the fire—and a rousing good one it was—where they roasted their corn and potatoes. And another one brought up the water from the spring that bubbled up clear and cold in the rocky ravine, so when all was ready it was a feast fit for a king, or rather the queen and her royal subjects.

And then Miss Salisbury and "sister" were escorted with all appropriate ceremonies down from their stone thrones —and one had the head and the other the foot of the feast spread on the grass—to sit on a stone draped with a shawl, and to be waited on lovingly by the girls, who threw them-

selves down on the ground, surrounding the snowy cloth.
And they sat two or three rows deep, and those in the front
row had to pass the things, of course, to the back-row girls.

"Oh, you're spilling jellycake crumbs all down my back,"
proclaimed Alexia, with a shudder. "Rose Harding," looking
at the girl just back of her, "can't you eat over your own lap,
pray tell?"

"Well, give me your seat then," suggested Rose, with
another good bite from the crumbly piece in her hand, "if
you don't like what the back-row girls do."

"No, I'm not going to," said Alexia. "Catch me! But you
needn't eat all over my hair. Ugh! There goes another," and
she squirmed so she knocked off the things in her neighbor's
as well as her own lap.

"Oh dear me! Keep your feet to yourself, Alexia Rhys,"
said the neighbor. "There goes my egg in all the dirt—and I'd
just gotten it shelled."

"All the easier for the bugs," observed Alexia sweetly.
"See, they're already appropriating it. And I guess you'd kick
and wriggle if someone put jellycake down your back,"
returning to her grievance. "Slippery, slimy jellycake," twisting again at the remembrance.

"Well, you needn't kick the things out of my lap. I didn't
put the jellycake down your back," retorted the neighbor,
beginning to shell her second egg.

Oh dear! Was ever anything quite so good in all this world
as that feast at the "Salisbury picnic"!

"I didn't suppose those baskets could bring out so much,
nor such perfectly delicious things," sighed Polly Pepper, in
an interval of rest before attacking one of Philena's chocolate
cakes.

"Polly, Polly Pepper," called a girl opposite, "give me one

of your little lemon tarts. You did bring 'em this year, didn't you?" anxiously.

"Yes, indeed," answered Polly. "Why, where are they?" peering up and down the festal, not "board," but tablecloth.

"Don't tell me they are gone," cried the girl, leaning over to look for herself.

"I'm afraid they are," said Polly. "Oh, I'm so sorry, Agatha!"

"You should have spoken before, my child," said a parlor boarder, who had eaten only three of Mrs. Fisher's tarts, and adjusting her eyeglasses.

"Why, I've only just gotten through eating bread and butter," said Agatha. "I can't eat cake until that's done."

"A foolish waste of time," observed the parlor boarder. "Bread and butter is for every day. Cake and custards and flummery for high holidays," she added with quite an air.

"Hush up, do," cried Alexia, who had small respect for the parlor boarders and their graces, "and eat what you like, Penelope. I'm going to ransack this table for a tart for you, Agatha."

She sent keen, birdlike glances all up and down the length of the tablecloth. "Yes, no—yes, it is." She pounced upon a lemon tart hiding under a spray of sweet fern and handed it in triumph across. "There you are, Agatha! Now don't say I never did anything for you."

"Oh, how sweet!" cried Agatha, burying her teeth in the flaky tart.

"I should think it was sour," observed Amy Garrett. "Lemons usually are."

"Don't try to be clever, Amy child," said Alexia. "It isn't expected at a picnic."

"It's never expected where you are," retorted Amy sharply.

"Oh dear, dear! That's pretty good," cried Alexia, nowise disconcerted, as she loved a joke just as much at herself as at the expense of anyone else, while the others burst into a merry laugh.

"There's one good thing about Alexia Rhys," the "Salisbury girls" had always said. "She can take any amount of chaff, and not stick her finger in her eye and whimper."

So now she smiled serenely. "Oh dear, dear! I wish I could eat some more," she said. "I haven't tasted your orange jelly, Clem, nor as much as looked at your French sandwiches, Silvia. What is the reason one can eat so very little at a picnic, I wonder?" She drew a long breath, and regarded them all with a very injured expression.

"Hear that, girls!" cried Silvia. "Isn't that rich, when Alexia has been eating every blessed minute just as fast as she could!"

"I suppose that is what we all have been doing," observed Alexia placidly.

Miss Salisbury had been a happy observer of all the fun and nonsense going on around her, and renewing her youth when she had dearly loved picnics, but it was not so with Miss Anstice. At the foot of the festal tablecloth, she had been viewing from the corners of her eyes the inroads of various specimens of the insect creation and several other peripatetic creatures that seemed to belong to no particular species but to a new order of beings originated for this very occasion. She had held herself in bravely, although eating little, being much too busy in keeping watch of these intruders, who all seemed bent on running over her food and her person, to hide in all conceivable folds of her white gown. And she was now congratulating herself on the end of the feast, which about this time should be somewhere in sight, when a goggle-eyed bug, at least so it seemed to her distraught vision, pranced with agile steps directly for her lap, to disappear at once. And it got on to her nerves.

"Oh—*ow!* Take it off." Miss Anstice let her plate fly, and skipped to her feet. But looking out for the goggle-eyed bug, she thought of little else, and stepped into some more of the jellycake—slipped, and precipitated herself into the middle of the feast.

Chapter 14

Miss Salisbury's Story

"**O**H, Miss Anstice!" cried the "Salisbury girls," jumping to their feet.

"*Sister!*" exclaimed Miss Salisbury, dropping her plate, and letting all her sweet, peaceful reflections fly to the four winds.

"I never did regard picnics as pleasant affairs," gasped Miss Anstice, as the young hands raised her, "and now they are—quite—quite detestable." She looked at her gown, alas! no longer immaculate.

"If you could wipe my hands first, young ladies," sticking out those members, on which were plentiful supplies of marmalade and jellycake, "I should be much obliged. Never mind the gown yet," she added with asperity.

"I'll do that," cried Alexia, flying at her with two or three napkins.

"Alexia, keep your seat." Miss Anstice turned on her. "It is quite bad enough, without your heedless fingers at work on it."

"I won't touch the old thing," declared Alexia, in a towering passion, and forgetting it was not one of the girls. "And I may be heedless, but I *can* be polite," and she threw down the napkins, and turned her back on the whole thing.

"Alexia!" cried Polly, turning very pale, and rushing up to her, she bore her away under the trees. "Why, Alexia Rhys, you've talked awfully to Miss Anstice—just think, the sister of our Miss Salisbury!"

"Was that old thing a Salisbury?" asked Alexia, quite unmoved. "I thought it was a rude creature that didn't know what it was to have good manners."

"Alexia, Alexia!" mourned Polly, and for the first time in Alexia's remembrance wringing her hands. "To think you should do such a thing!"

Alexia, seeing Polly wring her hands, felt quite aghast at herself. "Polly, don't do that," she begged.

"Oh, I can't help it." And Polly's tears fell fast.

Alexia gave her one look, as she stood there quite still and pale, unable to stop the tears racing over her cheeks, turned, and fled with long steps back to the crowd of girls surrounding poor Miss Anstice, Miss Salisbury herself wiping the linen gown with an old napkin in her deft fingers.

"I beg your pardon," cried Alexia gustily, and plunging up unsteadily. "I was bad to say such things."

"You were, indeed," assented Miss Anstice tartly. "Sister, that is quite enough. The gown cannot possibly be made any better with your incessant rubbing."

Miss Salisbury gave a sigh, and got up from her knees, and put down the napkin. Then she looked at Alexia. "She is very sorry, sister," she said gently. "I am sure Alexia regrets exceedingly her hasty speech."

"Hasty?" repeated Miss Anstice, with acrimony. "It was

quite impertinent; and I cannot remember when one of our young ladies has done such a thing."

All the blood in Alexia's body seemed to go to her sallow cheeks when she heard that. That she should be the first and only Salisbury girl to be so bad, quite overcame her, and she looked around for Polly Pepper to help her out. And Polly, who had followed her up to the group, begged, "Do, dear Miss Anstice, forgive her." And so did all the girls, even those who did not like Alexia one bit, feeling sorry for her now. Miss Anstice relented enough to say, "Well, we will say no more about it. I dare say you did not intend to be impertinent." And then they all sat down again, and everybody tried to be as gay as possible while the feast went on.

And by the time they sang the "Salisbury School Songs" —for they had several very fine ones, that the different classes had composed—there was such a tone of good humor prevailing, everybody getting so very jolly, that no one looking on would have supposed for a moment that a single unpleasant note had been struck. And Miss Anstice tried not to look at her gown, and Miss Salisbury had a pretty pink tinge in her cheeks, and her eyes were blue and serene, without the tired look that often came into them.

"Now for the story—oh, that is the best of all!" exclaimed Polly Pepper, when at last, protesting that they couldn't eat another morsel, they all got up from the feast, leaving it to the maids.

"Isn't it!" echoed the girls. "Oh, dear Miss Salisbury, I *am* so glad it is time for you to tell it." All of which pleased Miss Salisbury very much indeed, for it was the custom at this annual festival to wind up the afternoon with a story by the principal, when all the girls would gather at her feet to listen to it, as she sat in state in her stone chair.

"Is it?" she cried, the pink tinge on her cheek getting

deeper. "Well, do you know, I think I enjoy, as much as my girls, the telling of this annual story."

"Oh, you can't enjoy it *as much*," said one impulsive young voice.

Miss Salisbury smiled indulgently at her. "Well, now, if you are ready, girls, I will begin."

"Oh, yes, we are—we are," the bright groups, scattered on the grass at her feet, declared.

"Today I thought I would tell you of my schooldays, when I was as young as you," began Miss Salisbury.

"Oh—oh!"

"Miss Salisbury, I just love you for that!" exclaimed the impulsive girl, and jumping out of her seat, she ran around the groups to the stone chair. "I do, Miss Salisbury, for I did so want to hear all about when you were a schoolgirl."

"Well, go back to your place, Fanny, and you shall hear a little of my school life," said Miss Salisbury gently.

"No—no. The whole of it," begged Fanny earnestly, going slowly back.

"My dear child, I could not possibly tell you the whole," said Miss Salisbury, smiling. "It must be one little picture of my schooldays."

"Do sit down, Fanny," cried one of the other girls impatiently. "You are hindering it all."

So Fanny flew back to her place, and Miss Salisbury, without any more interruptions, began.

"You see, girls, you must know to begin with, that our father—sister's and mine—was a clergyman in a small country parish. And as there were a great many mouths to feed, and young, growing minds to feed as well, besides ours, why there was a great deal of considering as to ways and means constantly going on at the parsonage. Well, as I was the eldest, of course the question came first, what to do with Amelia."

"Were you Amelia?" asked Fanny.

"Yes. Well, after talking it over a great deal—and I suspect many sleepless nights spent by my good father and mother—it was at last decided that I should be sent to boarding school, for I forgot to tell you, I had finished at the academy."

"Yes, sister was very smart," broke in Miss Anstice proudly. "She won't tell you that, so I must."

"Oh, sister, sister," protested Miss Salisbury.

"Yes, she excelled all the boys and girls."

"Did they have boys at that school?" interrupted Philena, in amazement. "Oh, how very nice, Miss Salisbury!"

"I should just love to go to school with boys," declared ever so many of the girls ecstatically.

"Why don't you take boys at our school, Miss Salisbury?" asked Silvia longingly.

Miss Anstice looked quite horrified at the very idea, but Miss Salisbury laughed. "It is not the custom now, my dear, in private schools. In my day—you must remember that was a long time ago—there were academies where girls and boys attended what would be called a high school now."

"Oh!"

"And I went to one in the next town until it was thought best for me to be sent to boarding school."

"And she was very smart. She took all the prizes at the academy, and the principal said—" Miss Anstice was herself brought up quickly by her sister.

"If you interrupt so much, I never shall finish my story, Anstice," she said.

"I want the girls to understand this," said Miss Anstice with decision. "The principal said she was the best-educated scholar he had ever seen graduated from Hilltop Academy."

"Well, now, if you have finished," said Miss Salisbury, laughing, "I will proceed. So I was dispatched by my father to a town about thirty miles away, to a boarding school kept by the widow of a clergyman who had been a college classmate. Well, I was sorry to leave all my young brothers and sisters, you may be sure, while my mother—girls, I haven't even now forgotten the pang it cost me to kiss my mother good-bye."

Miss Salisbury stopped suddenly, and let her gaze wander off to the waving treetops, and Miss Anstice fell into a reverie that kept her face turned away.

"But it was the only way I could get an education, and you know I could not be fitted for a teacher, which was to be my life work, unless I went. So I stifled all those dreadful feelings which anticipated my homesickness, and pretty soon I found myself in the boarding school."

"How many scholars were there, Miss Salisbury?" asked Laura Page, who was very exact.

"Fifteen girls," said Miss Salisbury.

"Oh dear me, what a little bit of a school!" exclaimed one girl.

"The schools were not as large in those days," said Miss Salisbury. "You must keep in mind the great difference between that time and this, my dear. Well, and when I was once there, I had quite enough to do to keep me from being homesick, I can assure you, through the day, because in addition to lessons there was the sewing hour."

"Sewing? Oh my goodness me!" exclaimed Alexia. "You didn't have to sew at that school, did you, Miss Salisbury?"

"I surely did," replied Miss Salisbury, "and very glad I have been, Alexia, that I learned so much in that sewing hour. I have seriously thought, sister and I, of introducing the plan into our school."

"Oh, don't, Miss Salisbury," screamed the girls. "Please don't make us sew." Some of them jumped to their feet in distress.

"I shall die," declared Alexia tragically, "if we have to sew."

There was such a general gloom settled over the entire party that Miss Salisbury hastened to say, "I don't think, girls, we can do it, because something else equally important would have to be given up to make the time." At which the faces brightened up.

"Well, I was only to stay at this school a year," went on Miss Salisbury, "because, you see, it was as much as my father could do to pay for that time, so it was necessary to use every moment to advantage. So I studied pretty hard, and I presume this is one reason why the incident I am going to tell you about was of such a nature, for I was overtired. Though that should be no excuse," she added hastily.

"Oh, sister," said Miss Anstice nervously. "Don't tell them that story. I wouldn't."

"It may help them, to have a leaf out of another young person's life, Anstice," said Miss Salisbury, gravely.

"Well, but—"

"And so, every time when I thought I must give up and go home, I was so hungry to see my father and mother, and the little ones—"

"Was Miss Anstice one of the little ones?" asked Fanny, with a curious look at the crow's-feet and faded eyes of the younger Miss Salisbury.

"Yes, she was: there were two boys came in between; then Anstice, then Jane, Harriett, Lemuel, and the baby."

"Oh my!" gasped Alexia, tumbling over into Polly Pepper's lap.

"Eight of us. So you see, it would never do for the one who

was having so much money spent upon her, to waste a single penny of it. When I once got to teaching, I was to pay it all back."

"And did you—did you?" demanded curious Fanny.

"Did she? Oh, girls!" It was Miss Anstice who almost gasped this, making every girl turn around.

"Never mind," Miss Salisbury telegraphed over their heads, to "sister," which kept her silent. But she meant to tell sometime.

Polly Pepper, all this time, hadn't moved, but sat with hands folded in her lap. What if she had given up and flown home to Mamsie and the little brown house before Mr. King discovered her homesickness and brought Phronsie! Supposing she hadn't gone in the old stagecoach that day when she first left Badgertown to visit in Jasper's home! Just supposing it! She turned quite pale, and held her breath, while Miss Salisbury proceeded.

"And now comes the incident that occurred during that boarding-school year, that I have intended for some time to tell you girls, because it may perhaps help you in some experience where you will need the very quality that I lacked on that occasion."

"Oh, sister!" expostulated Miss Anstice.

"It was a midwinter day, cold and clear and piercing." Miss Salisbury shivered a bit, and drew the shawl put across the back of her stone seat closer around her. "Mrs. Ferguson— that was the name of the principal—had given the girls a holiday to take them to a neighboring town. There was to be a concert, I remember, and some other treats, and the scholars were, as you would say, 'perfectly wild to go,' " and she smiled indulgently at her rapt audience. "Well, I was not going."

"Oh, Miss Salisbury!" exclaimed Amy Garrett in sorrow,

as if the disappointment were not forty years in the background.

"No. I decided it was not best for me to take the money, although my father had written me that I could, when the holiday had been planned some time before. And besides, I thought I could do some extra studying ahead while the girls were away. Understand, I didn't really think of doing wrong then, although afterward I did the wrong thing."

"*Sister!*" reproved Miss Anstice. She could not sit still now, but got out of her stone chair, and paced up and down.

"No, I did not dream that in a little while after the party had started, I should be so sorely tempted, and the idea would enter my head to do the wrong thing. But so it was. I was studying, I remember, my philosophy lesson for some days ahead, when suddenly, as plainly as if letters of light were written down the page, it flashed upon my mind, 'Why don't I go home today? I can get back tonight, and no one will know it—at least, not until I am back again, and no harm done.' And without waiting to think it out, I clapped to my book, tossed it on the table, and ran to get my poor little purse out of the bureau drawer."

The girls, in their eagerness not to lose a word, crowded close to Miss Salisbury's knees, forgetting that she wasn't a girl with them.

"I had quite enough money, I could see, to take me home and back on the cars, and by the stage."

"The stage?" repeated Alexia faintly.

"Yes. You must remember that this time of which I am telling you was many, many years back. Besides, in some country places, it is still the only mode of conveyance used."

Polly Pepper drew a long breath. Dear old Badgertown, and Mr. Tisbett's stage. She could see it now, as it looked when the Five Little Peppers would run to the windows of the little brown house to watch it go lumbering by, and to hear the old stage driver crack his whip in greeting!

"The housekeeper had a day off, to go to her daughters, so that helped my plan along," Miss Salisbury was saying. "Well would it have been for me if the conditions had been less easy. But I must hasten. I have told you that I did not pause to think. That was my trouble in those days: I acted on impulse often, as schoolgirls are apt perhaps to do, and so I was not ready to stand this sudden temptation. I tied on my bonnet, gathered up my little purse tightly in my hand; and although the day was cold, the sun was shining brightly, and my heart was so full of hope and anticipation that I scarcely thought of what I was doing, as I took a thin little jacket instead of the warm cloak my mother had made me for winter wear. I hurried out of the house when there was no one to notice me, for the maids were careless in the housekeeper's absence, and had slipped off for the moment—at any rate, they said afterward they never saw me—so off I went.

"I caught the eight o'clock train just in time; which I considered most fortunate. How often afterward did I wish I had missed it! And reasoning within myself as the wheels bore me away, that it was perfectly right to spend the money to go home, for my father had been quite willing for me to take the treat with Mrs. Ferguson and the others, I settled back in my seat and tried not to feel strange at traveling alone."

"Oh dear me!" exclaimed the girls, huddling up closer to Miss Salisbury's knees. Miss Anstice paced back and forth. It was too late to stop the story now, and her nervousness could only be walked off.

"But I noticed the farther I got from the boarding school, little doubts would come creeping into my mind. First, was it very wise for me to have set out in this way? Then, was it right? And suddenly in a flash, it struck me that I was doing a very wrong thing, and that, if my father and my mother knew it, they would be greatly distressed. And I would have given worlds, if I had possessed them, to be back at Mrs. Ferguson's, studying my philosophy lesson. And I laid my head on the back of the seat before me, and cried as hard as I could."

Amy sniffed into her handkerchief, and two or three other girls coughed as if they had taken cold, while no one looked into her neighbor's face.

"And a wild idea crossed my mind once, of rushing up to the conductor and telling him of my trouble, to ask him if I couldn't get off at the next station and go back, but a minute's reflection told me that this was foolish. There was only the late afternoon train to take me to the school. I had started, and must go on."

A long sigh went through the group. Miss Anstice seemed to have it communicated to her, for she quickened her pace nervously.

"At last, after what seemed an age to me, though it wasn't really but half an hour since we started, I made up my mind to bear it as well as I could—father and mother would forgive me, I was sure, and would make Mrs. Ferguson overlook it—when I glanced out of the car window. Little flakes of snow were falling fast. It struck dismay to my heart. If it kept on like this—and after watching it for some moments, I had no reason to expect otherwise, for it was of that fine, dry quality that seems destined to last—I should not be able to get back to school that afternoon. Oh dear me! And now I began to open my heart to all sorts of fears: the train might be delayed, the stagecoach slow in getting through to Cherryfield. By this time I was in a state of nerves, and did not dare to think further."

One of the girls stole her hand softly up to lay it on that of the principal, forgetting that she had never before dared to do such a thing in all her life. Miss Salisbury smiled, and closed it within her own.

There was a smothered chorus of "Oh dears!"

"I sat there, my dears, in a misery that saw nothing of the beauty of that storm, knew nothing, heard nothing, except the occasional ejaculations and remarks of the passengers, such as, 'It's going to be the worst storm of the year,' and 'It's come to stay.'

"Suddenly, without a bit of warning, there was a bumping noise, then the train dragged slowly on, then stopped. All the passengers jumped up, except myself. I was too miserable to stir, for I knew now that I was to pay finely for my wrongdoing in leaving the school without permission."

"Oh—oh!" The girls gave a little scream.

" 'What is it—what is it?' the passengers one and all cried, and there was great rushing to the doors, and hopping outside to ascertain the trouble. I never knew, for I didn't care to ask. It was enough for me that something had broken, and the train had stopped, to start again no one could tell when."

The sympathy and excitement now were intense. One girl sniffed out from behind her handkerchief, "I—I should have—thought you would—have died—Miss Salisbury."

"Ah!" said Miss Salisbury, with a sigh, "you will find, Helen, as you grow older, that the only thing you can do to repair in any way the mischief you have done is to keep yourself well under control and endure the penalty without wasting time on your suffering. So I just made up my mind now to this, and I sat up straight, determined not to give way, whatever happened.

"It was very hard when the impatient passengers would

come back into the car to ask each other, 'How soon do you suppose we will get to Mayville?' That was where I was to take the stage.

" 'Not till night, if we don't start,' one would answer, trying to be facetious, but I would torture myself into believing it. At last the conductor came through, and he met a storm of inquiries, all asking the same question, 'How soon will we get to Mayville?'

"It seemed to me that he was perfectly heartless in tone and manner, as he pulled out his watch to consult it. I can never see a big silver watch to this day, girls, without a shiver."

The "Salisbury girls" shivered in sympathy, and tried to creep up closer to her.

"Well, the conductor went on to say that there was no telling—the railroad officials never commit themselves, you know—they had telegraphed back to town for another engine (he didn't mention that, after that, we should be sidetracked to allow other trains their right of way), and as soon as they could, why, they would move. Then he proceeded to move himself down the aisle in great dignity. Well, my dears, you must remember that this all happened long years ago, when accidents to the trains were very slowly made good. We didn't get into Mayville until twelve o'clock. If everything had gone as it should, we ought to have reached there three hours before."

"Oh my goodness me!" exploded Alexia.

"By this time, the snow had piled up fast. What promised to be a heavy storm had become a reality, and it was whirling and drifting dreadfully. You must remember that I had on my little thin jacket, instead—"

"Oh, Miss Salisbury!" screamed several girls. "I forgot that."

"Don't tell any more," sobbed another. "Don't, Miss Salisbury."

"I want you to hear this story," said Miss Salisbury quietly. "Remember, I did it all myself. And the saddest part of it is what I made others suffer, not my own distress."

"Sister, if you only *won't* proceed!" Miss Anstice abruptly leaned over the outer fringe of girls.

"I am getting on to the end," said Miss Salisbury, with a smile. "Well, girls, I won't prolong the misery for you. I climbed into that stage, it seemed to me, more dead than alive. The old stage driver, showing as much of his face as his big fur cap drawn well over his ears would allow, looked at me compassionately.

" 'Sakes alive!' I can hear him now. 'Hain't your folks no sense to let a young thing come out in that way?'

"I was so stiff, all I could think of was that I had turned into an icicle and that I was liable to break at any minute. But I couldn't let that criticism pass.

" 'They—they didn't let me—I've come from school,' I stammered.

"He looked at me curiously, got up from his seat, opened a box under it, and twitched out a big cape, moth-eaten, and well-worn otherwise. But oh, girls, I never loved anything so much in all my life as that horrible old article, for it saved my life."

A long-drawn breath went around the circle.

" 'Here, you just get into this as soon as the next one,' said the stage driver gruffly, handing it over to me where I sat on the middle seat. I needed no command, but fairly huddled myself within it, wrapping it around and around me. And then I knew by the time it took to warm me up, how very cold I had been.

"And every few minutes of the toilsome journey, for we

had to proceed very slowly, the stage driver would look back over his shoulder to say, 'Be you gittin' any warmer now?' And I would say, 'Yes, thank you, a little.'

"And finally he asked suddenly, 'Do your folks know you're comin'?' And I answered, 'No,' and I hoped he hadn't heard, and I pulled the cape up higher around my face, I was so ashamed. But he had heard, for he whistled, and oh, girls, that made my head sink lower yet. Oh, my dears, the shame of wrongdoing is so terrible to bear!

"Well, after a while we got into Cherryfield, along about half-past three o'clock."

"Oh dear!" exclaimed the young voices.

"I could just distinguish our church spire amid the whirling snow; and then a panic seized me. I must get down at some spot where I would not be recognized, for oh, I did not want any one to tell that old stage driver who I was and thus bring discredit upon my father, the clergyman, for having a daughter who had come away from school without permission. So I mumbled out that I was to stop at the Four Corners: that was a short distance from the center of the village, the usual stopping place.

"One of the passengers—for I didn't think it was necessary to prolong the story to describe the two women who occupied the back seat—leaned forward and said, 'I hope, Mr. Cheesewell, you ain't goin' to let that girl get out, half froze as she's been, in this snowstorm. You'd ought to go out o' your beat, and carry her home.'

" 'Oh, no—no,' I cried in terror, unwinding myself from the big cape and preparing to descend.

" 'Stop there!' roared Mr. Cheesewell at me. 'Did ye s'pose I'd desert that child?' he said to the two women. 'I'd take her home, ef I knew where in creation 'twas.'

" 'She lives at the parsonage—she's th' minister's daughter,' said one of the women quietly.

"I sank back in my seat—oh, girls, the bitterness of that moment!—and as well as I could for the gathering mist in my eyes, and the blinding storm without, realized the approach to my home. But what a homecoming!

"I managed to hand back the big cape and to thank Mr. Cheesewell, then stumbled up the little pathway to the parsonage door, feeling every step a misery, with all those eyes watching me. And lifting the latch, I was at home!

"Then I fell flat in the entry, and knew nothing more till I found myself in my own bed, with my mother's face above me. And beyond her, there was father."

Every girl was sobbing now. No one saw Miss Anstice, with the tears raining down her cheeks at the memory that the beautiful prosperity of all these later years could not blot out.

"Girls, if my life was saved in the first place by that old cape, it was saved again by one person."

"Your mother," gasped Polly Pepper, with wet, shining eyes.

"No, my mother had gone to a sick parishioner's, and father was with her. There was no one but the children at home; the bigger boys were away. I owe my life really to my sister Anstice."

"Don't!" begged Miss Anstice hoarsely, and trying to shrink away. The circle of girls whirled around to see her clasping her slender hands tightly together, while she kept her face turned aside.

"Oh, girls," cried Miss Salisbury, with sudden energy, "if you could only understand what that sister of mine did for me! I never can tell you. She kept back her own fright, as the small children were so scared when they found me lying there in the entry, for they had all been in the woodshed picking up some kindlings, and didn't hear me come in. And she thought at first I was dead, but she worked over me just as she thought mother would. You see we hadn't any near neighbors, so she couldn't call anyone. And at last she piled me all over with blankets just where I lay, for she couldn't lift me, of course, and tucked me in tightly. And telling the children not to cry, but to watch me, she ran a mile, or floundered rather—for the snow was now so deep—to the doctor's house."

"Oh, that was fine!" cried Polly Pepper, with kindling eyes, and turning her flushed face with pride on Miss Anstice. When Miss Salisbury saw that, a happy smile spread over her face, and she beamed on Polly.

"And then, you know the rest. For of course, when I came to myself, the doctor had patched me up. And once within my father's arms, with mother holding my hand—why, I was forgiven."

Miss Salisbury paused and glanced off over the young heads, not trusting herself to speak.

"And how did they know at the school where you were?" Fanny broke in impulsively.

"Father telegraphed Mrs. Ferguson, and luckily for me, she and her party were delayed by the storm in returning to the school, so the message was handed to her as she left the railroad station. Otherwise, my absence would have plunged her in terrible distress."

"Oh, well, it all came out rightly after all." Louisa Frink dropped her handkerchief in her lap, and gave a little laugh.

"*Came out rightly!*" repeated Miss Salisbury sternly, and turning such a glance on Louisa that she wilted at once. "Yes, if you can forget that for days the doctor was working to keep me from brain fever; that it took much of my father's hard-earned savings to pay him; that it kept me from school, and lost me the marks I had almost gained; that, worst of all, it added lines of care and distress to the faces of my parents; and that my sister, who saved me, barely escaped a long fit of sickness from her exposure."

"Don't, sister, don't," begged Miss Anstice.

"Came out rightly? Girls, nothing can ever come out rightly, unless the steps leading up to the end are right."

"Ma'am"—Mr. Kimball suddenly appeared above the fringe of girls surrounding Miss Salisbury—"there's a storm brewin'; it looks as if 'twas comin' to stay. I'm all hitched up, 'n' I give ye my 'pinion that we'd better be movin'.' "

With that, everybody hopped up, for Mr. Kimball's " 'pinion" was law in such a case. The picnic party was hastily packed into the barges—Polly carrying the little green botany case with the ferns for Phronsie's garden carefully on her lap—and with many backward glances for the dear Glen, off they went, as fast as the horses could swing along.

Chapter 15

The Broken Vase

*B*UT drive as they might, Mr. Kimball and his assistants, they couldn't beat that storm that was brewing. It came up rather slowly, to be sure, at first, but very persistently. Evidently the old stage driver was right. It was "coming to stay."

"Ye see, ma'am, ef we hadn't started when we did, like enough we couldn'ta got home tonight," he vouchsafed over his shoulder to Miss Salisbury, as they rattled on.

"Dear me!" she exclaimed at thought of her brood. Those young things were having the best of times. It was "wildly exciting," as Clem Forsythe said, to be packed in, those on the end seats huddling away from the rain as much as possible, under cover of the curtains buttoned down fast. And hilarity ran high. They sang songs, never quite finishing one, but running shrilly off to others, which were produced on several different keys maybe, according to the mood of the singers. And as every girl wanted to sing her favorite song, there were sometimes various compositions being produced in different quarters of the big stage, till no one particular melody could be said to have the right of way. And Miss Salisbury sat in the midst of the babel, and smiled as much as her anxiety would allow, at the merriment. And as it was in this stage, so the other stages were counterparts. And the gay tunes and merry laughter floated back all along the cavalcade, mingling harmoniously with the rainfall.

Suddenly an awful clap of thunder reverberated in the sky. The songs ended in squeals of dismay, and the laughter died away.

"Oh—oh—we're going to have a thunderstorm!" screamed more than one girl, huddling up closer to her next neighbor, to clutch her frantically.

"Oh, I'm so afraid of the thunder!" screamed Amy Garrett.

"You goose, it won't hurt you." Lucy Bennett, whom Amy had crouched against, gave her a little push.

"It will. It will. My uncle was struck once," said Amy, rebounding from the push to grasp Lucy frantically around the neck.

"You nearly choked me to death," exclaimed Lucy, untwisting the nervous hands. "Don't get so scared. Your uncle never was struck by the thunder, and we haven't had any lightning yet; so I wouldn't yell till we do."

"Well, there it is now," cried Amy, covering her eyes. And there it was now, to be sure, in a blinding flash, to be followed by deeper rolls of thunder, drowning the screams of the frightened girls, and the plunging of the horses that didn't like it much better.

Mr. Kimball peered out and squinted to the right and to the left through the blinding storm; then he turned his horses suddenly off from the road, into a narrow lane. "Oh, why do you—?" began Miss Salisbury. But this remonstrance wouldn't have done any good had the old stage driver heard it. At the end of the lane, he knew, in a few moments they would all arrive at a big old-fashioned mansion where shelter could not be refused them under such circumstances. Although—and Mr. Kimball shook within himself at his temerity—under any other conditions visitors would not be expected nor welcomed. For Mr. John Clemcy and his sister, Miss Ophelia, had never exhibited, since they settled down in this quiet spot after leaving their English home many years ago, any apparent desire to make friends. They were quite sufficient for themselves, and what with driving about—which they did in a big basket phaeton, or behind their solemn pair of black horses and the still more solemn coachman, Isaac, also black—and in the care of the large estate and the big brick mansion, they found ample occupation for their time and thoughts.

Up to this big red brick mansion now plunged Mr. Kimball with as much assurance as if he were not quaking dreadfully. And the other stages following suit, the sudden and unusual uproar brought two faces to the windows, and then to the door.

"May we all git out and go into your barn?" roared Mr. Kimball, peering at them from beneath his dripping hat.

There was an awful pause. Mr. Kimball clutched his old leather reins desperately, and Miss Salisbury, to whom had come faint rumors of the chosen isolation of the brother and sister, felt her heart sink woefully.

Mr. John Clemcy stepped out—slender, tall, with white hair and beard, both closely cropped. He had a pale, aristocratic face, and a pair of singularly stern eyes, which he now bent upon the old stage driver.

"Brother," remonstrated his sister—she looked as much

like him as possible in face and figure—"do not venture out in this driving storm."

"No," said Mr. Clemcy, "I cannot consent to your going into my stable. I—"

" 'Tain't Christian," blurted out the old stage driver, "to leave human bein's out in sech a pickle."

"No, I am aware of that," said Mr. John Clemcy, without a change of countenance, "and so I invite you all to come into my house." He threw wide the door. "My sister, Miss Clemcy."

Miss Ophelia stepped forward and received them as if she had specially prepared for their visit, and with such an air of distinction that it completely overwhelmed Miss Salisbury, so that her own manners, always considered quite perfect by parents and friends of her pupils, paled considerably in contrast. It was quite like entering an old baronial hall, as the courtly, aristocratic host ushered them in, and the girls, not easily overawed by any change of circumstance, who had tumbled out laughingly from the stages despite Miss Salisbury's nervous endeavors to quiet them, were now instantly subdued.

"Isn't it solemn!" whispered Alexia, hanging to Polly Pepper, her pale eyes roving over the armor and old family portraits almost completely covering the walls of the wide hall.

"Hush," whispered Polly back again.

"But I can't breathe: oh, look at that old horror in the ruff. Polly—look!" she pinched the arm she grasped.

Meantime, although there were so many girls, the big red brick mansion seemed quite able to contain them hospitably, as Mr. and Miss Clemcy opened door after door into apartments that appeared to stretch out into greater space beyond. When at last the company had been distributed, Miss Salisbury found her voice. "I am pained to think of all the trouble we are giving you, Miss Clemcy."

"Do not mention it." Miss Ophelia put up a slender arm, from which fed off a deep flounce of rare old lace. The hand that thus came into view was perfect; and Miss Salisbury, who could recognize qualities of distinction, fell deeply in love with the evidences before her.

"Do you suppose she dresses up like that every day, Silvia?" whispered Lucy Bennett, in an awestruck voice.

Silvia, in matters of dress never being willing to show surprise, preserved her composure. "That's nothing," she managed to say indifferently. "It can't be real, such a lot of it, and around her neck too."

Down into the old colonial kitchen, with its corner fireplace, wide and roomy, and bricked to the ceiling, Mr. Clemcy led the way. It was a big room, and not used for its original purpose, being filled with cabinets, and shelves on which reposed some of the most beautiful specimens of china and various relics and curiosities and mementos of travel Miss Salisbury thought she had ever seen. And she had been about the world a good bit, having utilized many of her vacations, and once or twice taking a year off from her school work, for that purpose. And being singularly receptive to information, she was the best of listeners, in an intelligent way, as Mr. Clemcy moved about from object to object explaining his collection. He seemed perfectly absorbed in it, and, as the girls began to notice, his listener as well.

Lucy Bennett was frightfully romantic, and jumped to conclusions at once. "Oh, do you suppose he will marry her?" she cried under her breath to Silvia, as the two kept together.

"Who? What are you talking about?" demanded Silvia, who was very matter-of-fact.

"Why, that old man—Mr. Whatever his name is," whispered Lucy.

"Mr. Clemcy? Do get names into your head, Lu," said Silvia crossly, who wanted to look at things and not be interrupted every minute.

"I can't ever remember names, if I do hear them," said Lucy, "so what is the use of my bothering to hear them, Sil?"

"Well, do keep still," said Silvia, trying to twist away her arm, but Lucy clung to it.

"Well, I can't keep still either, for I'm mortally afraid he is—that old man, whatever you call him—going to marry her."

"Who?" demanded Silvia sharply.

"Our Miss Salisbury, and—"

"Lu Bennett!" Silvia sat down in the first chair she could find. It was very fortunate that the other groups were so absorbed that nobody noticed them.

"Oh, you do say such perfectly silly things!" declared Silvia, smothering the peal of laughter that nearly escaped her.

"Well, it isn't silly," cried Lucy in an angry whisper, "and it's going to happen, I know, and she'll give up our school to Miss Anstice, and come and live here. Oh my!" She looked ready to cry on the spot. "Look at them!"

Now, Silvia had called Lucy Bennett "silly" hundreds of times, but now as she looked at Mr. Clemcy and Miss Salisbury, she began to have an uneasy feeling at her heart. "I won't go to school to Miss Anstice," she declared passionately. Then she began to plan immediately. "I'll get mother to let me go to boarding school."

"And I'll go with you," exclaimed Lucy radiantly. All this was in stage whispers, such a buzz going on around them that no one else could possibly catch a word. And so in just about two minutes they had their immediate future all planned.

"Well, you better get up out of that chair," said Lucy presently, and picking at Silvia's sleeve.

"I guess I'm not hurting the chair," said Silvia, squinting sideways at the high, carved back "They asked us in here—at least *he* did."

"Well, he didn't ask us to sit down," said Lucy triumphantly.

"And if he's going to marry her," said Silvia, in a convincing whisper, "I guess I can sit in all the chairs if I want to."

"Hush!" warned Lucy. "here comes Miss Anstice."

Miss Anstice, with her front breadth all stained with jellycake and marmalade, was wandering around, quite subdued. It was pitiful to see how she always got into the thickest of the groups to hide her gown, trying to be sociable with the girls. But the girls not reciprocating, she was at last taken in tow by Miss Ophelia, who set about showing her some rare old china, as a special attention.

Now, Miss Anstice cared nothing for rare old china, or indeed, for relics or curiosities of any sort, but she was very meek on this occasion, and so she allowed herself to be led about from shelf to shelf. And though she said nothing, Miss Ophelia was so enchanted by her own words and memories, as she described in a fluent and loving manner their various claims to admiration, that she thought the younger Miss Salisbury quite a remarkable person.

"Show her the Lowestoft collection, sister," called Mr. John Clemcy, from across the apartment, and breaking off from his animated discussion over an old Egyptian vase, in which Miss Salisbury had carried herself brilliantly.

"I will, Brother John," assented Miss Clemcy, with great affability. "Now here," and she opened the door to its cabinet, "is what will interest you greatly, I think."

Suddenly, a crash as of breaking porcelain struck upon the ear. Everyone in the old room jumped, save the persons who might be supposed to be the most interested—Mr. Clemcy and his sister. Their faces did not change.

Miss Salisbury deserted the Egyptian vase. "Who," she demanded, hurrying to the center of the apartment, a red spot on either cheek, "has done this?"

Mr. John Clemcy followed her. "Do not, I beg," he said quietly, "notice it."

"Notice it! After your extreme hospitality—oh! which one of my scholars can have forgotten herself enough to touch a thing?"

The groups parted a little, just enough to disclose a shrinking figure. It was Lily, whose curious fingers were clasped in distress.

"She is very young," said Miss Clemcy softly, as Miss Salisbury detached her from the group, and passed into another room, crying as if her heart would break.

Mr. John Clemcy then came up to his sister and her visitor. "Your sister must not take it so to heart," he said.

Miss Anstice was worn out by this time, what with her gown, and now by this terrible thing that would bring such discredit upon their school. And besides, it might take ever so much from their savings to replace, for Lily was poor, and was a connection, so they perhaps would have to help her out. She therefore could find no words at her command except "Oh dear me!" and raised her poor eyes.

Mr. John Clemcy searched her face intently, and actually smiled to reassure her. She thought he was looking at her gown, so she mumbled faintly, to draw off his attention, "I am afraid it was very valuable."

He didn't tell her it was one of the oldest bits in his collection, but while Miss Clemcy slipped off, and quietly picked up every piece of the broken treasure, he turned the conversation, and talked rapidly and charmingly upon something—for the life of her, Miss Anstice never could tell what.

And he was still talking when Miss Salisbury brought back Lily by the hand, red-eyed and still sniffling, to stumble over her pleas for pardon. And then, the storm having abated, there were instant preparations for departure set in motion. And Mr. Kimball and his associates helped them into their vehicles, Miss Clemcy's beautiful old lace showing off finely on the great porch as she bade them good-bye.

"It is real I guess," declared Silvia, looking closely from her seat next to Lucy. "And, oh dear me, isn't this too horrible, what Lily Cushing has done?"

Mr. John Clemcy helped the ladies in, Miss Anstice putting forth all her powers to enable her to ascend the steep steps without disclosing the front breadth of her gown. Despite her best endeavors, she felt quite sure that the keen eyes of both brother and sister had discovered every blemish.

Miss Salisbury sank back in her seat, as the barge rolled off, quite in despair, for she knew quite well that the broken vase was one of the gems of the collection.

"Oh, see the lovely rainbow!" The girls' spirits rose, now that they were once more on the move. What was one broken vase, after all? And they began to laugh and talk once more.

"Oh dear!" Polly Pepper glanced back. "Alexia, this will just about kill our dear Miss Salisbury!" she exclaimed.

"Well, I'm clear beat," Mr. Kimball was saying to himself, as nobody paid attention. "You might knock me over with a feather! To think o' that old *reecluse* that won't know nobody, him nor his sister, an' is so hifalutin' smart, a-bustin 'out so *polite* all of a suddint."

Chapter 16

New Plans

"**P**OLLY," said Jasper, "could you come into the den?"

"Why, yes, Jasper," she cried, in surprise at his face. "Oh, has anything happened?"

"No," he said, but the gloomy look did not disappear. "Oh, Polly, it's too bad to ask—were you going to study?" with a glance at her armful of books.

"No—that is, I can do them just as well after dinner." Polly dropped her books on the hall chair. "Oh, what is it, Jasper?" running after him into the den.

"It's just this, Polly, I hate to tell you—" He paused, and gloom settled worse than ever over his face.

"Jasper," said Polly quite firmly, and she laid her hand on his arm, "I really think you ought to tell me right away what is on your mind."

"Do you really, Polly?" Jasper asked eagerly.

"Yes, I do," said Polly, "unless you had rather tell Mamsie. Perhaps that would be best, Jasper."

"No, I don't really think it would in this case, Polly. I will tell you." So he drew up a chair, and Polly settled into it, and he perched on the end of the table.

"You see, Polly," he began, "I hate to tell you, but if I don't, why of course you can't in the least understand how to help."

"No, of course I can't," said Polly, clasping her hands together tightly, and trying to wait patiently for the recital. Oh, what could it be!

"Well, Pickering isn't doing well at school," said Jasper, in a burst. It was so much better to have it out at once.

"Oh dear me!" exclaimed Polly, in sorrow.

"No, he isn't," said Jasper decidedly. "It grows worse and worse."

"Dear me!" said Polly again.

"And now Mr. Faber says there isn't much hope for him, unless he picks up in the last half. He called me into his study to tell me that today—wants me to influence him and all that."

All the hateful story was out at last. Polly sprang out of her chair.

"You don't mean—you can't mean—that Pickering will be dropped, Jasper?" she cried as she faced him.

"Worse than that," answered Jasper gloomily.

"Worse than dropped!" exclaimed Polly with wide eyes.

"To be dropped a class wouldn't kill Pick. So many boys have had that happen, although it is quite bad enough."

"I should think so," breathed Polly.

"But Pick will simply be shot out of the school," said Jasper desperately. "There's no use in mincing matters. Mr.

Faber has utterly lost patience, and the other teachers as well."

"You don't mean that Pickering Dodge will be expelled?" cried Polly in a little scream.

"Yes." Jasper nodded his head, unable to utter another word. Then he sprang off from the table end and walked up and down the room, as Polly sank back in her chair.

"You see, it's just this way, Polly," he cried. "Pick has had warning after warning—you know, the teachers have a system of sending written warnings around to the boys when they fall behind in their work—and he hasn't paid any attention to them."

"Won't he pay attention to what the teachers write to him, Jasper?" asked Polly, leaning forward in her big chair to watch him anxiously as he paced back and forth.

"No, calls them rubbish, and tears them up. And sometimes he won't even read them," said Jasper. "Oh, it's awful, Polly."

"I should say it was," said Polly slowly. "Very awful indeed, Jasper."

"And the last time he had one from Herr Frincke about his German, Pick brought it into the room where a lot of us boys were, and read it out, with no end of fun over it, and it went into the scrap basket. And he hasn't tackled his grammar a bit better since; only the translations he's up a trifle on."

"Oh, now I know why you wouldn't go to ride with me for the last week," cried Polly, springing out of her chair to rush up to him, "you've been helping Pickering," she declared, with kindling eyes.

"Never mind," said Jasper uneasily.

"And it was splendid of you," cried Polly, the color flying

over her cheeks. "Oh, Jasper, I do believe you can pull him through."

"No, I can't, Polly." Jasper stood quite still. "No one can pull him through but you, Polly."

"I!" exclaimed Polly in amazement. "Why, Jasper King!" and she tumbled back a few steps to stare at him. "What *do* you mean?"

"It's just this way." Jasper threw back his hair from his hot forehead. "Pick doesn't care a bit for what I say: it's an old story; goes in at one ear, and out at the other."

"Oh, he does care for what you say," contradicted Polly stoutly, "ever and ever so much, Jasper."

"Well, he's heard it so much. Perhaps I've pounded at him too hard. And then again—" Jasper paused, turned away a bit, and rushed back hastily, with vexation written all over his face. "I must speak it: I can't help him any more, for somehow Mr. Faber has found it out, and forbids it. That's one reason of the talk this morning in his study—says I must influence him, and all that. That's rubbish; I can't influence him." Jasper dashed over to lay his head on the table on his folded arms.

"Polly, if Pick is expelled, I—" he couldn't finish it, his voice breaking all up.

Polly ran over to lay a hand on his shaking shoulders.

"What can I do, Jasper?" she cried brokenly. "Tell me, and I'll do it, every single thing."

"You must talk to him," said Jasper, raising his head. It filled Polly with dismay to see his face. "Get him in here. I'll bring him over and then clear out of the den."

"Oh, Jasper!" exclaimed Polly, quite aghast. "I couldn't talk to Pickering Dodge. Why, he wouldn't listen to me."

"Yes, he would," declared Jasper eagerly. "He thinks everything of you, Polly, and if you'll say the word, it will do more good than anything else. Do, Polly," he begged.

"But, Jasper," began Polly, a little white line coming around her mouth, "what would he think to have me talk to him about his lessons?"

"Think?" repeated Jasper. "Why, he'd like it, Polly, and it will be the very thing that will help him."

"Oh, I can't!" cried Polly, twisting her fingers. Then she broke out passionately, "Oh, he ought to be ashamed of himself not to study. And there's that nice Mr. Cabot, and his aunt—"

"Aunt!" exclaimed Jasper explosively. "Polly, I do believe if he hadn't her picking at him all the time, he would try harder."

"Well, his uncle is different," said Polly, her indignation by no means dying out.

"Yes, but it's his aunt who makes the mischief. Honestly, Polly, I don't believe I could stand her," said Jasper, in a loyal burst.

"No, I don't believe I could either," confessed Polly.

"And you see, when a boy has such a home, no matter what they give him, why, he doesn't have the ambition that he would if things were different. Just think, Polly, not to have one's own father or mother."

"Oh Jasper!" cried Polly, quite overcome. "I'll do it, I will."

"Polly!" Jasper seized her hands, and held them fast, his dark eyes glowing. "Oh, Polly, that's so awfully good of you!"

"And you better run right over and get him now," said Polly, speaking very fast, "or I may run away, I shall get so scared."

"You won't run away, I'll be bound," cried Jasper, bursting into a merry laugh, and rushing off with a light heart. And presently, in less time than one could imagine, though to

Polly it seemed an age, back he came, Pickering with him, all alive with curiosity to know what Polly Pepper wanted of him.

"It's about the play, I suppose," he began, lolling into an easy chair. "Jasper wouldn't tell me what it's all about—only seized me by the ear, and told me to come on. Draw up your chair, Jasper, and—why, hullo! Where is the chap?" swinging his long figure around to stare.

"Pickering," began Polly, and the den, usually the pleasantest place in all the house, was now like a prison, whose walls wouldn't let her breathe. "I don't know what to say. Oh dear me!" Poor Polly could get no further, but sat there in hopeless misery, looking at him.

"Eh—what? Oh, beg pardon," exclaimed Pickering, whirling back in his chair, "but things are so very queer. First Jasper rushes off like a lunatic—"

"And I am worse," said Polly, at last finding her tongue. "I don't wonder you think it's queer, Pickering, but Jasper does so love you, and it will just kill him if you don't study." It was all out now, and in the most dreadful way. And feeling that she had quite destroyed all hope, Polly sat up pale and stiff in her chair.

Pickering threw his long figure out of the easy chair, rushed up and down the den with immense strides, and came back to stand directly in front of her.

"Do you mean it, Polly?" His long face was working badly, and his hands were clenched, but as they were thrust deep within his pockets, Polly couldn't see them.

"Yes," said Polly. "I do, Pickering."

He stalked off again, but was back once more, Polly wondering how she could possibly bear to tell Jasper of her failure, for of course Pickering was very angry, when he said, "Polly, I want to tell you something."

"What is it?" Polly looked at him sharply, and caught her breath.

"I won't drag Jasper down, I tell you, with me. I'll get through somehow at school. I promise you that. Here!" He twitched out his right hand from its pocket, and thrust it out at her.

"Oh Pickering Dodge!" exclaimed Polly in a transport, and seizing his hand, it was shaken vigorously.

"There, that's a bargain," declared Pickering solemnly. "I'll get through someway. And say, Polly, it was awfully good of you to speak."

"It was awfully hard," said Polly, drawing a long breath. "Oh, are you sure you are not vexed, Pickering? Very sure?" And Polly's face drooped anxiously.

"Vexed?" cried Pickering. "I should rather say not! Polly, I'm lazy and selfish, and good for nothing, but I couldn't be vexed, for 'twas awfully hard for you to do."

"I guess it was," said Polly. Then she gave a little laugh, for it was all bright and jolly again, and she knew that Pickering would keep his word.

And that evening, after Jasper and she had a dance—they were so happy, they couldn't keep still—in the wide hall, Jasper burst out suddenly with a fresh idea.

"Polly," he said, drawing her off to rest on one of the high, carved chairs, "there's one more thing."

"Oh, what is it, Jasper?" she cried gaily, with flushed cheeks. "Oh, wasn't that spin just delicious?"

"Wasn't it?" cried Jasper heartily. "Well, now, Polly," flinging himself down on the next chair, "it's just this. Do you know, I don't believe we ought to have our play."

"Not have our play?" Polly peered around to look closely into his face. "What do you mean, Jasper?"

"You see, Polly, Pick was to take a prominent part, and he

ought not to, you know. It will take him from his lessons to rehearse and all that. And he's so backward there's a whole lot for him to make up."

"Well, but Pickering will have to give up his part, then," said Polly decidedly, "for we've simply got to have that play, to get the money to help that poor brakeman's family."

Jasper winced. "I know. We must earn it somehow," he said.

"We must earn it by the play," said Polly. "And besides, Jasper, we voted at the club meeting to have it. So there, now," she brought up triumphantly.

"We could vote to rescind that vote," said Jasper.

"Well, we don't want to. Why, Jasper, how that would look on our two record books!" said Polly in surprise, for Jasper was so proud of his club and its records.

"Yes, of course. As our two clubs united that evening, it must go down in both books," said Jasper slowly.

"Yes, of course," assented Polly happily. "Well, now, you see, Jasper, that we really *can't* give it up, for we've gone too far. Pickering will have to let someone else take the part of the chief brigand." For the little play was almost all written by Polly's fingers, Jasper filling out certain parts when implored to give advice, and brigands, and highway robberies, and buried treasures, and rescued maidens, and gallant knights figured generously, in a style to give immense satisfaction.

"And the play is so very splendid!" cried Jasper. "Oh dear me! What ought we to do, Polly?" He buried his face in his hands a moment.

"Pickering must give up his part," said Polly again.

"But, Polly, you know he has been in all our plays," said Jasper. "And he'll feel so badly, and now he's got all this trouble about his lessons on his mind," and Jasper's face fell.

Polly twisted uncomfortably on her chair. "Oh dear me!" she began, "I suppose we must give it up."

"And if we gave it up, not altogether, but put it off till he catches up on his studies," suggested Jasper, "why, he wouldn't be dropped out."

"But the poor brakeman's family, Jasper," said Polly, puzzled that Jasper should forget the object of the play.

"Oh, I didn't mean that we should put off earning the money, Polly," cried Jasper, quite horrified at such a thought. "We must do something else, so that we can sell just as many tickets."

"But what will it be?" asked Polly, trying not to feel crushed, and sighing at the disappearance of the beautiful play, for a time at least.

"Well, we could have recitations, for one thing," said Jasper, feeling dreadfully to see Polly's disappointment, and concealing his own, for he had set his heart on the play too.

"Oh dear me!" exclaimed Polly, wrinkling up her face in disdain. "Jasper, do you know, I am so tired of recitations!"

"So am I"—Jasper bobbed his head in sympathy—"but we boys have some new ones, learned for last exhibition, so Pick won't have to take a moment from his lessons. And then we can have music, and you will play, Polly."

"Oh Jasper, I've played so much," said Polly, "they're all tired of hearing me."

"They never would be tired of hearing you, Polly," said Jasper simply. "Every one of us thinks you play beautifully."

"And tableaux and an operetta take just as much time to rehearse," mused Polly, thinking very hard if there wasn't something to keep them from the dreaded recitations.

"And I just loathe an operetta or tableaux," exclaimed Jasper, with such venom that Polly burst out laughing.

"Oh, Jasper, if you could see your face!" she cried.

"I shouldn't want to." He laughed too. "But of all insipid things, an operetta is the worst. And tableaux—the way Miss Montague drilled and drilled *and* drilled us, and then stuck us up like sticks not to move for a half hour or so, nearly finished me."

"So it did me," confessed Polly. "And besides, it would take a great deal more time to go through all that drilling than to rehearse the play."

"Of course it would," said Jasper, "so tableaux, thank fortune, are not to be thought of. I think it will have to be recitations and music, Polly."

"I suppose so," she said with a sigh. "Oh, Jasper!" Then she sprang off from her chair, and clapped her hands. "I've thought of the very thing. I believe Mr. Hamilton Dyce would tell some of his funny stories and help out the program."

"Capital!" shouted Jasper, and just at this moment the big front door opened, and the butler ushered in Miss Mary Taylor and Mr. Dyce.

Polly and Jasper rushed up to the visitors, for they were prime favorites with the young people, and precipitated upon them all their woes. The end was, that they both promised beautifully to do whatever was wanted, for Miss Mary Taylor sang delightfully.

"And Pickering is safe, Polly, for I know now he'll go through the last half," cried Jasper as they ran off to study their lessons for the next day.

Chapter 17

Phronsie

*A*ND after that there was no more trouble about that program, for as luck would have it, the very next day a letter came from Joel, saying that Dr. Marks had given them a holiday of a week on account of the illness of two boys in their dormitory, and, "May I bring home Tom Beresford? He's no-end fine!" and, "Please, Mamsie, let me fetch Sinbad! Do telegraph 'Yes.' "

And Mother Fisher, after consultation with Mr. King, telegraphed "Yes," and wild was the rejoicing over the return of Joel and David and Percy and Van, and Tom, for Mother Fisher was ready to receive with open arms, and very glad silently to watch, one of Joel's friends.

"And to think that Sinbad is coming!" cried Polly, dancing about. "Just think, Phronsie, Joel's dear dog that Dr. Marks let him take to the little cobbler to keep for him!" And she took Phronsie's hand, and they spun around the hall.

"I shall get him a new pink ribbon," declared Phronsie breathlessly, when the spin was over.

"Do," cried Polly. "Dear me! That was a good spin, Phronsie!"

"I should think it was," said Ben. "Goodness me, Polly, Phronsie and you made such a breeze!"

"Didn't we, Pet!" cried Polly, with a last kiss. "Oh, Ben and Jasper, to think those boys will be here for our entertainment!"

"I know Tom is made of the right stuff," Mamsie said proudly to Father Fisher, "else my boy would not choose him."

"That's a fact, wife," the little doctor responded heartily. "Joel is all right. May be a bit heedless, but he has a good head on his shoulders."

The five boys bounded into the wide hall that evening— Joel first, and in his arms, a yellow dog, by no means handsome, with small, beady eyes, and a stubby tail that he was violently endeavoring to wag, under the impression that he had a good deal of it.

"Mamsie!" shouted Joel, his black eyes glowing, and precipitating himself into her arms, dog and all, "See Sinbad! See, Mamsie!"

"It's impossible not to see him," said Ben. "Goodness me, Joe, what a dog!" which luckily Joel did not hear for the babel going on around. Besides, there was Phronsie trying to put her arms around the dog, and telling him about the pink ribbon which she held in her hand.

"Joe," said Dr. Fisher, who had been here, there, and everywhere in the group, and coming up to nip Joel's jacket, "introduce your friend. You're a pretty one, to bring a boy home and—"

"I forgot you, Tom," shouted Joel, starting off, still hanging to his dog. "Oh, there you are!" seeing Tom in the midst of the circle, and talking away to Grandpapa and Polly.

"As if I couldn't introduce Tom!" sniffed Percy importantly, quite delighted at Joel's social omissions. "I've done it ages ago."

"All right," said Joel, quite relieved. "Oh, Phronsie, Sinbad doesn't want that ribbon on," as Phronsie was making violent efforts to get it around the dog's neck.

"I would let her, Joel," said Mother Fisher, "if I were you."

"But he hates a ribbon," said Joel in disgust, "and besides, he'll chew it up, Phronsie."

"I don't want him to chew it up, Joel," said Phronsie slowly, and pausing in her endeavors. And she looked very sober.

"I'll tell you, Phronsie." Mrs. Fisher took the pink satin ribbon that Phronsie had bought with her own money. "Now, do you want mother to tie it on?"

"Do, Mamsie," begged Phronsie, smoothing her gown in great satisfaction. And presently there was a nice little bow standing up on the back of Sinbad's neck, and as there didn't seem to be any ends to speak of, there was nothing to distract his attention from the responsibility of watching all the people.

"Oh, isn't he *beautiful!*" cried Phronsie in a transport, and hopping up and down to clap her hands. "Grandpapa dear, do look. And I've told Princey all about him, and given him a ribbon too, so he won't feel badly."

And after this excitement had died down, Joel whirled around. "Tom's brought his banjo," he announced.

"Oh!" exclaimed Polly.

"And he can sing," cried Joel, thinking it best to mention all the accomplishments at once.

"Don't, Joe," begged Tom, twitching his sleeve.

Polly looked over at Jasper, with sparkling eyes, and the color flew into her cheeks.

"Splendid!" his eyes signaled back.

"What is it?" cried Joel, giving each a sharp glance. "Now you two have secrets, and that's mean, when we've just got home. What is it, Polly?" He ran to her, shaking her arm.

"You'll see in time," said Polly, shaking him off, to dance away.

"I don't want to know in time," said Joel. "I want to know now. Mamsie, what is it?"

"I'm sure I haven't the least idea," said Mother Fisher, who hadn't heard Joel's announcement. "And I think you would do better, Joey, to take care of your guest, and let other things wait."

"Oh, Tom doesn't want to be fussed over," said Joel carelessly, yet he went back to the tall boy standing quite still in the midst of the general hilarity. "That's just the way Ben and Polly used to do in the little brown house," he grumbled—"always running away, and hiding their old secrets from me, Tom."

"Well, we had to, if we ever told each other anything," said Ben coolly. "Joel everlastingly tagged us about, Beresford."

"Well, I had to, if I ever heard anything," burst out Joel, with a laugh. "Come on, Tom," and he bore him off together with Sinbad.

"Polly," Jasper was saying, the two now being off in a corner, "how fine! Now, perhaps Tom Beresford will sing."

"And play," finished Polly, with kindling face. "Oh, Jasper, was anything ever so gorgeous!" she cried joyfully, for Polly dearly loved high-sounding words. "And we'll sell a lot more tickets, because he's new, and people will want to hear him."

"If he will do it," said Jasper slowly, not wanting to dampen her anticipation, but dreadfully afraid that the new boy might not respond.

"Oh, he'll do it, I do believe," declared Polly confidently. "He must, Jasper, help about that poor brakeman's family."

And he did. Tom Beresford evidently made up his mind, when he went home with Joel, to do everything straight through that the family asked him, for he turned out to be the best visitor they had entertained, and one and all pronounced him capital. All but Joel himself, who told him very flatly the second day that he wasn't half as nice as at school, for he was now running at everybody's beck and nod.

"Instead of yours," said Tom calmly. Then he roared.

"Hush up," cried Joel, very uncomfortable, and getting very red. "Well, you must acknowledge, Tom, that I want to see something of you, else why would I have brought you home, pray tell?"

"Nevertheless, I shall do what your sister Polly and your mother and Jasper and Mr. King ask me to do," said Tom composedly, which was all Joel got for his fuming. And the most that he saw of Tom after that was a series of dissolving views, for even Phronsie began to monopolize him, being very much taken with his obliging ways.

At last Joel took to moping, and Ben found him thus in a corner.

"See here, old fellow, that's a nice way—to come home on a holiday, and have such a face. I don't wonder you want to sneak in here."

"It's pretty hard," said Joel, trying not to sniffle, "to have a fellow you bring home from school turn his back on you."

"Well, he couldn't turn his back on you," said Ben, wanting very much to laugh, but he restrained himself, "if you went with him."

"I can't follow him about," said Joel, in a loud tone of disgust. "He's twanging his old banjo all the time, and Polly's got him to sing, and he's practicing up. I wish 'twas smashed."

"What?" said Ben, only half comprehending.

"Why, his old banjo. I didn't think he'd play it all the time," said Joel, who was secretly very proud of his friend's accomplishments, and he displayed a very injured countenance.

"See here, now, Joe," said Ben, laying a very decided hand on Joel's jacket, "do you just drop all this, and come out of your hole. Aren't you ashamed, Joe! Run along, and find Beresford, and pitch into whatever he's doing."

"I can't do anything for that old concert," said Joel, who obeyed enough to come "out of the old hole," but stood glancing at Ben with sharp black eyes.

"I don't know about that," said Ben. "You can at least help to get the tickets ready."

"Did Polly say so?" demanded Joel, all in a glow. "Say, Ben, did she?" advancing on him.

"No, but I do, for Polly asked me to do them. And you know, Joe, how busy I am all day."

He didn't say "how tired" also, but Joel knew how Ben was working at Cabot and Van Meter's, hoping to get into business life the sooner, to begin to pay Grandpapa back for all his kindness.

"Ben, if I can help you with those tickets I'll do it." Every trace of Joel's grumpiness had flown to the four winds. "Let me, will you?" he begged eagerly.

"All right." Ben had no need to haul him along, as Joel raced on ahead up to Ben's room to get the paraphernalia.

"I can't think what's become of Joel," said Polly, flying down the long hall in great perplexity. "We want him dreadfully. Have you seen him, Phronsie?"

"No," said Phronsie, "I haven't, Polly," and a look of distress came into her face.

"Never mind, Pet," said Polly, her brow clearing. "I'll find him soon."

But Phronsie watched Polly fly off, with a troubled face. Then she said to herself, "I ought to find Joey for Polly," and started on a tour of investigation to suit herself.

Meanwhile Ben was giving Joel instructions about the tickets, and Joel presently was so absorbed he wouldn't have cared if all the Tom Beresfords in the world had deserted him, as he bent over his task, quite elated that he was helping Polly, and becoming one of the assistants to make the affair a success.

"I guess it's going to be a great thing, Ben," he said, looking up a moment from the pink and yellow pasteboard out of which he was cutting the tickets.

"You better believe so," nodded Ben, hugely delighted to see Joe's good spirits, when the door opened, and in popped Phronsie's yellow head.

She ran up to Joel. "Oh, Joey!" she hummed delightedly, "I've found you," and threw herself into his arms.

Joel turned sharply, knife in hand. It was all done in an instant. Phronsie exclaimed, *"Oh!"* in such a tone that Ben, off in the corner of the room, whirled around to see Joel, white as a sheet, holding Phronsie. "I've killed her," he screamed.

Ben sprang to them. The knife lay on the table, where Joel had thrown it, a little red tinge along the tip. Ben couldn't help seeing it as he dashed by, with a groan.

"Give her to me," he commanded hoarsely.

"No, no—I'll hold her," persisted Joel, through white lips, and hanging to Phronsie.

"Give her to me, and run down for Father Fisher."

"It doesn't hurt much, Joey," said Phronsie, holding up her little arm. A small stream of blood was flowing down, and she turned away her head.

Joel took one look and fled with wild eyes. "I don't believe it's very bad," Ben made himself call after him hoarsely. "Now, Phronsie, you'll sit in my lap—there—and I'll keep this old cut together as well as I can. We must hold your arm up, so, child." Ben made himself talk as fast as he could to keep Phronsie's eyes on him.

"I got cut in the little brown house once, didn't I, Bensie?" said Phronsie, and trying to creep up further into Ben's lap.

"You must sit straight, child," said Ben. Oh, would Father Fisher and Mamsie ever come! For the blood, despite all his efforts, was running down the little arm pretty fast.

"Why, Ben?" asked Phronsie, with wide eyes, and wishing that her arm wouldn't ache so, for now quite a smart pain had set in. "Why, Bensie?" and thinking if she could be cuddled, it wouldn't be quite so bad.

"Why, we must hold your arm up stiff," said Ben, just as Mamsie came up to her baby, and took her in her arms. And then Phronsie didn't care whether the ache was there or not.

"Joe couldn't help it," said Ben brokenly.

"I believe that," Mother Fisher said firmly. "Oh, Ben, the doctor is away."

Ben started. "I'll go down to the office. Perhaps he's there.'"

"No, there's no chance. I've sent for Dr. Pennell. Your father likes him. Now Phronsie"—Mrs. Fisher set her white lips together tightly—"you and I and Ben will see to this arm of yours. Ben, get one of your big handkerchiefs."

"It doesn't ache so *very* much, Mamsie," said Phronsie, "only I would like to lay it down."

"And that is just what we can't do, Phronsie," said Mother Fisher decidedly. "All right," to Ben, "now tear it into strips."

Old Mr. King was not in the library when Joel had rushed down with his dreadful news, but was in Jasper's den, consulting with him and Polly about the program for the entertainment, as Polly and Jasper, much to the old gentleman's delight, never took a step without going to him for advice. The consequence was that these three did not hear of the accident till a little later, when the two Whitney boys dashed in with pale faces. "Phronsie's hurt," was their announcement, which wouldn't have been given so abruptly had not each one been so anxious to get ahead of the other.

Old Mr. King, not comprehending, had turned sharply in his chair to stare at them.

"Hush, boys," warned Polly, hoarsely pointing to him. "Is Mamsie with her?" She didn't dare to speak Phronsie's name.

"Yes," said Van, eager to communicate all the news, and hoping Percy would not cut in. But Percy, after Polly's warning, had stood quite still, afraid to open his mouth.

Jasper was hunting in one of his drawers for an old book his father had wished to see. So of course he hadn't heard a word.

"Here it is, father," he cried, rushing back and whirling the leaves. "Why, what?" for he saw Polly's face.

"Oh Jasper—don't," said Polly brokenly.

"Why do you boys rush in, in this manner?" demanded old Mr. King testily. "And, Polly, child, what is the matter?"

"Grandpapa," cried Polly, rushing over to him to put her arms around his neck, "Phronsie is hurt someway. I don't believe it is much," she gasped, while Jasper ran to his other side.

"Phronsie hurt!" cried old Mr. King in sharp distress. "Where is she?"

Then Percy, seeing it was considered time for communication of news, struck in boldly, and between the two, all that was known of Joel's wild exclamations was put before them. All this was told along the hall and going over the stairs, for Grandpapa, holding Polly's hand, with Jasper hurrying fast behind them, was making good time up to Ben's room.

"And Dr. Fisher can't be found," shouted Van, afraid that the whole would not be told. Polly gave a shiver that all her self-control could not help.

"But Joel's gone for Dr. Pennell," screamed Percy. "Mrs. Fisher sent him."

"He's very good" said Jasper comfortingly. So this is the way they came into Ben's room.

"Oh, here's Grandpapa!" cooed Phronsie, trying to get down from Mamsie's lap.

"Oh, no, Phronsie," said Mrs. Fisher, "you must sit still. It's better for your arm."

"But Grandpapa looks sick," said Phronsie.

"Bless me—oh, you poor lamb, you!" Old Mr. King went unsteadily across the room and knelt down by her side.

"Grandpapa," said Phronsie, stroking his white face. "See, it's all tied up high."

"Sit still, Phronsie," said Mrs. Fisher, keeping her fingers on the cut. Would the doctor ever come? Besides Joel, Thomas and several more messengers were dispatched with orders for Dr. Pennell and to find Dr. Fisher, with the names of other doctors if these failed. God would send some one of them soon, she knew.

Phronsie obediently sat quite still, although she longed to show Grandpapa the white bandages drawn tightly around her arm. And she smoothed his hair, while he clasped his hands in her lap.

"I want Polly," she said presently.

"Stay where you are, Polly," said her mother, who had telegraphed this before with her eyes, over Phronsie's yellow hair.

Polly, at the sound of Phronsie's voice, had leaned forward, but now stood quite still, clasping her hands tightly together.

"Speak to her, Polly," said Jasper.

But Polly shook her head, unable to utter a sound.

"Polly, you must," said Jasper, for Phronsie was trying to turn in her mother's lap, and saying in a worried way, "Where's Polly? I want Polly."

"Polly is over there," said Mamsie, "but I do not think it's best for her to come now. But she'll speak to you, Phronsie."

"How funny!" laughed Phronsie. "Polly can't come, but she'll talk across the room."

Everything turned black before Polly's eyes, but she began, "Yes, Pet, I'm here," very bravely.

"I am so glad you are there, Polly," said Phronsie, easily satisfied.

Footsteps rapid and light were heard on the stairs. Polly and Jasper flew away from the doorway to let Dr. Pennell, his little case in his hand, come in.

"Well, well!" he exclaimed cheerily, "so now it's Phronsie. I'm coming to her this time," for he had often dropped in to call or to dine since the railway accident.

"Yes," said Phronsie, with a little laugh of delight, for she very much liked Dr. Pennell. He always took her on his lap, and told her stories, and he had a way of tucking certain little articles in his pockets to have her hunt for them. So they had gotten on amazingly well.

"Why, where—" Phronsie began in a puzzled way.

"Is Dr. Fisher?" Dr. Pennell finished it for her, rapidly

going on with his work. "Well, he'll be here soon, I think. And you know he always likes me to do things when he isn't on hand. So I've come."

"And I like you very much," said Phronsie, wriggling her toes in satisfaction.

"I know that. We are famous friends, Phronsie," said the doctor, with one of those pleasant smiles of his that showed his white teeth.

"What's famous?" asked Phronsie, keeping her grave eyes on his face.

"Oh, fine. It means first-rate. We are fine friends, aren't we, Phronsie?"

"Yes, we are," declared Phronsie, bending forward to see his work the better, and taking her eyes from his face.

"There, there, you must sit quite straight. That's a nice child, Phronsie. And see here! I must take you sometime in my carriage when I go on my calls. Will you go, Phronsie?" and Dr. Pennell smiled again.

"Yes, I will." Phronsie nodded her yellow head, while she fastened her eyes on his face. "I used to go with Papa Fisher when I was at the little brown house, and I liked it, I did."

"Well, and now you will go with me," laughed Dr. Pennell. "Now, Phronsie, I think you are fixed up quite nicely," slipping the various articles he had used deftly into his little bag and snapping it to.

"Not a very bad affair," he said, whirling around to old Mr. King, drawn deeply within a big chair, having already telegraphed the same to Mother Fisher over Phronsie's head.

"Thank the Lord!" exclaimed the old gentleman.

"Well, now I'm going to send every one out of the room," announced Dr. Pennell, authoritatively. "Hurry now!" He clapped his hands and laughed.

Old Mr. King sat quite still, fully determined not to obey.

But the doctor, looking over him fixedly, seemed to expect him to leave, and although he still had that pleasant smile, he didn't exactly glve the impression that his medical authority could be tampered with. So the old gentleman found himself outside the door.

"And now, we must find Joel" Polly was saying to Jasper.

Chapter 18

Tom's Story

*J*OEL had no cause to complain now that Tom Beresford did not stick to him, for there he was hanging over him as he crouched into as small a heap as possible into a corner of Mamsie's sofa.

And there he had been ever since Joel had rushed in with Dr. Pennell, when, not daring to trust himself up in Ben's room, he had dashed for refuge to Mamsie's old sofa.

Tom had not wasted many words, feeling sure under similar circumstances he shouldn't like to be talked to, but he had occasionally patted Joel's stubby head in a way not to be misunderstood, and once in a while Joel thrust out a brown hand which Tom had gripped fast.

"It's all right, old boy, I verily believe," Tom cried with sudden energy, "so brace up. What's the use of your going to pieces, anyway?"

"It's Phronsie," gasped Joel, and burrowing deeper into the cushion.

"Well, I know it," said Tom, gulping down his sorrow, for he had petted Phronsie a good deal, so he was feeling the blow quite sharply himself, "but you won't help matters along any, I tell you, by collapsing."

"Go out into the hall, will you, Tom," begged Joel, huddling down, unwilling to listen himself, "and see if you can hear anything."

So Tom, skipping out into the wide upper hall, thankful for any action, but dreading the errand, stole to the foot of the stairs, and craned his ear to catch the faintest sound from above.

There was only a little murmur, for Dr. Pennell was in the midst of operations, and not enough to report. Thankful that it was no worse, Tom skipped back. "All's quiet along the Potomac."

"*Ugh!*" exclaimed Joel, burrowing deeper. Suddenly he threw himself up straight and regarded Tom out of flashing eyes. "I've killed Phronsie," he cried huskily, "and you know it, and won't tell me!"

"Joel Pepper!" cried Tom, frightened half out of his wits, and rushing to him, "lie down again," laying a firm hand on his shoulder.

"I won't," roared Joel wildly, and shaking him off. "You're keeping something from me, Tom."

"You're an idiot," declared Tom, thinking it quite time to be high-handed, "a first-class, howling idiot, Pepper, to act so. If you don't believe me, when I say I haven't anything to keep back from you, I'll go straight upstairs. Someone will tell me."

"Hurry along," cried Joel feverishly. But Tom had gotten no further than the hall when Joel howled, "Come back, Tom, I'll try—to—to bear it." And Tom flying back, Joel was buried as far as his face went, in Mamsie's cushion, sobbing as if his heart would break.

"It will disturb—them," he said gustily, in between his sobs.

Tom Beresford let him cry on, and thrust his hands in his pockets, to stalk up and down the room. He longed to whistle, to give vent to his feelings, but concluding that wouldn't be understood, but be considered heartless, he held himself in check, and counted the slow minutes, for this was deadly tiresome, and beginning to get on his nerves. "I shall screech myself before long, I'm afraid."

At last Joel rolled over. "Come here, do, Tom," and when Tom got there, glad enough to be of use, Joel pulled him down beside the sofa, and gripped him as only Joel could. "Do you mind, Tom? I want to hang on to something."

"No, indeed," said Tom heartily, vastly pleased, although he was nearly choked. "Now you're behaving better." He patted him on the back. "Hark, Joe! The doctor's laughing!"

They could hear it distinctly now, and as long as he lived, Joel thought, he never heard a sweeter sound. He sprang to his feet, upsetting Tom, who rolled over on his back to the floor.

Just then in rushed Polly and Jasper, surrounding him, and in a minute, "Oh, is Tom sick?"

"No," said Tom, picking himself up grimly, "only Joe's floored me, he was so glad to hear the doctor laugh."

"Oh, you poor, poor boy!" Polly was mothering Joel now, just as Mamsie would have done; and Tom, looking on with all his eyes, as he thought of his own home, with neither mother nor sister, didn't hear Jasper at first. So Jasper pulled his arm.

"See here, Beresford, you and I will go down to the library, I think."

"All right," said Tom, allowing himself to be led off, though he would much have preferred remaining.

"Now, Joel," said Polly, after they had gone, and the petting had continued for some minutes, "you must just be a brave boy, and please Mamsie, and stop crying," for Joel had been unable to stop the tears.

"I—I—didn't—see—Phronsie coming," wailed Joel afresh.

"Of course you didn't," said Polly, stroking his black curls. "Why, Joey Pepper, did you think for an instant that anyone blamed you?" She leaned over and set some kisses, not disturbing Joel that some of them fell on his stubby nose.

"N-no," said Joel, through the rain of drops down his cheeks, "but it was Phronsie, Polly." It was no use to try to check him yet, for the boy's heart was almost broken, and so Polly let him cry on. But she bestowed little reassuring pats on his shaking shoulders, all the while saying the most comforting thing she could think of.

"And just think, Joey," she cried suddenly, "you were the one who found Dr. Pennell. Oh, I should think you'd be so glad!"

"I am glad," said Joel, beginning to feel a ray of comfort.

"And how quickly you brought him, Joe!" said Polly, delighted at the effect of her last remark.

"Did I?" said Joel in a surprised way, and roused out of his crying. "I thought it was ever so long, Polly."

"I don't see how you ever did it, Joel, in all this world," declared Polly positively.

Joel didn't say that it was because he was a sprinter at school, he found himself equal to the job; nor did he think it of enough importance to mention how many people he had run into, leaving a great amount of vexation in his rear as he sped on.

"He was just going out of his door," he announced simply.

"Oh, Joey!" gasped Polly. Then she hugged him rapturously. "But you caught him."

"Yes, I caught him, and we jumped into his carriage, and that's all."

"But it was something to be always proud of," cried Polly, in a transport.

Joel, feeling very glad that there was something to be proud of at all in this evening's transactions, sat up quite straight at this, and wiped his eyes.

"Now that's a good boy," said Polly encouragingly. "Mamsie will be very glad." And she ran over to get a towel, dip it in the water basin, and bring it back.

"Oh, that feels so good!" said Joel with a wintry smile, as she sopped his red eyelids and poor, swollen nose.

"So it must," said Polly pitifully, "and I'm going to bring the basin here, and do it some more." Which she did, so that by the time Phronsie was brought downstairs to sleep in Mrs. Fisher's room, Joel was quite presentable.

"Here they come!" announced Polly radiantly, hearing the noise on the stairs, and running back to set the basin and towel in their places. " Now, Joey, you can see for yourself that Phronsie is all right."

And there she was, perched on Dr. Pennell's shoulder, to be sure, and Mamsie hurrying in to her boy, and everything was just as beautiful as it could be!

"See, Joel, I'm all fixed up nice," laughed Phronsie from her perch.

Joel's mouth worked dreadfully, but he saw Mamsie's eyes, so he piped up bravely, "I'm so glad, Phronsie." It so⌐⌐led very funnily, for it died away in his throat, and h⌐ have said another word possibly, but Phronsi⌐ and didn't notice. And then the doctor said out, so with a last glance at Phronsie, to be sure that she was all right, Joel went off, Polly holding his hand.

The next evening they were all drawn up before the library fire, Polly on the big rug with Joel's head in her lap, his eyes fixed on Phronsie, who was ensconced in an easy chair, close to which Grandpapa was sitting.

"Tell stories, do, Polly," begged Van.

"Yes, do, Polly," said little Dick, who had spent most of the day in trying to get near to Phronsie, keeping other people very much occupied in driving him off, as she had to be very quiet. "Do, Polly," he begged.

"Oh, Polly's tired," said Jasper, knowing that she had been with Phronsie all her spare time, and looking at the brown eyes which were drooping a bit in the firelight.

"Oh, no, I will," said Polly, rousing herself, and feellng that she ought not to be tired, when Phronsie was getting well so fast, and everything was so beautiful. "I'll tell you one. Let me see, what shall it be about?" and she leaned her head in her hands to think a bit.

"Let her off," said Jasper. "Do, boys. I'll tell you one instead," he said.

"No, we don't want yours," said Van, not very politely. "We want Polly's."

"For shame, Van!" said Percy, who dearly loved to reprove his brother, and never allowed the occasion to slip when he could do so.

"For shame yourself!" retorted Van, flinging himself down on the rug. "You're everlastingly teasing Polly to do things when she's tired to death. So there, Percy Whitney."

"Oh, I'll tell the story," Polly said, hastily bringing her brown head up, while Phronsie began to look troubled.

"I'd like to tell a story," said Tom Beresford slowly, where he sat just back of the big rug.

All the young folks turned to regard him, and Van was just going to say, "Oh, we don't want yours, Tom," when Polly leaned forward, "Oh, will you—will you, Tom?" so eagerly that Van hadn't the heart to object.

"Yes, I will," promised Tom, nodding at her.

"Well, get down on the rug, then," said Jasper, moving up. "The story teller always has to have a place of honor here."

"That so?" cried Tom. "Well, here goes," and he precipitated himself at once into the midst of things.

"Ow! Get out," cried Van crossly, and giving him a push.

"Oh Vanny!" said Polly reprovingly.

"Well, he's so big and long," grumbled Van, who didn't fancy anybody coming between him and Polly.

"I might cut off a piece of my legs," said Tom, "to oblige you, I suppose. They are rather lengthy, and that's a fact," regarding them as they stretched out in the firelight. "I'll curl 'em up in a twist like a Turk," which he did.

"Well, now," said Jasper, "we are ready. So fire ahead, Beresford."

Joel, who all this time had been regarding his friend curiously, having never heard him tell a story at Dr. Marks's school, couldn't keep his eyes from him, but regarded him with a fixed stare, which Tom was careful to avoid, by looking steadily into the fire.

"Well, now, I'm not fine at expressing myself," he began.

"I should think not," put in Joel uncomplimentarily.

"Joe, you beggar, hush up!" said Jasper, with a warning pinch.

"Yes, just sit on that individual, will you, Jasper?" said Tom, over his shoulder, "or I never will even begin."

So, Jasper promising to quench all further disturbance on Joel's part, the story was taken up.

"I can only tell a plain, unvarnished tale," said Tom, "but it's one that ought to be told, and in this very spot. Perhaps you don't any of you know that in Dr. Marks's school it's awfully hard to be good."

"Is it any harder than in any other school, Tom?" asked Mrs. Fisher quietly.

Tom turned, to reply. "I don't know, Mrs. Fisher, because I haven't been at any other school. But I can't imagine a place where everything is made so hard for a boy. To begin with, there is old Fox."

"Oh, Tom!" exclaimed Phronsie, leaning forward, whereat old Mr. King laid a warning hand upon the well arm.

"There, there, Phronsie. Sit back, child." So she obeyed.

"But, Grandpapa, he said there was an old fox at Joey's school," she declared, dreadfully excited, and lifting her face to his.

"Well, and so she is, Phronsie," declared Tom, whirling his long body suddenly around, thereby receiving a dig in the back from Van, who considered him intruding on his space. "A fox by name, and a fox by nature. But we'll call her, for convenience, a person."

"She's the matron," said Percy, feeling called upon to explain.

"Oh!" said Phronsie, drawing a long breath. "But I thought Tom said she was a fox, Grandpapa."

"That's her name," said Tom, nodding at her. "Jemima Fox—isn't that a sweet name, Phronsie?"

"I don't think it is a *very* sweet one, Tom," said Phronsie, feeling quite badly to be obliged to say so.

"I agree with you," said Tom, while the others all laughed. "Well, Phronsie, she's just as far from being nice as her name is."

"Oh dear me!" exclaimed Phronsie, looking quite grieved.

"But I have something nice to tell you," said Tom quickly, "so I'll hurry on, and let the other personages at Dr. Marks's slide. Well—but I want you all to understand, though"—and he wrinkled up his brows—"that when a fellow does real, bang-up, fine things at that school, it means something. You will, won't you?" He included them all now in a sweeping glance, letting his blue eyes rest the longest on Mrs. Fisher's face, while Phronsie broke in, "What's bang-up, Grandpapa?"

"You must ask Tom," replied Grandpapa, with a little laugh.

"Oh, that's just schoolboy lingo," Tom made haste to say, as his face got red.

"What's lingo?" asked Phronsie, more puzzled than before.

"That's—that's—oh, dear!" Tom's face rivaled the firelight by this time, for color.

"Phronsie, I wouldn't ask any more questions now," said Polly gently. "Boys say so many things, and it isn't necessary to know now. Let's listen to the story."

"I will," said Phronsie, feeling quite relieved that it wasn't really incumbent on her to ask for explanations. So she sat back quietly in her big chair, while Tom shot Polly a grateful look.

"Well, there are lots of chaps at our school," went on Tom—"I suppose there are at all schools, but at any rate we have them in a big quantity—who are mad when they see the other boys get on."

"Oh, Tom!" exclaimed Polly.

"Yes, they are—mad clear through," declared Tom positively. "And it's principally in athletics." Phronsie made a little movement at this word, but remembering that she was not to ask questions, for Polly had said so, she became quiet again.

"They simply can't hear that a boy gets ahead of 'em; it

just knocks 'em all up." Tom was rushing on, with head thrown back and gazing into the fire.

"Tom," said Joel, bounding up suddenly to take his head out of Polly's lap and to sit quite straight, "I wouldn't run on like this if I were you."

"You hush up, Pepper," said Tom coolly. "I haven't said a word about you. I shall say what I like. I tell you, it does just knock 'em all up. I know, for I've been that way myself."

This was getting on such dangerous ground that Joel opened his mouth to remonstrate, but Polly put her hand over it. "I'd let Tom tell his story just as he wants to," which had the effect of smothering Joel's speech for the time being.

"I thought, Jasper, you were going to quench Joe," observed Tom, who seemed to have the power to see out of the back of his head, and now was conscious of the disturbance. "You don't seem to be much good."

"Oh, Polly's doing it this time," said Jasper. "I'll take him in tow on the next offense."

"Yes, I have," declared Tom, "been that way myself. I'm going to tell you how, and then I'll feel better about it." His ruddy face turned quite pale now, and his eyes shone.

"Stop him," howled Joel, all restraint thrown to the winds, and shaking off Polly's fingers.

Jasper leaned forward. "I'm bound to make you keep the peace, Joe," he said, shaking his arm.

"But he's going to tell about things he ought not to," cried Joel in an agony. "Do stop him, Jasper."

Mother Fisher leaned forward and fastened her black eyes on Joel's face. "I think Tom better go on, Joel," she said. "I want to hear it."

That settled the matter; and Joel threw himself down, his face buried in Polly's lap, while he stuck his fingers in his ears.

"I'm going to tell you all this story," Tom was saying, "because I ought to. You won't like me very well after it, but it's got to come out. Well, I might as well mention names now, since Joe has got to keep still. You can't guess how he's been tormented by some of those cads, simply because he's our best tennis player, and on the football team. They've made things hum for him!" Tom threw back his head, and clenched his fist where it lay in his lap. "And the rest of us boys got mad, especially at one of them. He was the ring-leader, and the biggest cad and bully of them all."

No one said a word.

"I hate to mention names; it seems awfully mean." Tom's face got fiery red again. "And yet, as you all know, why, it can't be helped. Jenkins—well there, a fellow would want to be excused from speaking to him. And yet"—down fell Tom's head shamefacedly—"I let him show me how he was going to play a dastardly trick on Joe, the very day of the tennis tournament. I did, that's a fact."

No one spoke; but Tom could feel what might have been said had the thoughts all been expressed, and he burst out desperately, "I let that cad take Joe's racket."

A general rustle, as if some speech were coming, made him forestall it by plunging on. "His beautiful racket he'd been practicing with for this tournament. And I not only didn't knock the scoundrel down, but I helped the thing along. I wouldn't have supposed I could do it. Joe was to play with Ricketson against Green and me, and two minutes after it was done, I'd have given everything to have had it back on Joe's table. But the boys were pouring up, and it was hidden."

Tom could get no further, but hung his head for the reaction sure to set in against him by all this household that had welcomed and entertained him so handsomely.

"Has he got through? Has the beggar finished?" cried Joel lustily.

"Yes," said Polly, in a low voice. "I think he has, Joel."

"Then I want to say"—Joel threw himself over by Tom, his arms around him—"that he's the biggest fraud to spring such a trap on me, and plan to get off that yarn here."

"I didn't intend to when I came," said Tom, thinking it necessary to tell the whole truth. "I hadn't the courage."

"Pity you had now!" retorted Joel. "Oh, you beggar!" He laid his round cheek against Tom's. "Mamsie, Grandpapa, Polly," his black eyes sweeping the circle, "if I were to tell you all that this chap has done for me—why, he took me to the place where Jenk hid the racket."

"Pshaw! That was nothing," said Tom curtly.

"Nothing? Well, I got it in time for the tournament. You saw to that. And when Jenk and I were having it out in the pine grove that night, Tom thought he better tell Dave; though I can't say I thank you for that," brought up Joel regretfully, "for I was getting the best of Jenk."

Old Mr. King had held himself well in check up to this point. "How did you know, Tom, my boy, that Joel and er—this—"

"Jenk," furnished Joel.

"Yes—er—Jenk, were going to settle it that night?"

"Why, you see, sir," Tom, in memory of the excitement and pride over Joel's prowess, so far recovered himself as to turn to answer, "Joel couldn't very well finish there, for the dormitory got too hot for that sort of thing; although it would have been rare good sport for all the fellows to have seen Jenk flat, for he was always beating other chaps—I mean little ones, not half his size."

"Oh dear me!" breathed Polly indignantly.

"Yes. Well, Joe promised Jenk he would finish it some

other time, and Jenk dared him, and taunted him after the tournament. He was wild with rage because Joel won, and he lost his head, or he would have let Joe alone."

"I see," exclaimed Grandpapa, his eyes shining. "Well, and so you sat up and watched the affair."

"I couldn't go to bed, you know," said Tom simply.

"And he would have saved us, Dave and me, if that Jenk hadn't locked the door on us when he slipped in."

"Cad!" exclaimed Tom, between his teeth. "He ought to have been expelled for that. And then Joe shinned up the conductor—and you know the rest."

Mother Fisher shivered, and leaned over involuntarily toward her boy.

"Mamsie," exclaimed Joel, "you don't know what Tom is to me, in that school. He's just royal—that's what he is!" with a resounding slap on his back.

"And I say so too," declared Mother Fisher, with shining eyes.

"*What?*" roared Tom, whirling around so suddenly that Van this time got out of the way only by rolling entirely off from the rug. "Mrs. Fisher—you *can't*, after I've told you this, although I'm no-end sorry about the racket. I didn't want to tell—fought against it, but I had to."

"I stand by what I've said, Tom," said Mrs. Fisher, putting out her hand, when Tom immediately laid his big brown one within it. At this, Joel howled with delight, which he was unable to express enough to meet his wishes. So he plunged off to the middle of the library floor, and turned a brace of somersaults, coming up red and shining.

"I feel better now," he said. "That's the way I used to do in the little brown house when I liked things."

Chapter 19

The Grand Entertainment

"OUGHT we to, Mamsie?" asked Polly.

Jasper and she were in Mrs. Fisher's room, and they both waited for the reply anxiously.

"Yes, Polly, I think you ought," said Mother Fisher.

"Oh dear me! Phronsie can't have only a little bit of it," said Polly.

"I know it. But think, Polly, the boys have to go back to school so soon that even if other people didn't care if it were postponed, they would lose it. Besides, Tom is to be one of the chief people on the program. No, no, Polly, there are others to think of outside of ourselves. You must have your entertainment just as it is planned," Mrs. Fisher brought up very decidedly.

"Well," sighed Polly, "I am glad that Papa Fisher says that Phronsie can hear a little part of it, anyway."

"Yes," said her mother cheerfully, "and Helen Fargo is to

sit next to her. Mrs. Fargo is to take her home early, as she has not been very well. So you see, Polly, it will all turn out very good after all."

"But I did so want Phronsie to be there through the whole," mourned Polly.

"So did I," echoed Jasper. Then he caught Mother Fisher's eye. "But, Polly, the boys would lose it then," he added quickly.

"Oh!" cried Polly, "so they would. I keep forgetting that. Dear me! Why isn't everything just right, so that they all could hear it?" And she gave a little flounce.

"Everything is just right, Polly," said Mrs. Fisher gravely. "Don't let me hear you complain of things that no one can help."

"I didn't mean to complain, Mamsie," said Polly humbly, and she crept up to her, while Jasper looked very much distressed.

"Mother knows you didn't," said Mrs. Fisher, putting her arm around her, "but it's a bad habit, Polly, to be impatient when things don't go rightly. Now run away, both of you," she finished brightly, "and work up your program," and she set a kiss on Polly's rosy cheek.

"Jasper," cried Polly, with happiness once more in her heart as they raced off, "I tell you what we can do. We must change the program, and put those things that Phronsie likes, up first."

"That's so," cried Jasper, well pleased. "Now, what will they be, Polly?"

"Why, Mr. Dyce's story of the dog," said Polly, "for one thing. Phronsie thinks that's perfectly lovely, and always asks him for it when he tells her stories."

"All right," said Jasper. "What next?"

"Why, Tom must sing one of his funny songs."

"Yes, of course. That will please her ever so much," cried Jasper. "Don't you know how she claps her hands when he's rehearsing, Polly?"

"Yes. Oh, I wouldn't have her miss that for anything, Jasper," said Polly.

"No, indeed," cried Jasper heartily. "Well, Polly, then what ought to come next? Let's come into the den and fix it up now."

So they ran into the den, and Jasper got out the long program all ready to be pinned up beside the improvised stage, on the evening of the great event, and spread it on the table, Polly meanwhile clearing off the books.

"Let's see." He wrinkled up his brow, running his finger down the whole length. "Now, when I make the new program, Mr. Dyce goes first."

Polly stood quite still at that. "Oh, Jasper, we can't do it—no, never in all this world."

"Why, Polly"—he turned suddenly—"yes, we can just as easily. See, Polly."

"We can't spoil that lovely program that took you so long to make, for anything," said Polly, in a decisive fashion. "Phronsie wouldn't want it," she added.

"Phronsie isn't to know anything about it," said Jasper, just as decidedly.

"Well, but Jasper, you can't make another. You haven't the time," said Polly in great distress, and wishing she hadn't said anything about the changes. "I didn't think there would have to be a new program made."

"Oh, Polly, I think we'd better have a new one," said Jasper, who was very particular about everything.

"I thought we were going to have changes announced from the stage," said Polly. "Oh, why can't we, Jasper? I'm sure they do that very often."

"Well, that's when the changes come at the last moment," said Jasper reluctantly.

"Well, I'm sure this is the last moment," said Polly. "The entertainment is tomorrow night, and we've ever so much to do yet. *Please,* Jasper." That "Please, Jasper" won the day.

"All right, Polly," he said. "Well, now let's see what ought to come after Tom's song."

"Well, Phronsie is very anxious to hear Pickering's piece; I know, because I heard her tell Mamsie so."

"Why, she has heard Pick recite that ever so many times since he learned it for our school exhibition," said Jasper.

"And don't you know that's just the very reason why she wants it again?" said Polly, with a little laugh.

"Yes, of course," said Jasper, laughing too. "Well, she must have it then. So down goes Pick." He ran to the table drawer and drew out a big sheet of paper. "First, Mr. Dyce, then Tom Beresford, then Pickering Dodge," writing fast.

"And then," said Polly, running up to look over his shoulder, "Phronsie wants dreadfully to hear Tom play on his banjo."

"Oh, Polly"—Jasper threw back his head to look at her—"I don't believe there'll be time for all that. You know the music by Miss Taylor comes first as an overture. We can't change that."

"Why," exclaimed Polly in dismay, "we must, Jasper, get Tom's banjo in. And there's Percy's piece. Phronsie wouldn't miss that for *anything.*"

"Why, we shall have the whole program in if we keep on," said Jasper, looking at her in dismay.

"Oh, Jasper, Papa Fisher says that Phronsie may stay in twenty minutes. Just think. We can do a lot in twenty minutes."

"But somebody is bound to be late, so we can't begin on time. Nobody ever does, Polly."

"We must," said Polly passionately, "begin on time tomorrow night, Jasper."

"We'll try," said Jasper, as cheerfully as he could manage.

"And there's your piece. Why, Jasper, Phronsie told me herself that she *must* hear yours."

"Well, and so she told me that she'd rather hear you play your piece," said Jasper, "but you and I, Polly, as long as we change the program, can't come in among the first."

"No, of course not," said Polly. "But, oh, Jasper," and she gave a sigh, "it's too bad that you can't recite yours, for it is most beautiful!" Polly clasped her hands and sighed again.

"Well, that's not to be thought of," said Jasper. "Now I tell you how we'll fix it, Polly," he said quickly.

"How?" asked Polly gloomily.

"Why, we have twenty minutes that Phronsie can stay in. Now, let's mark off all those things that she wants, except yours and mine, even if they come beyond the time, and then we'll draw just those that will get into the twenty minutes."

"Oh, Jasper, what a fine idea!" exclaimed Polly, all her enthusiasm returning.

"Well, mark off half of 'em, and I'll write the others," said Jasper, tearing off strips from his big sheet of paper. So Polly and he fell to work, and presently "Pick," and "Tom" ("That's for the song," said Polly), and "Banjo," and "Mr. Dyce," and "Percy" went down on the little strips.

"Oh, and I forgot," said Polly, raising her head from her last strip. "Phronsie wanted to hear Clare very much indeed."

"Well, we should have had the whole program with a vengeance," said Jasper, bursting into a laugh. "Well, put him down, Polly."

So "Clare" went down on another strip, and then they were all jumbled up in a little Chinese bowl on the bookcase.

"Now, you draw first, Polly," said Jasper.

"Oh, no, let us choose for first draw," said Polly. "That's the way to be absolutely right."

So she ran back to the table and tore off two more strips, one short and the other long, and fixed them in between her hands.

"You didn't see?" she asked over her shoulder.

"Not a wink," said Jasper, laughing.

So Polly ran back, and Jasper drew the short one. "There! You have it, Polly!" he cried gleefully. "Oh, that's good!"

"Oh, I do hope I shall draw the right one, Jasper," she said, standing on tiptoe, her fingers trembling over the bowl.

"They are all of them good," said Jasper encouragingly. So Polly suddenly picked out one, and together they read, "Tom."

"Fine!" they shouted.

"Oh, isn't that perfectly splendid?" cried Polly, "because, you see, Phronsie did so very much wish to hear Tom sing," just as if she hadn't mentioned that fact before. "Now, Jasper."

"I'm in much the same predicament as you were," said Jasper, pausing, his hand over the bowl. "If I shouldn't choose the right one, Polly!"

"They are all of them good," said Polly, laughing at his face.

"Oh, I know, but it is a fearful responsibility," said Jasper, wrinkling his brows worse yet. "Well, here goes!"

He plunged his fingers in, and out they came with the strip, "Percy."

"Now, Jasper, you couldn't possibly have chosen better," declared Polly, hopping up and down, "for Phronsie did so want to hear Percy speak. And it will please Percy so. Oh, I'm so glad!"

"Well, I'm thankful I haven't to draw again," declared Jasper, "for we can't have but three pieces besides the overture, you know. So it's your turn now, Polly."

"Oh dear me!" exclaimed Polly, the color dying down in her cheek. "If I shouldn't draw the right one, Jasper King! And it's the last chance."

She stood so long with her hand poised over the Chinese bowl that Jasper finally laughed out, "Oh, Polly, aren't your tiptoes tired?"

"Not half so tired as I am," said Polly grimly. "Jasper, I'm going to run across the room and then run back and draw suddenly without stopping to think."

"Do," cried Jasper.

So Polly ran into the further corner and came flying up, to get on her tiptoes, thrust in her fingers, and bring out the third and last strip.

"The deed is done!" exclaimed Jasper. "Now, Polly, let's see who it is."

"Pick!" he shouted.

And "Pickering!" screamed Polly. And they took hold of hands and spun round and round the den.

"Oh, dear, we're knocking off your beautiful program," cried Polly, pausing in dismay.

"It hasn't hurt it any—our mad whirl hasn't," said Jasper, picking up the long program where it had slipped off the table to the floor. "Polly, you can't think how I wanted Pick to be chosen. It will do him so much good."

"And only think, if I hadn't chosen him out of that bowl!" cried Polly, in dismay at the very thought.

"Well, you did, Polly, so it's all right," said Jasper. "Now everything is fixed, and it's going to be the finest affair that ever was," he added enthusiastically. "And the best of it is—I can't help it, Polly—that Mrs. Chatterton isn't to come back till next week," he brought up in great satisfaction.

Mrs. Chatterton had gone to New York for some weeks, but was to return to finish her visit at "Cousin Horatio's."

"And I am so glad too," confessed Polly, but feeling as if she oughtn't to say it. "And isn't everything just beautiful, Jasper!"

"I should think it was!" cried Jasper jubilantly. "Just as perfect as can be, Polly."

And the next afternoon, when the last preparations for the grand entertainment were made, and everybody was rushing off to dress for dinner, a carriage drove up the winding driveway. There were big trunks on the rack, and two people inside.

Joel, racing along the hall with Tom at his heels, took one look. " Oh, whickets!" he ejaculated, stopping short, to bring his feet down with a thud.

"What's the row?" asked Tom, plunging up to him in amazement.

"That person." Joel pointed a finger at the carriage. "I must tell Polly," and off he darted.

Tom, not feeling at all sure that he ought to wait to see "that person," wheeled about and followed.

"Polly," roared Joel, long before he got to her. "She's come!"

"Has she?" Polly called back supposing he meant Alexia. "Well, tell her to come up here, Joe, in my room."

Joel took the stairs two at a time, Tom waiting below, and dashed into the blue and white room without ceremony.

"Polly, you don't understand," he blurted out. "She's come!"

Polly had her head bent over a drawer, picking out some

ribbons. At the sound of Joel's voice she drew it out and looked at him.

"Why, how funny you look, Joe!" she said. "What is the matter?"

"I guess you'd look funny," said Joel glumly, "if you'd seen Mrs. Chatterton."

"Not Mrs. Chatterton!" exclaimed Polly aghast, and jumping up, her face very pale, and upsetting her box of ribbons, she seized Joel's arm.

"Tell me this very minute, Joel Pepper," she commanded, "what do you mean?"

"Mrs. Chatterton has just come. I saw her coming up the drive. There's Johnson now letting her in." Joel had it all out now in a burst, ready to cry at sight of Polly's face, as the bustle in the hall below and the thin, high voice proclaimed the worst.

"Oh, Joel, Joel!" mourned Polly, releasing his arm to wring her hands. "What *shall* we do?"

"She's an old harpy," declared Joel. "Mean, horrid, old thing!"

"Oh, stop, Joel!" cried Polly, quite horrified.

"Well, she is," said Joel vindictively, "to come before we'd got back to school."

"Well, don't say so," begged Polly, having hard work to keep back her own words, crowding for utterance. "Mamsie wouldn't like it, Joey."

Joel, with this thought on his mind, only grumbled out something so faintly that really Polly couldn't hear as she ran out into the hall.

"Oh, Jasper!"

"Polly, did you know? What *can* we do?" It was impossible for him to conceal his vexation. And Polly lost sight of her own discomfiture in the attempt to comfort him.

"And father—it will just make him as miserable as can be," said Jasper gloomily. "And he was so happy over the beautiful time we were going to have this evening." He was so vexed he could do nothing but prance up and down the hall.

"Well, we must make him forget that she is here," said Polly, swallowing her own distress at the change of all the conditions.

"How can we, Polly?" Jasper stopped for a minute and stared at her.

"I mean," said Polly, feeling that it was a very hopeless case after all, "that we mustn't show that we mind it, her coming back, and must act as if we forgot it, and then that will keep him happy perhaps."

"If you only will, Polly," cried Jasper, seizing both of her hands, "it will be the best piece of work you ever did."

"Oh, I can't do it alone," exclaimed Polly, in consternation. "Never in all this world, Jasper, unless you help too."

"Then we'll both try our very best," said Jasper. "I'm sure I ought to. 'Twould be mean enough to expect you to go at such a task alone."

"Oh, you couldn't be mean, Jasper," declared Polly, in horror at the very thought.

"Well, I should be if I left you to tackle this by yourself," said Jasper, with a grim little laugh. "So Polly, there's my hand on it. I'll help you."

And Polly ran back to pick up her ribbons and dress for dinner, feeling somehow very happy after all, that there was something she could do for dear Grandpapa to help him bear this great calamity.

Tom Beresford, meanwhile, withdrew from the great hall when Johnson ushered in the tall, stately woman and her French maid, and took shelter in the library. And Mrs.

Whitney, coming over the stairs, saying, "Well, Cousin Eunice, did you have a pleasant journey?" in the gentle voice Tom so loved, gave him the first inkling of the relationship. But he wrinkled his brows at Joel's exclamation, and his queer way of rushing off.

"You know journeys always tire me, Marian. So that your question is quite useless. I will sit in the library a moment to recover myself. Hortense, go up and prepare my room," and she sailed into the apartment, her heavy silk gown swishing close to Tom's chair.

"Who is that boy?" she demanded sharply. Then she put up her lorgnette, and examined him closely as if of a new and probably dangerous species.

Tom slipped off from his chair and stiffened up.

"It's one of Joel's friends," said Mrs. Whitney, slipping her hand within the tall boy's arm. "The boys are at home from school for a week."

"Joel's friends," repeated Mrs. Chatterton, paying scant attention to the rest of the information. Then she gave a scornful cackle. "Haven't you gotten over that nonsense yet, Marian?" she asked.

"No, and I trust I never shall," replied Mrs. Whitney with a happy smile. "Now, Cousin Eunice, as you wish to rest, we will go," and she drew Tom off.

"My boy," she said, releasing him in the hall to give a bright glance up at the stormy, astonished face above her, "I know you and Joel will get dressed as rapidly as possible for dinner, for my father will not want to be annoyed by a lack of promptness tonight." She did not say, "because he will have annoyance enough," but Tom guessed it all.

"I will, Mrs. Whitney," he promised heartily. And thinking he would go to the ends of the earth for her, to be smiled on like that, he plunged off over the stairs.

"I've seen the old cat," he cried in smothered wrath to Joel, rushing into his room.

Joel sat disconsolately on the edge of his bed, kicking off his heavy shoes to replace with his evening ones.

"Have you?" said Joel grimly. "Well, isn't she a—" Then he remembered Mamsie, and snapped his lips to.

" 'A,' " exclaimed Tom, in smothered wrath, as he closed the door. "She isn't 'a' at all, Joe. She's 'the.' "

"Well, do be still," cried Joel, putting on his best shoes nervously, "or you'll have me saying something. And she's visiting here, and Mamsie wouldn't like it. Don't, Tom," he begged.

"I won't," said Tom, with a monstrous effort, "but—oh dear me!" Then he rushed into his own room and banged about, getting his best clothes out.

"Shut the door," roared Joel after him, "or you'll begin to fume, and I can't stand it, Tom. It will set me off."

So Tom shut the door, and with all these precautions going on over the house, all the family in due time appeared at dinner, prepared as best they could be to bear the infliction of Mrs. Chatterton's return.

And after the conclusion of the meal, why, everybody tried to forget it as much as possible, and give themselves up to the grand affair of the evening.

And old Mr. King, who had been consumed with fear that it would have a disastrous effect on Polly and Jasper, the chief getters-up of the entertainment, came out of his fright nicely, for there they were, as bright and jolly as ever, and fully equal to any demands upon them. So he made up his mind that, after all, he could put up with Cousin Eunice a bit longer, and that the affair was to be an immense success and the very finest thing possible.

And everybody else who was present on the eventful

occasion, said so too! And it seemed as if Mr. King's spacious drawing room, famous for its capacity at all such times, couldn't possibly have admitted another person to this entertainment for the benefit of the poor brakeman's family.

And Joel, who wasn't good at recitations, and who detested all that sort of thing, and Van, for the same reason, were both in their element as ticket takers. And the little pink and yellow squares came in so thick and fast that both boys had all they could do for a while—which was saying a good deal—to collect them.

And everybody said that Miss Mary Taylor had never played such a beautiful overture—and she was capable of a good deal along that line—in all her life. And Phronsie, sitting well to the front, between old Mr. King and Helen Fargo, forgot that she ever had a hurt arm, and that it lay bandaged up in her lap.

And little Dick, when he could lose sight of the fact that he wasn't next to Phronsie instead of Helen Fargo, snuggled up contentedly against Mother Fisher, and applauded everything straight through.

And old Mr. King protested that he was perfectly satisfied with the whole thing, which was saying the most that could be expressed for the quality of the entertainment, and he took particular pains to applaud Tom Beresford, who looked very handsome, and acquitted himself well.

"I must," said Tom to himself, although quaking inwardly, "for they've all been so good to me—and for Joel's sake!" So he sang at his very best. And he played his banjo merrily, and he was encored and encored. And Joel was as proud as could be, which did Tom good to see.

And Percy—well, the tears of joy came into his mother's eyes, for it wasn't easy for him to learn pieces, nor in fact to apply himself to study at all. But no one would have sus-

pected it to see him now on that stage. And Grandpapa King
was so overjoyed that he called "Bravo—bravo!" ever so
many times, which carried Percy on triumphantly over the
difficult spots where he had been afraid he should slip.

"If only his father could hear him!" sighed Mrs. Whitney
in the midst of her joy, longing as she always did for the time
when the father could finish those trips over the sea for his
business house.

Polly had made Jasper consent, which he did reluctantly,
to give his recitation before she played; insisting that music
was really better for a finale. And she listened with such
delight to the applause that he received—for ever so many of
the audience said it was the gem of the whole—that she
quite forgot to be nervous about her own performance, and
she played her nocturne with such a happy heart, thinking
over the lovely evening, and how the money would be, oh,
such a heap to take down on the morrow to the poor
brakeman's home, that Jasper was turning the last page of her
music—and the entertainment was at an end!

Polly hopped off from the music stool. There was a great
clapping all over the room, and Grandpapa called out, "Yes,
child, play again," so there was nothing for Polly to do but to
hop back again and give them another selection. And then
they clapped harder yet, but Polly shook her brown head and
rushed off the stage.

And then, of course, Grandpapa gave them, as he always
did, a fine party to wind up the evening with. And the camp
chairs were folded up and carried off, and a company of
musicians came into the alcove in the spacious hall, and all
through the beautiful, large apartments festivity reigned!

"Look at the old cat," said Tom in a smothered aside to
Joel, his next neighbor in the "Sir Roger de Coverley."
"Isn't she a sight!"

"I don't want to," said Joel, with a grimace, "and it's awfully mean in you, Tom, to ask me."

"I know it," said Tom penitently, "but I can't keep my eyes off from her. How your grandfather can stand it, Pepper, I don't see."

And a good many other people were asking themselves the same question, Madam Dyce among the number, to whom Mrs. Chatterton was just remarking, "Cousin Horatio is certainly not the same man."

"No," replied Madam Dyce distinctly, "he is infinitely improved. So approachable now."

"You mistake me," Mrs. Chatterton said angrily. "I mean there is the greatest change come over him. It's lamentable, and all brought about by his inexplicable infatuation over those low-born Pepper children and their designing mother."

"Mrs. Chatterton," said Madam Dyce—she could be quite as stately as Mr. King's cousin, and as she felt in secure possession of the right in the case, she was vastly more impressive—"I am not here to go over this question, nor shall I discuss it, anywhere with you. You know my mind about it. I only wish I had the Peppers—yes, every single one of them," warmed up the old lady—"in my house, and that fine woman, their mother, along with them."

Chapter 20

The Corcoran Family

*A*ND on the morrow—oh, what a heap of money there was for the poor brakeman's family! Four hundred and twelve dollars. For a good many people had fairly insisted on paying twice the amount for their tickets, and a good many more had paid when they couldn't take tickets at all, going out of town, or for some other good reason.

And one old lady, a great friend of the family, sent for Polly Pepper the week before. And when Polly appeared before the big lounge—for Mrs. Sterling was lifted from her bed to lie under the sofa blankets all day—she said, "Now, my dear, I want to take some tickets for that affair of yours. Gibbons, get my checkbook."

So Gibbons, the maid, brought the checkbook, and drew up the little stand with the writing case upon it close to the lounge, and Mrs. Sterling did a bit of writing, and presently she held out a long green slip of paper.

"Oh!" cried Polly, in huge delight, "I've never had one for my very own self before." There it was, "Polly Pepper," running clear across its face. And "Oh!" with wide eyes, when she saw the amount. "Twenty-five dollars!"

"Haven't you so?" said Mrs. Sterling, greatly pleased to be the first in one of Polly's pleasures.

"Oh!" cried Polly again. "Twenty-five dollars!" And she threw herself down before the lounge and dropped a kiss upon the hand that had made all this happiness for the brakeman's poor children.

"Well now, Polly, tell me all about it," said Mrs. Sterling, with a glow at her heart warm enough to brighten many a long invalid day. "Gibbons, get a cricket for Miss Mary."

"Oh, may I sit here?" begged Polly eagerly, as Gibbons, placing the little writing case back into position, now approached with the cricket. "It's so cozy on the floor."

"Why, yes, if you don't wish the cricket," said Mrs. Sterling with a little laugh, "and I remember when I was your age it was my greatest delight to sit on the floor."

"It is mine," said Polly, snuggling up to the sofa blankets.

Mrs. Sterling put out her thin hand and took Polly's rosy palm. "Now begin, dear," she said, with an air of content, and looking down into the bright face.

So Polly, realizing that here perhaps was need for help, quite as much as in the poor brakeman's home, though in a different way, told the whole story, how the two clubs, the Salisbury School Club and the boys' club, had joined together to help Jim Corcoran's children; how they had had a big meeting at Jasper's house, and promised each other to take hold faithfully and work for that object.

"We were going to have a little play," observed Polly, a bit sorrowfully, "but it was thought best not, so it will be recitations and music."

"Those will be very nice, I am quite sure, Polly," said Mrs. Sterling. "How I should love to hear some of them!" It was her turn to look sad now.

"Why—" Polly sat up quite straight now, and her cheeks turned rosy.

"What is it, my child?" asked Mrs. Sterling.

"Would you—I mean, do you want—oh, Mrs. Sterling, would you like us to come here some time to recite something to you?"

Mrs. Sterling turned an eager face on her pillow.

"Are you sure, Polly," a light coming into her tired eyes, "that you young people would be willing to come to entertain a dull, sick old woman?"

"Oh, I am sure they would," cried Polly, "if you would like it, dear Mrs. Sterling."

"Like it!" Mrs. Sterling turned her thin face to the wall for a moment. When she looked again at Polly, there were tears trickling down the wasted cheeks. "Polly, you don't know," she said brokenly, "how I just long to hear young voices here in this dreary old house. To lie here day after day, child—"

"Oh!" cried Polly suddenly, "it must be so very dreadful, Mrs. Sterling."

"Well, don't let us speak of that," said Mrs. Sterling, breaking off quickly her train of thought, "for the worst isn't the pain and the weakness, Polly. It's the loneliness, child."

"Oh!" said Polly. Then it all rushed over her how she might have run in before, and taken the other girls if she had only known. "But we will come now, dear Mrs. Sterling," she said aloud.

"Do," cried Mrs. Sterling, and a faint color began to show itself on her thin face, "but not unless you are quite sure that the young people will like it, Polly."

"Yes, I am sure," said Polly, with a decided nod of her brown head.

"Then why couldn't you hold some of your rehearsals here?" proposed Mrs. Sterling.

"Shouldn't we tire you?" asked Polly.

"No, indeed!" declared Mrs. Sterling, with sudden energy. "I could bear a menagerie up here, Polly." And she laughed outright.

Gibbons, at this unwonted sound, popped her head in from the adjoining room where she was busy with her sewing, to gaze in astonishment at her mistress.

"I am not surprised at your face, Gibbons," said Mrs. Sterling cheerily, "for you have not heard me laugh for many a day."

"No, madam, I haven't," said Gibbons, " but I can't help saying I'm rejoiced to hear it now," with a glance of approval on Polly Pepper.

"So, Polly, you see there is no danger of your bringing me any fatigue, and I should be only too happy to see you at your next rehearsal."

"We can come, I am almost sure," said Polly, "those of us who want to rehearse at all. Some of us, you see, are quite sure of our pieces: Pickering Dodge is, for one; he spoke at his last school exhibition. But I'll tell the others. Oh, thank you for asking us, Mrs. Sterling."

"Thank you for giving your time, dear, to a dull old woman," said Mrs. Sterling. "Oh, must you go?" She clung to her hand. "I suppose you ought, child."

"Yes," said Polly, "I really ought to go, Mrs. Sterling. And you are not dull, one single bit, and I like you very much," she added as simply as Phronsie would have said it.

"Kiss me good-bye, Polly," said Mrs. Sterling. So Polly

laid her fresh young cheek against the poor, tired, wasted one, hopped into her jacket, and was off on happy feet.

And the others said yes when they saw Polly's enthusiasm over the plan of holding a rehearsal at Mrs. Sterling's. And Jasper proposed, "Why couldn't we repeat the whole thing after our grand performance, for her sometime?" And before any one could quite tell how, a warm sympathy had been set in motion for the rich, lonely old lady in the big, gloomy stone mansion most of them passed daily on their way to school.

Well, the grand affair was over now, and a greater success than was ever hoped for. Now came the enjoyment of presenting the money!

"Grandpapa," said Polly, "we are all here."

"So I perceive," looking out on the delegation in the hall. For of course all the two clubs couldn't go to the presentation, so committees were chosen to represent them—Polly, Clem, Alexia, and Silvia for the Salisbury Club, and Jasper, Clare, Pickering, and Richard Burnett for the boys' club, while old Mr. King on his own account had invited Joel, Percy and Van, and, of course, Tom Beresford.

"My! What shall we do with such a lot of boys?" exclaimed Alexia, as they all met in the hall.

"You don't have to do anything at all with us, Alexia," retorted Joel, who liked her the best of any of Polly's friends, and always showed it by sparring with her on every occasion, "only let us alone."

"Which I shall proceed to do with the greatest pleasure," said Alexia. "Goodness me! Joe, as if I'd be bothered with you tagging on. You're much worse than before you went away to school."

"Come, you two, stop your quarreling," said Jasper, laughing. "A pretty example you'd make to those poor Corcoran children."

"Oh, we shan't fight there," said Alexia sweetly. "We'll have quite enough to do to see all that is going on. Oh, Polly, when do you suppose we can ever start?"

"Father has the bankbook," announced Jasper. "I saw him put it in his pocket, Polly."

Polly gave a little wriggle under her coat. "Oh, Jasper, isn't it just too splendid for anything!" she cried.

"I'm going to walk with Polly," announced Clem, seizing Polly's arm, "so, Alexia Rhys, I give you fair warning this time."

"Indeed, you're not," declared Alexia stoutly. "Why, I always walk with Polly Pepper."

"And that's just the reason why I'm going to today," said Clem, hanging to Polly's arm for dear life.

"Well, I'm her dearest friend," added Alexia, taking refuge in that well-worn statement, "so there now, Clem Forsythe."

"No, you're not," said Clem obstinately. "We're all her dearest friends, aren't we, Polly? Say, Polly, aren't we?"

"Hush!" said Jasper. "Father's coming."

"Well, I can't help it. I'm tired of hearing Alexia Rhys everlastingly saying that, and pushing us all away from Polly."

"Do hear them go on!" exclaimed Tom Beresford, off on the edge of the group. "Does she always have them carrying around like that?"

"Yes," said Joel, "a great deal worse. Oh, they're a lot of giggling girls. I hate girls!" he exploded.

"So do I," nodded Tom. "Let's keep clear of the whole lot, and walk by ourselves."

"Indeed, we will," declared Joel. "You won't catch me walking with girls when I can help it."

"Well, I wonder which of those two will get your sister

Polly this time," said Tom, craning his long neck to see the contest.

"Oh, Alexia, of course," said Joel carelessly. "She always gets her in the end."

But Joel was wrong. Neither of the girls carried off Polly. Old Mr. King marched out of his reading room. "Come, Polly, my child, you and I will walk together," and he waited on her handsomely out, and down the walk to the car.

Tom and Joel burst into a loud laugh, in which the others joined, at the crestfallen faces.

"Well, at least you didn't get her, Clem," said Alexia airily, coming out of her discomfiture.

"Neither did you," said Clem happily.

"And you are horrid boys to laugh," said Alexia, looking over at the two. "But then, all boys are horrid."

"Thank you," said Tom, with his best bow.

"Alexia Rhys, aren't you perfectly ashamed to be fighting with that new boy?" cried Clem.

"Come on, Alexia," said Jasper. "I shall have to walk with you to keep you in order," and the gay procession hurrying after old Mr. King and Polly caught up with them turning out of the big stone gateway.

And then, what a merry walk they had to the car! And that being nearly full, they had to wait for the next one, which luckily had only three passengers, and Mr. King and his party clambered on, to ride down through the poor quarters of the town, to the Corcoran house.

"Oh, misery me!" exclaimed Alexia, looking out at the tumbledown tenements, and garbage heaps up to the very doors. "Where *are* we going?"

"Did you suppose Jim Corcoran lived in a palace?" asked Pickering lazily.

"Well, I didn't suppose anybody lived like that," said

Alexia, wrinkling up her nose in scorn. "Dear me, look at all those children!"

"Interesting, aren't they?" said Pickering, with a pang for the swarm of ragged, dirty little creatures, but not showing it in the least on his impassive face.

"Oh, I don't want to see it," exclaimed Alexia, "and I'm not going to either," turning her back on it all.

"It goes on just the same," said Pickering.

"Then I am going to look." Alexia whirled around again, and gazed up and down the ugly thoroughfare, taking it all in.

"Ugh, how can you!" exclaimed Silvia Horne, in disgust. "I think it's very disagreeable to even know that such people live."

"Perhaps 'twould be better to kill 'em off," said Tom Beresford bluntly.

"Ugh, you dreadful boy!" cried Clem Forsythe.

"Who's fighting now with the new boy?" asked Alexia sweetly, tearing off her gaze from the street.

"Well, who wouldn't?" retorted Clem. "He's saying such perfectly terrible things."

Pickering Dodge gave a short laugh. "Beresford, you're in for it now," he said.

Tom shrugged his shoulders, and turned his back on them.

"What did you bring him home for, Joe?" asked Alexia, leaning over to twitch Joel's arm.

"To plague you, Alexia," said Joel with a twinkle in his black eyes.

"Oh, he doesn't bother me," said Alexia serenely. "Clem is having all the trouble now. Well, we must put up with him, I suppose," she said with resignation.

"You don't need to," said Joel coolly. "You can let us alone, Alexia."

"But I don't want to let you alone," said Alexia. "That's all boys are good for, if they're in a party, to keep 'em stirred up. Goodness me, Mr. King and Polly are getting out!" as the car stopped, and Grandpapa led the way down the aisle.

When they arrived at the Corcoran house, which was achieved by dodging around groups of untidy women gossiping with their neighbors, and children playing on the dirty pavements, with the occasional detour caused by a heap of old tin cans, and other debris, Mr. King drew a long breath. "I don't know that I ought to have brought you young people down here. It didn't strike me so badly before."

"But it's no worse for us to see it than for the people to live here, father," said Jasper quickly.

"That's very true—but faugh!" And the old gentleman had great difficulty to contain himself. "Well, thank fortune, the Corcoran family are to move this week."

"Oh, Grandpapa," cried Polly, hopping up and down on the broken pavement, and "Oh, father!" from Jasper.

"Polly Pepper," exclaimed Alexia, twitching her away, "you came near stepping into that old mess of bones and things."

Polly didn't even glance at the garbage heap by the edge of the sidewalk, nor give it a thought. "Oh, how lovely, Alexia," she cried, "that they won't have but a day or two more here!"

"Well, we are going in," said Alexia, holding her tightly, "and I'm glad of it, Polly. Oh, misery me!" as they followed Mr. King into the poor little house that Jim the brakeman had called home.

The little widow, thanks to Mr. King and several others interested in the welfare of the brakeman's family, had smartened up considerably, so that neither she nor her dwelling presented such a dingy, woebegone aspect as on the previous visit. And old Mr. King, being very glad to see this, still further heartened her up by exclaiming, "Well, Mrs. Corcoran, you've accomplished wonders."

"I've tried to," cried the poor woman, "and I'm sure 'twas no more than I ought to do, and you being so kind to me and mine, sir."

"Well, I've brought some young people to see you," said the old gentleman abruptly, who never could bear to be thanked, and now felt much worse, as there were several spectators of his bounty. And he waved his hand toward the representatives of the two clubs.

They all huddled back, but he made them come forward. "No, it's your affair today. I only piloted you down here," laughing at their discomfiture.

Meanwhile the whole Corcoran brood had all gathered about the visitors, to rivet their gaze upon them, and wait patiently for further developments.

"Polly, you tell her," cried Alexia.

"Yes, Polly, do," cried the other girls.

"Yes, Polly," said Pickering. "You can tell it the best."

"Oh, I never could," said Polly in dismay. "Jasper, you, please."

"No, no, Polly," said Van. "She's the best."

"But Polly doesn't wish to," said Jasper in a low voice.

"All right, then, Jappy, go ahead," said Percy.

There was a little pause, Mrs. Corcoran filling it up by saying, "I can't ask you to sit down, for there isn't chairs enough," beginning to wipe off one with her apron. "Here, sir, if you'd please to sit," taking it over to Mr. King.

"Thank you," said the old gentleman, accepting it with his best air. "Now then, Jasper"—he had handed a small parcel to him under cover of the chair-wiping—"go ahead, my boy."

So Jasper, seeing that there was no help for it, but that he was really to be the spokesman, plunged in quite bravely.

"Mrs. Corcoran, some of us girls and boys—we belong to two clubs, you know"—waving his hand over to the representatives—"wanted to show your boys and girls that we were grateful to their father for being so good and kind to the passengers that night of the accident."

Here the little widow put the corner of her apron up to her eye, so Jasper hurried on: "And we wanted to help them to get an education. And so we had a little entertainment, and sold the tickets, and here is our gift!" Jasper ended desperately, thrusting the package out.

"Take it, Arethusa," was all Mrs. Corcoran could say, "and may the Lord bless you all!" Then she put the apron over her head and sobbed loud.

"Bless me!" exclaimed old Mr. King, fumbling for his handkerchief. "Don't, my good woman, I beg of you."

"And oh, I do hope you'll learn to play on the piano," breathed Polly, as Arethusa took the package from Jasper and slid back to lay it in her mother's hand.

"Oh me! I'm going to cry," exclaimed Alexia, backing off toward the door.

"If you do, I'll throw you out," said Joel savagely.

"Well, I shall. I feel so sniffly and queer. Oh, Joel, what shall I do? I shall be disgraced for life if I cry here."

"Hang on to me," said Joel stoutly, thrusting out his sturdy arm.

So Alexia hung on to it, and managed to get along very well. And one of the children, the littlest one next to the baby, created a diversion by bringing up a mangy cat, and laying it on Mr. King's knees. This saved the situation as far as crying went, and brought safely away those who were perilously near the brink of tears.

"Oh dear me!" exclaimed Polly, starting forward, knowing how Grandpapa detested cats. But Jasper was before her.

"Let me take it, father." And he dexterously brought it off.

"Give it to me," said Polly. "Oh, what is its name?"

The little thing who seemed to own the cat toddled over, well pleased, and stuck his finger in his mouth, which was the extent to which he could go in conversation. But the other children, finding the ice now broken, all came up at this point, to gather around Polly and the cat.

"It's lucky enough that Phronsie isn't here," said Jasper in a low voice, "for she would never want to leave that cat."

"Just see Polly Pepper!" exclaimed Alexia, with a grimace. "Why doesn't she drop that dirty old cat?"

"Because she ought not to," howled Joel sturdily. Then he rushed over to Polly, and although he had small love for cats in general, this particular one, being extremely ill-favored and lean, met with his favor. He stroked her poor back.

Arethusa drew near and gazed into Polly's face, seeing which, the cat was safely transferred to Joel, and Polly turned around to the girl.

"Oh, do you want to learn to play on the piano?" asked Polly, breathlessly, under cover of the noise going on, for all the other members of the two clubs now took a hand in it. Even Percy unbent enough to interview one of the Corcoran boys.

"Yes, I do," said Arethusa, clasping her small red hands tightly.

Her eyes widened, and her little thin face, which wasn't a bit pretty, lightened up now in a way that Polly thought was perfectly beautiful.

"Well, I did, when I was a little girl like you"—Polly bent her rosy face very close to Arethusa's—"oh, *dreadfully*, and I used to drum on the table to make believe I could play."

"So do I," cried Arethusa, creeping up close to Polly's neck, "an' th' boys laugh at me. But I keep doin' it."

"And now, Arethusa, you are really going to learn to play on the piano." Polly thrilled all over at the announcement, just as she had done when told that she was to take music lessons.

"Not a really and truly piano?" exclaimed Arethusa, lost in amazement.

"Yes, a really and truly piano," declared Polly positively. "Just think, Arethusa, you can give music lessons and help to take care of your mother."

And just then Grandpapa, who had been talking to Mrs. Corcoran, was saying, "Well, well, it's time to be going, young people." And Joel put the cat down, that immediately ran between his legs, tripping him up as he turned, thereby making everybody laugh, and so the exit was made merrily.

"Wasn't that fun!" cried Alexia, dancing off down the broken pavement. "Oh, I forgot, I'm going to walk home with Polly," and she flew back.

"You take yourself away," cried old Mr. King, with a laugh. "I'm to have Polly to myself on this expedition."

"Well, at any rate, Clem, you haven't Polly," announced Alexia as before, running up to her.

"Neither have you," retorted Clem, in the same way.

"So we will walk together," said Alexia, coolly possessing herself of Clem's arm. "Those two boys can walk with each other. They're just dying to."

"How do you know I want to walk with you?" asked Clem abruptly.

"Oh, but do, you sweet thing you! Come on!" and Alexia dragged her off at a smart pace.

"Grandpapa," cried Polly, hopping up and down by his side, too happy to keep still, while she clung to his hand just as Phronsie would have done, "you are going to have the piano put into the house the very first thing after it is cleaned and ready—the *very* first thing?" She peered around into his face anxiously.

"The *very* first thing," declared the old gentleman. "Take my word for it, Polly Pepper, there shan't another article get in before it."

"Oh, Grandpapa!" Polly wished she could go dancing off into the middle of the thoroughfare for a regular spin.

"Take care, Polly," laughed old Mr. King, successfully steering her clear of an ash barrel. "This isn't the best dancing place imaginable."

"Oh, I beg your pardon, Grandpapa," said Polly, trying to sober down, "I didn't mean to: But oh, isn't it perfectly beautiful that Arethusa is going to take music lessons!"

"It is, indeed," said Grandpapa, with a keen, glance down at her flushed face. "And it really does seem to be an assured fact, for Miss Brown is engaged to begin as soon as the family move into their new home."

"Oh—oh!" Polly could get no further.

Jasper, ahead with Pickering Dodge, looked back longingly.

"Oh, I do wish, Grandpapa," said Polly, "that Jasper could walk home with us."

"So do I, Polly," said the old gentleman, "but you see he can't, for then I should have the whole bunch of those chattering creatures around me," and he laughed grimly. "You must tell him all about what we are talking of, as soon as you get home."

"Yes, I will," declared Polly, "the very first thing. Now, Grandpapa, please go on."

"Well, I had told Mrs. Corcoran all about the new house, you know, Polly, before."

"Yes, I know, Grandpapa," said Polly, with a happy little wriggle.

"And so today I explained about the bankbook; told her where the money was deposited, and showed her how to use it. By the way, Polly, Jasper made a good speech now, didn't he?" The old gentleman broke off, and fairly glowed with pride.

"Oh, didn't he!" cried Polly, in a burst. "I thought it was too splendid for anything! And he didn't know in the least that he had to do it. He thought you were going to give the bankbook, Grandpapa."

"I know it," chuckled Mr. King. "Well now, Polly, I thought I'd try my boy without warning. Because, you see, that shows what stuff a person is made of to respond at such a time, and he's all right, Jasper is. He came up to the demand nicely."

"It was perfectly elegant!" cried Polly, with glowing cheeks.

"And those two boys—the largest ones—are to begin in the other public school next week," continued the old gentleman.

"Everything begins next week, doesn't it, Grandpapa?" cried Polly.

"It seems so," said Mr. King, with a laugh. "Well, Polly, here we are at our car."

And having the good luck to find it nearly empty, the whole party hopped on, and began the ride back again.

"Now," said Jasper, when they had reached home, "for some comfort," and he drew Polly off into a quiet corner in the library. "Let's have the whole, Polly. You said you'd tell me what you and father were talking of all the way home."

"And so I will," cried Polly, too elated to begin at the right end. "Well, Jasper, you must know that Arethusa's piano is actually engaged."

"It is!" exclaimed Jasper. "Hurrah!"

"Yes," said Polly, with shining eyes, "and it's going into the new home the *very* first thing. Grandpapa promised me that."

"Isn't father good!" cried Jasper, a whole world of affection in his dark eyes.

"Good?" repeated Polly. "He's as good as good can be, Jasper King!"

"Well, what else?" cried Jasper.

"And the boys—the two biggest ones—are going into the other public school, the one nearest their new home, you know."

"Yes, I see," said Jasper. "That's fine, That will bring them in with better boys."

"Yes, and Grandpapa told Mrs. Corcoran all about the money we made at the entertainment, and that he put it in the bank for her this morning. And he showed her how to use the checkbook."

"Polly," said Jasper, very much excited, "what if we girls and boys hadn't done this for those children! Just think, Polly, only suppose it!"

"I know it," cried Polly. "Oh, Jasper!" drawing a long breath. "But then, you see, we did do it."

"Yes," said Jasper, bursting into a laugh, "we surely did, Polly."

Chapter 21

At the Play

"*O*H, Cathie!" Polly rushed out to meet the girl that Johnson was just ushering in. "I *am* so glad you've come!"

A pleased look swept over the girl's face, but she didn't say anything.

"Now come right upstairs. Never mind the bag. Johnson will bring that for you."

"I will take it up, miss," said Johnson, securing it.

"Mamsie is waiting to see you," cried Polly, as they ran over the stairs, Cathie trying to still the excited beating of her heart at the thought that she was really to visit Polly Pepper for three whole days! "Oh, Mamsie, here she is!"

"I am glad to see you, Cathie," said Mrs. Fisher heartily, taking her cold hand. "Now, you are to have the room right next to Polly's."

"Yes, the same one that Alexia always has when she stays here," said Polly. "See, Cathie," bearing her off down the hall. "Oh, it is so good to get you here," she cried happily. "Well, here we are!"

"You can't think," began Cathie brokenly. Then she turned away to the window. "It's so good of you to ask me, Polly Pepper!"

"It's so good of you to come," said Polly merrily, and running over to her. "There, Johnson has brought your bag. Aren't you going to unpack it, Cathie?—That is, I mean" —with a little laugh—"after you've got your hat and jacket off. And then, when your things are all settled, we can go downstairs and do whatever you like. Perhaps we'll go in the greenhouse."

"Oh, Polly!" exclaimed Cathie, quite forgetting herself, and turning around.

"And can't I help you unpack?" asked Polly, longing to do something.

"No," said Cathie, remembering her plain clothes and lack of the pretty trifles that girls delight in. Then seeing Polly's face, she thought better of it. "Yes, you may," she said suddenly.

So Polly unstrapped the bag and drew out the clothes, all packed very neatly. "Why, Cathie Harrison!" she exclaimed suddenly.

"What?" asked Cathie, hanging up her jacket in the closet, and putting her head around the door.

"Oh, what a lovely thing!" Polly held up a little carved box of Chinese workmanship.

"Isn't it?" cried Cathie, well pleased that she had anything worthy of notice. "My uncle brought that from China to my mother when she was a little girl, and she gave it to me."

"Well, it's too lovely for anything," declared Polly, running to put it on the toilet table. "I do think Chinese carvings are so pretty!"

"Do you?" cried Cathie, well pleased. "My mother has some really fine ones I'll show you sometime, if you'd like to see them, Polly."

"Indeed, I should," said Polly warmly. So Cathie, delighted that she really had something that could interest Polly Pepper, hurried through her preparations. And then the two went downstairs arm in arm, and out to the greenhouse.

"Polly Pepper!" exclaimed Cathie on the threshold, "I don't think I should ever envy you living in that perfectly beautiful house, because it just scares me to set foot in it."

"Well, it needn't," said Polly, with a little laugh. "You must just forget all about its being big and splendid."

"But I can't," said Cathie, surprised at herself for being so communicative, "because, you see, I live in such a little, tucked-up place."

"Well, so did I," said Polly, with a bob of her brown head, "before we came here to Grandpapa's. But oh, you can't think how beautiful it was in the little brown house—you can't begin to think, Cathie Harrison!"

"I know," said Cathie, who had heard the story before. "I wish you'd tell it all to me now, Polly."

"I couldn't tell it all, if I talked a year, I guess," said Polly merrily. "And there is Turner waiting to speak to me. Come on, Cathie." And she ran down the long aisle between the fragrant blossoms.

But Cathie stopped to look and exclaim so often to herself that she made slow progress.

"Shall I make her up a bunch, Miss Mary?" asked old Turner, touching his cap respectfully, and looking at the visitor.

"Oh, if you please," cried Polly radiantly, "and do put some heliotrope in, for Cathie is so fond of that. And please let her have a bunch every morning when I have mine, Turner, for she is to stay three days."

"It shall be as you wish, Miss Mary," said Turner, quite delighted at the order.

"And please let it be very nice, Turner," said Polly hastily.

"I will, miss. Don't fear, Miss Mary, I'll have it as nice as possible," as Polly ran off to meet Cathie.

"I should stay here every single minute I was at home if I lived here, Polly Pepper," declared Cathie. "Oh, oh!" sniffing at each discovery of a new blossom.

"Oh, no, you wouldn't, Cathie," contradicted Polly, with a laugh. "Not if you had to get your lessons, and practice on the piano, and go out riding and driving, and play with the boys."

"Oh dear me!" cried Cathie, "I don't care very much for boys, because, you see, Polly, I never know what in this world to say to them."

"That's because you never had any brothers," said Polly, feeling how very dreadful such a state must be. "I can't imagine anything without Ben and Joel and Davie."

"And now you've such a lot of brothers, with Jasper and all those Whitney boys. Oh, Polly, don't they scare you to death sometimes?"

Polly burst into such a merry peal of laughter that they neither of them heard the rushing feet until Cathie glanced up. "Oh dear me! There they are now!"

"Well, to be sure! We might have known you were here, Polly," cried Jasper, dashing up with Clare. "How do you do, Cathie?" putting out his hand cordially.

Clare gave her a careless nod, then turned to Polly. "It's to be fine," he said.

"What?" asked Polly wonderingly.

"Hold on, old chap." Jasper gave him a clap on the back.

"Father is going to tell her himself. Come on, Polly and Cathie, to his room."

"Come, Cathie," cried Polly. "Let's beat those boys," she said, when once out of the greenhouse. "We're going to race," she cried over her shoulder.

"Is that so?" said Jasper. "Clare, we must beat them," and they dashed in pursuit.

But they couldn't. The two girls flew over the lawn, and reached the stone steps just a breathing space before Jasper and Clare plunged up.

"Well done," cried Jasper, tossing back the hair from his forehead.

"I didn't know you could run so well," observed Clare, with some show of interest in Cathie.

"Oh, she runs splendidly," said Polly, with sparkling eyes. "Let's try a race sometime, Jasper. We four, down the Long Path, while Cathie's here."

"Capital! We will," assented Jasper. "But now for father's room."

There sat old Mr. King by his writing table. "Well, Polly—how do you do, Cathie? I am glad to see you," he said, putting out his hand kindly.

As well as she could for her terror at being actually in that stately Mr. King's presence, Cathie stumbled forward and laid her hand in his.

"Now, Polly," said the old gentleman, turning off to pick up a little envelope lying on the table, "I thought perhaps you would like to take your young friend to the play tonight, so I have the tickets for us five," with a sweep of his hand over to the two boys.

"Grandpapa!" cried Polly, precipitating herself into his arms. "Oh, how good you are!" which pleased the old gentleman immensely.

"Isn't that no-end fine!" cried Jasper in delight. "Father, we can't thank you!"

"Say no more, my boy," cried the old gentleman. "I'm thanked enough. And so, Polly, my girl, you like it," patting her brown hair.

"Like it!" cried Polly, lifting her glowing cheeks. "Oh, Grandpapa!"

"Run along with you then, all of you. Clare, be over in time."

"Yes, sir," cried Clare. "Oh, thank you, Mr. King, ever so much!" as they all scampered off to get their lessons for the next day, for going to a play was always a special treat, on condition that no studies were neglected.

"Oh, Cathie," cried Polly, before she flew into the window seat to curl up with her books, her favorite place for studying her lessons, "Grandpapa is taking us to the play because you are here."

"And I've never been to a play, Polly," said Cathie, perfectly overwhelmed with it all.

"Haven't you? Oh, I'm so glad—I mean, I'm glad you're going with us, and that Grandpapa is to take you to the first one. But, oh me!" and Polly rushed off to attack her books. "Now, don't let us speak a single word, Cathie Harrison," as Cathie picked out a low rocker for her choice of a seat. And pretty soon, if Miss Salisbury herself had come into the room, she would have been perfectly satisfied with the diligent attention the books were receiving.

But Miss Salisbury was not thinking of her pupils this afternoon. She was at this moment closeted with Miss Anstice, and going over a conversation that they frequently held, these past days, without much variation in the subject or treatment.

"If there were anything we could do to repay him, sister,"

said Miss Anstice mournfully, "I'd do it, and spend my last cent. But what is there?" Then she paced the floor with her mincing little steps now quite nervous and flurried.

"Sister," said Miss Salisbury, doing her best to be quite calm, "it isn't a matter of payment, for whatever we did, we never could hope to replace that exquisite little vase. Miss Clemcy had pointed out to me the fact that it was quite the gem in his collection."

"I know. I thought my heart would stop when I heard the crash." Miss Anstice wrung her little hands together at the memory. "Oh, that careless Lily!"

"Sister, pray let us look at this matter—"

"I am looking at it. I see nothing but that vase, smashed to pieces, and I cannot sleep at night for fear I'll dream how it looked in those very little bits."

"Sister—pray—pray—"

"And if you want me to tell you what I think should be done, I'm sure I can't say," added Miss Anstice helplessly.

"Well, then, I must think," declared Miss Salisbury, with sudden energy, "for some repayment must surely be made to him, although they utterly refused it when you and I called and broached the subject to them."

"It was certainly a most unfortunate day from beginning to end," said Miss Anstice, with a suggestion of tears in her voice, and a shiver at the remembrance of the front breadth of her gown. "Sister, I hope and pray that you will never have another picnic for the school."

"I cannot abolish that annual custom, Anstice," said Miss Salisbury firmly, "for the girls get so much enjoyment out of it. They are already talking about the one to come next year."

"Ugh!" shuddered Miss Anstice.

"And anything that holds an influence over them, I must

sustain. You know that yourself, sister. And it is most important to give them some recreations."

"But *picnics!*" Miss Anstice held up her little hands, as if quite unequal to any words.

"And I am very sorry that we were out when Mr. Clemcy and his sister called yesterday afternoon, for I am quite sure I could have arranged matters so that we need not feel under obligations to them."

Miss Anstice, having nothing to say, kept her private reflections mournfully to herself, and it being the hour for the boarding pupils to go out to walk, and her duty to accompany them, the conference broke up.

"Polly," called Mrs. Chatterton, as Polly ran past her door, her opera glasses Grandpapa had given her last Christmas in the little plush bag dangling from her arm, and a happy light in her eyes. Cathie had gone downstairs, and it was getting nearly time to set forth for that enchanted land—the playhouse!

Polly ran on, scarcely conscious that she was called. "Did you not hear me?" asked Mrs. Chatterton angrily, coming to her door.

"Oh, I beg pardon," said Polly, really glad ever since that dreadful time when Mrs. Chatterton was ill, to do anything for her. "For I never shall forget how naughty I was to her," Polly said over to herself now as she turned back.

"You may well beg my pardon," said Mrs. Chatterton, "for of all ill-bred girls, you are certainly the worst. I want you." Then she disappeared within her room.

"What is it?" asked Polly, coming in. "I shall be so glad to help."

"Help!" repeated Mrs. Chatterton in scorn. She was standing over by her toilet table. "You can serve me. Come here."

The hot blood mounted to Polly's brow. Then she thought, "Oh, what did I say? That I would do anything for Mrs. Chatterton if she would only forgive me for those dreadful words I said to her." And she went over and stood by the toilet table.

"Oh, you have concluded to come?" observed Mrs. Chatterton scornfully. "So much the better it would be if you could always learn what your place is in this house. There, you see this lace?" She shook out her flowing sleeve, glad to display her still finely molded arm, that had been one of her chief claims to distinction, even if nobody but this little country-bred girl saw it.

Polly looked at the dangling lace, evidently just torn, with dismay, seeing which, Mrs. Chatterton broke out sharply, "Get the basket, girl, over there on the table, and sew it as well as you can."

"Polly!" called Jasper over the stairs, "where are you?"

Polly trembled all over as she hurried across the room to get the sewing basket. Grandpapa was not ready, she knew, but she always ran down a little ahead for the fun of the last moments waiting with Jasper, when old Mr. King was going to take them out of an evening. And in the turmoil in her mind, she didn't observe that Hortense had misplaced the basket, putting it on the low bookcase, and was still searching all over the table as directed, when Mrs. Chatterton's sharp voice filled her with greater dismay.

"*Stupid!* If you would put heart into your search, it would be easy enough to find it."

"*Polly,* where *are* you!" Polly, in her haste not to displease Mrs. Chatterton by replying to Jasper before finding the basket, knocked over one of the small silver-topped bottles with which the dressing table seemed to be full, and before she could rescue it, it fell to the floor.

"Go out of this room," commanded Mrs. Chatterton, with blazing eyes. "I ought to have known better than to call upon a heavy-handed, low-born country girl, to do a delicate service."

"I didn't mean—" began poor Polly.

"Go out of this room!" Mrs. Chatterton, now thoroughly out of temper, so far forgot herself as to stamp her foot, and Polly, feeling as if she had lost all chance in her future encounters with Mrs. Chatterton, of atoning for past short-comings, went sadly out, to meet, just beside the door, Jasper, with amazement on his face.

"Oh, Polly, I thought you were never coming." Then he saw her face.

"That old—" he said under his breath. "Polly, don't ever go into her room again. I wouldn't," as they hurried off downstairs.

"She won't let me," said Polly, her head drooping, and the brightness all gone from her face. "She won't ever let me go again, I know."

"Won't let you? Well, I guess you'll not give her a chance," cried Jasper hotly. "Polly, I do really wish that father would tell her to go away."

"Oh, Jasper," cried Polly, in alarm, "don't say one word to Grandpapa. Promise me you won't, Jasper."

"Well, father is tired of her. She wears on him terribly, Polly," said Jasper gloomily.

"I know," said Polly sadly. "And oh, Jasper, if you say one word, he will really have her go. And I was so bad to her, you know," and the tears came into Polly's brown eyes.

"Well, she must have been perfectly terrible to you," said Jasper.

"Polly—Jasper—where are you?" came in old Mr. King's voice.

"Here, father," and "Here, Grandpapa," and Clare running up the steps, the little party was soon in the carriage.

"Promise me, Jasper, do," implored Polly, when Grandpapa was explaining to Cathie about the great actor they were to see, and Clare was listening to hear all about it, too.

"Oh, I won't," promised Jasper, "if you don't wish me to."

"I really wouldn't have you for all the world," declared Polly, and now that this fear was off from her mind, she began to pick up her old, bright spirits, so that by the time the carriage stopped at the theater, Polly was herself again.

Jasper watched her keenly and drew a long breath when he saw her talking and laughing with Grandpapa.

"You are going to sit next to me, Polly," said the old gentleman, marshaling his forces when well within. "And Jasper next. Then, Cathie, you will have a knight on either side."

"Oh, I can't sit between two boys," cried Cathie, forgetting herself in her terror.

"I won't bite you," cried Clare saucily.

"I will see that Clare behaves himself," said Jasper.

"You'll do nicely, my dear," said Mr. King encouragingly to her, then proceeded down the aisle after the usher. So there was nothing to do but to obey. And Cathie, who would have found it a formidable thing to be stranded on the companionship of one boy, found herself between two, and Polly Pepper far off, and not the least able to help.

"Now, then," said Jasper, taking up the program, "I suppose father told you pretty much all that was necessary to know about Irving. Well—" And then, without waiting for a reply, Jasper dashed on about the splendid plays in which he had seen this wonderful actor, and the particular one they

were to enjoy tonight, and from that he drifted off to the
fine points to be admired in the big playhouse, with its
striking decorations, making Cathie raise her eyes to take it
all in, until Clare leaned over to say:

"I should think you might give Cathie and me a chance to
talk a little, Jasper."

"Oh, I don't want to talk," cried Cathie in terror. "I
don't know anything to say."

"Well, I do," said Clare, in a dudgeon. "Only Jasper goes
on in such a streak tonight."

"I believe I have been talking you both blue," said Jasper,
with a laugh.

"You certainly have," said Clare, laughing too.

And then Cathie laughed, and Polly Pepper, looking over,
beamed at her, for she had begun to be worried.

"The best thing in the world," said old Mr. King, "was to
turn her over to those two boys. Now, don't give her another
thought, Polly. She'll get on."

And she did. So well that before long she and Clare were
chatting away merrily, and Cathie felt it was by no means
such a very terrible experience to be sitting between two
boys at a play. And by the time the evening was half over
she was sure that she liked it very much.

And Polly beamed at her more than ever, and Jasper felt
quite sure that he had never enjoyed an evening more than
the one at present flying by so fast. And old Mr. King, so
handsome and stately, showed such evident pride in his
young charges, as he smiled and chatted, that more than one
old friend in the audience commented on it.

"Did you ever see such a change in anyone?" asked a
dowager, leveling her keen glances from her box down upon
the merry party.

"Never. It was the one thing needed to make him quite

perfect," said another one of that set. "He is approachable now—absolutely fascinating. So genial and courteous."

"His manners were perfect before," said a third member of the box party, "except they needed thawing out—a bit too icy."

"You are too mild. I should say they were quite frozen. He never seemed to me to have any heart."

"Well, it's proved he has," observed her husband. "I tell you that little Pepper girl is going to make a sensation when she comes out," leaning over for a better view of the King party, "and the best of it is that she doesn't know it herself."

And Clare made up his mind that Cathie Harrison was an awfully nice girl, and he was real glad she had moved to town and joined the Salisbury School. And as he had two cousins there, they soon waked up a conversation over them.

"Only I don't know them much," said Cathie. "You see I haven't been at the school long, and besides, the girls didn't have much to say to me till Polly Pepper said nice things to me, and then she asked me to go to the bee."

"That old sewing thing where they make clothes for the poor little darkies down south?" asked Clare.

"Yes, and it's just lovely," said Cathie, "and I never supposed I'd be asked. And Polly Pepper came down to my desk one day and invited me to come to the next meeting, and I was so scared, I couldn't say anything at first. And then Polly got me into the Salisbury Club."

"Oh, yes, I know." Clare nodded, and wished he could forget how he had asked one of the other boys on that evening when the two clubs united, why in the world the Salisbury Club elected Cathie Harrison into its membership.

"And then Polly Pepper's mother invited me to visit her— Polly, I mean—and so here I am"—she forgot she was talking to a dreaded boy, and turned her happy face toward him—"and it's just lovely. I never visited a girl before."

"Never visited a girl before!" repeated Clare, in astonishment.

"No," said Cathie. "You see, my father was a minister, and we lived in the country, and when I visited anybody, which was only two or three times in my life, it was to papa's old aunts."

"Oh dear me!" exclaimed Clare faintly, quite gone in pity.

"And so your father moved to town," he said, and then he knew that he had made a terrible mistake.

"Now she won't speak a word—perhaps burst out crying," he groaned within himself, as he saw her face. But Cathie sat quite still.

"My papa died," she said softly, "and he told mamma before he went, to take me to town and have me educated. And one of those old aunts gave the money. And if it hadn't been for him, I'd have run home from the Salisbury School that first week, it was so perfectly awful."

Clare sat quite still. Then he burst out, "Well, now, Cathie, I think it was just splendid in you to stick on."

"Do you?" she cried, quite astonished to think any one would think she was "just splendid" in anything. "Why, the girls call me a goose over and over. And sometimes I lose my temper, because they don't say it in fun, but they really mean it."

"Well, they needn't," said Clare indignantly, "because I don't think you are a goose at all."

"Those two are getting on quite well," said Jasper to Polly. "I don't think we need to worry about Cathie any more."

"And isn't she nice?" asked Polly, in great delight.

"Yes, I think she is, Polly," said Jasper, in a way that gave Polly great satisfaction.

But when this delightful evening was all over, and the good-nights had been said, and Mother Fisher, as was her wont, had come into Polly's room to help her take off her things, and to say a few words to Cathie too, Polly began to remember the scene in Mrs. Chatterton's room, and a sorry little feeling crept into her heart.

And when Mamsie had gone out and everything was quiet, Polly buried her face in her pillow, and tried not to cry. "I don't believe she will ever forgive me, or let me help her again."

"Polly," called Cathie softly from the next room, " I did have the most beautiful time!"

"Did you?" cried Polly, choking back her sobs. "Oh, I am so glad, Cathie!"

"Yes," said Cathie, "I did, Polly, and I'm not afraid of boys now. I think they are real nice."

"Aren't they!" cried Polly. "And weren't our seats fine! Grandpapa didn't want a box tonight, because we could see the play so much better from the floor. But we ought to go to sleep, Cathie, for Mamsie wouldn't like us to talk. Good night."

"Good night," said Cathie. "A box!"she said to herself, as she turned on her pillow. "Oh, I should have died to have sat up in one of those. It was quite magnificent enough where I was."

Chapter 22

Pickering Dodge

"*J*ASPER!"

Jasper, rushing down the long hall of the Pemberton School, books in hand, turned to see Mr. Faber standing in the doorway of his private room.

"I want to see you, Jasper."

Jasper, with an awful feeling at his heart, obeyed and went in. "It's all up with Pick," he groaned, and sat down in the place indicated on the other side of the big round table, Mr. Faber in his accustomed seat, the big leather chair.

"You remember the conversation I had with you, Jasper," he said slowly. And picking up a paper knife he began playing with it, occasionally glancing up over his glasses at the boy.

Jasper nodded, unable to find any voice. Then he managed to say, "Yes, sir."

"Well, now, Jasper, it was rather an unusual thing to do, to set one lad, as it were, to work upon another in just that way. For I am sure I haven't forgotten my boyhood, long past as it is, and I realize that the responsibilities of school life are heavy enough, without adding to the burden."

Mr. Faber, well pleased with this sentiment, waited to clear his throat. Jasper, in an agony, as he saw Pickering Dodge expelled, and all the dreadful consequences, sat quite still.

"At the same time, although I disliked to take you into confidence, making you an assistant in the work of reclaiming Pickering Dodge from his idle, aimless state, in which he exhibited such a total disregard for his lessons, it appeared after due consideration to be the only thing left to be done. You understand this, I trust, Jasper."

Jasper's reply this time was so low as to be scarcely audible. But Mr. Faber, taking it for granted, manipulated the paper knife a few times, and went on impressively.

"I am very glad you do, Jasper. I felt sure, knowing you so well, that my reasons would appeal to you in the right way. You are Pickering's best friend among my scholars."

"And he is mine," exploded Jasper, thinking wildly that it was perhaps not quite too late to save Pickering. "I've known him always, sir." He was quite to the edge of his chair now, his dark eyes shining, and his hair tossed back. "Beg pardon, Mr. Faber, but I can't help it. Pickering is so fine: he's not like other boys."

"No, I believe you." Mr. Faber smiled grimly and gave the paper knife another whirl. And much as Jasper liked him, that smile seemed wholly unnecessary, and to deal death to his hopes.

"He certainly is unlike any other boy in my school in regard to his studying," he said. "His capacity is not wanting, to be sure; there was never any lack of that. For that reason I was always hoping to arouse his ambition."

"And you can—oh, you can, sir!" cried Jasper eagerly, although he felt every word he said to be unwelcome, "if you will only try him a bit longer. Don't send him off yet, Mr. Faber."

He got off from his chair, and leaned on the table heavily.

"Don't send him off?" repeated Mr. Faber, dropping the paper knife, "what is the boy talking of! Why, Jasper—I've called you in here to tell you how much Pickering has improved and—"

Jasper collapsed on his chair.

"And is it possible that you haven't seen it for yourself, Jasper?" exclaimed Mr. Faber. "Why, every teacher is quite delighted. Even Mr. Dinsmore— and he was in favor of at least suspending Pickering last half—has expressed his opinion that I did well to give the boy another trial."

"I thought—" mumbled Jasper, "I was afraid." Then he pulled himself together, and somehow found himself standing over by Mr. Faber's chair, unbosoming himself of his fright and corresponding joy.

"Pull your chair up nearer, Jasper," said Mr. Faber, when, the first transport having worked off, Jasper seemed better fitted for conversation, "and we will go over this in a more intelligent fashion. I am really more pleased than I can express at the improvement in that boy. As I said before"—Mr. Faber had long ago thrown aside the paper knife, and now turned toward Jasper, his whole attention on the matter in hand—"Pickering has a fine capacity. Take it all in all, perhaps there is none better in the whole school. It shows to great advantage now, because he has regained his place so rapidly in his classes. It is quite astonishing, Jasper." And he took off his glasses and polished them up carefully, repeating several times during the process, "Yes, very surprising indeed!"

"And he seems to like to study now," said Jasper, ready to bring forward all the nice things that warranted encouragement.

"Does he so?" Mr. Faber set his glasses on and beamed at him over them. The boys at the Pemberton School always protested that this was the only use they could be put to on the master's countenance. "Well, now, Jasper, I really believe I am justified in entertaining a very strong hope of Pickering's future career. And I see no reason why he should not be ready for college with you, and without conditions, if he will only keep his ambition alive and active, now it is aroused."

"May I tell him so?" cried Jasper, almost beside himself with joy. "Oh, may I, Mr. Faber?"

"Why, that is what I called you in here for, Jasper," said the master. "It seemed so very much better for him to hear it from a boy, for I remember my own boyhood, though so very long since. And the effect will, I feel sure, be much deeper than if Pickering hears it from me. He is very tired of this study, Jasper," and Mr. Faber glanced around at the four walls, and again came that grim smile. "And even to hear a word of commendation, it might not be so pleasing to be called in. So away with you. At the proper time, I shall speak to him myself."

Jasper, needing no second bidding, fled precipitately—dashed in again. "Beg pardon, I'd forgotten my books." He seized them from the table, and made quick time tracking Pickering.

"Where is Pick?" rushing up to a knot of boys on a corner of the playground, just separating to go home.

"Don't know. What's up, King?"

"Can't stop," said Jasper, flying back to the schoolroom. "I must get Pick."

"Dodge has gone," shouted a boy clearing the steps, who had heard the last words. So Jasper, turning again, left school and playground far behind, to run up the steps of the Cabot mansion.

"Pickering here?"

"Yes." The butler had seen him hurrying over the stairs to his own room just five minutes ago. And in less than a minute Jasper was up in that same place.

There sat Pickering by his table, his long legs upon its surface, and his hands thrust into his pockets. His books sprawled just where he had thrown them, at different angles along the floor.

"Hullo!" cried Jasper, flying in, to stop aghast at this.

"Yes, you see, Jasper, I'm played out," said Pickering. "It isn't any use for me to study, and there are the plaguey things," pulling out one set of fingers to point to the sprawling books. "I can't catch up. Every teacher looks at me squint-eyed as if I were a hopeless case, which I am!"

"Oh, you big dunce!" Jasper clapped his books on the table with a bang, making Pickering draw down his long legs, rushed around to precipitate himself on the rest of the figure in the chair, when he pummeled him to his heart's content.

"If you expect to beat any hope into me, old boy," cried Pickering, not caring in the least for the onslaught, "you'll miss your guess."

"I'm hoping to beat sense into you," cried Jasper, pounding away, "though it looks almost impossible now," he declared, laughing. "Pick, you've won! Mr. Faber says you've come up in classes splendidly, and—"

Pickering sprang to his feet. "What do you mean, Jasper?" he cried hoarsely, his face white as a sheet.

"Just what I say."

"Say it again."

So Jasper went all over it once more, adding the other

things about getting into college and all that, as much as Pickering would hear.

"Honest?" he broke in, his pale face getting a dull red, and seizing Jasper by the shoulders.

"Did I ever tell you anything that wasn't so, Pick?"

"No, but I can't believe it, Jap. It's the first time in my life I've—I've—" And what incessant blame could not do, praise achieved. Pickering rushed to the bed, flung himself face-down upon it, and broke into a torrent of sobs.

Jasper, who had never seen Pickering cry, had wild thoughts of rushing for Mrs. Cabot; the uncle was not at home. But remembering how little good this could possibly do, he bent all his energies to stop this unlooked-for flood.

But he was helpless. Having never given way in this manner before, Pickering seemed determined to make a thorough job of it. And it was not till he was quite exhausted that he rolled over, wiped his eyes and looked at Jasper.

"I'm through," he announced.

"I should think you might well be," retorted Jasper. "What with scaring me almost to death, you've made yourself a fright, Pick, and you've just upset all your chances to study today."

Pickering flung himself off the bed as summarily as he had gone on.

"That's likely, isn't it?" he cried mockingly, and shame-facedly scrabbling up the books from the floor. "Now, then," and he was across the room, pouring out a basinful of water, to thrust his swollen face within it.

"Whew! I never knew it used a chap up so to cry," he spluttered. "Goodness me!" He withdrew his countenance from the towel to regard Jasper.

"How you look!" cried Jasper, considering it better to rail at him.

Whereupon Pickering found his way to the long mirror. "I never was a beauty," he said.

"And now you are less," laughed Jasper.

"But I'm good," said Pickering solemnly, and flinging himself down to his books.

"You can't study with such eyes," cried Jasper, tugging at the book.

"Clear out!"

"I'm not going. Pick, your eyes aren't much bigger than pins."

"But they're sharp—just as pins are. Leave me alone." Pickering squirmed all over his chair, but Jasper had the book.

"Never mind, I'll fly at my history, then," said Pickering, possessing himself of another book. "That's the beauty of it. I'm as backward in all of my lessons as I am in one. I can strike in anywhere."

"You are not backward in any now," cried Jasper in glee, and performing an Indian war dance around the table. "Forward is the word henceforth," he brought up dramatically with another lunge at Pickering.

"Get out. You better go home."

"I haven't the smallest intention of going," replied Jasper, and successfully coming off with a second book.

"Here's for book number three," declared Pickering—but too late. Jasper seized the remaining two, tossed them back of him, then squared off.

"Come on for a tussle, old fellow. You're not fit to study—ruin your eyes. Come on!" his whole face sparkling.

It was too much. The table was pushed to one side. Books and lessons, Mr. Faber and college, were as things never heard of. And for a good quarter of an hour, Pickering, whose hours of exercise had been much scantier of late, was hard pushed to parry all Jasper's attacks. At the last, when the little clock on the mantel struck four, he came out ahead.

"I declare, that was a good one," he exclaimed in a glow.

"Particularly so to you," said Jasper ruefully. "You gave me a regular bear hug, you scamp."

"Had to, to pay you up."

"And now you may study," cried Jasper gaily, and snatching his books, he ran off.

"Oh, Pick," putting his head in at the door.

"Yes?"

"If the lessons are done, come over this evening, will you?"

"All right." The last sound of Jasper's feet on the stairs reached Pickering, when he suddenly left his chair and flew into the hall.

"Jap—oh, I say, Jap!" Then he glunged back into his room to thrust his head out of the window. "Jap!" he howled, to the consternation of a fat old gentleman passing beneath, who on account of his size, finding it somewhat inconvenient to look up, therefore waddled into the street, and surveyed the house gravely.

Pickering slammed down the window, leaving the old gentleman to stare as long as he saw fit.

"I can't go over there tonight, looking like this." He pranced up to the mirror again, fuming every step of the way, and surveyed himself in dismay. There was some improvement in the appearance of his countenance, to be sure, but not by any means enough to please him. His pale blue eyes were so small, and their surroundings so swollen, that they reminded him of nothing so much as those of a small pig he had made acquaintance with in a visit up in the country. While his nose, long and usually quite aristocratic-looking, had resigned all claims to distinction, and was hopelessly pudgy.

"Jasper knows I can't go in this shape," he cried in a fury. "Great Caesar's ghost! I never supposed it banged a fellow up so, to cry just once!" And the next moments were spent in sopping his face violently with the wet towel, which did no good, as it had been plentifully supplied with that treatment before.

At last he flung himself into his chair. "If I don't go over, Jap will think I haven't my lessons, so that's all right. And I won't have them anyway if I don't tackle them pretty quick. So here goes!" And presently the only sound to be heard was the ticking of the little clock, varied by the turning of his pages, or the rattling of the paper on which he was working out the problems for tomorrow.

"Oh dear me! Jasper," Polly exclaimed about half-past seven, "I don't believe Pickering is coming."

"He hasn't his lessons, I suppose," said Jasper. "You know I told him to come over as soon as they were done. Well, Polly, we agreed, you know, to let him alone as to invitations until the lessons were out of the way, so I won't go over after him."

"I know," said Polly, "but oh, Jasper, isn't it just too elegant for anything, to think that Mr. Faber says it's all right with him?"

"I should think it was," cried Jasper. "Now if he only keeps on, Polly."

"Oh, he must. He will," declared Polly confidently. "Well, we can put off toasting marshmallows until tomorrow night."

About this time, Pickering, whose lessons were all done, for he had, as Mr. Faber had said, "a fine capacity" to learn, was receiving company just when he thought he was safe from showing his face.

"Let's stop for Pickering Dodge," proposed Alexia, Clare having run in for her to go over to Polly Pepper's, "to toast marshmallows and have fun generally."

"All right. So we can," cried Clare. So they turned the corner and went down to the Cabot mansion, and were let in before the old butler could be stopped.

Pickering, whose uncle and aunt were out for the evening, had felt it safe to throw himself down on the library sofa. When he saw that John had forgotten what he told him, not to let anybody in, he sprang up, but not before Alexia, rushing in, had cried, "Oh, here you are! Come on with us to Polly Pepper's!" Clare dashed in after her.

"Ow!" exclaimed Pickering, seizing a sofa pillow, to jam it against his face.

"What is the matter?" cried Alexia. "Oh, have you a toothache?"

"Worse than that," groaned Pickering behind his pillow.

"Oh, my goodness me!" exclaimed Alexia, tumbling back. "What can it be?"

"You haven't broken your jaw, Pick?" observed Clare. "I can't imagine that."

"I'll break yours if you don't go," said Pickering savagely, and half smothered, as he tried to keep the pillow well before the two pairs of eyes.

This was a little difficult, as Clare, seeing hopes of running around the pillow, set himself in motion to that end. But as Pickering whirled as fast as he did, there was no great gain.

"Well, if I ever did!" exclaimed Alexia, quite aghast.

And the next moment Pickering, keeping a little opening at one end of the pillow, saw his chance, darted out of the door, and flinging the pillow the length of the hall, raced into his own room and slammed the door, and they could hear him lock it.

"Well, if I ever did!" exclaimed Alexia again, and sinking into the first chair, she raised both hands.

"What's got into the beggar?" cried Clare in perplexity, and looking out into the hall, as if some help to the puzzle might be found there.

"Well, I guess you and I, Alexia, might as well go to Polly Pepper's," he said finally.

"And if I ever come after that boy again to tell him of anything nice that's going to happen, I miss my guess," declared Alexia, getting herself out of her chair, in high dudgeon. "Let's send Jasper after him. He's the only one who can manage him," she cried, as they set forth.

"Good idea," said Clare.

But when Alexia told of their funny reception, Jasper first stared, then burst out laughing. And although Alexia teased and teased, she got no satisfaction.

"It's no use, Alexia," Jasper said, wiping his eyes, "you won't get me to tell. So let's set about having some fun. What shall we do?"

"I don't want to do anything," pouted Alexia, "only to know what made Pickering Dodge act in that funny way."

"And that's just what you won't know, Alexia," replied Jasper composedly. "Well, Polly, you are going to put off toasting the marshmallows, aren't you, till tomorrow night, when Pick can probably come?"

"Oh, I wouldn't wait for him," Alexia burst out, quite exasperated, "when he's acted so. And perhaps he'd come with an old sofa pillow before his face, if you did."

"Oh, no, he won't, Alexia," said Jasper, going off into another laugh. But although she teased again, she got no nearer to the facts. And Polly proposing that they make candy, the chafing dish was gotten out, and Alexia, who was quite an adept in the art, went to work, Jasper cracking the nuts, and Polly and Clare picking out the meats.

And then all the story of Pickering's splendid advance in the tough work of making up his lessons came out, Jasper pausing so long to dilate with kindling eyes upon it, that very few nuts fell into the dish. So Polly's fingers were the only ones to achieve much, as Clare gave so close attention to the story that he was a very poor helper.

In the midst of it, Alexia threw down the chafing-dish spoon, and clapped her hands. "Oh, I know!" she exclaimed.

"Oh," cried Polly, looking up from the little pile of nutmeats, "how you scared me, Alexia!"

"I know—I know!" exclaimed Alexia again, and nodding to herself wisely.

Jasper threw her a quick glance. It said, "If you know, don't tell, Alexia." And she flashed back, "Did you suppose I would?"

"What do you know?" demanded Clare, transferring his attention from Jasper to her. "Tell on, Alexia; what do you know?"

"Oh, my goodness me! This candy never will be done in time for those meats," cried Alexia, picking up the spoon to stir away for dear life. And Jasper dashed in on what Mr. Faber said about Pickering's chances for college, a statement that completely carried Clare off his feet, so to speak.

"You don't mean that he thinks Pick will get in without conditions?" gasped Clare, dumfounded.

"Yes, I do." Jasper nodded brightly. "If Pick will only study. Keep it up, you know, I mean to the end. He surely said it, Clare."

It was so much for Clare to think of, that he didn't have any words at his command.

"Now isn't that perfectly splendid in Pickering!" cried Alexia, making the spoon fly merrily. "Oh dear me! I forgot to put in the butter. Where—oh, here it is," and she tossed in a big piece. "To think that—oh dear me, I forgot! I *did* put the butter in before. Now I've spoilt it," and she threw down the spoon in despair.

"Fish it out," cried Polly, hopping up and seizing the spoon to make little dabs at the ball of butter now rapidly lessening.

"But it's melted—that is, almost—oh dear me!" cried Alexia.

"No, it isn't. There, see how big it is." Polly landed it deftly on the plate and hopped back to her nutmeats again.

"And I should think you'd better shake yourself, Clare," said Jasper, over at him. "We shouldn't have any nuts in this candy if it depended on you."

"You do tell such astounding stories," cried Clare, setting to work at once. And Jasper making as much noise as he could while cracking his nuts, Alexia's secret was safe.

But when the candy was set out to cool, and there was a pause in which the two boys were occupied by themselves, Alexia pulled Polly off to a corner.

"Where are they going?" asked Clare, with one eye after them.

"Oh, they have something to talk over, I presume," said Jasper carelessly.

"Nonsense! They've all the time every day. Let's go over and see."

"Oh, no," said Jasper. "Come on, Clare, and let's see if the candy is cool." But Clare didn't want to see if the candy was cool, nor anything else but to have his own way. So he proceeded over to the corner by himself.

"Oho! You go right away!" cried Alexia, poking up her

head over Polly's shoulder. "You dreadful boy! Now, Polly, come." And she pulled her off into the library.

"You see, you didn't get anything for your pains," said Jasper, bursting into a laugh. "You'd much better have stayed here."

"Well, I don't want to know, anyway," said Clare, taking a sudden interest in the candy. "I believe it is cold, Jasper. Let's look."

"Polly," Alexia was saying in the library behind the portieres, "I know now; because I did it once myself: it was when you first promised you'd be a friend to me, and I went home and cried for very joy. And I didn't want to see anybody that night."

"Oh, Alexia!" exclaimed Polly, giving her a hug that satisfied even Alexia.

"No, I didn't. And I remember how I wanted to hold something up to my face. I never thought of a sofa pillow, and I couldn't have gotten it if I had thought, 'cause aunt had it crammed against her back. Oh, my eyes were a sight, Polly, and my nose was all over my face."

Chapter 23

The Clemcy Garden Party

"**Y**OU may go on those errands, Hortense, but first send Polly Pepper to me," commanded Mrs. Chatterton sharply.

The French maid paused in the act of hanging up a gown. "I will *re*-quest her, Madame. I should not like to send Mees Polly Peppaire."

"*Miss* Polly Pepper!" Mrs. Chatterton was guilty of stamping her foot. "Are you mad? I am speaking of Polly Pepper, this country girl, who is as poor and low-born here in this house, as if in her little brown house, wherever that may be."

Hortense shrugged her shoulders and hung up the gown.

"Has Madame any further commands for me?" she asked, coming up to her mistress.

"Yes. Be sure to get the velvet at Lemaire's, and take back the silk kimono. I will send to New York for one."

"Yes, Madame."

"That is all—besides the other errands. Now go." She dismissed her with a wave of her shapely hand. "But first, as I bade you, *send* Polly Pepper to me."

Hortense, with another elevation of her shoulders, said nothing, till she found herself the other side of the door. Then she shook her fist at it.

"It ees not Miss Polly who will be sent for; it ees Madame who will be sent out of dees house, *j'ai peur*—ha, ha, ha!"

She laughed softly to herself all the way downstairs, with an insolent little fling to her head, that boded ill for her mistress's interests.

Meanwhile, Mrs. Chatterton was angrily pacing up and down the room. "What arrant nonsense a man can be capable of when he is headstrong to begin with! To think of the elegant Horatio King, a model for all men, surrounding himself with this commonplace family. Faugh! It is easy enough to see what they are all after. But I shall prevent it. Meanwhile, the only way to do it is to break the spirit of this Polly Pepper. Once do that, and I have the task easy to my hand."

She listened intently. "It can't be possible she would refuse to come. Ha! I thought so."

Polly came quietly in. No one to see her face would have supposed that she had thrown aside the book she had been waiting weeks to read, so that lessons and music need not suffer. For she was really glad when Mrs. Chatterton's French maid asked her respectfully if she would please be so good as to step up to her mistress's apartments, *"s'il vous plait,* Mees Polly."

"Yes, indeed," cried Polly, springing off from the window seat, and forgetting the enchanted storyland immediately in the rush of delight. "Oh, I have another chance to try to please her," she thought, skimming over the stairs. But she was careful to restrain her steps on reaching the room.

"You may take that paper," said Mrs. Chatterton, seating herself in her favorite chair, "and read to me. You know the things I desire to hear, or ought to." She pointed to the society news, *Town Talk*, lying on the table.

Polly took it up, glad to be of the least service, and whirled it over to get the fashion items, feeling sure that now she was on the right road to favor.

"Don't rattle it," cried Mrs. Chatterton, in a thin, high voice.

"I'll try not to," said Polly, wishing she could be deft-handed like Mamsie, and doing her best to get to the inner page quietly.

"And why don't you read where you are?" cried Mrs. Chatterton. "Begin on the first page. I wish to hear that first."

Polly turned the sheet back again and obeyed. But she hadn't read more than a paragraph when she came to a dead stop.

"Go on," commanded Mrs. Chatterton, her eyes sparkling. She had forgotten to play with her rings, being perfectly absorbed in the delicious morsels of exceedingly unsavory gossip she was hearing.

Polly laid the paper in her lap, and her two hands fell upon it. "Oh, Mrs. Chatterton," she cried, the color flying from her cheek, "please let me read something else to you. Mamsie wouldn't like me to read this." The brown eyes filled with tears, and she leaned forward imploringly.

"Stuff and nonsense!" exclaimed Mrs. Chatterton passionately. "I command you to read that, girl. Do you hear me?"

"I cannot," said Polly, in a low voice. "Mamsie wouldn't like it." But it was perfectly distinct, and fell upon the angry ears clearly. And storm as she might, Mrs. Chatterton knew that the little country maiden would never bend to her will in this case.

"I would have you to know that I understand much better than your mother possibly can, what is for your good to read. Besides, she will never know."

"Mamsie knows every single thing that we children do," cried Polly decidedly, and lifting her pale face. "And she understands better than any one else about what we ought to do, for she is our mother."

"What arrant nonsense!" exclaimed Mrs. Chatterton passionately, and unable to control herself at the prospect of losing Polly for a reader, which she couldn't endure, as she thoroughly enjoyed her services in that line. She got out of her chair, and paced up and down the long apartment angrily, saying all sorts of most disagreeable things, that Polly only half heard, so busy was she debating in her own mind what she ought to do. Should she run out of the room, and leave this dreadful old woman that everyone in the house was tired of? Surely she had tried enough to please her, but she could not do what Mamsie would never approve of. And just as Polly had about decided to slip out, she looked up.

Mrs. Chatterton, having exhausted her passion, as it seemed to do no good, was returning to her seat, with such a dreary step and forlorn expression that she seemed ten years older. She really looked very feeble, and Polly broke out impulsively, "Oh, let me read the other part of the paper, dear Mrs. Chatterton. May I?"

"Read it," said Mrs. Chatterton ungraciously, and sat down in her favorite chair.

Polly, scarcely believing her ears, whirled over the sheet, and determined to read as well as she possibly could, managed to throw so much enthusiasm into the fashion hints and social items, that presently Mrs. Chatterton's eyes were sparkling again, although she was deprived of her unsavory morsels.

And before long she was eagerly telling Polly to read over certain dictates of the Paris correspondent, who was laying down the law for feminine dress, and calling again for the last information of the movements of members of her social set, till there could be no question of her enjoyment.

Polly, not knowing or caring how long she had been thus occupied, so long as Mrs. Chatterton was happy, was only conscious that Hortense came back from the errands, which occasioned only a brief pause.

"Put the parcels down," said Mrs. Chatterton, scarcely glancing at her, "I cannot attend to you now. Go on, Polly."

So Polly went on, until the fashionable and social world had been so thoroughly canvassed that even Mrs. Chatterton was quite convinced that she could get no more from the paper.

"You may go now," she said, but with a hungry glance for the first page. Then she tore her gaze away, and repeated more coldly than ever, "You may go."

Polly ran off, dismayed to find how happy she was at the release. Her feet, unaccustomed to sitting still so long, were numb, and little prickles were running up and down her legs. She hurried as fast as she could into Mamsie's room, feeling in need of all the good cheer she could find.

"Mrs. Fisher has gone out," said Jane, going along the hall.

"Gone out!" repeated Polly. "Oh, where? Do you know, Jane?"

"I don't exactly know," said Jane, "but she took Miss Phronsie, and I think it's shopping they went for. Mr. King has taken them in the carriage."

"Oh, I know it is," cried Polly, and a dreadful feeling

surged through her. Why had she spent all this time with that horrible old woman, and lost this precious treat!

"They thought you had gone to the Salisbury School," said Jane, wishing she could give some comfort, "for they wanted you awfully to go."

"And now I've lost it all," cried Polly at a white heat— "all this perfectly splendid time with Grandpapa and Mamsie and Phronsie just for the sake of a horrible—"

Then she broke short off, and ran back into Mamsie's room, and flung herself down by the bed, just as she used to do by the four-poster in the bedroom of the little brown house.

"Why, Polly, child!" Mother Fisher's voice was very cheery as she came in, Phronsie hurrying after.

"I don't see her," began Phronsie in a puzzled way, and peering on all sides. "Where is she, Mamsie?"

Mrs. Fisher went over and laid her hand on Polly's brown head. "Now, Phronsie, you may run out, that is a good girl." She leaned over, and set a kiss on Phronsie's red lips.

"Is Polly sick?" asked Phronsie, going off to the door obediently, but looking back with wondering eyes.

"No, dear, I think not," said Mrs. Fisher. "Run along, dear."

"I am so glad she isn't sick," said Phronsie, as she went slowly off. Yet she carried a troubled face.

"I ought to go and see how Sinbad is," she decided, as she went downstairs. This visit was an everyday performance, to be carefully gone through with. So she passed out of the big side doorway, to the veranda.

"There is Michael now," she cried joyfully, espying that individual raking up the west lawn. So skipping off, she flew over to him. This caught the attention of little Dick from the nursery window.

"Hurry up there!" he cried crossly to Battles, who was having a hard time anyway getting him into a fresh sailor suit.

"Oh, Dicky—Dicky!" called mamma softly from her room.

"I can't help it, mamma. Battles is slow and poky," he fumed.

"Oh, no, dear," said his mother. "Battles always gets you ready very swiftly, as well as nicely."

Battles, a comfortable person, turned her round face with a smile toward the door. "And if you was more like your mamma, Master Dick, you'd be through with dressing and make everything more pleasant to yourself and to everyone else."

"Well, I'm not in the least like mamma, Battles. I can't be."

"No, indeed, you ain't. But you can try," said Battles encouragingly.

"Why, Battles Whitney!" exclaimed Dick, whirling around on her. In astonishment, or any excitement, Dicky invariably gave her the whole name that he felt she ought to possess; "Mrs. Maria Battles" not being at all within his comprehension. "What an *awful* story!"

"Dicky—Dicky!" reproved Mrs. Whitney.

"Well, I can't help it, mamma." Dick now escaped from Battles's hands altogether, and fled into the other room, the comfortable person following. "She said"—plunging up to her chair in great excitement—"that I could be like you."

"I said you could try to be," corrected Battles, smoothing down her apron.

"And she knows I can't ever be, in all this world," declared Dick, shaking his short curls in decision, and glancing back to see the effect, "for you're a woman, and I'm always going to be a man. Why, see how big I am now!" He squared off and strutted up and down the little boudoir.

"And you'd be bigger if you'd let me fix your blouse and button it up," declared Battles, laughing, and bearing down on him to fasten the band and tuck in the vest. "And if you was more like your mother in disposition—that's what I mean—'twould be a sight comfortabler for you and every one else. Now, says I, your hair's got to be brushed." And she led him back into the nursery, laughing all the way.

"What makes you shake so when you laugh, Battles?" asked Dick suddenly, and ignoring all references to his disposition.

"Can't help it," said Battles, beginning work on the curls. "That's because there's so much of me, I suppose." And she laughed more than ever.

"There's so very much of you, Battles," observed Dick with a critical look all over her rotund figure. "What makes it?"

"Oh, I don't know," said Battles. "Stand still, Dicky, and I'll be through all the sooner. Some folks is big and round, and some folks is little and scrawny."

"What's scrawny?" asked Dick, who always got as many alleviations by conversation as possible out of the detested hair-brushing.

"Why, thin and lean."

"Oh, well, go on, Battles."

"And I'm one of the big and round ones," said Battles, seeing no occasion in that statement to abate her cheerfulness. So she laughed again.

"I like you big and round, Battles," cried little Dick affectionately, and whirling about so suddenly as to endanger his eye with the comb doing good execution. And he essayed to put his arms around her waist, which he was always hoping to be able to accomplish.

"That's good," said Battles, laughing, well pleased. "But you mustn't jump around so. There now, in a minute you shall be off." And she took up the brush.

"I must," declared Dick, remembering his sight of Phronsie running across the lawn. "Do hurry, Battles," he pleaded, which so won her heart that she abridged part of the brushing and let him scamper off.

Phronsie was kneeling down in front of Sinbad's kennel.

"Can't you untie him today, Michael?" she asked, a question she had propounded each morning since the boys went back to school.

"Yes, Miss Phronsie, I think I can. He's wonted now, and the other dogs are accustomed to him. Besides, I've locked up Jerry since he fit him."

"I know," said Phronsie sorrowfully. "That was naughty of Jerry when Sinbad had only just come."

Michael scratched his head. He couldn't tell her what was on his mind, that Sinbad was scarcely such a dog as anyone would buy, and therefore his presence was not to be relished by the high-bred animals already at home on the place.

"Well, you know, Miss Phronsie," he said at last, "it's kinder difficult like, to expect some dogs to remember their manners. And Jerry ain't like all the others in that respect."

"Please tell him about it," said Phronsie earnestly, "how good Prince is to Sinbad, and then I guess he'll want to be like him." For Phronsie had never swerved in her allegiance to Prince ever since he saved her from the naughty organ man in the little-brown-house days. And in all her conversations with the other dogs she invariably held up Jasper's big black dog, his great friend and companion since pinafore days, as their model.

And just then Dicky ran up breathlessly.

"Dick," announced Phronsie excitedly, "Michael is going to let Sinbad out today." And she clasped her hands in delight.

"Jolly!" exclaimed Dick, capering about.

"Now, Master Dick, you must let the dog alone," cried Michael. "It's time to try him with his freedom a bit. He's chafin' at that chain." He looked anxiously at Dick. "Stand off there, both of you," and he slipped the chain off.

Sinbad gave a little wiggle with his hind legs, and stretched his yellow body. It was too good to be true! But it was, though; he was free, and he shot out from his kennel, which was down in the gardener's quarters, and quite removed from the other dogs, and fairly tore—his ragged little tail straight out—across the west lawn.

"Oh, he'll run back to Joel at school," cried Dick, who had heard Joel say he must be tied at first when everything was strange, and he started on a mad run after him.

"You stay still," roared Michael. "That dog is only stretchin' his legs. He'll come back." But as well tell the north wind to stop blowing. Dicky's blouse puffed out with the breeze, as his small legs executed fine speed.

"Oh, Michael!" cried Phronsie in the greatest distress. "Make Dicky come back."

"Oh, he'll come back," said Michael reassuringly, though he quaked inwardly. And so Dicky did. But it was now a matter of Sinbad chasing him, for as Michael had said, the dog, after stretching his legs as the mad rush across the lawn enabled him to do, now was very much pleased to return for a little petting at the hands of those people who had given him every reason to expect that he should receive it. And supposing, from Dick's chase after him, that a race was agreeable, he set forth, his ears, as ragged as his tail, pricked up in the fullest enjoyment of the occasion.

But Dick saw nothing in it to enjoy. And exerting all his strength to keep ahead, which he couldn't do as well for the reason that he was screaming fearfully, Sinbad came up with him easily. Dicky, turning his head in mad terror at that instant, stumbled and fell. Sinbad, unable to stop at short notice, or rather no notice at all, rolled over with him in a heap.

This brought all the stableboys to the scene, besides Mrs. Whitney, who had seen some of the affair from her window. And finally, when everything was beginning to be calmed down, Battles reached the lawn.

Sinbad was in Phronsie's lap, who sat on the grass, holding him tightly.

"Oh, Phronsie!" gasped Mrs. Whitney at that. "Michael, do take him away," as she fled by to Dick. One of the stableboys was brushing off the grime from his sailor suit.

"The dog is all right, ma'am," said Michael. "'Twas only play; I s'pose Master Joel has raced with him."

"'Twas only play," repeated little Dick, who, now that he found himself whole, was surprised the idea hadn't occurred to him before. "Hoh! I'm not hurt, and I'm going to race with him again."

"Not today, Dicky," said Mrs. Whitney, looking him all over anxiously.

"He's all right, ma'am," declared Michael. "They just rolled over together, 'cause, you see, ma'am, the dog couldn't stop, he was a-goin' so fast, when the youngster turned right in his face."

And Dick, to prove his soundness of body and restoration of mind, ran up to Phronsie, and flung himself down on the grass by her side.

Sinbad received him as a most pleasant acquaintance, cocked up his ragged ears, and tried to wag his poor little scrubby tail, never quite getting it into his head that it wasn't long and graceful. And then he set upon the task of licking Dick's hands all over, and as much of his face as was possible to compass.

"See that now," cried Michael triumphantly, pointing. "That dog mayn't be handsome, but he hain't got a bad bone in his body, if he does look like the Evil One hisself."

This episode absorbing all their attention, nobody heard or saw Alexia Rhys, running lightly up over the terrace. "Oh, my! what *are* you doing? And where's Polly?" she asked of Mrs. Whitney.

It being soon told, Alexia, who evidently had some exciting piece of news for Polly, ran into the house.

"Polly," she called. "Oh, Polly Pepper, where *are* you?" running over the stairs at the same time.

But Polly, as we have seen, was not in her room.

"Now then," Mother Fisher said at sound of Alexia's voice, "as we've finished our talk, Polly, why, you must run down and see her."

But Polly clung to her mother's neck. "Do you think I ought to go next Saturday morning out shopping, Mamsie, after I've been so naughty?"

"Indeed, you ought," cried Mrs. Fisher, in her most decisive fashion. "Dear me! That would be very dreadful, Polly, after we put it off for you, when we thought you had gone down to the Salisbury School. Why, we couldn't get along without you, Polly."

So Polly, with a happy feeling at her heart that she was really needed to make the shopping trip a success, and best of all for the long talk with Mamsie, that had set many things right, ran down to meet Alexia, brimming over with her important news.

"Where *have* you been?" demanded Alexia, just on the point of rushing out of Polly's room in despair. "I've looked everywhere for you, even in the shoe box." And without waiting for a reply, she dragged Polly back. "Oh, you can't possibly guess!" her pale eyes gleaming with excitement.

"Then tell me, do, Alexia," begged Polly, scarcely less wrought up.

"Oh, Polly, the most elegant thing imaginable!" Alexia dearly loved to spin out her exciting news as long as possible, driving the girls almost frantic by such methods.

"Well, if you are not going to tell me, I might as well go back again, up in Mamsie's room," declared Polly, working herself free from the long arms, and starting for the door.

"Oh, I'll tell, Polly—I'll tell," cried Alexia, plunging after. "Miss Salisbury says—I've just been up to the school after my German grammar—that Mr. John Clemcy and Miss Ophelia have invited the whole Salisbury School out there for next Saturday afternoon. Think of it, after that smashed vase, Polly Pepper!"

Polly Pepper sat down on the shoe box, quite gone in surprise.

It was as Alexia had said: a most surprising thing, when one took into consideration how much Mr. John Clemcy had suffered from the carelessness of a Salisbury pupil on the occasion of the accidental visit. But evidently one of his reasons—though by no means the only one—was his wish to salve the feelings of the gentlewomen, who were constantly endeavoring to show him their overwhelming sorrow, and trying to make all possible reparation for the loss of the vase.

And he had stated his desire so forcibly on one of the many visits to the school that seemed to be necessary after the accident, that Miss Salisbury was unable to refuse the invitation, although it nearly threw her, self-contained as she usually was, into a panic at the very idea.

"But why did you promise, sister?" Miss Anstice turned on her on the withdrawal of the gentleman, whose English composure of face and bearing was now, in its victory, especially trying to bear. "I am surprised at you. Something dreadful will surely happen."

"Don't, Anstice," begged Miss Salisbury, nervous to the last degree, since even the support of "sister" was to be withdrawn. "It was the least I could do, to please him—after what has happened."

"Well, something will surely happen," mourned Miss Anstice. "You know how unfortunate it has been from the very beginning. I've never been able to look at that gown since, although it has been washed till every stain is removed."

"Put it on for this visit, sister," advised Miss Salisbury, with a healthy disapproval of superstitions, "and break the charm."

"Oh, never!" Miss Anstice raised her slender hands. "I wouldn't run such a chance as to wear that gown for all the world. It will be unlucky enough, you will see, without that, sister."

But as far as anybody could see, everything was perfectly harmonious and successful on the following Saturday afternoon. To begin with, the weather was perfect, although at extremely short intervals Miss Anstice kept reminding her sister that a tremendous shower might be expected when the expedition was once under way.

The girls, when they received their invitation Monday morning from Miss Salisbury in the long schoolroom, were, to state it figuratively, "taken off their feet" in surprise, with the exception of those fortunate enough to have caught snatches of the news always sure to travel fast when set going by Alexia. And wild was the rejoicing, when they could forget the broken vase, at the prospect of another expedition under Miss Salisbury's guidance.

"If Miss Anstice only weren't going!" sighed Clem. "She is such a fussy old thing. It spoils everybody's fun just to look at her."

"Well, don't look at her," advised Alexia calmly. "For my part, I never do, unless I can't help it."

"How are you going to help it," cried Amy Garrett dismally, "when you are in her classes? Oh dear! I do wish Miss Salisbury would get rid of her as a teacher, and let Miss Wilcox take her place."

"Miss Wilcox is just gay!" exclaimed Silvia. "Well, don't let's talk of that old frump any more. Goodness me! Here she comes," as Miss Anstice advanced down the long hall, where the girls were discussing the wonderful invitation after school.

And as the day was perfect, so the spirits of the "Salisbury girls" were at their highest. And Mr. Kimball and his associates drove them over in the same big barges, the veteran leader not recovering from the surprise into which he had been thrown by this afternoon party given to the Salisbury School by Mr. Clemcy and his sister.

"Of all things in this world, this is th' capsheaf," he muttered several times on the way. "A good ten year or more, those English folks have been drawin' back in them pretty grounds, an' offendin' every one; an' now, to get a passel o' girls to run over an' stomp 'em all down!"

Being unable to solve the puzzle, it afforded him plenty of occupation to work away at it.

Mr. Clemcy and Miss Ophelia, caring as little for the opinion of the stage driver as for the rest of the world, received the visitors on the broad stone piazza, whose pillars ran the length of the house, and up to the roof, affording a wide gallery above. It was all entwined with English ivy and creepers taken from the homestead in Devonshire, and brought away when the death of the old mother made it impossible for life to be sustained by Miss Ophelia unless wrenched up from the roots where clustered so many memories. So brother John decided to make that wrench, and to make it complete. So here they were.

"I didn't know it was so pretty," cried Clem, after the ladies had been welcomed with the most gracious, old-time hospitality, and the schoolgirls tumbled out of the barges to throng up. "It rained so when we were here before, we couldn't see anything."

"Pretty?" repeated Alexia, comprehending it all in swift, birdlike glances. "It's perfectly beautiful!" She turned, and Mr. Clemcy, who was regarding her, smiled, and they struck up a friendship on the spot.

"Miss Salisbury, allow me." Mr. Clemcy was leading her off. Miss Anstice, not trusting the ill-fated white gown, rustled after in the black silk one, with Miss Ophelia, down the wide hall, open at the end, with vistas of broad fields beyond, where the host paused. "Let the young ladies come," he said, and the girls trooped after, to crowd around the elder people.

Amongst the palms and bookcases, with which the broad hall was lined, was a pedestal, whose top was half covered with a soft, filmy cloth.

Mr. Clemcy lifted this, and took it off carefully. There stood the little vase, presenting as brave an appearance as in its first perfection.

Miss Salisbury uttered no exclamation, but preserved her composure by a violent effort.

"I flatter myself on my ability to repair my broken collection," began Mr. Clemcy, when a loud exclamation from the girls in front startled every one. Miss Anstice, on the first shock, had been unable to find that composure that was always "sister's" envied possession; so despite the environment of the black silk gown, she gave it up, and sank gradually to the ground.

"I told you so," cried Clem, in a hoarse whisper to her nearest neighbors; "she always spoils everybody's fun," as Miss Anstice, at the host's suggestion, his sister being rendered incapable of action at this sudden emergency, was put to rest in one of the pretty chintz-covered rooms above, till such time as she could recover herself enough to join them below.

"I couldn't help it, sister," she said. "I've been so worried about that vase. *You* don't know, because you are always so calm. And then to see it standing there—it quite took away my breath."

Oh, the delights of the rose-garden! In which every variety of the old-fashioned rose seemed to have had a place lovingly assigned to it. Sweetbrier clambered over the walls of the gardener's cottage, the stables, and charming summer-houses, into which the girls ran with delight. For Mr. Clemcy had said they were to go everywhere and enjoy everything without restraint.

"He's a dear," exclaimed Lucy Bennett, "only I'm mortally afraid of him."

"Well, I'm not," proclaimed Alexia.

The idea of Alexia being in any state that would suggest fear, being so funny, the girls burst out laughing.

"Well, we shan't any of us feel like laughing much in a little while," said Clem dolefully.

"What is the matter?" cried a dozen voices.

"Matter enough," replied Clem. "I've said so before, and now I know it's coming. Just look at that."

She pushed aside the swaying branches of the sweetbrier and pointed tragically. "I don't see anything," said one or two of the girls.

"There!" "There" meant Mr. Clemcy and Miss Salisbury passing down the rose walk, the broad central path. He was evidently showing her some treasured variety and descanting on it, the principal of the Salisbury School from her wide knowledge of roses, as well as of other subjects, being able to respond very intelligently.

"Oh, can't you see? You stupid things!" cried Clem. "He's going to marry our Miss Salisbury, and then she'll give up our school; and—and—" She turned away, and threw herself off in a corner.

A whole chorus of "No—no!" burst upon this speech.

"Hush!" cried Alexia, quite horrified. "Polly, do stop them. Miss Salisbury is turning around, and she's been worried quite enough over that dreadful Miss Anstice," which had the effect of reducing the girls to quiet.

"But it isn't so," cried the girls in frantic whispers, "what Clem says." And those who were not sure of themselves huddled down on the summerhouse floor. "Say, Alexia, you don't think so, do you?"

But Alexia would give them no comfort, but wisely seizing Polly's arm, departed with her. "I shall say something that I'll be sorry for," she declared, "if I stay another moment longer. For, Polly Pepper, I do really believe that it's true, what Clem says."

And the rest of that beautiful afternoon, with rambles over the wide estate, and tea with berries and cream on the terraces, was a dream, scarcely comprehended by the "Salisbury girls," who were strangely quiet and well behaved. For this Miss Salisbury was thankful.

And presently Miss Anstice, coming down in the wake of Miss Ophelia, was put carefully into a comfortable chair on the stone veranda, where she sat pale and quiet, Miss Clemcy assiduously devoting herself to her, and drawing up a little table to her side for her berries and cream and tea.

"Now we will be comfortable together," said Miss Ophelia, the maid bringing her special little pot of tea.

"I am so mortified, my dear Miss Clemcy," began Miss Anstice, her little hands nervously working, "to have given way," all of which she had said over and over to her hostess in the chintz-covered room. "And you are so kind to overlook it so beautifully."

"It is impossible to blame one of your delicate sensibility," said Miss Ophelia, with her healthy English composure, quite in her element to have someone to fuss over and to make comfortable in her own way. "Now, then, I trust that tea is quite right," handing her a cup.

Chapter 24

The Piece of News

"**P**EPPER, you're wanted!" Dick Furness banged into Joel's room, then out again, adding two words, "Harrow—immediately."

"All right," said Joel, whistling on, all his thoughts upon Moose Island and the expedition there on the morrow. And he ran lightly down to the second floor, and into the underteacher's room.

Mr. Harrow was waiting for him, and pushing aside some books, for he never seemed to be quite free from them even for a moment, he motioned Joel to a seat.

Joel, whose pulses were throbbing with the liveliest expectations, didn't bother his head with what otherwise might have struck him as somewhat queer in the underteacher's manner. For the thing in hand was what Joel principally gave himself to. And as that clearly could be nothing else than the Moose Island expedition, it naturally followed that Mr. Harrow had to speak twice before he could gain his attention.

But when it was gained, there was not the slightest possible chance of misunderstanding what the underteacher was saying, for it was the habit of this instructor to come directly to the point without unnecessary circumlocution.

But his voice and manner were not without a touch of sadness on this occasion that softened the speech itself.

"Joel, my boy," Mr. Harrow began, "you know I have often had you down here to urge on those lessons of yours."

"Yes, sir," said Joel, wondering now at the voice and manner.

"Well, now today, I am instructed by the master to send for you for a different reason. Can you not guess?"

"No, sir," said Joel, comfortable in the way things had been going on, and wholly unable to imagine the blow about to fall.

"I wish you had guessed it, Joel," said Mr. Harrow, moving uneasily in his chair, "for then you would have made my task easier. Joel, Dr. Marks says, on account of your falling behind in your lessons, without reason—understand this, Joel, *without reason*—you are not to go to Moose Island tomorrow."

Even then Joel did not comprehend. So Mr. Harrow repeated it distinctly.

"*What!*" roared Joel. In his excitement he cleared the space between them, and gained Mr. Harrow's side. "*Not go to Moose Island, Mr. Harrow?*" his black eyes widening, and his face working fearfully.

"No," said Mr. Harrow, drawing a long breath, "you are not to go; so Dr. Marks says."

"But I *must* go," cried Joel, quite gone in passion.

" 'Must' is a singular word to use here, Joel," observed Mr. Harrow sternly.

"But I—oh, Mr. Harrow, do see if you can't help me to

go." Joel squirmed all over, and even clutched the under-teacher's arm piteously.

"Alas, Joel! It is beyond my power." Mr. Harrow shook his head. He didn't think it necessary to state that he had already used every argument he could employ to induce Dr. Marks to change his mind. "Some strong pressure must be brought to bear upon Pepper, or he will amount to nothing but an athletic lad. He must see the value of study," the master had responded, and signified that the interview was ended, and his command was to be carried out.

"Joel"—Mr. Harrow was speaking—"be a man, and bear this as you can. You've had your chances for study, and not taken them. It is a case of *must* now. Remember, Dr. Marks is doing this in love to you. He has got to fit you out as well as he can in this school, to take that place in life that your mother wants you to fill. Don't waste a moment on vain regrets, but buckle to your studies now."

It was a long speech for the underteacher, and he had a hard time getting through with it. At its end, Joel, half dazed with his misfortune, but with a feeling that as a man, Dr. Marks and Mr. Harrow had treated him, hurried back to his room, dragged his chair up to the table, and pushing off the untidy collection of rackets, tennis balls, boxing gloves, and other implements of his gymnasium work and his recreation hours, lent his whole heart with a new impulse to his task.

Somehow he did not feel like crying, as had often been the case with previous trials. "He said, 'Be a man,' " Joel kept repeating over and over to himself, while the words of his lesson swam before his eyes. "And so I will. And he said, Dr. Marks had got to make me as Mamsie wanted me to be," repeated Joel to himself, taking a shorter cut with the idea. "And so I will be." And he leaned his elbows on the table, bent his head over his book, and clutching his stubby crop by both hands and holding on tightly, he was soon lost to his misfortune and the outside world.

"Hullo!" David stood still in amazement at Joel's unusual attitude over his lesson. Then he reflected that he was making up extra work, to be free for the holiday on the morrow. Notwithstanding the need of quiet, David was so full of it that he couldn't refrain from saying jubilantly, "Oh, what a great time we'll have tomorrow, Joe!" giving him a pound on the back.

"I'm not going," said Joel, without raising his head.

David ran around his chair to look at him from the farther side, then peered under the bunch of curls Joel was hanging to.

"What's—what's the matter, Joe?" he gasped, clutching the table.

"Dr. Marks says I'm not to go," said Joel telling the whole at once.

"*Dr. Marks said you were not to go!*" repeated David. "Why, Joel? Why?" he demanded in a gasp.

"I haven't studied. I'm way behind. Let me alone," cried Joel. "I've got a perfect lot to make up," and he clutched harder than ever at his hair.

"Then *I* shall not go," declared David, and rushing out of the room he was gone before Joel could fly from his chair; which he did, upsetting it after him.

"Dave—*Dave!*" he yelled, running out into the hall, in the face of a stream of boys coming up from gymnasium practice.

"What's up, Pepper?" But he went through their ranks like a shot. Nevertheless David was nowhere to be seen, as he had taken some shortcut, and was lost in the crowd.

Joel bent his steps to the underteacher's room, knocked, and in his excitement thought he heard "Come in." And with small ceremony he precipitated himself upon Mr. Harrow, who seemed to be lost in a reverie, his back to him, leaning his elbow on the mantel, and his head upon his hand.

"Er—oh!" exclaimed Mr. Harrow, startled out of his usual composure, and turning quickly to face Joel. "Oh, it's you, Pepper!" which by no means lifted him out of his depression.

"Dave says he won't go without me. You must make him," said Joel in his intensity forgetting his manners.

"To Moose Island?" asked Mr. Harrow.

Joel nodded. He couldn't yet bring himself to speak the name.

"All right. I will, Joe." Mr. Harrow grasped the brown hand hanging by Joel's side.

"Really?" said Joel, swallowing hard.

"Really. Run back to your books, and trust me."

So Joel dashed back, not minding the alluring cries from several chums, "Come on—just time for a game before supper," and was back before his table in the same attitade, and hanging to his hair.

"I can study better so," he said, and holding on for dear life.

One or two boys glanced in. "Come out of this hole," they cried. "No need to study for tomorrow. Gee whiz! Just think of Moose Island, Joe."

No answer.

"Joe!" They ran in and shook his shoulders. "Moose Island!" they screamed, and the excitement with which the whole school was charged was echoing it through the length of the dormitory.

"Go away," cried Joel at them, "or I'll fire something at you," as they swarmed around his chair.

"Fire your old grammar," suggested one, trying to twitch

away his book, and another pulled the chair out from under
him.

Joel sprawled a moment on the floor, then he sprang up,
hanging to his book, and faced them. "I'm not going. Clear
out." And in a moment the room was as still as if an
invasion had never taken place. In their astonishment they
forgot to utter a word.

And in ten minutes the news was all over the playground
and in all the corridors, "Joe Pepper isn't going to Moose
Island."

If they had said that the corner stone of the dormitory was
shaky, the amazement would not have been so great in some
quarters, and the story was not believed until they had it
from Joe himself. Then amazement changed to grief. Not to
have Joe Pepper along was to do away with half the fun.

Percy ran up to him in the greatest excitement just before
supper. "What is it, Joe?" he cried. "The fellows are trying to
say that you're not going to Moose Island." He was red with
running, and panted dreadfully. "And Van is giving it to
Red Hiller for telling such a whopper."

"Well, he needn't," said Joel "for it's perfectly true. I'm
not going."

Percy tried to speak, but what with running, and his
astonishment, his tongue flapped up idly against the roof of
his mouth.

"Dr. Marks won't let me," said Joel, not mincing matters.
"I've got to study, so there's an end of it." But when Davie
came in, a woebegone figure, for Mr. Harrow had kept his
promise, then was Joel's hardest time. And he clenched his
brown hands to keep the tears back then, for David gave way
to such a flood in the bitterness of his grief to go without Joel,
that for a time Joel was in danger of utterly losing his own
self-control.

"I'm confounded glad." It was Jenk who said it to his small following, and hearing it, Tom Beresford blazed at him. "If you weren't quite so small, I'd knock you down."

"Well, I am glad"—Jenk put a goodly distance between himself and Tom, notwithstanding Tom's disgust at the idea of touching him—"for Pepper is so high and mighty, it's time he was taken down," but a chorus of yells made him beat a retreat.

Dr. Marks paced up and down his study floor, his head bent, his hands folded behind him.

"It was the only way. No ordinary course could be taken with Pepper. It had come to be imperative. It will make a man of him." He stepped to the desk and wrote a few words, slipped them into an envelope, sealed and addressed it.

"Joanna!" He went to the door and summoned a maid, the same one who had shaken her broom at Joel when he rushed in with the dog. "Take this over to the North Dormitory as quickly as possible." It seemed to be especially necessary that haste be observed, and Dr. Marks, usually so collected, hurried to the window to assure himself that his command was obeyed.

Mrs. Fox took the note as Joanna handed it in, and sent it up at once, as those were the orders from the master. It arrived just at the moment when Joel was at the end of his self-mastery. He tore it open. "My boy, knowing you as I do, I feel sure that you will be brave in bearing this. It will help you to conquer your dislike for study and make a man of you. Affectionately yours, H. L. Marks."

Joel swung the note up over his head, and there was such a glad ring to his voice that David was too astonished to cry.

"See there!" Joel proudly shook it at him "Read it, Dave."

So David seized it, and blinked in amazement.

"Dr. Marks has written to me," said Joel importantly, just as if David hadn't the note before him. "And he says, 'Be a man,' just as Mr. Harrow said, and, 'affectionately yours.' Now, what do you think of that, Dave Pepper?"

David was so lost in the honor that had come to Joel, that the grief that he was feeling in the thought of the expedition to be made to Moose Island tomorrow without Joel began to pale. He smiled and lifted his eyes, lately so wet with tears. "Mamsie would like that note, Joe."

Tom Beresford rushed in without the formality of a knock, and gloomily threw himself on the bed. "Poor Joe!" was written all over his long face.

"Oh, you needn't, Tom," said Joel gaily, and prancing up and down the room, "pity me, because I won't have it."

"It's pity for myself as well," said Tom lugubriously, and cramming the pillow end into his mouth. "What's a fellow to do without you, Joe?" suddenly shying the pillow at Joel.

Joe caught it and shied it back, then twitched the master's note out of David's hand. "Read it, Tom," he cried, with sparkling eyes.

"I'd much rather stay back with you, Joe," Tom was saying.

"Well, you won't," retorted Joel. "Dave tried that on, but it was no good. Read it, I tell you." So Tom sat up on the bed, and spread Dr. Marks's note on his knee.

"Great Caesar's ghost! It's from the master himself! And what does he say?" Tom rubbed his eyes violently, stared, and rushed over the few sentences pellmell; then returned to take them slowly to be sure of their meaning.

"Joe Pepper!" He got off from the bed.

"Isn't it great!" cried Joel. "Give me my note, Tom."

"I should say so!" cried Tom, bobbing his head. "I shouldn't in the least mind being kept back from a few things, to get a note like that. Think of it, Joe, from Dr. Marks!"

"I know it," cried Joel, in huge satisfaction. "Well, now, you must take yourself off, Tom. I've got to study like a Trojan." He ran to the closet and came back with his arms full of books.

"All right," said Tom, shooting out. Then he shot back, gave Joel a pat—by no means a light one—"Success to you, old fellow!" and was off, this time for good.

And Davie dreamed that night that Joel took first prize in everything straight through, and that he himself was sailing, sailing, over an interminable sea (going to Moose Island probably), under a ban never to come back to Dr. Marks's school. And the first thing he knew, Joel was pounding him and calling lustily, "Get up, Dave. You know you are to start early."

And then all was bustle and confusion enough, as how could it be helped with all those boys getting off on such an expedition?

And Joel was the brightest of them all, here, there, and everywhere! You never would have guessed that he wasn't the leading spirit in the whole expedition, and its bright particular star!

And he ran down to the big stone gate to see them off. And the boys wondered, but there was no chance to pity him, with such a face. There was only pity for themselves.

And somebody started, "Three cheers for Joe Pepper!" It wasn't the underteacher, but he joined with a right good will, and the whole crowd took it up, as Joel ran back to tackle his books, pinching Dr. Marks's letter in his pocket, to make sure it really was there!

Just about this time, Alexia Rhys was rushing to school. She was late, for everything had gone wrong that morning from the very beginning. And of course Polly Pepper had started for school when Alexia called for her, and feeling as if nothing mattered now, the corner was reached despairingly, when she heard her name called.

It was an old lady who was a friend of her aunt's, and Alexia paused involuntarily, then ran across the street to see what was wanted.

"Oh, my dear, I suppose I ought not to stop you, for you are going to school."

"Oh, it doesn't matter," said Alexia indifferently. "I'm late anyway. What is it, Miss Seymour?"

"I want to congratulate you—I *must* congratulate you," exclaimed old Miss Seymour, with an excited little cackle. "I really must, Alexia."

Alexia ran over in her mind everything for which she could, by any possibility, be congratulated, and finding nothing, she said, "What for?" quite abruptly.

"Oh, my dear! Haven't you heard?" Old Miss Seymour put her jewelled fingers on the girl's shoulder. She had gathered up her dressy morning robe in her hand, and hastened down her front steps at the first glimpse of Alexia across the way.

Alexia knew of old the roundabout way pursued by her aunt's friend in her narrations. Besides, she cared very little anyway for this bit of old women's gossip. So she said carelessly, "No, I'm sure I haven't, and I don't believe it's much anyway, Miss Seymour."

" 'Much anyway'? Oh, my dear!" Old Miss Seymour held up both hands. "Wait, what would you say if you should be told that your teacher was going to be married?"

Alexia staggered backward and put up both hands. "Oh, don't, Miss Seymour," she cried, the fears she had been fighting so many weeks now come true. Then she burst out passionately, "Oh, it isn't true—it *can't* be!"

"Well, but it is," cried Miss Seymour positively. "I had it not ten minutes since from a very intimate friend, and as you were the first Salisbury girl I saw, why, I wanted to congratulate you, of course, as soon as I could."

"Salisbury girl!" Alexia groaned as she thought how they should never have that title applied to them any more, for of course the beautiful school was doomed. "And where shall we all go?" she cried to herself in despair.

"Oh, how could she go and get engaged!" she exclaimed aloud.

"You haven't asked who the man is," said Miss Seymour in surprise.

"Oh, I know—I know," said Alexia miserably. "It's Mr. John Clemcy. Oh, if we hadn't had that old picnic!" she burst out.

"Eh—what?" exclaimed the little old lady quickly.

"Never mind. It doesn't signify who the man is. It doesn't signify about anything," said Alexia wildly, "as long as Miss Salisbury is going to get married and give up our school."

"Oh, I don't suppose the school will be given up," said Miss Seymour.

"What? Why, of course it will be. How can she keep it after she is married?" cried Alexia impatiently. She longed to say, "You goose you!"

"Why, I suppose the other one will keep it, of course, and it will go on just the same as it did before."

"Oh dear me! The idea of Miss Anstice keeping that school!" With all her misery, Alexia couldn't help bursting into a laugh.

"Miss Anstice?"

"Yes. If you knew her as we girls do, Miss Seymour, you never'd say she could run that school."

"I never said she could."

"Oh, yes, you did," Alexia was guilty of contradicting. "You said distinctly that when Miss Salisbury was married, you supposed Miss Anstice would keep it on just the same."

Little old Miss Seymour took three or four steps down the pavement, then turned and trotted back, the dressy morning robe still gathered in her hand.

"Who do you think is engaged to Mr. John Clemcy?" she asked, looking up at the tall girl.

"Why, our Miss Salisbury," answered Alexia, ready to cry, "I suppose. That's what you said."

"Oh, no, I didn't," said the little old lady. "It's Miss Anstice Salisbury."

Alexia gave her one look; then took some flying steps across the street, and away down to the Salisbury School. She met a stream of girls in the front hall; and as soon as she saw their faces, she knew that her news was all old.

And they could tell her something more.

"Miss Wilcox is going to be the assistant teacher," cried Amy Garrett.

"And Miss Salisbury announced it. Why were you late, Alexia?" It was a perfect buzz around her ears. "And then she dismissed school; and we're all going down to the drawing room now, to congratulate Miss Anstice."

Alexia worked her way to Polly Pepper and clung to her.

"Oh, Alexia, you've got here!" cried Polly delightedly. "And only think, we can keep our Miss Salisbury after all."

Chapter 25

"The Very Prettiest Affair"

*A*ND Mr. John Clemcy, having put off any inclination to marry till so late in life, was, now that he had made his choice, in a ferment to hurry its consummation. And Miss Ophelia, who was still to keep the house and run the old-fashioned flower garden to suit herself—thus losing none of her honors—and being in her element, as has been stated, with someone "to fuss over" (her self-contained brother not yielding her sufficient occupation in that line), begged that the wedding might take place soon. So there was really no reason on earth why it should not be celebrated, and Miss Wilcox be installed, as assistant, and thus all things be in running order for the new year at the Salisbury School.

"And they say he has heaps of money—Mr. Clemcy has," cried Alexia, in the midst of the excitement of the next few days, when everybody was trying to adjust themselves to this new condition of affairs. A lot of the girls were up in Polly Pepper's room. "And it's an awful old family back of him in

England," she went on, "though for my part, I'd rather have something to do with making my name myself."

"Oh, Alexia," cried Clem, "think of all those perfectly elegant old family portraits!"

"Moldy old things!" exclaimed Alexia, who had small reverence for such things. "I should be ashamed of them, if I were Mr. John Clemcy and his sister. They don't look as if they knew anything to begin with. And such arms and hands, and impossible necks! Oh my! It quite gives me a turn to look at them."

"We are quite distinguished—the Salisbury School is," said Silvia, with an elegant manner, and a toss of her head. "My mother says it will be splendid capital to Miss Salisbury to have such a connection."

"And, oh, just think of Miss Anstice's engagement ring!" exclaimed another girl. "Oh my, on her little thin finger!"

"It's awful old-fashioned," cried Silvia, "set in silver. But then, it's big, and a *very* pure stone, my mother says, and quite shows that the family must have been something, for it is an heirloom."

"Oh, do stop about family and heirlooms," cried Alexia impatiently. "The main thing is that our Miss Salisbury isn't going to desert us."

"Miss Anstice is. Oh, goody!" Amy Garrett hopped up and down and softly beat her hands while she finished the sentence.

"Hush!" Alexia turned on her suddenly. "Now, Amy, and the rest of you girls, I think we ought to stop this nonsense about Miss Anstice. She's going, and I, maybe, haven't treated her just rightly."

"Of course you haven't," assented Clem coolly. "You've worried her life nearly out of her."

"And oh, dear me! I'm sorry now," said Alexia, not

minding in the least what Clem was saying. "I wonder why it is that I'm forever being sorry about things."

"Because you're forever having your own way," said Clem. "I'll tell you."

"And so I'm going to be nice to her now," said Alexia, with a perfectly composed glance at Clem. "Let's all be, girls. I mean, behind her back."

Polly Pepper ran over across the room to slip her arm within Alexia's and give her a little approving pat.

"It will be so strange not to make fun of her," observed Amy Garrett, "but I suppose we can't now, anyway, that she is to be Mrs. John Clemcy."

"Mrs. John Clemcy, indeed!" exclaimed Alexia, standing very tall. "She was just as nice before, as sister of our Miss Salisbury, I'd have you to know, girls."

"Well, now, what are we to give her as a wedding present?" said Polly Pepper. "You know we, as the committee, ought to talk it over at once. Let's sit down on the floor in a ring and begin."

"Yes," said Alexia. "Now all flop." And setting the example, she got down on the floor, and the girls tumbling after, the ring was soon formed.

"Hush now, do be quiet, Clem, if you can," cried Alexia, to pay up old scores.

"I guess I'm not making as much noise as some other people," said Clem, with a wry face.

"Well, Polly's going to begin, and as she's chairman, we've all got to be still as mice. Hush!"

"I think," said Polly, "the best way would be, instead of wasting so much time in talking, and—"

"Getting into a hubbub," interpolated Alexia.

"Who's talking now," cried Clem triumphantly, "and making a noise?"

"Getting in confusion," finished Polly, "would be, for us each to write out the things that Miss Anstice might like, on a piece of paper, without showing it to any of the other girls. Then pass them in to me, and I'll read them aloud. And perhaps we'll choose something out of all the lists."

"Oh, Polly, how fine! Just the thing."

"I'll get the paper."

"And the pencils." The ring was in a hubbub; Alexia, as usual the first to hop out of her place.

"Sit down, girls," said Polly as chairman. So they all flew back again.

"There, you see now," said Alexia, huddling expeditiously into her place next to Polly, "how no one can stir till the chairman tells us to."

"Who jumped first of all?" exclaimed Clem, bursting into a laugh.

"Well, I'm back again, anyhow," said Alexia coolly, and folding her hands in her lap.

"I'll appoint Lucy Bennett and Silvia Horne to get the paper and pencils," said Polly. "They are on my desk, girls."

Alexia smothered the sigh at her failure to be one of the girls to perform this delightful task, but the paper being brought, she soon forgot her disappointment, in having something to do.

"We must all tear it up into strips," said the chairman, and, beginning on a sheet, "Lucy, you can be giving around the pencils."

And presently the whole committee was racking its brains over this terribly important question thrust upon them.

"It must be something that will always reflect credit on the Salisbury School," observed Alexia, leaning her chin on her hand while she played with her pencil.

"Ugh! Do be still." Lucy, on the other side, nudged her. "I can't think, if anybody speaks a word."

"And fit in well with those old portraits," said Clem, with a look at Alexia.

"Well, I hope and pray that we won't give her anything old. I want it spick, span, new; and to be absolutely up to date." Alexia took her chin out of her hand, and sat up decidedly. "The idea of matching up those moldy old portraits! —and that house just bursting with antiques."

"Ugh! Do hush," cried the girls.

"And write what you want to, Alexia, on your own slip, and keep still," said Silvia, wrinkling her brows. "You just put something out of my head; and it was perfectly splendid."

"But I can't think of a thing that would be good enough," grumbled Alexia, "for the Salisbury School to give. Oh dear me!" And she regarded enviously the other pencils scribbling away.

"My list is done." Amy Garrett pinched hers into a little three-cornered note and threw it into Polly's lap.

"And mine—and mine." They all came in fast in a small white shower.

"Oh my goodness!" exclaimed Alexia, much alarmed that she would be left out altogether. "Wait, Chairman—I mean, Polly," and she began scribbling away for dear life.

"Oh dear me!" The chairman unfolded the first strip, and began to read. "A piano—why, girls, Miss Anstice can't play."

"Well, it would look nice in that great big drawing room," said Clem, letting herself out with a very red face.

"Oh, my! you wrote a *piano!*" Alexia went over backward suddenly to lie flat on the floor and laugh. "Besides, there is one in that house."

"An old thing!" exclaimed Clem in disdain.

"Well, let's see; here's something nice"—Polly ran along the list—"a handsome chair, a desk, a cabinet. Those are fine!"

"Clem has gone into the furniture business, I should think," said Philena.

"And a cabinet!" exclaimed Amy Garrett, "when that house is just full of 'em."

"Oh, I mean a jewel cabinet, or something of that sort," explained Clem hastily.

"That's not bad," announced Silvia, "for I suppose he'll give her all the rest of those heirlooms. Great strings of pearls probably he's got, and everything else. Dear me, don't I wish we girls could see them!" and she lost herself in admiration over the fabulous Clemcy jewels.

"Well, Chairman—Polly, I mean"—Alexia flew into position—"what's the next list?"

"This is quite different," said Polly, unrolling it. "some handsome lace, a fan, a lorgnette, a bracelet."

"It's easy enough to see that's Silvia's," said Alexia. "All that finery and furbelows."

"Well, it's not fair to tell what you think and guess," said Silvia, a pink spot coming on either cheek.

" 'Twouldn't make any difference, my guessing. We all know it's yours, Silvia," said Alexia coolly.

"Well, I think that's a lovely list," said Amy, with sparkling eyes, "and I for one would be willing to vote for any of those things."

"My mother says we better give her something to wear," said Silvia, smoothing down her gown. "Miss Anstice likes nice things; and that great big house is running over with everything to furnish with."

Polly was reading the third list, so somebody pulled Alexia's arm and stopped her. "A watch and chain—that's all there is on this list," announced Polly.

"Oh!"—there was a chorus of voices. "that's it—that's it!" and "Why didn't I think of that?" until the whole ring was in a tumult again.

It was no matter what was on the other lists. The chairman read them over faithfully, but the items fell upon dull ears. They might make suitable tributes for other brides; there was but one mind about the present for this particular bride going forth from the Salisbury School. The watch and chain was the only gift to be thought of.

"And she wears that great big old-fashioned thing," declared Silvia. "Looks like a turnip—oh, oh!"

"And I do believe that's always made her so impressive and scary whenever she got into that black silk gown," said Amy Garrett. "I never thought of it before, but it was that horrible old watch and chain."

"Girls," said the chairman, "I do really believe that it would be the very best thing that we could possibly give her. And now I'm going to tell who it was who chose it."

"Do—oh, do!" The whole ring came together in a bunch, as the girls all crowded around Polly.

"Alexia!" Then Polly turned and gave a loving little pat on the long back.

"Don't," said Alexia, shrinking away from the shower of congratulations on having made the best choice, and thought of the very thing that was likely to unite the whole school on a gift. "It's nothing. I couldn't help but write it. It was the only thing I thought of."

"Well, it was just as clever in you as could be, so there now!" Clem nodded over at her, and buried all animosity at once.

"And think how nice it will be, when it's all engraved

inside the case with what we want to say," said Polly, with shining eyes.

"And a great big monogram outside," said Silvia, with enthusiasm, "and one of those twisted chains—oh, how fine!" She shook out her silver bracelets till they jingled all her enthusiasm, and the entire committee joining, the vote was taken to propose to the rest of the "Salisbury girls," on the morrow, the gift of a watch and chain to the future Mrs. John Clemcy.

And the watch and chain was unanimously chosen by the "Salisbury girls" as the gift of all gifts they wanted to bestow upon their teacher on her wedding day; and they all insisted that Polly Pepper should write the inscription. So there it was, engraved beautifully on the inner side of the case: "Anstice Salisbury, with the loving regard of her pupils." And there was a beautiful big monogram on the outside; and the long chain was double and twisted, and so handsome that Silvia's mother protested she hadn't a word to say but the very highest praise!

Oh, and the presentation of it came about quite differently from what was expected, after all. For the gift was to be sent with a little note, representing the whole school, and written as was quite proper, by Polly Pepper, the chairman of the committee. But Miss Salisbury, to whom the precious parcel had been entrusted, said suddenly, "Why don't you give it to her yourselves, girls?"

It was, of course, the place of the chairman of the committee to speak. So Polly said, "Oh, would she like to have us, Miss Salisbury?"

"Yes, my dears. I know she would. She feels badly to go and leave you all, you know," and there were tears in the blue eyes that always looked so kindly on them. "And it would be a very lovely thing for you to do, if you would like to."

"We should *love* to do it," cried Polly warmly. "May we go now, dear Miss Salisbury?"

"Yes," said Miss Salisbury, very much pleased. "She is in the red parlor."

So the committee filed into the red parlor. There sat Miss Anstice, and—oh dear me!—Mr. John Clemcy!

There was no time to retreat; for Miss Salisbury, not having heard Mr. Clemcy come in, was at the rear of the procession of girls. "Here, my dears—Anstice, the girls particularly want to see you—oh!" and then she saw Mr. John Clemcy.

Miss Anstice, who seemed to have dropped all her nervousness lately, saved the situation by coming forward and greeting them warmly. And when Mr. John Clemcy saw how it was, he went gallantly to the rescue, and was so easy and genial, and matter-of-course, that the committee presently felt as if a good part of their lives had been passed in making presentations, and that they were quite up to that sort of thing.

And Polly made a neat little speech as she handed her the packet; and Miss Anstice's eyes filled with tears of genuine regret at leaving them, and of delight at the gift.

"Girls, do you know"—could it be Miss Anstice who was talking with so much feeling in her voice?—"I used to imagine that you didn't love me."

"Oh, that could never be!" cried Mr. Clemcy.

"And I got so worried and cross over it. But now I know you did, and that I was simply tired, for I never could teach like sister"—she cast her a loving glance—"and I didn't really love my work. And, do you know, the thing I've longed for all my life was a watch and chain like this? Oh, girls, I shall love it always!"

She threw the chain around her neck, and laid the little watch gently against her cheek.

"Oh!" It was Alexia who pressed forward. "You'll forgive us all, won't you, Miss Anstice, if we didn't love you enough?"

"When I want to forgive, I'll look at my dear watch," said Miss Anstice brightly, and smiling on them all.

" 'Twas that horrible old black silk gown that made her so," exclaimed Alexia as all tumbled off down the hall in the greatest excitement. "You see how sweet she is now, in that white one."

"And the red rose in her belt," said Clem.

"And her diamond ring," added Silvia.

"And we're different, too," said Clem. "Maybe we wouldn't love to teach a lot of girls any better either, if we had to."

"Well, and now there's the wedding!" exclaimed Amy Garrett, clasping her hands. "Oh!"

"What richness!" finished Alexia.

And everybody said it was "the very prettiest affair. And so picturesque!" "And those dear Salisbury girls—how sweet they looked, to be sure!" Why, St. John's blossomed out like a veritable garden, just with that blooming company of girls, to say nothing of the exquisite flowers, and ropes of laurel, and palms, and the broad white satin ribbons to divide the favored ones from the mere acquaintances.

"And what a lovely thought to get those boys from the Pemberton School for ushers, with Jasper King as their leader!"

They all made such a bright, youthful picture, to be followed by the chosen eight of the "Salisbury girls," the very committee who presented the gift to the bride-elect. There they were in their simple white gowns and big white hats.

And then came the little assistant teacher of the Salisbury School, in her pearl gray robe; singularly enough, not half so much embarrassed as she had often been in walking down the long schoolroom before the girls.

And Mr. John Clemcy never thought of such a thing as embarrassment at all, but stood up in his straightforward, manly, English composure, to take his vows that bound him to the little schoolteacher. And Miss Salisbury, fairly resplendent in her black velvet gown, had down deep within her heart a childlike satisfaction in it all. "Dear Anstice was happy," and somehow the outlook for the future, with Miss Wilcox for assistant teacher, was restful for one whose heart and soul were bound up in her pupils' advancement.

Miss Ophelia Clemcy blossomed out from her retirement, and became quite voluble, in the front pew before the wedding procession arrived.

"You see, it was foreordained to be," she announced, as she had before declared several times to the principal of the Salisbury School. "The first moment he saw her, Brother John was fully convinced that here was a creature of the greatest sensibility, and altogether charming. And, my dear Miss Salisbury, I am only commonplace and practical, you know, so it is all as it should be, and suits me perfectly. And we will always keep the anniversary of that picnic, that blessed day, won't we?"

And old Mr. King invited the eight ushers from the Pemberton School and the committee from the Salisbury School to a little supper to top off the wedding festivities. And Grandpapa sat at the head of the table, with Mother Fisher at the other end, and Dr. Fisher and Mrs. Whitney opposite in the center. And there were wedding toasts and little speeches; and everybody got very jolly and festive. And the little doctor looked down to the table end where he could see his wife's eyes. "It reminds me very much of our own wedding day, wife," his glance said. And she smiled back in such a way as to fill him with great content.

"And wasn't that reception in the school parlors too perfectly beautiful for anything!" cried Polly Pepper, in a lull, for about the fiftieth time the remark had been made.

"Yes, and didn't Alexia make an awful blunder with her paper of rice!" said Clem sweetly.

"I can't help it," said Alexia, nowise disturbed. "The old paper burst, and I had to put it in my handkerchief. You couldn't expect me, girls, to keep my wits after that."

"Well, you needn't have spilt it all over Miss Anstice's bonnet," said Philena, laughing.

"Mrs. Clemcy's, you mean," corrected Jasper.

"Oh dear me! I never shall get used to her new name," declared Philena.

"And I think I got my rice deposited as well as some of the rest of you girls," declared Alexia airily.

"Mine struck Mr. Clemcy full in the eye," said Silvia. "Then I ducked behind Polly Pepper."

"Oh, that was a great way to do!" exclaimed Jasper.

"Oh, I saw her," said Polly, with a little laugh, "and I jumped away; and Mr. Clemcy saw her, too."

"Horrors!" cried Silvia. "Did he? Oh, I'm frightened to death! What did he look like, Polly?"

"Oh, he laughed," said Polly.

Just then came a ring at the doorbell, sharp and sudden.

"What is going to happen?" cried Polly, her face like a rose. "Everything has been beautiful today, and now I just know something perfectly lovely is coming to finish off with."

"A telegram, sir." Johnson held out a long yellow envelope to Mr. King.

"It's for Mrs. Fisher," said the old gentleman.

So the yellow envelope went down the table length, the color going out of Polly's cheek; and she didn't dare to look at Mamsie's eyes.

"Oh—the boys!" gasped Polly. "Jasper, do you suppose?" —What, she didn't finish, for Mother Fisher just then cried out, and passed the yellow sheet to the little doctor. "Read it aloud," was all she said. But how her black eyes shone!

"David took first prize classics. I'm picking up a bit.

JOEL PEPPER."

Afterword

Barbara Cooney

*L*et me tell you how I met The Five Little Peppers and why I loved them.

Now and then, when I was a little girl, my grandmother came in her big car to fetch me and take me back with her for a visit to the city where she lived. You may think I was a spoiled little girl because I did not enjoy being tucked under the navy blue plush lap robe, that I did not appreciate the little cut-glass vase always filled with fresh sweet peas and asparagus fern that hung between the two left-hand rear windows nor the little telephone between the two right-hand ones through which my grandmother issued orders to the chauffeur. I would rather have sat with him up front. Only boys, however, got to ride in front.

When we got to the city, we went up to the top floor of a hotel and walked down a long hall to a door bearing the number 1127. Behind that door was my grandmother's apartment. It had a beautiful view looking over the East

River and across to Manhattan. But little girls don't look at views for very long. After thumping out "The Happy Farmer" a few times on the big rosewood piano and looking for the millionth time into the curio cabinet at bits of melted glass from Pompeii, I would press my nose to the window and stare out at the Statue of Liberty standing in the harbor and wish the visit would hurry and be over so that I could be back home with my brothers and my friends.

And then one day, in the library, I came across a shelf holding the books my mother had read when she was my age. On that day I became launched on a long lifetime of reading books that came in series. First I came across the complete works of Sophie May, which had begun to appear in 1863, the Flaxie Frizzle Stories and the Little Prudy Series. Next came the Elsie Dinsmore books, the first one appearing in 1868. Despite Flaxie Frizzle's baby talk and Elsie Dinsmore's tears, which "trembled on her eyelashes through-out . . . [her] childhood, her adolescence, her marriage, her widowhood, and her grandmotherhood," I was hooked. I had become a series addict.

Last of all, in a set of The Five Little Peppers books, my home away from home was found. I ceased being homesick. I had Ben and Joel and Polly and Davie and Phronsie for companionship; I had Mamsie to comfort me. I followed them in their adventures and in their sometimes big but usually small catastrophes and shared their happiness and their sorrows. And I shared the little brown house they lived in.

I loved that little brown house. I promised myself that when I grew up I too would live in the real country all the time and have a house full of merry laughing children. And so I did. My house was yellow (still is) and filled with children (alas, no longer). It is not far from Concord, Massachusetts, where Margaret Sidney, the author of *Five Little Peppers*, lived.

Today Margaret Sidney is chiefly revered in Concord, not for writing *Five Little Peppers*, but for preserving the house she lived in, The Wayside, the former home of Nathaniel Hawthorne and, before that, of Louisa May Alcott. It seems appropriate that, although writing a generation apart—*Little Women* appearing in 1868 and *Five Little Peppers and How They Grew* in 1881—the creators of those two beloved families, the Marches and the Peppers, should have lived in the same house. The two families had much in common. They were truly good, although they had to work at it. They struggled against adversity and had to "make do" to make ends meet. They were always up to something: outings and festivities and good-works projects. Above all they loved each other and had pluck. This is what I remembered about the Five Little Peppers and why I did not hesitate to undertake writing this afterword to *Five Little Peppers at School*.

Upon rereading it, however, I was totally surprised by several things, things I had never noticed or that had washed over me or perhaps I had forgotten. Certainly they did not get in the way of my loving the books when I was a little girl.

The first, and this was not a very big hurdle, was that the people, especially the children, talked differently from the way they do in books today. Nowadays boys, when angry, do not called each other "mean beggars" or "beastly cowards" or "cads." Nor do they triumphantly shout "Tippety Rickety!" or exclaim "Oh, whickets!" That is interesting but not important. One gets used to the talk.

The second surprise was the amount of tears that spilled down the Peppers' cheeks. Like Elsie Dinsmore the Peppers did a great deal of crying. Hardly a chapter goes by without someone sobbing. But unlike Elsie the Peppers had pluck. Almost immediately smiles would break through the tears, eyes would shine, and they would spin each other around in a merry dance. These kids were definitely not laid back. At first, upon rereading, the rapid mood swings disturbed me. It had been the pluck, the gumption, not the tears, that I had remembered and admired. And still do.

The third surprise (how could I have forgotten this?) was the atmosphere of snobbishness in which they now were living. It was the loving merry family, truly happy though poor, and the little brown house that had enthralled me. I did remember the rags-to-riches fairytale ending of the first book, when a rich relative, old Mr. King, "the powerful millionaire railroad director," arrived on the scene to save them all from poverty. Polly could have her own piano at last. No longer did she have to drum on the kitchen table.

In *Five Little Peppers at School* the fairytale ending continues. The book opens with the lives of Joel and Davie, now in a boys' private boarding school. The story moves on to Polly and "a bevy" of girls, all students at Miss Salisbury's select school, who are on an outing to have tea in the country and a sail on a steam yacht.

Can the ideals implanted in the Five Little Peppers by Mamsie in the little brown house survive in an atmosphere of wealth and inequality? Yes.

Polly is a caring person. She has been doing charitable work for a poor southern family. ("Poor little southern darkies," Jasper calls them; "disgusting pickaninnies," says his snotty friend Pickering, to whom Polly gives a cold shoulder.)

Coming home on the train from tea in the country, there is an accident. Someone has been killed. "A brakeman," says the governess in charge of the girls. "Don't be frightened. None of the passengers." But Polly immediately thinks of helping the family of the poor brakeman. She rallies the Peppers and all their friends to her cause. And she enlists the aid of old Mr. King, who buries "his aristocratic old face in his handkerchief" as they ride through the slums to the house of the brakeman.

So brush aside the trappings. Love and fairmindedness, generosity and pluck remain. The happy spirit of the little brown house lives on.